VADIM

Donald James is the author of the bestselling novels *Monstrum*, *The Fortune Teller* and also *The Fall of the Russian Empire* and the *Penguin Dictionary of the Third Reich*. He lives in London.

Also by Donald James

Monstrum
The Fortune Teller
The Fall of the Russian Empire
Penguin Dictionary of the Third Reich

VADIM

Donald James

Published by Arrow Books in 2001

3 5 7 9 10 8 6 4 2

Copyright © Donald James 2000

Donald James has asserted his right under the Copyright, Designs
and Patents Act 1988 to be identified as the author of this work

First published in Great Britain in 2001 by Century

Arrow Books
The Random House Group Limited
20 Vauxhall Bridge Road, London SW1V 2SA

Random House Australia (Pty) Limited
20 Alfred Street, Milsons Point, Sydney,
New South Wales 2061, Australia

Random House New Zealand Limited
18 Poland Road, Glenfield,
Auckland 10, New Zealand

Random House (Pty) Limited
Endulini, 5a Jubilee Road, Parktown 2193, South Africa

The Random House Group Limited Reg. No. 954009

www.randomhouse.co.uk

A CIP catalogue record for this book
is available from the British Library

Papers used by The Random House Group Limited are natural,
recyclable products made from wood grown in sustainable forests.
The manufacturing processes conform to the environmental
regulations of the country of origin

ISBN 0 09 941064 8

Typeset by Palimpsest Book Production Limited,
Polmont, Stirlingshire
Printed and bound in Great Britain by
Bookmarque Ltd, Croydon, Surrey

To Phyllis Beatrice Wheal (1910–1999)

All limits are self-imposed.

ICARUS – who flew too close to the sun
and fell to earth.

PLAGUE

The Russian poor called it *Dog Death*, as their peasant forebears had before them. Tuberculosis seemed too formal a name for the destruction of lungs, or the frightening facial disfigurements of the disease. By the turn of the twenty-first century the pestilence was already spreading from the prisons to the towns and ancient villages of Mother Russia. A report by Harvard Medical School warned that without the immediate expenditure of up to a billion dollars, an epidemic would sweep Russia as the new millennium progressed.

The following years saw a familiar Russian nightmare of incompetence, corruption and the theft of Western medical aid funds. With no belief in their government, thousands of Russians now saw the stark choice before them as *emigrate or die*. Some fled by train or air, often on counterfeit visas; the poor sold up to pay to be smuggled West in crowded trailers full of emigrants, many already infected.

In the US, a sense of crisis was surprisingly slow to build. For several months the media had carried stories of Russian illegal immigration, but it was only when, in August, a listing cargo ship, packed with four hundred sick Russians, was stopped by the US Coast Guard in Long Island Sound, that the crisis exploded. The following day the mayor of New York ordered preparations be made for the immediate reopening of Ellis Island for the vaccination and repatriation of Russian illegal immigrants. Within days, what had been a distant Russian problem was front page news throughout the United States.

All this in the year when Americans were in the throes of choosing a new president.

I

First, brothers . . . a few facts. Broadly sketched in. Just to clear up any misunderstanding about who I am and what I think I'm doing here tonight. Maybe, even, to put a slightly more flattering gloss on how I got myself into the whole thing.

So . . . My name is Constantin Vadim. Age, just past forty. Profession, police inspector from the far Russian Arctic city of Murmansk, voluntarily retired. By birth sign a Capricorn, impulsive, too easily swayed by whim and women – although today, fortune-telling, the zodiac, necromancy, all that sort of thing, is something else I've voluntarily retired from. That was yesterday's man.

It is late. The true middle of the night, though still an hour or two before dawn, late August, 2020. And the place – the one-time capital of Russia. I am in the city Peter the Great built – St Petersburg.

I move along the base of a high pink stucco wall, silent as the shadow I throw before me. But I am not alone. Another shadow follows me. Although absurdly dressed in a coat to his ankles, an overlarge felt hat and a ski mask underneath it, my companion is a man of some importance. He is in fact Regional Governor of the far northern province of Kola. Not a man to draw a truthful picture of. I present my old school friend Roy Rolkin to you as an amiable buffoon. It seems easier this way. But he is far from a buffoon – and sometimes very far from amiable.

Like a disgruntled child's, his feet scrape the pavement and I half-turn as he reaches out to catch my elbow. 'How much further, fuck your mother?' he snarls at me.

I look at the map, but I find it difficult not to laugh. If furtiveness has a Platonic form, at this moment Roy Rolkin is its embodiment. Only his weird wrap-around eyes are visible in the slit of the ski mask. One gloved hand is braced against the pink stucco wall. His head turns anxiously from side to side. Like me, he is more than a little drunk.

'Walking is *your* choice, Roy,' I tell him. 'We could have taken a cab all the way from the airport,' I say reasonably.

'And have the driver know where we were going? I am a well-known face, an elected provincial governor. I can't *afford* to be involved in something like this.'

'Something like what?'

'You'll find out soon enough. Just believe me, I can't afford for anybody to see me here.'

Roy standing on his dignity is almost endearing. This time I can't resist a sputter of laughter.

He glares at me. 'Are you a friend or what?' he asks fiercely, nearly unbalancing me with his grip on my arm. There's nothing endearing about him now. This is a question he *means* me to answer.

There's no time to search my conscience. 'Of course I'm a friend,' I say. 'Wherever we're going – let's just get you there, for God's sake.'

In St Petersburg tonight, moonlight strikes hard shadows off the corners of the grand buildings; even in the narrowest streets it shafts through arrowhead railings, revealing cobbled courtyards, challenging the soft light from old copper lamps.

In Petersburg, of course, you expect such refinements as old copper lamps. Up in brash, ugly, ice-hard Murmansk where we come from, we favour the concrete, goose-neck style of lighting, as we favour the barrack-block style of worker accommodations. But all that seems very distant from the soft hiss of the yellow gas lights, and the view from the Kazan Canal Bridge of Petersburg's great

Church of the Resurrection, rising floodlit, its nine enamelled domes twirling and pirouetting against the night sky.

We creep forward. I point down the side street to stone pillars supporting fine cast-iron gates. The gates are open. Beyond is an enclosed courtyard and a broad path which leads to the tall black-painted doors at the top of a semicircle of stone steps. Our destination, according to the map.

We pass through the iron gates, cross the courtyard and mount the stone steps. 'They do know you're coming – whoever they are?' I ask him.

'Of course they know.'

'At this time of night?'

He nods irritably. I reach for the brass bell. I am close enough now to read the most discreet of polished brass plates: The St Petersburg Institute of Cosmetology.

Through this tall black door sidles the Russian world of business, entertainment, sport and now politics. All anxious for one less wrinkle or fold of flesh than the years are giving them. So . . . I say to myself, if Roy is caught on the steps now, his secret's out.

It took a half-litre of vodka, passed back and forth between us during this afternoon's disastrous football match, for him to persuade me to accompany him to Petersburg. Even standing outside the door of the cosmetic-surgery institute I still don't believe a facelift is what Roy's here for. He's barely into his forties. So what is he doing here? Roy Rolkin is a man whose surprises are not all pleasant ones. I try again. My tone is deliberately accusatory. 'You've got something else in mind . . . is that it?'

He stands beside me trying to sink his head into his shoulders for greater concealment. 'Just ring the fucking bell,' he mutters.

I shrug and reach out and press the ivory button in the centre of the brass surround. At that very second the great bell of the Kazan cathedral thunders half past the hour, a reverberation that dislodges dust from the portico above our heads. The effect on Roy is dramatic. He ducks and whirls round in search of cover. For a moment I think he's going to run for it.

I look at the lines I have just written. Again, you see, I'm trying to turn Roy into a figure of farce. I suppose I somehow think I can humanise him like this, make the real Roy unreal. Or perhaps excuse my presence here, excuse my being with Roy Rolkin at all.

In the meantime, one of the black double doors has opened and a porter in a long white Russian shirt, belted at the waist, conducts us across a tiled hall, lit by muted chandeliers, towards a mahogany reception desk.

Roy refuses to remove his ski mask or to give his name or any other details to the girl in the sharply cut black suit who stands to greet us. He tells her the number of his reserved room and requires to be taken there immediately. Within minutes we're alone in Roy's suite. In the centre of the room, on a blood-red porphyry base, a naked bronze maiden subdues a rearing stallion; it could be Vienna, 1905, overheated, overstuffed, over-carpeted, waiting for Dr Freud.

'So,' I say. 'It's time I knew what we're really doing here.'

He doesn't answer. He's busily checking for cameras in the bronze centrepiece. Reluctantly satisfied, he begins to strip off his outer clothing. He's more relaxed now, caressing the huge TV set. 'I ordered this for us,' he says. 'So we can watch a rerun of this afternoon's match.'

I groan. This afternoon, from the directors' stand in Murmansk, we had watched our home side, Murmansk Dynamo, devastated 9-1 in a friendly against the English. Of course, Manchester United are just about the best soccer club in the world. But a lifelong love for Murmansk Dynamo, our own team of losers, is one of the things that binds Roy and myself together.

What *separates* us is Roy's belief, as the chairman and

proprietor of Dynamo, that Murmansk can ever make it into the European Premier League. But I say nothing. I leave him to his dreams.

We sit in the suite at the Cosmetology Institute and watch the video of the game. It is painful. I have that feeling in the first half that the English club have sneaked an extra man or two onto the field. Roy, too. Twice, I see him counting.

'So?' Roy says at half-time. 'You're a director of the club. Analyse it. Where's the weak link?'

I don't even hesitate. 'Borleone. Italy's the best natural footballing nation in Europe and we have to get Borleone.'

Roy scowls at me. It was his choice to spend six million dollars of city money on buying the ageing player from Juventus. But Juventus already knew Borleone was just cruising over the top. Since then, for Murmansk, Borleone's performance has been all downhill.

'So what do we do?' I say. 'Break his legs, collect the insurance and buy a really good striker?'

He sideglances me. 'I'll think about it.'

'For Christ's sake,' I protest in alarm, 'I didn't mean it. Seriously, what are you going to do?'

'There's a very good young striker playing for Bronx United.'

'Bronx are an up-and-coming team.'

'Someone would have to go over and check him out, of course.' He looks at me. 'One of the directors.'

'It's a thought,' I say casually, watching on screen the misery on the faces of the Murmansk supporters as they head for the exits. A visit to the United States! A dream since I came of age. Since even before my big ugly sister Olga went there and enjoyed something for the first time in her life.

'An American visa's not easy to come by,' I say carefully.

Roy nods soberly. 'You've had your BCG?'

'For tuberculosis? Of course. When I was in the police.'

'Good. Just make sure you take your attestation. When can you leave?'

Something turns over in my chest. 'What about an American visa?'

'Collect it at the US Consulate here tomorrow morning. A standard one-week *business* visa. It's all arranged. First-class flight booked. All formalities taken care of. Hotel carefully selected for its central position.' He struts the room to the whistled tune of 'Yankee doodle dandy'. He looks like a portly version of James Cagney.

All arranged! All right. Don't even think to warn me I'm being manipulated. I *know*. And I'm not complaining. New York! I try not to let my delight show. I'll deal with whatever he wants out of me when the time comes.

Roy checks the time and picks up the phone. 'Are they ready?' he asks someone on the end of the line. He holds a clear bottle in his other hand and is necking it as he waits for an answer.

What is this? Are they going to operate tonight? With Roy half afloat on vodka?

'OK,' Roy says. 'We'll go down now.'

He gets up and puts on his ski mask. On top he puts his black felt hat. Then the long overcoat. 'Get your coat,' he says. 'This is it. We're going down.'

I know he's bought me with the offer of a trip to America, but this is too much. 'I'm not going down to the operating theatre,' I say. 'I'm not going to watch while they slit your throat.'

He ignores me and leads the way. I grab up my overcoat and struggle into it as we go down the back stairs where we are met by the same white-shirted porter. I stand in the background while Roy gives him money. Perhaps a hundred dollars or more.

An old stone passage smells of two hundred years of cooking cabbage. The door at the end has an iron-barred grille through which cold air dilutes the cooking smell.

When the porter unbars the grilled door I see a private ambulance, an old battered model with a very low chassis. The front nearside fender is crushed and the driving-side door just about hangs on. The ambulance has been in a class B accident in the last few hours.

'I'll drive,' Roy says. In one hand he has a map which flaps like an unruly flag tugged by the wind.

'Just tell me, Roy. What's going on?'

'We're leaving,' he says. 'Fast as we can.'

So Roy's nerve has failed him. Thank God. I move towards the passenger seat but he shakes his head. 'You get in the back, Costya. OK?'

I get into the back without argument. It is low and dark here and, strangely, smells strongly of alcohol. I can hear Roy climb into the driver's seat and see a narrow angle of his head through the connecting flap. 'There's no light back here,' I say.

He starts the engine. 'Let's get onto the road first.' The bald ambulance tyres churn on the wet asphalt before we slew away, charging through the open wooden back gates of the institute and out onto the road. I am kneeling on the jump seat, craning to see where we're going but I can't make out much through the flap, mostly the bright white dog-toothing of the eaves of the palaces and great houses we're passing. Sometimes a church or a few hanging lamps. Copper, of course, every last one. We make a few turns, then Roy picks up speed and I lose all sense of direction.

I turn my attention to the interior of the ambulance. In the darkness, I hear something. I listen for a moment, then freeze. Below the swish of tyres and the cough and grumble of the old engine, I think I hear breathing. I turn my head. There is definitely somebody or something in here with me.

Straining my eyes I can now see an auxiliary light switch above the connecting flap. I flip on low blue lights. At about the level of my knees a man is lying on an aluminium trolley. A blanket covers him to the shoulders. Above that, his head is tightly bandaged to leave only his eyes and a small mouth aperture. I lean down towards him. The eyes, I see, are closed. But he's breathing, thank God.

'Roy,' I say in a totally unnecessary stage whisper. 'There's a man in here.'

'I know.'

'He's unconscious.'

'Thank Christ for that.'

The man groans, muffled by the bandages. 'He's groaning,' I say.

'So would you in similar circumstances. Unwrap his face.'

'He's a patient from the institute, Roy. He's probably been cut and sewn just an hour or two ago.'

'Trust me, Costya,' Roy's voice floats confidently through the flap, our roles completely reversed from a few hours earlier. 'If he's still alive, everything's going according to plan.'

'Plan? What plan? Why don't we just leave the bandages and take him straight back?'

'Get them off, Costya. Give him a chance to breathe for God's sake and let me concentrate on this map.'

I know Roy. I'm not going to get more out of him in this sort of mood. He likes to focus on one problem at a time.

The bandaging is secured with a tuck. I lift the head and, with infinite care, begin to unwrap the face below me. As I do it I glance up at the connecting grille. I catch a glimpse of the tops of large modern buildings slipping past, different structures from those back there closer to the river Neva, different lamps, balled in mist. But the man on the trolley is groaning with more strength now. I test the tenderness of his head by moving it gently. Strangely he doesn't groan any louder. I have the impression that his pain, which is considerable, isn't coming from his head.

We've slowed down. 'Hold on tight in the back there, Costya.' Roy's voice floats through, casual, unalarmed. 'Very tight.'

I leave the unbandaging and seize a handrail as I feel the wheels lock as Roy hits the brakes.

Roy is a very good driver. So why the hell is he jabbing at the brakes on an old vehicle with worn tyres? We slide across the road, the back of the ambulance moving away gently. I brace myself for the impact and suddenly we hit something with a tremendous clatter of tearing metal. We stop dead. The back doors fly open. I hang onto the rail; our patient screams with pain; Roy mutters to himself in a tone I can hear is approving. 'Not bad. Locked on like radar.'

I get out. We are in a part of St Petersburg I don't recognise at all. Industrial: long low silent brick buildings, their roofs made shapeless by backdrops of mist, tinted orange by the light of sodium lamps. I notice all this as I round the ambulance to see what we have run into.

I stop in alarm. A superb green Mercedes is radiator to radiator with our old ambulance. Roy has a hammer wrapped in a cloth and seems to be battering dents into the bodywork of the car. 'What d'you think?' he asks me.

I can't speak. I just don't understand. We are on an ordinary slip road, a ramp wide enough to pass a tank and we have apparently crashed head-on with an *empty* Mercedes.

Which Roy, completely without ire, is now attacking with a hammer.

He stops hammering and levers a piece of torn metal from the ambulance to overlap the smashed eye socket of one of the Mercedes' headlights. 'OK,' he says. 'Let's get him out.'

I follow him to the back of the ambulance. We lift the gurney and push it round to the driving seat of the

Mercedes. The man is in real pain. Roy lifts his head and quickly untwirls the remaining bandages round his face. I look down at him.

You've guessed already, brothers.

Borleone's dark Italian eyes stare up at me. There are no cuts or sutures on his handsome face. But waves of intense pain cause him to flinch as we move him.

'Lift him into the driving seat,' Roy says. 'Watch his legs. They're broken.'

Tinnitus is singing in my ears. I feel I'm about to retch. Maybe I'm making some noise in the back of my throat.

Roy looks at me. 'He agreed the deal,' he says reasonably. 'A half-million dollars' worth of insurance to him. The rest to the club for a new striker. My uncle's a surgeon at the cosmetology clinic. He broke Borleone's legs under full anaesthetic. Absolute secrecy – and painless . . .' he shrugs as Borleone twists in agony. 'Well . . . until now maybe. For Borleone this is a dream ticket.'

I look at the pallor of the player's face, at the anguished grimaces as we arrange him behind the wheel of the Mercedes. It's *his* own Mercedes, I now recognise. He is conscious but still groaning. I tell him, on no authority at all, that everything's going to be all right.

Roy uses his cellphone to call an ambulance, a real ambulance, and before it arrives he goes to pick up the old Renault Economy he has had hidden behind the factory building.

Borleone's face is draining of blood. I lean close. 'Did you really agree to this?' I ask him. 'Did you really do a deal with Roy for half a million dollars?'

He closes and opens his eyes, a sort of nod.

'But did he give you a choice?'

He tries a wry smile. 'Either they break my legs – or my neck.'

He is looking bad. I tell him an ambulance is on its way. Roy calls to me from the getaway car.

'He's in real pain,' I say. 'He looks as if he's going to faint.'

Roy nods approval. 'Authentic,' he says. 'The man's a born fucking actor.'

2

Roy slipped away that morning into the mists that seemed to surround his life, leaving me with three thousand dollars and an international money card with a credit for another five thousand. Among measures to increase entry control American airports were only accepting Russian flights originating in Moscow. My instructions were therefore first to take a train to Moscow; from there a flight to New York; make an evaluation and first discreet contact with Bronx United's striker Bradley Lister; and deliver a full report a week later in Murmansk. How could I even call it work?

I bought myself a duffel bag and a light suit and a few shirts and other items of clothing in the smart shops along the Nevsky Prospekt. Then, at the American Consulate, with the help of Roy's signature, I was invited to bypass a line of less fortunate applicants trailing down the street. In the enormous waiting room, a TV set blared the empty reassurances of Deputy Prime Minister Anna Popova. 'The Government confidently expects adequate supplies of vaccination and drug treatments to become available in the immediate future. It is officially stated that there are sufficient stocks in Russia to treat all those infected with TB, twice over. Minor problems of distribution are now being surmounted. The Prime Minister personally insists that the condition is to be known as TB or tuberculosis. Those using peasant terms from the last century, particularly the offensive Dog Death, risk a fine of up to a thousand roubles.'

The Russian clerk behind the desk paused in the act of pushing my visa into an envelope. 'The consul wants to see you before you leave,' he said. He lifted a phone and spoke into it: 'He's here now, ma'am.' Then he got up and led me along a high-ceilinged corridor to a set of double doors. Knocking, he opened the doors for me and stood aside.

The consul, Margaret Burns, was about fifty, a Junoesque figure with a big American smile. 'I'm being translated to Murmansk this month,' she said, after we had shaken hands. 'As a Murmansker, I wondered if you could give me any tips on how to deal with your Governor Rolkin.'

'No attractive woman needs tips on how to deal with the governor,' I said.

She smiled. 'He's done well, no doubt about it. The World Health Organisation has commended Murmansk for its TB vaccination programme.'

'We've got the Dog Death up in Murmansk, too. But it's true Governor Rolkin has kept most of the racketeers at bay,' I said. 'On the whole, the vaccine gets through to those who need it.'

'And yet I detect something in your voice. Less than satisfaction with your governor.'

'Roy Rolkin's an old friend, Mrs Burns,' I said. 'We grew up together. What you hear is nothing more than a touch of natural envy at his undoubted success.'

She smiled – doubtfully. 'Washington is asking consuls for a whole raft of reports on the big cities. This is election year, remember, and the Russian epidemic has become a big election issue. Infected Russians fleeing to the US are a threat to American health. If they're healthy enough they're turning to crime.'

'How can I help?'

'You were a senior police officer. Who do I go to for accurate health statistics in Murmansk?'

'That's easy. Forget the Department of Health. Forget the mayor and especially forget the governor's office. Go straight to the Lermontov Hospital, the best in Western Russia.'

'You have a personal interest?'

I took it slowly. 'My wife worked there,' I said. 'When I had a wife.'

I was to take the overnight train to the capital that same evening. With a valid vaccination certificate from my militia service, my US visa in my pocket and the day to kill before making my way to the Moscow Station, I felt uneasily triumphant.

To a man born in the far north, the real Arctic north, the north of pollution clouds and waste mountains, St Petersburg truly is an enchanted city. It shows well by day, colourful, well proportioned, studded with great museums and statuary. And what a history! Built by a six-foot-six czar determined to wrench Russia's head round from Moscow to face the West, for two centuries St Petersburg was the nation's capital, the home of commerce with Western Europe, and the final resting place of men like Dostoevsky, Tchaikovsky and Rachmaninov.

But there's no forgetting, either, that Petersburg has another history. It was here at the Winter Palace in 1917 that Lenin's Revolution was born; in this city, renamed Leningrad, a million people went to their deaths from shelling or starvation in the nine-hundred-day siege in World War Two. During much of that terrible time, Shostakovich continued to compose, and the Conservatoire continued to play great music; there was defiant heroism to be seen on every street corner – and cannibalism along the blacked-out quays at night.

But that's the Russian enigma for you, brothers. We are a huge and restless tribe, roaming history, still looking for our place in the world. Perhaps what happened here could even stand as a metaphor for the relentless energy of the Russian personality. We might enchant with our arts, or inspire with our courage. But we have never lost the need to *feed upon* each other.

*   *   *

I was drinking a last cup of coffee on the concourse of St Petersburg's Moscow Station with less than twenty minutes before the overnight express left for the capital. On the table in front of me was a copy of *Iskra*, the Petersburg sex-and-sport evening paper. Borleone's accident had made a big inside spread but mostly because it gave a chance to publish nude pictures of six of his girlfriends from the Texas Chorale, Murmansk's not entirely adequate answer to the Folies Bergère. The story, dwarfed by the pictures, told of a girl's purse with make-up scattered about the interior of the car and a pair of briefs discovered in the passenger seat-well. Borleone denied he was playing dangerous games at the time of the crash and insisted that the items of clothing and make-up dated from several hours before. The insurance company had already agreed to treat the matter as a straightforward accident. With Roy on the board, this was of course a likely outcome.

As I closed the paper, my cellphone rang. Offhand, I couldn't think of any other more likely caller than Roy, with more frenetic advice on how to spot a master striker, but when I pressed the button there was a woman's voice on the line. 'Is that you, Constantin?' she asked.

I frowned at the wholly strange voice coming from the phone in my hand.

'Costya, is that you? You recognise me, don't you?' A pause. 'Surely, Costya.'

There *was* perhaps something here I recognised, something in the tone, but I was muttering under my breath, still unable to put a name to the voice, when to my astonishment I heard the words: 'It's your sister, dolthead.'

Dolthead? I bridled at that. I hadn't seen my sister for fifteen years or more, hadn't heard from her except for a few postcards from America. How was I to be expected to recognise her voice on a scratchy cellphone? But I had to admit the tone was pure Olga.

'Listen, Costya. You have to do something for me.'

17

'Wait a minute, Olga,' I said. 'Wait a minute. Splash out on the extra copeck. Just take a moment to say hello after fifteen years, just a bare minimum of the civilities, OK?'

I could almost hear the teeth grind. 'All right . . . all right. Hello, Constantin. I trust you're keeping well. Now . . .'

'How did you get this number anyway?' I interpolated.

'Roy Rolkin gave it to me. This is an emergency. I called him at his office. He may be grand now, Regional Governor of Kola Province, but he was as helpful as an old friend could be.'

I dropped two rouble notes on the table for my coffee and, with my free hand, picked up my bag. 'Old friend? Roy Rolkin? You detest him. You detested all my friends.'

'People change. I hear the news even over here. He's doing a good job ridding Murmansk of corrupt business-men with their clubs and girls.'

'He's just leading the pack.' I started across the con-course, phone to my ear.

'Now listen, Costya . . .'

'Olga,' I said. 'I'm catching a train. It's leaving in a few minutes – the Arrow Express to Moscow.'

'Roy told me. It's nothing short of an act of God.'

'How's that?'

'Because it's in Moscow I need your help.'

I was silent. Or silenced. 'You're back in Russia, then?' I asked without enthusiasm.

'Of course not. I'm here in New York. That's to say nearby in Connecticut. You've heard of Connecticut? Good. But I need your help in Moscow. And thank the Virgin Mary, Costya, that, at the very moment you can be of service, you're stepping onto the Arrow Express to the capital.'

I thanked the Virgin Mary. I showed my ticket at the barrier and walked along beside the train, phone to my ear, my eyes seeking out sleeping car 42. When we were children Olga had been a classical big-sister bully. Even in my twenties I had been delighted (though a little envious too I have to admit) when she had emigrated to the United States. Since then, her rare postcards suggested she had, over the years, done well for herself. I would do what I could for her in Moscow if it took no more than an hour or so, but I didn't feel I owed her any big favours.

Ahead of me was sleeping car 42. 'What is it you want me to do?' I asked Olga.

'Listen carefully, Costya. I have an important friend . . .' She paused as if she had made a mistake. 'She's not an important person in herself you understand, but she's important to me. A friend in trouble . . .'

'In trouble . . . That usually only has one meaning. You mean she's been arrested. She's in jail?'

'Militia Station 13. Do you know it?'

'Know it? It was my old station when I served in Moscow. The Virgin Mary again.'

'Exactly,' she said with that smug confidence I find so difficult to take in the unquestioningly faithful.

'What the Virgin Mary might, or might not be up to date on,' I said, 'is that in the last few years, the Red Presnya police district has become the cesspit of Moscow. When was this friend of yours pulled in?'

'An hour or so ago.'

'What for – drugs, violence, drunkenness, theft, prostitution?'

'A mistake,' Olga said firmly, 'whatever the charge.'

'You mean you don't know the charge but you want me to get her out.'

'Of course I want you to get her out. But you must act with discretion. This is of the greatest importance.'

I stopped at car 42. 'So you said before. D'you mind telling me why?'

'I can't do that.' Her voice actually softened. 'But it's important to me, Constantin. Couldn't be more important.'

Did I really want to know why? 'What's her name?'

'I'm not at liberty to tell you that.'

'She must have given a name to the duty sergeant at Station 13.'

'She refused.'

'She won't make it easy on herself,' I said. 'Is she Russian or American?'

She hesitated. 'American.'

'A wealthy American woman goes for a night on the town. Gets friendly with a handsome young thug ... He robs her and accuses *her* of robbing him. This is *the* Moscow twenty-first-century love story. Something like this was it?'

'I've told you I know nothing of the charge. Can you get her out?'

I let the silence hang. I didn't want to make it look too easy. 'I'm no longer a member of the militia,' I said. 'I'll have to get help. There's someone I know ... a good friend. He took over my job when I left Moscow. Ilya Dronsky. I'll ask him to help.'

'Whatever it costs.'

'Olga, for Christ's sake, not everybody can be bought. Even in Moscow. Certainly not Dronsky.'

'I'm sorry, Costya. I didn't mean to insult your friend ... I'm out of touch with things at home. But you'll do something as soon as you reach Moscow. I have your word on it?'

On the strength of the first apology she'd ever made to me in her life, I promised.

Moscow's St Petersburg Station was in chaos when we rolled slowly into it next morning.

Living up in Murmansk, the refugee crisis in Moscow had been just another media story. Here, it seemed as if half Russia was fleeing from the plague. Cooking fires had been lit in the middle of the station forecourt. People with huge backpacks jostled each other angrily as they struggled to reach trains going West. Fights broke out along the length of the west-bound train on the next platform.

I stood on the step of my train as it slowed to a stop, aware of a sense of deep shock. With tears in my eyes, I watched something flowing away from us. I watched Russians, after centuries of fighting, of holding on, of repelling invaders and outliving tyrants, now struggle to abandon the land that made them Russians. I've been a lover of most things American since my teenage years, brothers, but I could still never think of leaving Russia for good. Some things are bred in the bone.

I joined the phalanx of passengers making for the exit. Younger refugees, their eyes fixed on our bags, fell back slowly to let us pass. But every so often a passenger leaving the first-class compartments was pulled aside and cigarettes, or the price of a pack, was demanded. The refugees were not quite ready to take whatever they wanted. They were testing reactions, their own as much as those of the people they were harassing. Later in the day, when vodka had emboldened their spirits, I could guess the mood would be different. By then I'd be well on my way to New York.

During the Moscow siege at the end of our recent Civil War, Militia Precinct Station 13 had suffered several near misses, which had shaken the early-nineteenth-century building to its foundations. The stone porch, barely supported on its Doric columns, was tilted sideways like a drunkard's opera hat. Ground-floor windows were still boarded up and the broad stone approach steps undulated brokenly from left to right. Bizarre and unstable as it was, this building held memories for me.

Memories shared by Ilya Dronsky who was waiting for me at the top of the steps. As ever he was wearing a black polo neck and a grey check jacket. Dronsky is neither tall, nor in any other way physically impressive on first meeting. He has pouched cheeks and cropped hair and Groucho eyebrows that threaten to join across the bridge of his nose. But since I first worked with him in Moscow almost five years ago, I recognised him as someone who knows what friendship is. To receive it from him is a privilege, hard to define. As a man, he is not in any way spectacular. But when I'm with him I know that if there is to be a civilised Russia tomorrow, if there is ever to be a civilised Russia at all, it will be because of people like Dronsky.

We shook hands and looked around at the old building, both I suspect in need of some brief camouflage for our emotion.

'Good to see you, Chief,' he said lugubriously, checking me over as if I might have been missing a limb since we last met. Although he's a captain now, and I'm no longer even a militia officer, he still calls me *Chief*, a sort of deliberate homage to the old days together. 'So . . . going to America then,' he said slowly.

'I'm going for a week, Dronsky. I'm not a fucking refugee.'

'Ah . . . Just the week?'

'I'm a Russian, for Christ's sake.'

'Right.' His face seemed to lighten. 'I'm not worried, Chief. You're the last man to desert a sinking ship.'

'OK,' I said. 'So how are we going to handle this?'

'The American woman?' he said. 'Shouldn't take more than a few minutes.'

'Then we'll relax with a good thumb or two of pepper vodka before I have to catch my plane.'

Through the double doors we passed into the huge reception room, where a circle of high columns supported a modest dome. I looked up. Still painted in gold leaf on blue above the columns were the legends: MURDER, ASSAULT, ROBBERY, PETTY OFFENCES, FRAUD – that familiar dedication to the crimes of Red Presnya.

I shook hands with the duty sergeant whose name I

couldn't remember but who was a familiar face from my brief posting to the district four or five years back. He signalled to his deputy and took his keys from the lock-hook. 'We've booked her as Madame X,' he said. 'She doesn't speak more than a few words of Russian. And she refuses to give her name and date of birth.'

'What's she look like?' Dronsky asked.

'Good-looking I'd say, in different circumstances.' He turned to me. 'She's not a friend of yours, Chief?'

I shook my head. 'Never met her as far as I know.'

We started down the basement steps, the sergeant leading the way. 'Last time I looked in on her she was sleeping it off.'

'She was drunk?'

'You could say that,' the sergeant grinned. 'Quite a sight for a well-dressed piece of ass like that.'

'What are the charges?' Dronsky asked.

'None so far. But it won't just be drunk and disorderly.'

Dronsky stopped him with a hand on his arm. 'What happened?'

'Lieutenant Bitov's squad brought her in. They arrested her in one of the big hotels. It's in the book, the Royal American, I think it was.'

'And what was the offence?'

We were standing at the entrance to the corridor that led to the cells. The sergeant looked down. Then at me. 'You're sure she's not a friend of yours, Chief?'

'I promise.'

'She was fighting some woman. Over a man. A young man. The son of the Minister of the Interior, as it happened. Yuri Solikov. Already, at nineteen, he's a lad about town.' The sergeant scratched his jaw. 'The girls go mad over him.'

'The American in custody,' I said. 'She's a youngster?'

'She's not seventeen you understand.' The sergeant paused. 'Closer fifty.'

'Jesus,' I said. 'And fighting over a nineteen-year-old.'

'Is that Inspector Vadim?' a woman's voice said in English.

I walked forward until I stood before the middle cell in a line of three. A woman was facing me, holding the bars. A black silk evening coat was crumpled in a corner of the cell's bare cinder-block bed behind her. Pale dust from the bed had left abstract patterns on her black dress and there was a bad tear at the collar. Her blonde hair hung lank; her face was lined with the traces of last night's make-up. Despite her hung-over appearance, it wasn't difficult to see the outline of a woman of striking looks. Fifty was about right. Maybe a little more.

'Have you brought an interpreter with you?' she said. 'Or do you speak English?'

'Enough. Why don't you tell me about last night?'

'A squalid business,' she said. Her manner was cool, Lauren Bacall. It didn't sit well with her dishevelled appearance.

'You don't deny an assault?'

'Not really. Can you get me out of here?'

'That depends how co-operative you are. Where do you live in the United States?'

'I come from New York City.'

'You were born there?'

'If you like.'

'It's not a matter of what I like.'

'You speak *good* English.'

'Enough to know you're not an American. At least not an American by birth. You certainly weren't born in New York.' I came closer to the bars. 'You're Russian.'

'I'm an American citizen.' The Lauren Bacall image cracked. I could see the tension about her eyes.

'Then you have a passport.'

'Not with me.'

'Your name?'

She shook her head.

'Place of birth. In *Russia*.'

Again she refused to answer.

'We'll speak in Russian,' I said, reaching for one of the bars and leaning my weight on it. 'That way we can all understand.'

'I have nothing to say, in English or in Russian.'

Dronsky was leaning, back to the wall, arms folded, an unlit cigarette between his lips. He removed the cigarette. 'We can keep you until you provide identifying details,' he said. 'I think we should tell her that's the law, Chief.'

She glared at him and then turned to me. 'I thought Olga sent you to get me out.'

'How do you know Olga?'

She shook her head in refusal to answer.

'A friend?'

Her blank face turned away.

'A neighbour?'

'A friend of a friend, if you like. I've never even met her.'

'Olga is not a woman to do favours for someone she's never met.' I pushed my weight off the bars. 'OK, if you won't talk, you won't. Doesn't matter. But if I'm going to do anything for you I do need your name and marital status. You have a husband?'

She hesitated. 'Yes.'

'An American?'

'An American.'

'Name?'

'I love my husband, Inspector. Why would I give you his name?'

'Your own name, then. Your unmarried name. How about that?'

'I've already refused.'

'Listen,' I said. 'There are forms to fill in. Any name you like.' I stared hard at her. 'You look like a Margaret Smith to me.'

'Right first time.'

'Now, just a few details. You'd had a lot to drink.'

The woman waved the accusation aside with a hand that flashed jewellery.

'How long had you been at the Royal American before the incident took place?'

She made an irritable shape of her lips. 'God knows. I'd had dinner somewhere. Where I can't remember.'

'Alone?'

'No . . . probably with several people. Several *boring* people.'

'And you slipped away.'

'Exactly.'

'To find somewhere it was more fun.'

'What an understanding policeman!'

'In the Royal American you were drinking with a young man named Solikov. A government minister's son.'

'My mistake.'

'You accused another woman of trying to make off with young Solikov,' the sergeant said.

'A simple misunderstanding,' she said. 'I'll explain. I'd just come back from powdering my nose and I found another woman with her arms round him. A fat whore.'

'You attacked her?'

'Attacked her? Hardly. It was no more than a gesture.'

'What sort of a gesture?' Dronsky asked mildly.

'I believe I ripped the shoulder straps off her dress. There was pandemonium. The dress fell to the ground.' She smiled. 'Fat thighs.'

'She was one of the bar girls at the Royal American?' I said.

Her lips twisted. '*That* was the misunderstanding.' She paused. '*My* misunderstanding. The woman embracing him was Minister Solikov's wife. Bidding her *youngest son* an affectionate goodnight.' Her voice dropped. 'The fat whore was his *mother*.'

3

It was early evening and less than three hours to my plane to New York. Dinner and a few drinks with Dronsky was out. He had spent most of the afternoon at the Procurator's office smoothing the way to the woman's release. I had been to the Royal American Hotel and received the manager's assurance that Minister Solikov's wife had no wish to press charges, fearful that reporters would never believe it was her son she was kissing goodnight. As far as she was concerned the incident in the bar had never occurred.

I asked the manager if the American woman was a regular at the bar but he told me he had never seen her before she had arrived alone at about ten o'clock. Young Solikov had been at the bar with a noisy party of young friends and the American had taken a place near them. 'She was looking for a pickup,' the manager said. 'That was obvious enough.'

'You're not saying she was a professional?'

'Definitely not. No tart would go out for a night's work wearing jewellery like that. In any case professional girls get bought drinks, don't they? They don't order bottles of Bollinger for young men at the bar.'

I thanked him for his help and left to meet up with Dronsky, just back from the Procurator's office. The rain which had threatened all day had now started to fall and I was forced to say goodbye to Dronsky over a hurried thumb of vodka in his office at Station 13 as he put together the documentation that secured the American woman's release. He had that familiar worried look. There are times when I think he worries more about me than he does about his office cat, V. I. Lenin as the cat is known because of his wisp of goatee beard and a conviction you can sense in him; that he has revolutionary leadership qualities yet to be fully recognised.

V. I. Lenin is not a comradely cat, though some people consider he has a dour charm of his own. This mostly derives from his habit of greeting you with a raised paw, lifted above shoulder height like his namesake on the podium. He and I have a stand-off relationship that is polite at best. He once came to stay a spell in Murmansk but it was a relationship that never worked out. This hasn't entirely deterred Dronsky. I know he still harbours the hopes of us bonding, man and beast, but I would be highly doubtful of that on either side.

'Listen, Chief,' Dronsky said as he prepared the truly disgusting fishburgers he had brought in for V. I. Lenin's supper. 'You want me to wait and drive you out to the airport? I get reports of tens of thousands camping round the perimeter,' he said. 'All trying to get out with fake papers they've spent a fortune on. What in God's name is happening to us?'

'Panic,' I said. 'It's short-term.'

He shook his head. 'There's nothing short-term about the epidemic *or* the panic it causes, Chief. It's more than just a government that can't cope. The evidence is that this is a man-made crisis.'

I felt a surge of shock pass through me. 'You're saying the *racketiry* are deliberately spreading the disease?'

'Wherever they can. In Moscow, they burn down warehouses storing treatment drugs. They hijack convoys carrying vaccine and keep it in short supply. They've even been known to force infected sputum down the throats of vagrants and drunks to widen the market.'

I felt sickened. 'With the right drugs, the disease is curable?'

'Even the resistant forms are curable. But it takes six months to two years regular medication. It could cost you all you have. But for your own health, your family's health, you'd do anything, right? You'd find five thousand dollars any way you could. It's been building since the Harvard report. It's a twenty-first-century Russian tragedy, Chief.'

'The *racketiry* are really deliberately infecting people?'

He nodded sombrely.

I tipped my glass. 'And we fought the Civil War to bring us together.' I poured another quick thumb of vodka each.

'Listen Chief,' he said. 'This woman. You've done all you can for her. Leave it there. I have an instinct about her.' His eyebrows knitted with concern. 'This woman is really trouble.'

'You think that?'

'I know it.'

I woke up. 'You're a fox, Dronsky. You managed to pull her fingerprints. Am I right?'

He shrugged. 'I took her pail from the cell. We lifted a clear set of right-hand prints.'

'And?'

'And there's where we come to a juddering halt, Chief. So far we've confirmed she has a record . . .'

'For what?'

'It could be up to a month at least before we get the details. If ever.'

'A *month*?'

'Central Records has just been taken over by refugees. It all depends if they decide to take our computers with them when they move on.' He stapled sheets of paper together and handed them to me. 'She's all yours, Chief. That makes it official.'

We parted, regretting the loss of an opportunity to spend a little more time together, and arranging to meet as I passed through Moscow on my way back from New York.

Within five minutes I stood on the broken steps of the

precinct station, watching the rain with the woman who had taken up the best part of my day. She had somehow arranged the tear in her dress and renewed her make-up and brushed her hair. Perhaps she had had an hour or two's sleep as well. She looked different.

It was not only the years that had peeled off her. The personality had changed too. The sardonic, young Lauren Bacall manner had gone, almost as if she had become more mature with her loss of years. She nodded towards the falling rain. 'Where I come from it would be snow.'

'Beginning of September?' I said doubtfully.

'Why not?' she said. 'I come from the north.'

I was going to tell her I was a northerner too, then decided against it.

'A good fall of snow covers everything,' she said wistfully. 'Where I grew up the village grandmothers came out and nodded and genuflected to the first snows, praying that they would cover the horrors of the past year. As I got older, I learnt to hope the same.'

I knew she was offering some oblique explanations, but I was bearing in mind, too, what Dronsky had said. 'Keep her at arm's length, Chief. This woman's trouble.'

'Russians need to put their snow to use,' I said. 'It's because we produce so much more of it than anything else.'

'You're a cynic.'

'If only.'

She grimaced up at me and offered her hand. 'I have to thank you, Constantin,' she said slowly. 'You've saved me from a great deal of embarrassment.'

'Thank my sister.'

'I will.'

'So you do know her? Tell me, at least, how.'

'We're two Russians in New York. Isn't that enough?'

'Except with all the illegal immigration you must be two Russians there among two million.'

'In the US today, Russians get blamed for everything.

30

Yesterday it was blacks. Today, it's Russians.' She looked along the street. 'One last favour,' she said. 'I have no money for a cab. I lost my purse outside the hotel last night in the scuffle with your colleagues.'

'Cabs don't cruise this neighbourhood,' I gestured back to the station behind us. 'But I've the loan of a Station 13 car. I can take you somewhere if you like.'

She gave me a quick smile and shook her head. 'That way you'll know the hotel I'm staying in.'

'Is it that important to keep your identity hidden?'

'To me it is.'

'Because your husband wouldn't be pleased to hear last night's story.'

'What husband would?'

I took her arm. 'Listen, no questions. I'll drive you to Tverskaya Street, or the Arbat or wherever and give you twenty roubles. That way you can get yourself a cab and nobody will know which is your hotel. How's that?'

We walked to the parking lot and got into a Renault squad car. 'Olga's brother is a gentleman,' she said.

As we pulled away I offered her my cellphone. 'Do you want to call someone? I said no questions . . . but your husband maybe.'

'You assume I have one.'

'You do, don't you?'

She looked at me for a moment. 'Yes,' she said. 'I have a husband.'

'Here in Moscow?'

She smiled. 'Turn left here,' she said. 'And first right. I'm looking for a church. You can drop me there.'

We were in a narrow cobbled lane with brightly lit fast-food bars and vibrant clubs on either side. I drove slowly down to the end.

'There,' she said. 'Pull into the courtyard of that church.'

It was obvious enough the church was no longer used. Most of the windows were smashed and part of the wooden wall to one side of the main door had been burnt away. 'I have to leave,' I said. 'I have to get to the airport by eight.'

'Just come into the church with me a moment,' she said. 'Then I'll pick up a cab . . .' She laughed. 'And be off your hands for ever.'

We left the car and walked through the great charred gap in the wall into the church. Light fell through holes in the roof, oddly angled beams from neon club-signs and street lamps outside. There was very little left to see inside. Carved wood was burnt black, the remains of what might have been a gilded screen. Painted walls had peeled to leave saints' faces beyond recognition. 'Why are we here?' I said, turning to her as she crunched her way across the broken glass and plaster on the floor. 'It means something to you?'

She nodded. 'It did.'

'Do I ask why it's important to you?'

'Something happened here once. A very long time ago.' She stood below a sagging section of roof, a street lamp shining through onto her face.

'Did you know it before it was burnt down?'

'Yes.'

'How did it happen?'

'Somebody threw a grenade. Timbers caught. Within minutes it was blazing.'

'Were you here?'

She took a long time to answer. 'Yes, I was here. I escaped unhurt.'

I could tell, by her tone, that some others, or some *other*, didn't. I looked at her, her face white against the charred blackness around us. 'I'm sorry,' I said. 'Was it someone close to you?'

She nodded acknowledgement of my meaning. 'When the grenade was thrown I was standing on the steps with my eight-year-old daughter.'

Christ!

I drew a deep breath. 'And your daughter . . . ?'

She turned around and looked past me. 'My daughter was blinded. Partially blinded, perhaps I should say.'

I put my arm round her shoulder. 'Forget the cab,' I said. 'I'll run you to the hotel. I won't even *look*.'

She smiled, her face wan. 'How about if, instead, you spare a few moments for us to go on talking.'

I looked at my watch. 'OK,' I said, hesitantly. 'A few minutes. Then I have to get up to the airport.'

'I know I shouldn't importune you like this, but I really am desperate to talk.'

'About your daughter?'

'No. About myself.' She paused, not looking at me. 'I'm in trouble. And the truth is I feel completely alone.'

We walked forward to where we stood out of the falling rain. She turned to face me. 'I won't ask you why you gave up the police.'

'I probably couldn't answer, anyway,' I said. 'In any case, I thought you wanted to talk about yourself.'

'I do.' She took a deep breath. 'I don't know how to start. I'm in danger, Constantin. My life is being threatened.'

'Threatened? Who by?'

'God knows. There are several possibilities.'

It was the way she said it. Her tone carried such an aura of unreality, a theatricality that didn't ring true. Standing here in this ruined church, it suddenly occurred to me that this could be a woman whose life was playing games, a woman, nameless for no real purpose. Perhaps there was no husband. No blinded daughter. Perhaps she was a woman protecting a mystery that just didn't exist. Perhaps to her to be secretive was just fun.

'There's a doubting look on your face, Constantin. You think me just another Moscow fantasist.'

'Do you do drugs?'

'Vodka.'

'Who doesn't?'

'What I'm telling you is true,' she said. 'Believe me.'

She reached out and held the front of my topcoat with both hands. 'Believe me, Constantin. What I've told you is the truth. More than that, I risk everything every time I do things like chase after this boy Solikov. I risk my life even! You hear what I'm saying to you?'

'Then why do it? Why take the risk?' I just said the words. What else was I to say?

She kept her voice low but it throbbed with fury. 'God knows,' she said. 'God knows why I take a risk like last night. All right, I was drunk, feeling hot . . . and alone. Haven't you ever turned to sex to salve the pain?'

She had me there.

'Or who knows, maybe every time I do something like this I'm throwing out a challenge to them.'

'Them?'

'Whoever's threatening me.'

Well, maybe . . . I sneaked a look at my watch.

'I have something to ask you, Constantin. I want you to call me. When you get to New York. I might have a proposition for you.'

Oh Christ. I looked up at the rain, falling again through the roof. I felt the need to bring this back to earth. 'Listen,' I said. 'I really have to go.'

She shoved her hands deep in the pockets of her coat and paced in front of me, kicking small pieces of burnt debris aside with the toe of her expensive shoe. 'All right,' she said suddenly, lifting her head. 'But contact me in New York.'

I took her arm and we walked towards the door.

'I wish we had more time to talk, Constantin. You're a man who knows. I believe you could help me. And I could help you.'

Perhaps I shrugged my doubt. 'I really do have a plane to catch,' I said. 'Now.'

'I know.'

34

'Let me find you a cab,' I said. I reached the steps ahead of her.

She looked around at the charred woodwork, the crumbling stones and broken windowpanes. It was a sort of goodbye.

I was searching the crowded alley for a cab.

'Take this,' she said. She tore the top off a business card. 'Use this number. Ask for Katerina. Don't give any details. No mention of tonight. Agreed?'

'Agreed,' I said, not even looking at the card. 'You're trusting me?'

'Yes. As I said before,' she walked past me, her rich silk coat swinging, 'Olga's brother is a gentleman.'

Not such a gentleman. When I'd hailed her cab outside the church, I got into the Economy and took a right and right again to come out behind the taxi carrying her. I was curious, I admit, to see which hotel she was staying in. One of the most expensive, I'd no doubt.

But I was wrong. Within a few hundred metres she had changed taxis, directing her new cab back towards the ring road. The last I saw of her, before I headed my borrowed militia car towards the airport, was as she paid off the taxi outside the residence of the American Embassy.

I called Dronsky as I drove up the old Leningrad Prospekt. We call it Tsar Ivan Way now. That's Ivan the Terrible. Russia, of course, has a wide selection of murderers to choose from.

Dronsky answered just as I was turning into the short-stay parking lot where I was to leave the Renault Economy for Station 13 to pick up.

'You got rid of her, Chief?' Dronsky asked. I could hear the kids playing in the background and his wife, Irina, talking to them. I was looking forward to staying there a few days on my way back from New York.

'I put her in a taxi, then followed the cab.'

35

'And?'

'She drove to the US Ambassador's residence. She paid off the taxi and walked straight in. The Marine Guard saluted her, Dronsky. No questions asked, no papers demanded. They just let her straight through.'

'And yet we're talking about a woman with some sort of criminal record, according to our files.'

'A record you can't access for a month or more.'

'I could get some pressure put on to find out what's in her file while you're in America.'

'I'll live without it,' I said. 'As far as I'm concerned the matter is closed.'

'Very wise. Call me as soon as you're back in Moscow, Chief. See a few good games. And have a good trip.'

I settled down in my first-class seat on the Air Russia Boeing 777 as we reached twenty-five thousand feet and the nose was pointed towards New York. I put aside the *New York Times* with its headlines on the coming lacklustre presidential election and the *Daily News* with its scare story of one million illegal Russian immigrants flooding into New York City this year and turned my attention to more serious things. The stewardess placed a thumb of vodka in one hand. On my lap, I opened *World Football Magazine* at an article: 'World's choice for the hundred best strikers'. Number twenty-eight was my target – the young up-and-coming Bradley Lister of Bronx United.

4

They did everything but shave our heads. Hardly had we landed at Newark International Airport at ten p.m. local time, than we were bussed to a cavernous hangar. There, we joined other Russian flights and were formed into six or seven lines of perhaps a hundred people each. Great menacing overhead hoardings announced that this was a joint operation of US Immigration and the US Department of Health.

The body heat of several hundred anxious Russians compounded the humidity of the night. Trickles of sweat ran down faces hungry for information. People protested they had relatives meeting them, hotel rooms booked. Questions in broken English were blankly ignored by the blue-uniformed men organising the lines. Older women began to cry; children huddled into their mothers' skirts. Chillingly I was reminded of our own Russian methods of crowd control. Was this really the America whose images I had nurtured since my teens?

The shuffle forward took an hour before I reached the high, seaweed-green painted barrier. I could now see that it was inset with a row of booths each with a turnstile next to it, copied you might think from the entrance to one of the dog-racing stadiums that had become popular in Russian cities in the last few years.

A family of four or five passed through the turnstile in front of me, the children cowed, the woman in silent tears. I stepped forward. I needed to get this over quickly before anger boiled.

The immigration officer in the booth in front of me wore a dark blue sleeveless padded jacket that rode up round his ears. His thin face showed that terrible blankness that humans develop when dealing with lesser humans. Or those they consider lesser humans. I offered my passport and visa and he examined both at length and set them aside. 'Vadim, uh? Constantin Vadim.'

I nodded.

'Clearance certificate,' he demanded, hand already out.

I took my Murmansk Militia health card from my wallet. It showed X-ray dates and results and a stamped and signed clearance attestation.

'What's this?' he said, thin nose lifted. 'It's in Russian.'

'It's a Russian certificate,' I said. 'Murmansk Police District. I was a former inspector.'

'How come you speak such good English?' he wanted to know.

'University. And a special course on Anglo-American vernacular in the navy.'

He frowned doubtfully. 'You were in the navy?'

'The *Russian* navy.'

He glanced down at my health card and pushed it back at me. 'This is no good to us,' he said casually.

The woman in the adjoining booth was crying as she tried to make sign language to convey some point. I felt for a brief moment impossibly sorry for her, impossibly sorry for all immigrants everywhere. Then I turned back to the problem in front of me.

'You can see by the photograph it's me. OK?'

'Could be anything.'

'But not anyone. Let's start there.'

He looked at me, his tongue in his cheek. 'You know, one thing I really can't take is wise-ass Russians,' he said with quiet menace. 'Admission to the United States requires a consular or equivalent stamp on all Russian medical documentation. I see your consular stamp on your visa – but not on your medical documentation, Mr Vadim.'

'The first I've heard of it.'

'It's a requirement,' he intoned, not displeased. 'New.'

'So what happens now?'

'Your passport and visa are in order. So you have a choice.' He smiled as he sat back in his chair. 'You can take the next plane back to Moscow . . .'

I could feel for all those men who had wanted to jump across the table at the Jack in Office in front of them. I clenched my fists. 'Or what?' I asked.

'Or you can accept voluntary X-ray examination and quarantine at Ellis Island.'

The early twentieth-century immigrants called it the Isle of Tears. 'Ellis Island,' I said. 'Quarantine?'

'Until you're cleared.' He ran his tongue over his bottom lip. 'You can always go back home to Russia, Mr Vadim. Make that choice – and you won't get any sort of hard time from me.'

'I'll take Ellis Island,' I said. To spite him. Don't tell me. My problem is that I have a childish streak.

In the green navigation lights, I unfolded my map in the wind. The immigration-authority ferry had brought us along the Elizabeth Channel from Newark International, butting past Staten Island and into the dark choppy waters of Upper New York Bay. The Statue of Liberty rose before us, moody and magnificent against the dark sky. The glittering square-cut black diamonds in the distance were unmistakably the outlines of Manhattan Island. Leaning against the rail, into the tug of wind, I watched Ellis Island rise from the darkness ahead. Hard to imagine the low, dark mass as landfall to so many millions of European immigrants at the turn of the twentieth century.

At the end of that century the crumbling brick buildings of the reception years had been refurbished and for a while had served as a museum, some sort of Shrine to the Melting Pot. But as the hugely successful melting-pot philosophy faded before the ragbag claims of separatist ethnicity, Ellis Island's museum had again fallen into disuse. Until rescued by the need to examine and quarantine Russian immigrants arriving without suitable documentation.

As we approached it, Ellis Island now seemed a small mass in a darkness surrounded by the glitter of a wealthy and comfortable New York. There were lights there too, of course. But they held no welcome. The familiar curve of the gooseneck directed their harsh white beams efficiently down onto a bare wharf. Men and women in dark blue uniform paced, awaiting us.

All around me, people were sobbing. Others stood with blank faces, baffled by the sudden decline in their circumstances.

Me among them.

Our instructions were to check in all cellphones and luggage but to retain wallets and money. We were then offered a shower, a basic hamburger and coffee meal in the old Immigration Center dining rooms and assigned a bunk in a long bare dormitory. Don't misunderstand me brothers, it was clean and well organised but, for Russians perhaps more than any people on earth except Jews, it carried the sharp face-slap of history with it.

I soon found the first shortage was interpreters. I had until tomorrow night to get out of here and get to my soccer match. I looked at all the troubled adult faces around me, the children with frightened eyes and trembling lips. My problems were nothing compared with theirs. I volunteered for a shift or two interpreting for new arrivals.

It was harrowing work.

I met people from Rostov-on-Don, from Sevastopol, from Omsk and Novgorod. I met people from villages I had never heard of and would never hear of again. I met carpenters and dentists and writers and actors. I met truck drivers and computer specialists and even a few peasants. What all had in common was a faked medical document, some rough attestation written in

English with an official-looking stamp – and a terrible sense of despair that the new life in America on which they had spent everything was denied them.

I gathered people in a brick, unplastered room, thirty or forty at a time, and tried to explain what was happening. Most of them were decent people with a dream of a new life. Some were criminals straight from a Russian jail. Many had received a water injection and a casually forged certificate in some Moscow back-alley 'clinic' before they left. Often they were unaware that this was not a vaccination, that their documents were worthless. At Ellis Island all would be medically examined and X-rays would be taken. Anybody requiring treatment would be supplied with a course of drugs. Others would be vaccinated and given clearance certificates. They would then be returned to Russia on the grounds of attempted illegal entry.

Perhaps I gave this speech twenty, perhaps forty times. Sometimes men became violent and tried to pull me off the desk I was standing on. Each announcement that they would, either way, be sent home, was received with cries of anguish that took a thick, choking hold on my throat.

In the early hours, I was exhausted. A young woman immigration officer, her shirt tagged with the name Rosalie M. Pope, showed me a small office I could sit in and gave me a cup of coffee. 'I must check the TV,' she said. 'Things have been happening in the city today.'

I drank coffee as she switched on and ran through the channels. She stopped at New-2-You screening a perfectly proportioned woman's face in close-up. The woman was speaking but I wasn't hearing.

'Catch this,' the immigration officer said.

I forced myself to raise my head. The newscaster's voice was increasing in clarity. '*As the temperature rose in New York this afternoon, disturbances broke out in several parts of the city. The immigrant encampments in Central Park were the scene of fierce fighting between Russians and neo-Nazis carrying Hitler's Name banners. At several points luggage was dragged from its owners and piled up before being sprayed with gasoline and ignited.'*

On screen, clothing, broken bottles and open suitcases were spread across the grass. Police sirens whooped. A great pile of cases and bags was burning fiercely. Men with white face masks were hurling more bags onto the fire. Others were fighting groups of men and women for possession of more bags.

'Oh my God,' Rosalie Pope was saying. 'Oh my good God.'

'*American Unity Party chairman Ben Rushton,*' the marble-faced presenter said, '*was among the first on the scene.*' The screen cut to a tall middle-aged man in a pale suit. He had grey hair and a long, sharply cut good-looking face. The police had recovered control by now and had separated the Hitler's Name group from the immigrants. Rushton stood there, taller than most, in the centre of a small crowd of stunned men and sobbing women. To my surprise I heard him speak a few simple words of Russian.

New-2-You switched to tennis and Rosalie turned off the set. 'This is just the beginning of it,' she said.

'The beginning?'

'Trouble. Here we are in election year and neither main party presidential candidate even wants to talk about Russian immigration and about the way Americans are beginning to think about it. Well, events are going to force it down everybody's throat before this election's over. There's just too much fucking suffering,' she said.

I sipped my coffee. She had a small, intense face, made, I think, smaller and even more intense by the loose fit of the uniform shirt round her slim neck. She pulled a pack of cigarettes from her breast pocket. 'I've started smoking again since I came here,' she said apologetically. She cocked her head at the sounds outside in the passage, the sound of crying women and children that I would always associate with this place – and probably always had been associated with this place. It wasn't known as the Isle of Tears for nothing.

She took a cigarette, offered me one as an afterthought and lit them for both of us. 'I've arranged leave from the service,' she said. 'I'm going to get involved.'

I was too tired to follow closely. And what I wanted was not coffee but a generous thumb of vodka to cut through the echoing desolation of this place.

'Involved . . . ?'

'In the campaign. The American Unity Party . . . On TV just now.'

I nodded.

'A tiny outfit run by the guy you saw there, Ben Rushton. He runs no ads. He doesn't stand a snowball's chance in hell of getting elected. He hasn't even declared himself a candidate. But he's using the election to say things the American people need to hear. Listen,' she wound up like a pitcher. 'On the day before Super Tuesday . . . OK, he wasn't offering himself, but Ben Rushton couldn't get 10 per cent voter recognition in the polls . . .'

My eyes closed but I don't think she noticed. I was fighting myself awake. 'The American people need to hear, you said. What was that they need to hear?'

'Like what's about to happen when two million Russians, many of them infected, arrive in the eastern seaboard ports and cities. And maybe another million drop into California.'

'There are a lot of people on the move in Russia,' I said. 'But three million . . .'

'It's barely started. That's what Ben Rushton says.'

'You mean it's a plague of locusts?'

She looked at me seriously. 'No,' she said. 'Ben Rushton doesn't look at it in those terms. Apart from anything else he has a Russian wife.'

'You're right,' I said. I pushed myself to my feet. I felt

I had to say something to her to encourage her innocence and goodwill. 'If the good people don't get involved,' I said, 'the others get away with murder. It's always been like that.'

It wasn't inspired but with eyelids this heavy it was the best I could do. 'Listen Officer,' I said. 'I'd better get back to telling these people the good news.'

She stretched out her hand. 'Rosalie,' she said.

I shook her hand. 'Constantin.'

She smiled. 'Hi.'

The small friendly gesture had me swallowing hard.

I worked through to dawn then stood in line in an endless corridor for the one call we were allowed to make. I was saved by the young immigration girl, Rosalie, who hauled me off to her office and offered the phone.

'I just faxed my resignation,' she said. 'Effective, end of the week.'

'Resignation? I thought you were taking leave.'

'Not after talking to you,' she said. 'You made me see I had to go all the way.'

'I did?'

Americans are strange people.

Russians are stranger. On the phone I got Roy Rolkin in the bath.

'Offshore,' he said. 'Where offshore? Coney Island? Fire Island? Where, for Christ's sake?'

'*Ellis* Island.'

'What in God's name you doing there?' he said. 'I get you a first-class air ticket, first-class papers. I get you a class A visa. You swore to me you had militia vaccination clearance. Right? Did you tell me that, Costya – or not?'

'I told you that.'

'So what went wrong, fuck your mother? What are you doing in there with the huddled millions? You work for me, you don't have to huddle, for Christ's sake?'

'Simple thing,' I said. 'Your office failed to pick up on the fact that medical clearance certificates need an officially stamped cover note *in English*.'

There was a long silence. 'Listen,' he said. 'I'll pull teeth for this. I'm sorry, Costya. I am truly sorry. What a friend I turn out to be! Tell you what. Find some American immigration vek. Slip him a thousand dollars and watch his eyes light up.'

'This call is being monitored,' I said.

Another long silence. 'It was a joke, of course, Costya. Come to think of it, I've heard better. A lot better.'

'They'll understand that,' I said. 'They're very understanding people here.'

'When will you get out?' His voice was hushed now.

'You're still not with this situation, Roy. They have withdrawn my visa. Why? Because I was trying to enter the US with an incomplete set of documents. I am about to be returned to Moscow. Not on the next flight because I have to undergo medical examinations for a disease I have already been vaccinated against. And there's a five-day wait for results.'

'You'll miss the match.'

'I'll miss the match.'

'That's OK. There's another on the weekend. Return you to Russia – no! Leave this to me, Costya. Will you do that?'

'I don't have any choice, do I?' I said savagely.

'I'll call the US Commercial Attaché's office in Moscow. I'll explain you're on a commercial mission of importance. They'll come round.'

I didn't believe it, then, or several nights later, when I was still addressing sad roomfuls of new arrivals. Roy's writ just didn't run this far. And the more I got to know Ellis, the more sad and shocking I found it to be. Camp life evolves quickly. The strong thrive. Mostly by theft and rape, or at least pressure for sexual favours. I talked to far too many girls who were at the mercy of the gangs within hours of arriving here. Ellis Island was an instant, vicious ghetto.

I'd told Roy I had no choice but to leave it to him to arrange my release. I was lying. There was one slender choice. In my top pocket was a calling card, the name and address torn off – only a phone number remaining.

Katerina's number.

Rosalie was prepared to help with another phone call made from her office as she moved in and out packing up. I punched in the number on the crumpled card. No answer. Just a brisk *Leave a message and I'll call you back.* But it was definitely Katerina's voice.

I tried again after addressing another new group of arrivals. The pain and dismay on the faces of the people I'd been talking to stayed with me as I punched in Katerina's number. She had said we might be able to help each other. Just at this moment, she could certainly help me.

I had to get free of Ellis Island. Katerina was surprised, maybe even shocked to hear me on the line. I explained to her as quickly as possible my situation. 'Shoe's on the other foot,' I said. 'Is there anything you can do?'

She said there was.

Rosalie came and woke me. I was sleeping, fully dressed, on my bunk. I'd worked almost every hour there was since I arrived here, trying to reassure frightened, sometimes angry, people. The immigration officers were doing their best. They weren't the hard-faced toughs in the reception booths. There were a lot of women here with sympathetic faces and soft voices, but it was still detention.

'Listen,' Rosalie said, her voice low. 'You've been sprung.'

Heads hung over the side from the top bunks. Legs appeared from the lower bunks. Lawyers, doctors, dentists, peasants, industrial workers, all thirsting for information.

'Apparently they're going to accept your Murmansk

Militia vaccination certificate. You've got friends,' she whispered.

I rolled up onto one arm. 'It was friends got me into this,' I said. I got up and walked towards the door with her. In the baggage room I collected my duffel and cellphone. I was about to sign a clearance that I had received back all valuables when an alarming lightness around the area usually occupied by my inside pocket brought me upright. I delved a hand and, to my astonishment, watched it burst through the leather of the front of my jacket. I withdrew it slowly, like a ventriloquist operating his puppet.

'It's a favourite Russian pastime,' one of the immigration people said. 'Any big crowd, they move in close and slit your jacket just enough to ease out your wallet. They've done a good clean job there. Not too much damage to the leather that can't be put right.'

I tucked back the shredded lining into the long gaping slit and scowled at him. In the corridor Rosalie was waiting to say goodbye. I asked her if she'd let me have thirty dollars on my very expensive watch and she promised it would be recoverable at any time.

'Remember,' she said, 'it's all about politics now.'

'What does that mean?'

'It means just what you said. If the good guys don't work at it, the bad guys get away with murder. That's why I'm quitting to join the Rushton team. We have to take on Colson and Bass.' Rosalie had a nice one-track mind.

Governor Colson and Senator Henry Bass were names I'd heard endlessly repeated on the ubiquitous 24-hour-a-day TV that was a feature of the corridors of the island. Dozens of ads seemed to pour from the screen every hour. Colson, recent winner of the Republican nomination at the convention at Houston, emphasised his cool, clean-cut western background. His own lifestyle said it all. An efficient, prosperous, Republican America. Russian immigration was a problem for the immigration authorities. Senator Bass, the overweight Democratic candidate, gave immigration a brief, inconclusive mention. Russia's crisis might not have existed. His pitch was a calculated giveaway programme for society in need. Farmers balanced inner-city dwellers. There would be tax cuts *and* more public services. The Henry Bass commercials were plentiful but lacked conviction.

I hadn't seen a single Unity Party commercial. But their candidate was the one that figured most for me on Ellis Island. Rosalie had given Ben Franklin Rushton a gloss of his own. I was already a partisan.

A Bureau of Immigration liberty launch set out across the bay on a bright sea-sparkling afternoon. Water slashed past my shoulder as I sat in the bow. Every now and again I wiped a light spray from my cheek. I found the image of all that misery behind me hard to dispel. An unbeatable view of the clustered towers of New York City rose before me, but I wasn't really in the mood to be impressed.

5

My plan had been to take a cab to my hotel, the Chelverton, on West Forty-eighth Street, a slow shower with a thumb or two of ice-cold vodka and a change of clothes before hitting the thrills and spills of New York City. But with Rosalie's thirty dollars to cover everything but my dowry, these were such things as dreams are made on. Instead, I was going to have to go begging right away.

I used my cellphone from the prow of the launch. In seconds I was explaining, trying to explain, my predicament to Roy, who was in bed with a pair of clinking champagne glasses and at least one irrepressible giggler.

'Yes, Roy,' I said. 'They make a slit in the outside of your jacket and ease out the wallet.'

'Christ on the Cross!' he exploded. 'First Ellis Island. Now you fall for an amateur pickpocket while under the protection of US immigration officials. What were you doing?'

'What do you think I was doing? I was trying to get a few minutes' sleep in crowded, lousy, frightening conditions, surrounded by crying women and children and shouting men. OK, I wasn't my old watchful self. Mea fucking culpa!'

'All right, Costya. All right. Calm down. Did you call the police?'

'Will you remember where I was, for Christ's sake?'

'Sure, sure,' he said, close as he could get to soothingly. 'Listen, I'll cancel the money card straight away. No use crying over spilt milk. I'll have another card for you . . .

49

Too late to do anything for tomorrow. So it's going to be Monday morning.'

'And I miss tonight's game.'

'Hey, come on. Walk to the fucking stadium, it can't be that far.'

From several thousand miles away a girl giggled in my ear. 'The Microsoft International Stadium is a few blocks from the hotel, Roy,' I said with not much patience. 'But a ticket to the game costs seventy-five dollars. Didn't you hear me, Roy? I've had my wallet lifted. I don't *have* seventy-five dollars.'

'OK, OK,' he said placatingly. 'I'll think of something.' The champagne glasses clinked.

I didn't tell him that his effort to spring me from Ellis Island had fallen flat. That I was out through the good offices of someone else. That I had not much faith in Roy's long-range influence just at the moment. That was one I wanted to keep back, to use against him later.

'Listen,' he said after a few moments of nuzzling noises. 'After tonight, Lister's next match is against the Chicago Lakesiders. Is that right?'

'Next Thursday.'

'Catch that instead. See something of the Windy City. He'll be up against a stronger defence. I'll get a whole potful of new money to you by then.'

I said OK, I'd wait. But I had no real intention of sitting penniless in a room in the YMCA for two or three whole days while my time in New York dribbled away. I didn't like calling Katerina again but I had no choice. Really no choice this time.

She was good. 'Constantin,' she said. 'A free man again. I'm so pleased. We Russians love our freedom, don't we? – why, I wonder, do we spend so much of our history in jail? Now darling, money is no problem to me at all. But getting it to you is. Tonight important people are coming to my house. Can you come over right away? Where are you now?'

'I'm on an immigration launch headed for Battery Park.'

'Come out right away then and you'll be here before the party begins. I live at a place called Observatory Point, Greenwich, Connecticut. An hour's train ride from Grand Central. Then about a mile north of Greenwich Station. Do you think you can find it?'

'I'll find it.'

She hesitated. 'I'd hoped you wanted to discuss my proposition.'

'Just the loan.'

'OK, Constantin. But ask for Olga.'

'She lives there too?'

'She'll get the money to you. I won't see you but I send you my love. And my gratitude. Call me again in a couple of days.' She stopped. 'But one thing, Constantin. I rely on your discretion. Nobody shall know about how we met, uh? Your help to me, mine to you. Nobody. Never. You understand?'

'Got it. I deal with my sister. I know no-one else at the house. Rely on me.'

'Call me,' she said.

My problem became apparent when I saw that the launch was no longer headed for Battery Park. That, in fact, it was steering sharp to starboard away from Manhattan Island, heading pretty well due south. My father used to say best learn early that, however warming, the sun doesn't shine for you alone. The liberty boat was dropping off fifteen immigration officers. Fifteen officers at different points around the coastline of Upper New York Bay. One reprieved Russian was getting no priority here. Katerina had urged speed. I could do nothing about it but duck the spray and hope most of the officers were heading for homes in Manhattan.

We came down between Liberty and Governor's Island to drop off three officers who planned to spend the rest of the day fishing where the bridge links Staten Island and Brooklyn. When the captain shouted our first destination, Verrazano Bridge, the hair tingled on the back of my neck. The shoreline here is the real graveyard of old New York. On a ledge of land above Lower New York Bay, old immigrant, rowdy, diseased, creative New York lies. When the great city slums of Manhattan were cleared in the 1930s the detritus of hundreds of thousands of tenement lives was dumped here, forming the so-called Doorknob Grounds below Verrazano Bridge. The crushed-brick remains of what was crudely called the Lung block are here. Among all the other untreatable diseases, in those days, the Dog Death was New York's leading killer. The tuberculosis rate was higher in that one city block, the Lung block, than in any other part of the city, and for a half-century it remained an inescapable contagion of the very poor. But that was long ago.

I stand wedged against the gunwale of the launch thinking of the tuberculosis epidemic rampant in Russian cities today and I can't avoid the fact that even this crudest of comparisons places us close to a full century behind the United States.

We drop off our fishermen. Long rays of sun shine on the glittering Atlantic. We swoop round to Brighton Beach, beloved of generations of Russian immigrants, before doubling back to make another drop at Tomkinsville, Staten Island. Then churning north we duck under Brooklyn Bridge to berth briefly on the right bank of the river, somewhere in Queens. Twenty minutes later we've rounded the tip of Manhattan and made our last drop at Battery Park. This is where I jump ship.

Wall Street towered above me. People streamed along the sidewalks. Not an inch of wasted space. All possible nooks and wedges between buildings occupied by harassed-looking smokers. I had no watch to check but

I was conscious, even in the canyons of the financial district, that the afternoon was growing older. Katerina's party time was approaching.

Hefting my duffel bag I made for the nearest subway.

Grand Central Station was a dream shattered. In black and white films of the Forties and Fifties I'd watched dozens of meetings and partings here, usually of uniformed men and neatly dressed girls with curled hair and silk bows at their throat. In the back of my mind I was looking out for June Alyson or Loretta Young waving tentatively as the steam trains hissed and spat behind them. But it wasn't like that. The first impact was more like the Belorussian Station in Moscow. Hundreds of shabby people filled the giant foyer, gathered in groups of up to twenty or thirty around piles of equally shabby luggage. Some were stretched out sleeping, some eating, many shouting and waving their arms, many crying. Police wearing white gauze disinfected face masks were trying to corral them, trying to get them on their feet with their baggage, trying to move them on.

It was with deep and bitter shock that I recognised that the civilian with the loudspeaker at a window above the Champagne Bar was speaking in Russian. The police were there to help, he was saying. No decisions had yet been made by the Bureau of Immigration about their asylum status. They were first to be transported to Ellis Island for medical processing.

Perhaps it was the use of the word *transported* but a terrible ululation rose from the huge mass, now pressed by the police into the centre of the concourse. Fighting broke out between police and some of the younger men. Television crews ran and ducked between struggling men. Tear gas was used at short range. The rest of us, American citizens, Western tourists and a few frauds like myself, were escorted between lines of police without gauze masks to buy tickets or check luggage before a way was cleared to the trains.

Nearly two hours after I had first entered Grand Central, I was boarding the train for Greenwich. I was conscious that I was now running seriously late.

Two or three businessmen and women were my companions as we pulled out of the terminal. A few people talked about the scenes they'd just witnessed. Most seemed confused at the speed with which this crisis was exploding among them. Within a few minutes stories were being recounted of similar incidents in train and bus stations in Baltimore, Chicago, Philadelphia . . . Here, someone claimed that this morning Central Park resembled a vast gypsy encampment and Ellis Island was said to be overflowing. The mayor was arranging to make part of Governor's Island available for the processing of Russian illegals. Those words from the middle of the last century again, *transport*, *processing*.

I kept quiet, uncertain whether my accent was strong enough to be recognisable. Borne north towards Connecticut, I tried not to peer too eagerly from the window. But once clear of the Bronx, Metro North carried me through increasingly well-kept suburban areas as we approached the Connecticut state line, areas that might be spurned by guide books and tourists. But not by tourists from Murmansk.

I got out at a modern station at Greenwich and checked my duffel. No point in carrying it the last stage of the journey. I should be back here as soon as I'd picked up the money. Down the steps to the main street, I turned my back on the last of the setting sun blazing dark red on the waters of Long Island Sound and walked out of Greenwich along a street of country-size shops. Most were closed or closing for the night. Passing fashion boutiques with price tags that made me wince, bookshops, coffee shops, a shop advertising fragrant bayberry candles, I seemed to be, quite suddenly, into deep country, surrounded by high birch and sycamores. Substantial houses soon gave way to the outline of even more substantial properties glimpsed among the trees. A small township named Observatory Village, with a founding date of 1730 displayed, was posted a mile ahead. The houses became fewer, bigger, richer. By now there were lights in most of them.

There was a richness about the countryside too, the undergrowth on either side of the road a dense growth of blackberry and highly scented honeysuckle. I was on the north side of Long Island Sound, of course, but with every step now I felt I was being drawn deeper and deeper into a Gatsby landscape. Then, before the last light dissolved, I caught an occasional tourette capped with grey slate or the roof line of an English country house shyly exposing itself among the trees. Any one of these mansions might have been chosen by Fitzgerald for Gatsby's last summer.

It was dark as I made my way through the scattered community of Observatory Village. I followed a shallow incline on a narrowing road and a white-painted sign told me Observatory Point was half a mile distant.

For a country road there was no lack of traffic. The cars which caught me in their headlights and cruised past were long absurd limos, or Jaguars, Rolls-Royces and Mercedes. So that when I heard an engine slowing beside me, it was something of a surprise to see that it was a nondescript Ford. Surprise turned quickly to an edgy, familiar alarm as three men jumped out. Their uniforms, dark blue with a puff jacket and eight-cornered cap, spoke cop, but they weren't police. Tiny embroidered lettering inside impressive shoulder badges identified them as Cooper Nightwatch Security.

'You mind if I ask you,' the first man said, 'have you had a breakdown, sir?'

The other two men blocked my way, front and rear.

I was baffled. The technique was pure Murmansk

militia; the polite tone wasn't. 'No,' I shook my head, 'no breakdown.' I was working on the assumption he meant automotive. Anything else might have taken too long to explain. 'I'm headed for a house called Observatory Point. It can't be far from here.'

'You've an invitation for the party then?' One of the back-ups eased forward. 'You won't mind showing it to us?'

Slight irritation rose in me. 'As soon as you tell me who pays your wages,' I said.

'Our salaries are no part of this.' They were getting closer now, crowding me into the headlights of their car, none of them more than a nightstick away.

'OK.' I decided to make things simple for myself. 'I'm visiting my sister, Olga Vadim. She lives at Observatory Point.' I looked at the leader. 'I know nothing about a party there.'

The leader looked at his comrades, feeling my claim bore repetition. 'He says he's Olga's brother,' he said to the other man.

'You know Olga?' I asked him.

His nod was a fractional movement of the tip of his nose.

'So the matter's settled,' I said.

The man in front of me looked from one of his colleagues to the other, then back to me. His tone halfway changed. 'May I just have your name, sir?'

'Constantin Vadim,' I said. 'Now I suggest you offer me a ride up to the house where any sorting out that's necessary can be done.'

'Well, yes sir. We'll call in and tell them you're coming. Wouldn't like to cross Olga,' the man said with a grin that I was meant to take as a joke. But I could see he meant it.

Observatory Point was visible only as lights through the trees. But as we swept up the last hundred yards of road I was treated to the floodlit façade, a pleasing jumble of early-eighteenth-century brick with Victorian greystone flanks, much of it bearded with ivy. A stone tower with a brightly lit glass and copper-domed observatory rose two or three storeys above the roof line. I was, I admit, pretty much dumbstruck. I had expected Katerina to be well off but all this was way beyond the scale of well off.

I was getting out of the car when a tall, stringy figure came out of the gatehouse. I watched him as he approached me. In his early fifties, he still had the balanced look of an athlete about him. He was wearing a grey suit and dark tie as if he were just slightly less than comfortable in it, but his most arresting features were the sharp cut of his deeply pockmarked face and his long grey hair, shaped in a widow's peak and held in a curling ponytail. I know a hard man when I see one.

The man's thin mouth, I soon saw, was used sparingly when he spoke. 'You'll be Olga's brother,' he said. 'I'm Stack,' he added, as if that would fix his place in the landscape for me.

'Olga lives here?'

He nodded briskly. 'She does.'

While we were speaking, large cars were sweeping past us into the drive, the flash of a gold-printed invitation enough to get a salute from the uniformed gatemen.

'Olga didn't mention a party tonight,' I said cautiously. 'I hope I'm not interrupting.'

He gave me a narrow-eyed look, then terminated it by a derisive snort. When he laid his hand on my forearm it was with a grip like a crane claw. 'I've heard a thing or two from Olga about you,' he said.

He released my arm and we began walking. The closer we got to the house, the grander the whole structure seemed. Cars, silent except for the pop and crackle of tyres on gravel, moved slowly past us and pulled to a stop under a striped awning. Beneath it was an arched entrance to a courtyard or perhaps former stable yard which I supposed stood at the centre of the building. The guests, the men in dinner jackets, the women in long dresses, left their cars and made their way on a purple carpet under the archway.

Between the main doors and the archway a confusion of entrances of different sizes had resulted from the building additions at different periods. Stack headed for one of them. 'You'd better wait here,' he said.

He had placed me somewhat to the side of the brilliantly lit archway, at an angle that prevented me from seeing what was happening beyond. He turned at the low door he was about to pass through, looking me over doubtfully. 'Just stay there,' he said. 'Enjoy watching the lady guests arrive.'

Look but don't touch. He disappeared into the house and I stood there on the edge of the drive watching the cars draw up. Watching the chauffeurs leap out to open doors and the guests, exuding opulence, pass across the purple carpet into the archway from which I could hear a band playing 1940s dance music.

I stood for two minutes listening to good imitation Tommy Dorsey and watching bare, tanned shoulders pass under the awning. The jewellery, the clothes, the shoes, the *teeth* were extraordinary. The mix of perfumes heady as a distillery. It was the most polished procession of human beings I had encountered in my life.

Was it a mild resentment rising in me, brothers, as I stood there? Was it a sense of exclusion? Was it a sense of *Russian* exclusion?

At least half of my life's many mistakes can be safely put down to impetuosity: the other half derive from inertia. A decision was what I needed. I was certainly not in the mood to have a slim fold of dollars pressed into my hand by my sister and a firm pressure in the centre of the back from Stack, steering me towards the gate. I had wasted one of my rare days with Dronsky in Moscow to help Katerina get out of jail. That alone, surely, deserved a

few minutes at her party. A thumb of vodka or two . . .
a discreet glimpse of this other life . . .

The decision was made. As the next two cars drew up,
I walked across the drive, mingled, fairly smoothly, with
the new guests and passed with them on the magic purple
carpet under the archway.

It might have been through the looking glass. Imagine
passing across the purple carpet into a warm fairyland
of brightness and music, a paved courtyard under great,
coloured canopies stretched on light metal frames. From
where I stand, I see long pink-clothed trestles of salmon
and lobster and pies and salads and foie gras and Château
d'Yquem and chilled champagne. And, among bright-
coloured pennants from every state in the Union, I watch
dozens of well-dressed people, in groups, in huddles, in
clutches, drinking, greeting, laughing, waving . . .

I get a tremendous kick of excitement. Ellis Island is an
ocean away. Perfumed air rolls around me. I am carried
forward on a huge surge of emotion. My heart drums. My
smile widens. *Oh, my America! My new found land!*

6

I joined the glittering company before me. It wasn't difficult to make friends.

'Some party,' a man at my shoulder volunteered. 'Looks like the whole of one hundred twenty-one has turned out in force.'

I frowned incomprehension.

'The Upper East Side postcode,' he said. 'One hundred thousand Manhattan luminaries representing the densest concentration of campaign contributions in America. Without them there can't be a campaign.'

He moved on.

'I'll wager a bottle of champagne that that suit's cut by Martina-Martina Lopez,' a mature blonde woman murmured as I eased past her.

'It's just well-slept in,' I said in her ear.

She smiled and pinched me where it hurt and I turned to find myself standing in a loose circle of guests. A man with silver hair and an expensive tan was saying that Ben Rushton's record running UN agencies made him a natural to negotiate this Russian immigration horror . . .

I moved to get into the conversation . . . and stopped.

'Something wrong?' the silver-haired man said. I knew I was staring across the heads of the crowd. I felt his hand on my back. 'Something wrong, guy?' he repeated, friendly concern in his voice.

He followed the direction I was looking. Katerina was less than twenty feet away. She hadn't seen me and I thought it better she didn't. But the silver-haired man picked up on my expression. 'Have you met Katerina?'

'Not yet,' I said. I eased away. Katerina had just

turned from the man she was talking to and with a fluttery wave of her free hand she was heading towards a waiter carrying a tray of champagne glasses. She was also heading towards me.

I bent my head forward as if I was studying the paving stones at her feet.

'No need,' she said. She was standing next to me. 'I saw you come under the arch.'

'I'm sorry,' I said. 'I was just taking a peek. I didn't intend you to see me.'

'No harm done. You've spoken to Olga?'

'Not yet. Stack's gone to get her. You employ him too?'

'He's general factotum,' she said. 'And Olga's fancy man.'

'Jesus, no.'

My memory of Olga was of someone who, before she turned thirty, already resembled a babushka with a snow-sweeping detachment, a stocky woman with an inflated bosom and hips that looked as if she wore a truck tyre for a girdle. In today's market for svelte Russian brides, or whatever, she wouldn't command premium prices. But if Stack liked what he saw . . .

Katerina was smiling. 'Cruel thoughts,' she said. She put out her hand. 'Good to see you again, Constantin.'

'Where will I find Olga?'

She gestured to a passing waiter and took a glass from the tray. He stood there, I noticed, while she downed it quickly and efficiently. She took another and gestured to me to help myself.

'Olga lives in a separate part of the house,' she said. 'She looks after my young sister, Alexandra.' She paused. 'Alexandra needs special help.'

'Special help.'

In Moscow she'd told me of a daughter, partially blinded. Now a sister needing 'special help'? My doubts about her came flooding back. I waited for her to say more about Alexandra but she seemed to have no such intention. She looked at me. Not a young woman, not a young face. But a good face. Honest? God knows.

'Finish up your drink,' she said. 'Best go now.'

'On my way.' I lifted my glass.

She watched me. 'Olga told me two things about you, Constantin, when she sent you to help me in Moscow,' she said. 'One was that women find you attractive.' She paused. 'That's not hard to see.'

'What was the other thing?'

'The other thing she said was that you weren't really clever enough to *cause* trouble. But all your life you've attracted it.'

'Maybe.'

'So you're no stranger to trouble.'

'No . . .'

'Then come and work for me, Constantin. I need help . . .'

'What kind of help?'

'What would you call it? Protection. Someone to look after me . . .'

I could see, behind the party-talk dimension, something that might have been real fear, might have been theatrical. But none of it was anything I wanted to get into. There were no outstanding favours owed between us.

'I already have a job,' I said. 'I'm talent-spotting at tonight's soccer match between Manhattan and the Bronx.'

'I'll pay you more.'

I shook my head.

She smiled then. The only lines under her eyes were now those of age, and, probably an overfondness for alcohol in its more expensive manifestations. 'I shouldn't even have offered. Didn't I discover in Moscow that Olga's brother was a gentleman?'

Very formally, she shook hands with me and made off, with no more than a slight swaying motion, through the crowd. As I watched her I caught a movement at a window next to one of the low mock-medieval doorways of the courtyard. A long barbecue grill had been set up in front of the window and it was only through the rising smoke that I could see the demonically angry face of Olga as she tapped on the pane to demand my attention.

I was about to cross to the window when the band brought their version of 'Mood Indigo' to an early stop. There was a rattle of drums and the guests all turned towards the dais where a stocky man in his early fifties was walking towards the platform. His dark grey hair was cropped short, giving him a retired-military look. His cheeks were deeply incised by lines down both sides of his mouth. He looked fit, and confident as he ran up the steps to the platform. Standing before the microphone, accepting the applause, his face, I noticed, was carefully composed like the presenter at an awards ceremony, trying not to give the good news away. Our host? Katerina's husband?

There was a last flutter of applause, rippling away uncertainly as he lifted his hand. We were on the edge of an announcement, that much was clear.

'Ladies and gentlemen,' the man at the microphone said, one hand still raised aloft. 'Most of us know each other here of course, but just let me introduce myself to our new friends joining us tonight. Congressman Jack Yado, adviser, unofficial chief of staff, planner, plotter . . . major-domo, grand vizier . . . No real title yet, but what the heck, that'll come. One and all of those things to the man who, I am absolutely certain, is about to occupy a very significant place . . .' and here he smiled as if we were all sharing a private joke . . . 'a very significant place indeed on the American political scene in the coming months – ladies and gentlemen . . .' His hand shot out, finger pointing. 'I give you *Ben Franklin Rushton*.'

There was a storm of applause at this and I looked round to follow the direction most of the guests were looking in. A tall, slim, broad-shouldered man with well-cut coarse grey-white hair was moving through the crowd, waving with both hands, but preserving a serious, determined look. The man I had seen on TV, talking to the Russians outside the burning hostel. Of course. The man Rosalie was turning in her career with Immigration to help.

He wore a dark blue business suit, almost certainly, apart from me, the only man at the party without a dinner jacket. The man about to occupy a very significant place on the American political scene? I studied his face. Rosalie could have been right. He was different, no doubt about that. He seemed to have nothing of the ready smile, the anxiety to please I had come to associate with pictures of American politicians. If it was an image he cultivated, it worked. You'd see him as tough, straight-speaking, in contrast to the flawless pocket-lining politicos running for office all over the world these days.

Did Katerina see him like that, I wondered, as I caught a strange, almost questioning look on her face. Ben Rushton dropped his arms, smiling now for the first time, then half-turned and extended both hands to someone making their way through the guests. The applause changed to a rhythmic clapping. The band took it up. I watched the throng part before a flash of red and Katerina swung through a double line of applauding guests, ran up the steps onto the platform and reached up to kiss Rushton full on the lips.

I was watching Katerina, wondering how much champagne she'd already put away, when a hand took my arm. I winced at the identifying strength of the grip. 'Stack,' I said, without turning.

'I told you to wait outside,' a voice said low in my ear.

I turned to face Stack, his pocked face close to mine. 'And I decided not to.'

There was a hard look in his eyes, but he nodded. 'OK, no harm done.'

'But, in passing,' I said, 'Mrs Rushton's dangerously near the edge of the platform given the party mood.'

He looked bleakly towards the platform where Katerina Rushton, glass in hand, was bending forward, ordering up champagne for the band.

'I see what you mean,' he said. At that moment a waiter began mounting the steps with a full tray of glasses and Katerina stepped aside, her back to the guests, to allow him to pass.

I was already moving forward when one high-heeled ankle turned, her hand reached out to recover her balance, and half the glasses on the waiter's tray were swept to the ground, champagne spurting across guests. Katerina Rushton pitched backwards, turning in the air.

I was there to break her fall. Not really a neat save-the-lady catch, no, I can't claim that. But enough to keep her head above her heels. Enough to prevent her sprawling, legs wide, on the ground below the dais. Enough to keep her dignity.

'Are you *always* on hand?' she murmured in my ear in a voice masked by the outburst of applause.

I removed my hand. I stood her upright. 'Stop drinking, for Christ's sake,' I muttered in her ear. 'You can't take any more.'

I knew of course that no drunk in history had ever been restrained by telling them they're drunk. Certainly not me.

She had refixed her smile. Guests were pressing round her to ask if she was hurt. I withdrew back towards Stack. 'They'll be offering you a job here, if you carry on like this,' he said. I think he already knew.

I looked towards the platform. Katerina was back in place. Rushton, I noticed, had an arm round her shoulder, lightly restraining. I turned back to Stack.

'You saved the day,' he said, unsmiling.

'What day is that?'

'Have you never heard of Ben Rushton?'

'I've seen him on TV. A sort of McGovern. The choice for the young.'

'He's a straight talker,' Stack said forcefully. 'Listen, I don't know politics. But what to do with the Russians has become the big issue in America.'

'What to do with the Russians has been the number one issue in Russia for centuries.'

'Maybe. But you believe me. This man's catching the voters' imagination.'

'As the third party candidate? The traditional loser?'

'You don't understand. He hasn't declared yet,' he said cantankerously. 'He's not officially in the running even.'

'So it's anybody's guess where he stands.'

'In a few moments we'll find out, OK? There's only one poll that counts these days. The big one, the one they're all waiting for – the Bernheimer.'

'That's what tonight's all about?'

'In the first Bernheimer he came nowhere. Three per cent. But tonight, if Mr Rushton gets within spitting distance of either main candidate, Republican or Democrat, he'll be on his way.'

'You keep abreast.'

'Olga makes sure I do.'

'And what chance has Mr Rushton got?'

'Enough for Olga to put a month's salary on it.'

'She must be crazy.'

He gave me a hard look. 'Come and tell her that to her face.'

I peered through the smoke rising from the cooking grills at the window behind. Olga was still there. This was something I wasn't going to be able to put off any longer. I swayed right and scooped a champagne glass from one of the waiters' trays. 'I'm ready,' I said.

* * *

I was led by Stack through a low stone doorway, down a carpeted corridor and into what felt like, from the different atmosphere and furnishings, a large apartment within the house. We turned into a spacious sitting room decorated in a taste that immediately seemed to me utterly familiar. It took me a moment to pick up the tsarist flavour from the small bear-hunting oils from the Caucasus on the walls and the one or two pieces of Alexandrine furniture.

Olga turned from the window and came towards me with a cold look in her eye. Her clothes were markedly different from those she used to favour but still short of stylish. Her dark blue dress was plain but obviously good quality. Her hair was as I remembered it – pulled back into a greying bun. She had, I admit, lost a good many kilos but she was still a substantial woman. On her feet she wore knitted house-mules of a distinctly unfetching kind.

'First of all,' she said in English, 'you'll explain what you were doing at the party.'

Stack, I noticed, had followed me into the room, closed the door behind him. Perhaps the English was for his benefit.

'I was just taking my first look at American opulence. As a tourist, nothing more. Now hand me the money Mrs Rushton offered and I'll get out of here. I have a soccer game to catch.'

'You should not have attended the party,' Olga insisted furiously.

'Do I have to grovel to my sister for the price of a ticket to a soccer game?'

'You should have followed Stack's instructions.'

'Olga,' I said, barely placatory, 'let me have the money and a phone to call a cab and I'll leave you to whatever you do here . . . and whoever you do it for.'

There was, at that moment, a clatter from the room beyond the part-open double doors and an exclamation of mild irritation. I saw the immediate look of concern on Olga's face as Stack stepped forward. 'You see to

Alexandra,' he said. 'I'll make sure your young brother doesn't take to wandering through the guests again.' A narrowing of the eyes accompanied the assurance.

Olga nodded rapidly and moved quickly through the double doors. I heard her speaking soothingly in Russian, as you might to a frightened child, before she closed them behind her.

I pointed to the double doors. 'Who's Alexandra?'

Stack surveyed me for a moment. 'Alexandra is Mrs Rushton's kid sister.'

'Her sister? Does Mrs Rushton have a young daughter?'

'No.'

So what was the story she told me in the ruined church in Moscow?

'Olga's Alexandra's nurse. Is that right?'

He twisted his lips in what I suppose was an affirmative. 'Olga looks after her, yes. Has since the accident.'

'Accident?' I said.

Stack finished rolling his liquorice-paper cigarette and lit it. 'Talk to Olga,' he said. 'If there's anything to tell about Alexandra, she'll be the one to tell you. OK?'

I shrugged. 'How long will it take me by cab to get back to the city?'

He drew on the thin brown tube as if considering. Blowing smoke through pursed lips, he surprised me. 'No need to call a cab,' he said. 'I'm off duty early. I'll give you a lift. I'm a big fan of the Bronx myself.'

I pocketed five hundred dollars from what seemed to me a highly reluctant Olga. I suppose I wasn't very gracious about it myself, offering minimal thanks which she shook off like a dog emerging from a pond. We were back to our old brother-sister relationship.

'How will you return it to Mrs Rushton?' she wanted to know.

'I'll send it to you before I leave New York,' I said. 'Promise.'

She narrowed her blue eyes fiercely and led me to the door. 'Now slip through the guests without making a nuisance of yourself.' In the corridor she paused. Facing me, she patted my chest. Her expression softened. 'If you wanted to bring the money back yourself, bratkin,' she said, 'sometime when there's no party on, we could share a half-litre of Kuban together up in my apartment.'

Not an easy woman to know, I was thinking as I stepped out into the covered courtyard and the whoops of delight of what must have been close to three hundred guests.

Jack Yado was up on the bandstand talking again. Next to him, Rushton and Katerina. This time she wasn't carrying a champagne glass. But small movements, a step back here or sideways there, suggested she was still having difficulty with her balance. It was nothing obvious, perhaps only visible to a fellow sufferer. Among the six or seven people, men and women, crowded behind them, I doubt if any noticed. Except those who realised her fall from the dais earlier was caused by something more than an ankle twisting in a strap heel.

'Here we go, ladies and gentlemen. Silence please,' Yado said. 'The result we've been waiting for.'

'The result we hope we've been waiting for,' Rushton said, his voice, half-meant to be under his breath, magnified by the microphone.

Now the noise seemed to seep out of the courtyard. The guests stopped roaming, their eyes turned towards the platform. Then the curtains behind the band parted to reveal a screen six feet across. A glossily presented young man sat behind a dark red table. The sound came up. '. . . and this is tonight's Newsdesk *presented by Jamie Lee O'Brien. The big news of the evening of course is the Bernheimer poll result the whole nation has been waiting for. In the last month State polls have shown Governor Colson of California pulling slightly ahead of the Democratic Party choice, Senator Henry Cabot Bass of Massachusetts, by up to eight points. But tonight professional pollsters are beginning to believe that this most prestigious of polls could be set to deliver a seriously heavy blow to both party candidates. Third party leader Ben Rushton has been moving up in the last month. Certainly from 7 per cent he has a long way to go to join the leaders. But it looks as though the result's with us now . . .'* A show was made of Jamie Lee receiving the news through his earpiece. He dropped his eyes, nodded gravely, then raised his face to camera. *'Well, we anticipated the two candidates could find themselves seriously threatened. But nobody expected this result. It is as follows: of those responding, Governor Colson and Senator Bass are neck and neck, each commanding exactly 31 per cent of the nation's vote according to tonight's Bernheimer.*

'Now this is itself an extraordinary result. Governor Colson well down – Senator Bass down but level pegging. But this is far from the whole of tonight's remarkable story: third party leader, we can't call him candidate yet, Ben Franklin Rushton, has come from nowhere, has moved up from 7, to an astounding 28 per cent of votes.'

The cheering killed Jamie Lee's next words.

'Jesus,' Stack said next to me. 'Our man's up with the front runners. Do you understand what I'm saying?' His rough face seemed transformed by an almost religious moment. 'He's just four fuckin' points short of the White House.'

I looked from him back to the platform. The men were reorganising themselves in the small space available to let Ben Rushton get to the microphone. There was no sign of Katerina.

'Listen, Vadim,' Stack said. 'We'd better be going. It's a good drive into Manhattan. We don't want to miss the kick-off.'

I nodded. We began walking towards the arch. We had almost reached it when I picked up a splash of red somewhere in my peripheral vision. I turned my head to see Katerina standing in deep shadow near the archway. She was talking to a young blond man. One of the waiters. However muffled the words, there was no mistaking the direction of the conversation. Nor the direction of her left hand, concealed from the guests, where the pale wrist disappeared into his fly.

'There's nothing we can do about it,' Stack said roughly. From his angle he had seen less than me. 'She won't do anything with everybody round her.'

I eased my way through the crowd. As I reached the edge of the shadow the young man stepped back quickly. It's not something I can easily explain but his face caused me a quick shiver of recognition. Reminded me immediately of the hungry, ruthless adult-children of Moscow's streets. Easy, Constantin, I said to myself. So many times I've been wrong about things like this – but sometimes right too. The boy's face was narrow, sharp, good-looking I suppose, but smug with something deeply disturbing.

'You're not my keeper,' Katerina hissed the words at me.

'Get going,' I said to the waiter.

'Mother of God! What's it got to do with you?' Katerina said in Russian. 'I'm not in jail this time.'

The young guy gave me a quick, wolfish grin and for a moment I thought he was going to stand his ground. Then he melted away into the darkness.

'You're right,' I said to her after enough time had elapsed for the boy to have disappeared. 'Nothing to do with me. I just came to thank you for the loan and say goodnight. Just came to tell you how much I'd enjoyed the party.'

'Thank you,' she said coldly.

I looked towards the platform where Rushton was

about to speak. 'And to congratulate you on your husband's success in the Bernheimer, of course.'

This time she gave me a smile, a bitter smile. Strange, I thought.

'Enjoy your soccer match,' she said in English.

'I will.'

'Listen,' she squeezed my hand. 'Thanks.'

TV cameras seemed to appear from every corner of the darkness. Lights had been rigged and crews were jockeying for position. On the platform, Ben Rushton was looking relaxed and confident.

'Let's go,' I said to Stack.

'Just hear this,' he said. 'A historic moment.' Stack's eyes were turned towards the stage where Rushton took in the applause, his eyes travelling the upturned faces of the guests.

'Just say the word, Ben,' a woman's voice rose from somewhere close to the back.

'We're with you all the way, Ben,' a man called.

Slowly Rushton nodded his thanks. He was a performer, I could see that. He stood there for a moment, head down, hands not clasped but resting on the front of his thighs. He looked part oriental priest, part sportsman psyching himself for the incredible moment. He looked, I thought, terrific.

Then a tall, bald-headed man took the microphone.

'Mr Clint Maddox,' Stack said in my ear. 'Chairman of the Unity Party. A Southern gentleman as you can probably hear.'

'Ladies and gentlemen . . . as Unity Party chairman, it's appropriate for me to make the next announcement. We're a small party. A minnow compared with the Republican and Democrat monsters of the deep. But with a striking advantage. We have Ben Franklin Rushton.'

There was a brief, intense burst of applause, like canned audience reaction in a comedy show, before Maddox continued in a toneless, formal voice. 'This afternoon it was proposed by me to the party committee that we should take the step of inviting Ben Rushton to be our candidate for the coming presidential election, with Jack Yado joining him on the ticket. That we duly resolved. And I now publicly invite Ben Rushton's acceptance.'

The guests fell silent. Rushton came forward as Maddox faded from the spotlight on the microphone. Faces around me, I saw, were set, almost anxious. When he began, Rushton's voice was low but distinct, his words brief, anticipated, but even so, with a visible impact on the faces upturned to him. 'Early this evening, in full knowledge of the fierce struggle that lies before us, I accepted the invitation of Chairman Maddox and members of the committee.'

He allowed a long punctuating silence. 'So my friends . . . it is with great pride – and great humility – that I, Benjamin Franklin Rushton, hereby declare myself to the American people a candidate for this November 2020 election for the office of President of the United States of America.'

Women around me were dabbing away tears. Olga, and a tall, shadowy figure of a woman beside her, both had handkerchiefs to their faces. When the band struck up the relief of tension was like a gusher. From all around me red white and blue balloons bobbed and floated into the air.

7

This is a boy with truly wonderful ball control. In his white shirt and black shorts he slides, slithers, weaves, jumps, races, stops, turns, hurtles, plunges through the red-shirt barrier of Manhattan Islander players at will. The floodlights catch his muscled thigh as he turns on a copeck, whirls, dupes and speeds ahead again, crossing the ball in a flicker of movement, to drop it at the foot or head of a team mate.

But again and again some variant of this brilliant manoeuvre is plucked from the air by the Manhattan goalkeeper, a true ebony giant of six foot eleven inches. His arms seem to span the goalmouth, his height means he's easily capable of looping a wrist over the bar awaiting the next attack. He has a lazy, mocking confidence.

By half-time it has become personal. The crowd feels it. As they struggle for a crucial goal, the two men now play each other: Lister versus the goalkeeper Paxton. I am either on the edge of my seat – or up on my feet, arms waving, hoarse with shouting for Lister. Football in the twenty-first century has never been better than this.

Half-time. Score, still Manhattan Islanders o – Bronx United o. The players return to the pitch. Ends have now changed. The crowd draws a communal breath as Lister appears at the mouth of the tunnel. Then another, a gasp, as Paxton strolls to his goalmouth. The man's physique is extraordinary. The image of a predator, a black panther perhaps, can't be far from thirty thousand spectators' minds as Paxton roams back and forth, back and forth, between the goalposts. Perhaps I should try to persuade Roy to buy him too.

The second half begins. For over half an hour both sides skirmish back and forth, neither coming within any distance of scoring. The work rate is attritional as both defences fight to deprive the strikers of the ball. Less than ten years ago, Stack tells me, you'd never have raised thirty thousand American spectators for a soccer game if you'd paid them to come. Bronx United didn't exist and even the Manhattan Islanders were no more than a fifth-rate team on the global soccer scene. But the world spins. Faster in America than most places. Tonight the tension crackles in American veins every time Lister comes even close to getting possession.

And now, from a position in the mid-field that doesn't seem particularly dangerous, Lister takes a high ball, chests it down, flicks it left, receives it back and is moving down the wing . . . Moving? No, the man's flying . . .

In the Manhattan goal Paxton is already calculating the danger. He stands, legs astride, crouched, neck strained forward, head moving side to side, eyes on Lister, on his movement across the field, on his feint left, then on his sudden electrifying break through the centre.

Three defenders are led into space left almost immediately empty as Lister's acceleration takes him past them, past a blocking fullback, to confront Paxton across fifty feet of gleaming turf. Everybody on the pitch knows this has to be it. Even Paxton, I suspect, knows his skills and size can't take the coming shot.

Are the spectators looking on in awed silence or are they on their feet cheering their heads off? I don't know. I'm too absorbed in the moment of confrontation to say. When the shot comes, it is long and low, rocketing inside the left-hand post before it rattles triumphantly round the net.

And now the brand new, floodlit stadium erupts. Take the word at its face value, brothers. Like a volcano, this stadium *erupts*.

* * *

Stack's phone rang before the cheering of the Bronx supporters died away. I was aware of him pulling the phone from his pocket and slipping low on his seat. I was watching Lister, the modest bearing as he walked back to the centre line, his restrained handshake with the Bronx captain, the easy smile towards his coach and manager on the touchline. Everything in the relaxed slightly pigeon-toed walk spoke of goal after goal to come for Murmansk Dynamo.

Stack was saying something, concern on his raddled face, but I didn't pick up the words.

Manhattan kicked off. 1–0 to Bronx United and another twenty minutes to the whistle. There was every chance of a 3–0 result here. Every chance to see two more perfectly delivered goals by young Lister.

'Somebody actually saw them leave together?' Stack was crouched low in the seating well now, his voice floating up to me.

The first attack by Manhattan was a desperate surge towards the Bronx goal. But the attack was neatly held by the Bronx defence, and the ball was swung back and forth across the field to slow the pace of the game, to let the Manhattan adrenaline seep away. And then Lister had possession again.

Stack said, 'It'll be a bitter blow leaving a match like this. But I'm on my way.'

Lister boxed by three men. Lister flipping the ball over heads, breaking between them and streaking clear. And now only the huge panther between him and a second goal. His speed over the AstroTurf would not disgrace the 100-metre dash. And now the panther made his fatal decision – to narrow Lister's shooting angle, to race forward himself, arms wide, eyes white and huge, almost visibly calculating the odds: would it be a deftly rolled ball, a hard left-foot shot, a delicate chip above even his enormous reach . . . ? Or an in-swinger that would curve wide past his right hand and like a planet in orbit respond to the gravity pull of the goalmouth to slip into that corner formed by post and crossbar?

Nobody, I swear, had an eye for the Manhattan defender running at an angle across the pitch. He had no hope, no intention of going for the ball. The collision impact with Lister's body was tremendous. A shocked groan from thirty thousand throats, Manhattan and Bronx supporters alike, acknowledged the ferocity of the foul.

Somewhere in the back of my mind, the rough shape of Stack's words boomed. '. . . *leave a match like this.*' Leave the match? Was the man mad? He was pulling at my shoulder now, not even looking at the pitch. I tore my arm from him. Lister was sailing through the air. The giant was diving towards him, trying to break the other man's fall. The ball was rolling safely wide, unattended. 'We're going,' Stack said.

'You go,' I said.

'Listen, Vadim. They specifically asked for you.'

'It's a penalty,' I yelled at him. 'You want me to leave before a penalty? Who specifically asked for me?'

The roar of the crowd died away. I looked again at the goalmouth. The ball was out of play. Sportingly, the Manhattan goalkeeper was helping Lister to his feet.

'Olga's desperate,' Stack said. 'Mr Rushton's out of his mind with worry.' He was dragging me from my seat. 'Mrs Rushton's missing again.'

Like so many critical moments in my life I didn't actually make a decision. I was already moving. With barely time to glance back to see Lister and Paxton shaking hands, I made it to the end of the line of seats and plunged down the stairs. 'What's happened?' I asked Stack as he set off at a jog for Exit P where we had left the car.

'Olga thinks she might have had some sort of arrangement with the waiter we saw her with at the party. She doesn't miss a lot, your sister.' Stack slowed and took two or three deep breaths. 'She says she's not sure but she thinks Katerina could have made some sort of sign to him a few minutes after we'd gone.' He bared his big teeth, savage in his concern. 'Tonight of all nights, when the boss is climbing the Bernheimer!'

I said nothing until we were in the car. I could hear wild, thunderous crowd noise from the stadium. The penalty being taken? 2–0 to Bronx?

'Listen,' I said as Stack pulled away. 'It's late. I've had a long day. All this has nothing to do with me. If Mrs Rushton can't keep out of trouble, there's nothing I can do about it.'

'You did before.'

'That was in Moscow.'

'Mr Rushton was very grateful.'

'He knows?'

'She told him. Apparently she usually does.'

'How does he take it?'

Stack gave me a bleak look.

'Listen,' I said. 'I'm sorry Rushton's got problems but it's nothing to do with me. Drop me off. I've got a hotel reserved on West Forty-eighth Street. I ought to be able to catch the highlights of the game.'

'God help me,' Stack said. 'I never thought I'd hear myself saying there were things more important than soccer. But there are. And you're in it now whether you like it or not.'

He reached under his seat and withdrew a bottle of Glenmorangie single malt. 'I don't have vodka but I don't think you'll be disappointed by this.'

I took the bottle and necked a good two or three mouthfuls before passing it back. 'I'm in it now, you said. In what?'

He drank, corked the bottle and handed it to me. 'Ben Rushton's a good man,' he said slowly. 'As good a man as Americans are likely to get as president this century. Unless his wife blows him out of the water before he even gets to the election.' He paused.

I knew there was more coming. I waited.

'You did a brilliant job in Moscow,' he said. 'Some could see your coming to New York as salvation.'

'Oh no . . .'

'The Rushtons need you. She's already spoken to him about you and he's all in favour. Are you going to turn them down?'

Turn them down? I'm a fool for flattery, brothers. I know it and I still don't resist. The sheer flattery of being needed by a presidential candidate and his wife was too much for me. I settled back with the bottle as the city lights streaked past us. As we crossed the Triborough Bridge it never occurred to me that I was, in fact, crossing my own particular Rubicon.

8

The security men on the gate told us that Katerina's Mercedes had left the house just after midnight and taken the road south towards the coast. Both men, phrasing their replies carefully, said that Mrs Rushton *could* have been alone.

I sat at the wheel of a dark blue 4×4 Ford Foxbat, engine running. Stack stood beside the open window, searching through his pockets, coming up with a pen and an invitation to tonight's party which he folded into the palm of his hand. 'The chances are,' he said, 'she's gone out for a drive, no more. She does that quite a lot.'

'You mean you think she's alone?'

'I'm saying she could be.'

'And that's what we've rushed back for?'

'These are sensitive times, my friend. A stab at the American presidency means a once in a lifetime investment of time and reputation for everyone concerned. Everybody on Mr Rushton's team is terrified of what that woman could do to his chances.'

I glanced at him but he hadn't recognised the ferocity in his own voice.

'I'll take the local bars and taverns.' He was scribbling a rough map as he spoke. 'If she's pulling tonight it'll be one of these she goes for. If she's with someone from the party here, then they're more likely up on the Old Sheepshead Road where she rents a small timber lodge in the woods there.'

'What's the lodge for? Officially?'

'She's something of a musician. She uses it to practise her music. On the way up, you'll pass a club a mile or two before Stamford. Called the Pirate. She's been there before a couple of times. It's a rough-tough place used by the kids from East Stamford. Worth checking,' Stack added as he turned for his own car.

I took the Sheepshead Road down towards Stamford, a drive through thick woods. The Pirate was discreetly set back from the road, an old Victorian coastguard station or barracks perhaps. I drove in and parked the Foxbat and heard some not very good music seeping through the brickwork.

I had no problem getting in once I'd laid two twenties in the pirate doorman's hand. In fair exchange I got a choice of a cardboard pirate hat, a cardboard moustache and beard, or a parrot with a spring clip that would keep it perched on my shoulder. I chose the parrot.

It was a very long, dark room with a heavy atmosphere of cigar smoke and strong weed. Mostly men roamed the tables, a bottle of Indian Cobra, this year's high-fashion beer, in hand. They wore jeans with heavy decorated belts. Sometimes an expensive leather jacket covered the tee shirt or a fashion safari jacket with leather ammunition pouches high on the chest. A surprising number retained the pirate hats or moustaches they had been given at the door. Underfoot there were a lot of trampled cardboard parrots.

The women were mostly equally young but there were fewer of them. Dressed tight and tarty, they might or might not have been hookers. They sat in pairs or three-somes at tables around the wall talking to the boys, sometimes being joined by them, sometimes leaving with them. Very few girls wore a pirate hat, I noticed. But one or two sat drinking with green parrots on their shoulders.

I didn't really expect to find her here, although the large numbers of unattached young men prevented me from leaving before I had a serious look around. At the bar I ordered vodka – without ice, or orange twists, or lemon slices or mint sauce. The barman looked at me as if I was putting him out of a job. 'We *specialise* in vodka,' he said, shooting his eyebrows.

'So do I,' I told him and downed the glass he put in front of me. Then I ordered a Cobra beer and a Winterman slim cigar, got a light for it and began to travel.

People were trying to dance. I looked them over quickly. Sometimes, in the smoky darkness, someone looked possible for a moment or two, the height or hair misleading me, then I passed on to cover the room starting at the bar end.

I talked as I travelled, exchanged a few words with girls, some of whom definitely were professional, and boys who were friendly or fierce as the mood took them. I was necking the bottle of Cobra in the mode du jour when I saw him. The slender-faced blond boy, now wearing white shirt and leather jacket, was sitting alone at one of the side tables, smoking something that seemed considerably more satisfying than a Marlboro.

I picked up another Cobra from the bar and walked across to him. He didn't look up until I put the beer on the table and slid onto the bench next to him. 'Are you alone?' I asked him. 'Or is she here somewhere?'

There was shock on his face as he looked up at me. His hand was trembling so much the joint he was holding was shaking out smoke signals. He had pulled the cardboard moustache and beard back off his face until it lay flat on his head. 'What I'm doing here, or who with,' he said, with nervous bravado, 'is absolutely no fucking business of yours.'

'Wrong,' I said. I moved up closer, squeezing him into the booth. 'Is she here with you?' I said slowly.

He didn't answer. His mouth was moving as he sucked his teeth, ran his tongue across his upper lip, all the international signs of agitation in a witness.

At that moment the overhead lighting changed from red to blue. Suddenly I could see more. At the same time, by chance, the dancers in the long room had parted somewhat. Katerina, in jeans and tee shirt now, was making her way across the room, a cut-out pirate hat at an angle, a pirate eyepatch in place.

I got up quickly and moved towards her.

'Holy Mother, what are you doing here?' she said, stopping dead.

She'd had a lot to drink. Standing still was more difficult than walking. She tottered a little. I steadied her. It was a good excuse to keep hold of her arm.

'Are you completely out of your mind?' I said in Russian.

She laughed. 'Sometimes I think so. But what is this – Constantin to the rescue again?' She was good-humoured and easy about it.

'I've come to take you home, yes.'

'Oh no, not yet. Ben's got nothing to fear,' she slurred a little there. 'My eyepatch is as firmly fixed as my pants. More firmly.'

'He's worried about you, Katerina,' I said urgently.

'My husband's worried about himself. What does he really care now that I've outlived my usefulness.' She pushed her way past me and I followed. On the edge of the dance floor she stopped and looked around. Surprisingly, she smiled to herself. 'You seem to have frightened off my young man, Constantin. Buy me a drink,' she said. 'He'll be around somewhere.'

I waited until she slid into a booth, then shouldered my way through to the bar. When I came back she had taken off the pirate hat. The eyepatch, I was pleased to see, was in place.

I put the beer in front of her. She lifted it, sipped at it, grimaced. 'Why do I get so drunk? Answer me that.'

I knew better than to try.

'You like him, don't you?' she said. 'You like Ben.'

'What I know of him.'

'What if I tell you he's not so admirable as you think?'

'In Moscow you told me you loved him.'

'I did. Maybe still do. I don't know.'

I certainly didn't.

'While I was useful to him, essential to him even, he was the perfect husband.' She took Russian cigarettes from her jeans back pocket and slid one from the pack.

'Useful? Essential? What does that mean?'

She let her eyes wander the room. 'How much do you think it costs to reach the stage Ben has reached in an electoral year? I'm talking about dollars. Millions of dollars.'

'How would I know?'

'Yado's a snake. But he's conducted a brilliant campaign on Ben's behalf. Nobody denies that.' She was slurring her words slightly but I could see the effort of concentration was there. 'Yado's tactic allowed Ben to pace himself, financially. Spend what he had, but not be forced to spend more just to keep up. Yado saw that. He made *lack* of money work for us. And got the vice-presidential candidature as a reward.'

'With all Yado's tactics, it still costs money to get where your husband is tonight,' I said.

'Of course. Just to maintain voter recognition still costs. To date, twenty million dollars.'

I was impressed, even though not too much surprised. 'Your husband has that sort of money to gamble?'

She lifted her beer, swirled it round and put it down again. Somehow she made a negative of the gesture.

'So where did the money come from?'

'From me,' she said. 'Ben didn't have it.'

'And you did?'

She raised her one visible eyebrow. 'When my father died I thought he'd long ago sold off what little he had. A broken-down vineyard in the south, a rat-ridden apartment in St Petersburg. But there was also a strip of factory wasteland in Moscow comfortably inside the Garden Ring. Split into building lots for auction, it proved to be very desirable.'

'You're saying you bankrolled your husband's campaign.'

'Twenty million dollars of it so far. Ben may not have officially declared until tonight, but Yado and Maddox have already set up committee organisations in every major city in the States. But let me tell you, you pay rent even on mothballed offices.'

'So how have you outlived your usefulness? You've run through your money? Or the campaign has no further need?'

'It'll need ten times more than we've spent so far.' She made a gesture with her hand that slopped beer onto the table. 'You saw the party tonight. You saw the people there ... Up till two days ago we hadn't received more than thirty-five acceptances. They were backed up five deep waiting to see what the word was on the Bernheimer result. Then pollsters polling the possible outcome of the Bernheimer – that's the way they do things here – began suggesting Ben might just get up there close to the other two. The next day we got a landslide of acceptances. Politicos, journos, CEOs, moneyed New York. The signal that the business world is about to beat a path to Ben's door.'

'With campaign funds on offer.'

'Their pockets will be stuffed with money, darling. And Ben will need every penny for his TV campaign. He's doing brilliantly. But remember no third party candidate ever won a US presidential election.'

'Where does all this leave you?'

'Here, Constantin. Some crummy place like the Pirate with a cocked hat and a cardboard eyepatch.'

I looked around us, at the crowded bar and the now heaving dance floor, then back at Katerina. It all had a quality far more than just bizarre. Reluctant as I am to use the word, I could find nothing else but *surreal*. I told her. 'Your husband stands every chance of becoming president of the United States,' I said carefully. 'By far the most important position in the world. And you're sitting in some teenage pickup with a pirate eyepatch, swilling beer that you don't even enjoy. How does that make you feel?'

She shot an angry glance at me. 'It's time for you to leave, Constantin.'

'Time for *you* to leave.'

'Back to my loving husband?' There was steel in her voice.

'He wants you back home, Katerina.'

'And you're the messenger boy,' she taunted.

'Delivery man,' I corrected her.

There was a loud thwack as her palm hit my cheek. 'Jesus Christ,' I said. But she was already moving across the room to double doors, one marked *Pirates* (with an appropriate picture) and the other decorated with the picture of a leggy, barefoot girl in drawstring blouse inscribed: *Doxies*.

I looked across the room. The blond boy was scrambling towards the exit. As he passed the bar, he ripped off the moustache and eyepatch which had slipped round his neck. At the door he glanced quickly round, caught my eye – and disappeared into the darkness.

I took my beer and walked across, finding a corner at the bar where I could comfortably lean and cover the door decorated with the pirate's doxy. Katerina had not left the ladies' room.

Perhaps five minutes passed. Hard to say in such a busy atmosphere. Girls went through to the doxy room and came out a little later. Katerina stayed in there.

'Are you going to buy me a drink?' A voice asked the international call girl's question number one next to my elbow. I glanced at her – a very young, crop-hair tan-faced girl with a disconcertingly large gold ring in her nose. Like a prize heifer.

I bought her a beer.

'We could go out in your car for a hundred dollars, no holds barred. You like the idea of that?'

'What's no holds barred?'

'What it says, man. You got an imagination, don't you?'

'I'll pay you fifty but I'm looking for something special,' I said. 'Go across to the ladies' room there. There's a woman, an older woman there. Tell her there's a guy waiting to drive her home. And he's not planning to leave until she reappears.'

'What's she got that I haven't?'

I winked meaninglessly. 'Will you do that little thing for me?' I produced the money.

'Why not? Makes an easy fifty.'

She came out a couple of minutes later and crossed to the bar. 'Since there's no sign of your lady love in there,' she said, 'how about we go back to our first conversation.'

'Wait a minute, wait a minute,' I said. 'She must be in there. She didn't come through that door.'

The girl shrugged thin, indifferent shoulders. 'Then she took the back door. Only way to go.'

'There's a back door?'

'Onto the parking lot. So . . . can we get back to what we were talking about?'

But I was already moving through the broad shoulders, bewhiskered faces, the pirate hats and the bobbing green parrots . . .

Dawn was no more than an hour or two away when I picked up the Sheepshead Road. There were a few cars on it and I cruised, checking the plates of each one that passed me. But there was still no sign of Katerina's blue Mercedes when I turned off the road into the narrow Low Meadow Lane which Stack had told me led straight down to the lodge. I decided that if her car wasn't there I'd contact Stack on his cellphone and call it a night. I could be riding these back roads for ever . . .

After a few hundred yards the blacktop ended and

gravel crunched beneath the wheels. Here the lane narrowed and the old oaks clustered tight to the edge of the track. Three or four sharp bends cut off the possibility of seeing lights from the main road above.

As I drove slowly down I began to play out in my mind the scene when I arrived at the lodge. The hammering on the door, the furious, drunken woman inside. The young guy doing what? Dressing with quick embarrassed movements – or throwing himself at me as an unwelcome intruder. The truth, I suppose, is that events had suddenly caught up with me. What was I thinking of, almost a complete stranger bursting into the love nest? If Katerina told me to get lost I'd have no choice.

Thinking of these things didn't release enough concentration for the driving. My speed had increased without my being aware of it. In the Foxbat's lights the way ahead was suddenly confused by thick overhanging bushes. The road turned sharply. I swung the wheel and saw to one side a drop of about twenty feet and the gleam of running water. I put on the brakes as the front wheels rolled onto a plain planked bridge. As the tyres bit on the timberwork, I saw I was angled across the planking, inches only from a fragile timber railing and a plunge over into the water.

I was taking a few deep breaths and fervently wishing I'd come equipped with a bottle of vodka when the cellphone rang. Stack's voice grated in my ear: 'She's not at the Lamplighter or any of the other places I've checked on this road.'

'She was at the Pirate,' I said.

'The Pirate? What happened?'

'She gave me the slip.'

'Was she by herself?'

'No. With the young blond guy.'

'From the party?'

'The same,' I said.

'What's his game?'

'Not love at first sight. He was so nervous he couldn't get his joint to his lips.'

'Blackmail maybe.'

'Maybe,' I said. 'We'll find out soon enough.'

'But you don't think she was recognised by anybody else?'

'I'm sure not. If they'd recognised her, the place'd be swarming with journos and TV crews. My guess is that to them she's an eccentric local matron. Rich and with a taste for booze and boys.'

'I'll pass it on here. Listen, did you find your way down to the lodge? Did you find the lane?'

'I almost found the river too. I'm sitting on the bridge now, slewed across the planking.'

'I had it in mind to warn you,' he said coolly. 'That's a bad bridge.'

'So how far am I from the lodge?'

'It's about fifty yards on down. You might just see lights through the trees if she's there.'

I manoeuvred back and forth a few times to straighten myself out. Then I drove very slowly to the other bank and on down the gravel track. Another turn brought me, quite suddenly, to a small shingle house, set back into the woods. There was a small porch in front and a house area that would hardly have amounted to a pair of rooms. A dacha. But there were no lights inside. No car on the small parking area outside the garage. I stopped the Foxbat and switched off my lights.

I took a flashlight from the door pocket and went up to the house. From the time I reached the bridge, my headlights would, of course, have warned anybody here that a car was coming down the lane. Time for Katerina to turn the lights off, if her Mercedes had already been put in the garage.

I crunched across the gravel and climbed the steps onto the porch. From here I could look through the front windows. The moonlight was enough to show me a comfortably furnished room. Nobody was hiding in the shadows. I flicked on the flashlight . . . A music stand, a piano, a violin in an open black leather case . . . But no trail of shoes into the bedroom, no empty rolling bottles, or bras and briefs scattered over the furniture. No tokens of Russian wantonness.

I came back down the steps and walked along the side of the garage. There was a small grille window there and I hauled myself up to look in. No Mercedes.

I think it was at that moment, as I dropped down from the window and turned back to my car, that I saw the flash of light touch the front gable of the house. For a moment or two I stood, straining my ears to listen. The sound of the cars passing along the Sheepshead Road came down to me. But I could swear there was also something closer, a car approaching at some speed down the lane. No more than a low hum. Then in quick sequence: the carried roar of an over-revved engine; the rasping of brakes applied on gravel and the tumbrel sound of heavy wheels across the bridge planking.

There was a silence of two, maybe three seconds before more sounds split the night, a woman's scream, the crash of colliding rock and metal, the shattering of glass and the long blast of a car's horn, trapped under the chin or chest of the driver.

I thought of driving, decided against it. Seconds later I was running like a madman towards the bridge. The moment I turned the bend I saw, in the moonlight, a gap burst in the low railing on the right side of the bridge. Part of the planking had been ripped out of place so that timbers stuck up at odd angles. There was no sign of Katerina's Mercedes, no sign of her headlights poking into the woods to one side.

My feet thundered across the woodwork. I stopped dead on the damaged side of the narrow bridge, breathing heavily. I leaned out on the shattered railing. The car was directly below me, the moonlight catching the ripple of water as it flowed across the top of the Mercedes, the headlights burning for a few more seconds under the water in short fingers of waving light that revealed green stones and ancient tree boles. Then darkness.

I moved two or three yards closer to the bank and vaulted the undamaged section of rail. Ten feet is an endless drop in the darkness but I hit a flat patch of grass, slid sideways, lost and found again the flashlight and turned to where the Mercedes stood submerged, angled but upright, in maybe six or seven feet of water.

Perhaps I mentioned, brothers, that even in the submarine service I never learnt to swim. I switched on the flashlight and waded into the river. Weeds and underwater grasses twisted round my legs, sometimes a brushing caress, sometimes an almost live jerking movement that made me gasp in alarm. Less than six feet in I was already at chest height. I took two more steps and the water level rose to my shoulders.

The flashlight was a big rubber, heavy-duty model. I switched on underwater. The beam poked forward, undulating and waving greenly, like a less powerful version of the Mercedes' headlights. I knew I needed three or four more steps to the driver's door. For a second I hesitated, then plunged forward.

The river bed fell away under my feet. My hands stretched before me. I gripped something with no time even to think what it might be and my feet found a foothold beneath me.

I had dropped the flashlight but I was hanging onto the open driver's door. For a moment I held up my head, drawing deep spluttering breaths. Then ducking below the surface I opened my eyes. In submarine-escape training, swimming is no use whatsoever to the submariner. But the ability to open your eyes underwater and to concentrate without panic for a few vital seconds is everything.

What I saw before me was a scene from the Lair of the River Monster. Light from the dropped torch imparted a glowing green eeriness to the interior of the car. A page of a newspaper floated lazily from the front towards the back seats. The pressure on my chest became acute. I could hold out no more than a few seconds. A deflated airbag hung from the steering wheel. But there was no-one in the driver's seat.

I had seen enough crashes to know that a driver without a seat belt could be thrown into the back seat. I hauled myself over and peered down. The back was dark and empty. I had to get out now, had to get into the air. I was backing out of the driver's door when I saw something was moving in the well of the passenger seat. I stared hard, concentrating as I had never concentrated before. Hair, like pale seaweed, lifted and fell with the turbulence caused by my outstretched hand. I took a handful and pulled. A white face turned up towards me, eyes open. Changing my grip to a collar I pulled harder. The body lifted, floated, seemed to rush towards me with outstretched arms. As I let go, it moved past, up to break the surface above my head.

I was close to drowning as I hit the surface. Water streamed from my nose and mouth. I was aware of a voice shouting, shouting and a huge splash nearby but I was unable to register anything coherently. Somehow I managed to hook my arm over the open door and keep the body above the surface. Time functioned like a broken watch. In front of me, a figure, blurred by the stinging water in my eyes, was wading towards me. 'Hang on there,' Stack was calling. 'I'm with you, Vadim.'

I think it was only then that I realised the figure I'd pulled from the Mercedes was not Katerina, that the chin I was holding clear of the water, and the strained face above it, belonged to the young blond man she had been with at the Pirate.

I dragged him towards the bank while Stack jackknifed below the surface and began to pull himself into the car. Reaching the bank, I hauled the body just clear of the river.

He lay half floating in the shallows. I still had no idea whether he was alive or dead. His eyes were closed. I worked his arms in the Barlinkov method and water poured out of his clothes, his ears and his mouth. To stop him slipping back into the water, I put my arms round his chest and hauled him roughly higher up the bank. Suddenly he coughed, choked, spluttered and rolled over hawking onto the grass. He didn't look wolfish now. But he was, at least, alive.

Stack broke the surface with a thunderous noise and glancing shafts of light from the cascading water. 'There's nothing,' he shouted at me. 'There's nobody down there.'

'There must be, for Christ's sake,' I screamed at him. I was shivering so much my words warbled across the space between us. 'I heard her crash . . .' I was catching my breath now, slowing down . . . 'I was here within a minute, seconds.'

Stack waded towards me. 'She's not here, Vadim. I'll swear to it.'

I slithered down the bank. I was still blowing water. 'The driver's door was open,' I said. 'When I jumped in the door was already open . . .'

'You think she made it?'

'We can ask *him*,' I turned to the man on the bank. 'Take one more look down there, Stack, just beyond the door.'

I clambered up the bank. The young guy was up on one elbow, staring at me red-eyed. I dropped on one knee beside him. I pulled his upper body up by his leather jacket. 'She was with you? She was in the car with you?'

He nodded his head but it wobbled as if he had lost control of his neck.

'And she got out?'

'Maybe.'

'The driving door was open. Is that what happened, somehow she got out?'

'I didn't see what happened to her,' he said, wiping his mouth and spitting water. 'I was thrown every which way, for Christ's sake. I panicked as the water came rushing in.'

In desperation I looked down into the water. Stack had picked up the flashlight I'd dropped and was scouring the riverbed. The man was an eel.

He came thrashing to the surface and hung for a moment over the top of the car door. 'There's no sign of her, Vadim,' he shouted up to me. 'I swear she's not down there.'

I scrambled up the last slope of the bank and round onto the bridge. From there I looked down on the other bank of the narrow river.

What did I expect?

A crumpled shape among the thick water grasses? Or maybe, higher up, a figure doubled over, water streaming from her clothes and hair? Stack tossed me up the flashlight and I played the beam all over the bank. He stood chest-high in the river watching the spool of light as I made it climb from the surface of the water, through the rushes, then up the twenty feet of bushes into the oak wood. I did it again to make sure, but I saw nothing.

Then suddenly he was shouting something from below. I went to the edge of the bridge to make out what he was saying.

'There's signs of something,' he was yelling. He pointed. 'Shine your torch down at the base of that tree there.'

I did as he said. Like him I could see the gleam of wetness on the crushed grass and sliding footmarks in the mud.

He climbed up the bank and together we searched the oak wood around the bridge. There was a trail of water on one path and at one point I found a shoe, a woman's expensive black high heel. We stood together, looking along the path. 'She ran away from it,' I said. 'She must have known the boy was still in the car.'

Stack nodded, heavy with disappointment at what she had done. 'Looks like it,' he said. 'Looks like she ran away and left the young fellow to drown.'

We walked back towards the bridge. The bank beyond looked, in the moonlight, as though a stampede of beavers had slithered down into the water. But of the blond boy there was no sign. Like Katerina, he had disappeared into the night.

9

Both Stack and myself were certain that at least Katerina had made for the lodge. Maybe the boy too. But when we got there, there were no lights inside, no trail made by dripping clothes up the wooden stairs. I made a fist and hammered hard on the door. Anybody inside who wanted to hear, would have heard. Stack circled the small timber building and came back and reported no sign of movement through the rear windows.

We looked at each other, baffled. 'She's soaking wet and cold as hell,' I said. 'She's lost one shoe. And this is her place, fifty yards away. Why the hell isn't she here?'

Stack shook his head. 'Unless her keys are still in the car.'

'Maybe. You go back and report to whoever you report to at Observatory Point. I'll wait on here a while.'

When Stack had gone I went down the lane and backed the Foxbat deep into the bushes to where I could see clearly in the moonlight the whole front of the lodge. Switched off the engine, held the flashlight at the ready, then settled down to try to keep as warm as I could without the heater.

Perhaps I dozed off. Certainly my head was brought upright by the sound of breaking glass. I blinked and peered ahead. The moon was out from behind the clouds. No darker shape in the house shadows. Nothing moved in the area between me and the front of the house.

I waited, expecting a light to go on. But three, four minutes later I was still waiting. I edged the Foxbat's door open, ready to make a quick move towards the house. Held it like that for another full minute. But there was still no light, no sound.

If the boy was in there with Katerina I didn't want him to escape by a back window until I had had a word with him. I climbed out of the car and staying off the gravel in front of the house, I moved across the grass verge to a point where I could reach the steps. From here on I was going to be seen by anybody.

I ran up the steps. There was just enough light in the sky to see, through the window to the side of the door, Katerina, sprawled in an armchair, her head sagging to the right, her wet clothes blackened with mud. Everything about her spelled out that utter exhaustion that would enable her, compel her even, to be asleep within seconds of collapsing into the chair.

I knocked on the front door and went back to the window next to it. There was no movement in the figure sprawled in the chair. I stared at the angle of the sagging head, the arm hanging loose towards the floor. Like a cold hand crawling up my back, an idea took possession of me. Could she be dead? I switched on my torch. The beam, through the window, hit her full in the face. I started back as I saw the quick flicker of a spasm before she rose, sheer terror on her face.

'It's Constantin,' I said. I spoke in Russian, somehow thinking it would reassure her but she was already out of the chair and backing towards the far side of the room.

I turned off the torch. 'It's all right, Katerina, it's Constantin,' I repeated. 'Just come and open the door.' I stood there a moment, reluctant to turn the flashlight on again. I could see the shadowy figure pressed into a corner of the room but little more.

I stepped back to the door. 'Just open up, Katerina,' I said. 'I've got a car here. I'll drive you back home.'

There was a soft click and the door opened. Close up she looked terrible, her hair hanging, smudges of dried mud on her face, her shirt and jeans still wet and smelling of river water. And in her hand, down at her side, she carried a small blue-steel pistol.

I looked down at it. 'You won't need that,' I said, reaching for it.

She pulled away and backed unsteadily into the room. I switched on the torch and played the beam behind her. There was a bottle of lemon vodka on the table by the armchair and a full-size tumbler – empty.

'I'll put the lights on,' I said, flipping the switch by the door.

I don't know if it was a shout or scream that escaped her. 'Turn off the light, you fool,' she spat at me. 'Do you want to get me killed?'

The gun, I saw, was no longer pointed at the floor. I turned off the lights. We stood, facing each other. She was drunk. She had been drunk enough in the Pirate. But she was something more than that. Afraid, yes. But also not functioning properly, switching the gun from one hand to the other as she tried to decide which one she would use to pick up the bottle to refill her vodka glass. Shock, I suppose, she was suffering from.

My eyes were on the gun and the casual way her finger covered and uncovered the trigger. 'Katerina,' I said as gently as possible, in English this time. 'How about if you pour me a drink?'

'Pour it yourself.' She gestured with the gun and walked over to the sofa and collapsed into it. 'Holy Mother,' she said, taking a mouthful of vodka. 'Holy Mother, what happened to him? Is he dead? Is Luke dead?'

'Luke?' I sat on the edge of the wet armchair, reached over for the vodka and necked a good thumb from the bottle. 'He's alive,' I said. 'You've no need to worry. We pulled him out.'

'Where is he now?'

I expected guilt but I looked up and saw her face was stricken with fear.

'Where is he?' she said again.

98

'I don't know. He didn't hang around. But he's OK, I promise you. Nobody's going to be charging you with murder.'

'Charging *me* with murder?' She laughed. A theatrical shrillness. 'No murder charge for me? Well, that's a relief, I suppose.'

I stood up. 'Let's find a blanket to wrap round you and get you back home. And you won't need that gun.' Again I reached for it – and again she pulled away. Like a child refusing to share a toy, I thought.

'I'm not going home,' she said. 'I can't trust anybody there. I'm never going back to Observatory Point again.'

I looked at her. The tensions were visible in the drawn, white face, the wide eyes. Childlike. Like this she seemed to me clearly, perhaps even dangerously, unbalanced.

As if reading my mind, she said, 'I'm not the one who's crazy. If one of us is crazy, it's my husband. It's Ben.'

What to say? I tilted my head to one side to indicate contemplation of the possibility.

'My life has been threatened, Constantin. I told you that in Moscow.'

'You've told Mr Rushton?'

'I tell Ben and he calls it Russian melodrama. Why? Why does he take it so lightly? Well, I could tell you a thing or two.'

Had she really been threatened? I hadn't believed her in Moscow. Did I really believe her now? 'You're talking about a phone threat, or what?'

'Two separate threats. Two calls . . .' She waved the gun dangerously.

'Recently.'

'The first about a month ago,' she said slowly. 'The second just before we left for Moscow.'

'And you don't know who it was? You've no idea who it might have been?'

She hesitated a moment, then shook her head, the wet

strands of her hair falling like dreadlocks over her face. She either knew – or suspected someone.

'You get a threat, there's usually an *unless* attached to it,' I said.

She pushed her hair back. 'There was. Unless I stopped my fooling around. Unless I led a quiet, well-behaved *political* life, I would be killed.'

'Could he have been a crank?'

She stood up. The silence hung heavily in the room as she moved back and forth. There was fear in her restlessness. But real fear or fantasy fear? 'It was no crank.' Her cheeks flared red with anger. 'You have no understanding of the commitment men – and women – make to winning elections here. Elections to the senate, governorships . . . People work their asses off. They throw in time, effort, relationships, marriages, anything. And when it's the presidency at stake, when there's even a whiff in the air of the presidency . . .'

'And you've put all that at risk by carrying on with Luke?'

She didn't answer.

'You're saying that one of your husband's team would do this because you're a threat to his election chances?'

She lifted her head defiantly. 'Who knows? People have been murdered for less – much, much less.'

I stood awkwardly in the room half-lit by moonbeams. It seemed appropriate.

'Believe me,' she urged. 'At Observatory Point there are motives scattered like grass-seed.'

Did she mean that? Was it possible she was including her husband? Was she saying her husband wanted her dead?

She crossed the room to what I supposed was the bedroom door, dropping her glass with a clatter on the tray on the side table. She turned at the door, hand on the doorknob. 'I've got dry clothes here. I'll change.'

'I'll wait outside for you.'

'I'm not going back to the house, Constantin. I'm not taking that risk.'

'Risk?' I felt a surge of annoyance. 'You're talking in riddles, Katerina. Either you know who's threatening you. Or you don't.'

'I talk in riddles to protect those I love,' she said.

Perhaps I shrugged dubiously. I'm not sure. But the flush of anger came back to her cheeks. 'You still don't understand, Constantin. A brutally murdered wife could arouse great sympathy from the American public.'

'Brutally murdered?'

She laughed coldly. 'You know, once you receive a death threat the mind becomes extraordinarily fertile in devising ways it could be carried out. After the first threat I used to lie awake at night working out how I was going to die.'

'Now I *do* think you're crazy,' I said bluntly.

'Think hard before you say that. By the time of the second phone call I had more details. A man would be sent for me, a Russian. A specialist.'

'A specialist?'

'A specialist hangman, Constantin. They have a man already under orders. He does these things for people who pay him. A sort of travelling hangman.'

I said nothing. I could think of nothing to say.

'A man who could be out there in the woods now,' she said.

I did, I admit, take a quick glance over my shoulder out into the moon-shadowed woods. 'Katerina,' I said. 'You should see a doctor.'

'You think I need to see a doctor because you don't believe a word of what I'm telling you. You think I'm a cold-hearted bitch who's just trying to cover for leaving a boy to drown in her car.'

'Leaving me to pull him out,' I said.

'Yes,' she said, her voice dropping. 'Tonight you saved the hangman's apprentice.'

'For God's sake, Katerina,' I said.

'You think I got free of the car and left a totally innocent boy to drown there? God's balls! Of course I didn't.'

'Tell me,' I said stiffly.

'He made me pull over, just before the bridge. He was holding a knife to my side. I think it was a knife.'

'Luke was holding a knife . . .'

She nodded, fighting for control of her lips. 'He tried to pull something over my head. A bag of some sort. A hood. I fought him but he was much stronger. As he pulled the hood down I pushed the car into drive. It started moving forward and I saw it was my only chance. I hit the accelerator. The car jumped forward onto the bridge, crashed through the barrier and tipped into the water.'

I looked at her, struggling to make up my mind. 'Is this true?' I said. 'Did this really happen?'

'I swear by the Holy Mother.'

'OK. His name. Luke what?'

She shrugged. 'Just Luke. For what I wanted from him I didn't need to know more than that.'

I watched the movements in her features, her eyes. This wasn't acting, I swear. But it could of course have been the reaction of a seriously sick mind.

'Was it Luke who threatened you on the phone?'

She refilled her glass. 'No. Someone else.'

I was right out of my depth. She was paranoid, there was no doubt in my mind about that. But even paranoids can have life-threatening experiences.

'Help me get away, Constantin,' she said urgently. 'For God's sake, say you'll help me. I daren't go back to Observatory Point. I don't know who's behind this. I have money but I have to get away.' She was drinking, great gulps of lemon vodka. I could smell the citrus tang from where I stood.

'You'll be safe at the house,' I said.

She waved the idea aside angrily. 'If you don't help . . .'

She took another mouthful and it was as if she was fighting for breath. 'If you won't help me, what are you doing here in the middle of the night? What do you want with me? What men have always wanted. You want to fuck me? Is that it?'

'No,' I said.

She hurled the remains of the vodka in my face. 'Oh yes you do. You want to fuck me when it's help I need.' Her voice rose to a scream. 'Help . . . help is what I need!'

While her eyes filled with tears I grabbed the gun from her and tossed it across the room. The glass dropped from her other hand and shattered on the floor. Then, as her arms flailed, I fought them down as she began to scream in uncontrollable panic.

It took minutes to calm her. Five minutes at least until I had wrestled her onto the sofa, talking to her quietly, insistently. Her face was white, ravaged as she stared at me. 'Take me to bed,' she said in a voice not much above a whisper. 'It's better than vodka, better than dope. For me it's the only way to forget.'

I told her I'd stay with her if that was what she wanted. But I'd sleep in a chair. She should take some aspirin, get into bed, alone, and sleep for a few hours. She'd feel different, I said, in the morning.

I'd forgotten the gun on the floor. As I released her she jumped from the sofa and snatched it up.

'You won't stay with me – then just go,' she said. Her accent was strong and sultry. She sat on the sofa and let her head fall back. The gun, waved in front of her, gave a powerful sense of security. Powerful but probably false. Her wrist was weighed down by the small-calibre weapon. Her eyes were glazed with drink or sleep. 'Just get out of my house, Constantin. Get out of my life. Leave me. Leave me to fend for myself. But make no mistake. Out there, there are beasts in the forest.'

It might have been a scene from a Stalin romance-of-socialism movie of the 1930s.

I made sure she was comfortable. I checked the big main lock and found she could securely lock herself in. I checked the small broken pane in the back door which was how she had got the key in the lock. Relocked, the key now on the table beside her, the back door was safe enough. I asked her if anybody else had a key but she seemed too far gone to remember. 'Luke, for instance,' I said. 'Did you give him a key?'

'Maybe,' she said. 'Sometime. Anyway,' she said with an angry movement of the shoulders, 'I have the gun. That counts more than any key.'

I stood for a moment, dazed by lack of sleep and maybe pure exhaustion. I didn't know what to believe of the story she had told me. She was having an affair with the young guy, Luke, that was accepted. But had he tried to force a hood over her head? Had someone threatened her on the phone? My inclination is to believe anything a woman tells me. Usually a younger woman. But tonight, not just because of her age, I found I wasn't sure about anything.

I told her I would let them know at Observatory Point that she was safe and I let myself out and listened to her lock the door behind me. I stood for a moment on the porch and used my phone. Stack answered.

I kept my voice low. 'She's here,' I said. 'At the lodge.'

'Is she OK?'

'She's OK.' But there was tone enough to tell him there was something wrong.

'I'm going to put you onto Mr Rushton,' he said. 'He's right here.'

I swallowed. Rushton came on the line and I recognised

the voice. 'Vadim? Rushton here. You say she's at the lodge?'

'Yes sir.' In as few words as possible I told him what had happened since Stack left.

'She's not hurt?'

'No, she's not hurt. But she wants to stay at the lodge. More than that, she refuses to come back.'

He thought for a moment. 'Do you believe she was attacked in her car?'

'If you're pinning me down, I suppose the answer's no. But if she was, the hood she claims he tried to force over her head must be down there in the car somewhere. I suggest we handle it this way. I'll look for the hood. If it's there I think she should have protection. I can't see that anything can happen while I'm looking for the hood. She's locked in. She's got a gun there. The bridge is only fifty yards from the lodge.'

'And . . . ?'

'If there's nothing down there, then I'd say it was safe for her to stay in the lodge. I'll stay outside in the Foxbat. If there's a hood, I'll call you right away and I guess you'll want to call the police.'

'OK, Mr Vadim. I go along with that. And I don't have to tell you how grateful I am . . .'

I grunted nothingness and hung up.

I went down the steps and turned. She was standing, framed in the moonlight, at the long window beside the door. She lifted a hand and blew me a slow kiss. I found myself strangely moved by this woman of so many exaggerations, so many moods, of so many natures, even, contained in one body. I waved to her and she raised a grim smile. Then I walked past the Foxbat and on down the gravel lane towards the bridge. Did she, I wondered, know what I was going to do?

A thick pre-dawn mist hung just above the river. Standing on the bridge I shone my flashlight into the white cloudiness below me. It was, I could see, a moving mass, swirling and lifting on some journey, it seemed, with the water it concealed, downstream to Long Island Sound.

I crossed the bridge and slid down the bank to stand on the edge of the river. From here, I could see the water, over the top of the car and a piece or two of the broken railing of the bridge trapped in the rushes on the other bank.

I shone the torchlight into the water. It penetrated perhaps a foot or two below the surface, to about the level of the bottom of the Mercedes' windows. What I knew I had to do, had to be done. I waded forward in the freezing stream, so much colder it seemed than last time.

The water reached my knees, then rose the length of my thighs to strike like a single heavy blow to my balls. I gasped in pain, stepped forward, almost losing my balance, and again like earlier in the night grasped for the support of the open car door. Secure there for a moment, my chin just above the water level, my teeth chattering almost beyond control, I gathered the will to make the dive, then pointing the flashlight I plunged.

I was better at it this time round, further from panic, further from a fatal loss of control. I shone the light before me and, moving forward, I ducked into the car. If there *had* been a hood, it might have floated anywhere as Katerina struggled to tear it off underwater. Worse, a thought that hadn't occurred to me, she might have dragged it with her clear of the car so that it was now floating far downriver or had snagged on a branch lying in the water.

I was about to pull clear when the beam of the flashlight, no more than a foot long underwater, caught something in the passenger seat well. Reaching for it, still uncertain what exactly it was, I closed my hand round it. Something smooth and long enough to grip. Like the handle of a knife.

I surfaced, close to exhaustion, suddenly affected more

perhaps than I was aware by this apparent confirmation of Katerina's story. Holding my head clear of the water, I breathed deeply. I was holding a six-inch-long lipstick brush in a clear plastic tube. I dropped it back into the water. I braced myself on the door sill. I would try, I decided, one more dive.

Underwater, I saw it straightaway. Hooked by the rear-view mirror, just above my line of concentration on the earlier dives, was a shapeless black cloth. I snatched at it, came back to the surface and waded back to the bank.

For a moment I sat, breathing heavily, the black cloth, obscene by association, hanging from my hand. Moon-light touched the top of the trees and a misty greyness still hugged the earth. I lifted the cloth, a black bag. It was about a foot across, a little more in length. At the neck was a thick drawstring. Could there be any doubt that the bag was designed for the purpose Katerina had described? As a hood?

I rolled up the bag. Here and there a bird trilled tentatively. Frogs or toads began to croak and plop into the narrow river. Somewhere, not too far away, I heard a car engine start up. I stood up, listening. Seconds later the crunch of tyres on gravel gave way to the rumble of a vehicle above me. As it began to cross the planking of the bridge, the headlights flicked on.

I was standing, staring up at the broken railing, as the Foxbat passed a few feet above my head and, hurling gravel back at me, accelerated for the Sheepshead Road.

I call Stack to come and get me. For a few moments I stand on the bridge where the Mercedes has burst through the railing and open the black bag in my hands. Of course it could be a bag fashioned for a dozen purposes. A shoe bag is an obvious possibility, supplied by one of those expensive fashion boutiques on Fifth Avenue where I imagine Katerina shops. I have no way of knowing.

The mist hangs around me, no wetter than my clothes,

but cold and with a full dampness in the nostrils. Perhaps it's the drip of moisture from the trees or the slithering of small animals on the riverbank that puts me on edge, makes me anxious to get away from here. Whatever. But a chilling conviction grows on me as I begin to walk up between the overarching trees to the Sheepshead Road. Is there any basis for this idea which is beginning to envelop me? I can tell myself, and perhaps believe it, that the sinister black hood I'm carrying in my pocket is nothing more than a Fifth Avenue shoe bag. I can tell myself I am overaffected by tiredness and diving in a cold dawn to a drowned Mercedes. Or that my disturbing foreboding is the result of association with the high-key fantasy world that Katerina inhabits.

Yet either way, brothers, what grips me in these minutes is the overwhelming conviction that Katerina Rushton, fantasist or not, cannot be long for this world. How Russian, you'll say, with a faintly deprecating smile even. And maybe you'll be right. But don't tell me that you don't sense it too, sense that, for whatever reason, Katerina Rushton is a woman whose time has come?

11

'Chappaquiddick,' Yado snarled. Fury showed on his face in bloodless striations from the bridge of his nose. 'This will go down as our own fucking Chappaquiddick, nothing less.'

Clothes still plastered to my body, I had walked into as grand a room as I'd seen in a private house. Shoulder-high white-painted panelling offset oak furniture. Sofas and armchairs were arranged around two low oak tables at opposite ends of the room. A log fire burnt in the fireplace opposite us. A low hum suggested the room temperature was kept comfortable with air conditioning. Leather-bound books filled the alcoves of shelves either side of the fire. The library, Olga had called it, but more decorative than working.

Yado and the tall, bald, round-faced chairman of the Unity Party, Clint Maddox, stood at the left end of the room. There were two women, one I hadn't seen at the party, in her early forties, casually dressed in jeans and a tee shirt, her hair short and blonde. The other, a young woman with striking red-haired good looks, sat in a black party dress on the arm of a sofa at the right-hand end, as if holding herself deliberately separate from the others. At one point, I seemed to remember, she had been on the platform during the party. All four were so still and eyes-front that they might have been posed by a photographer just moments before our entry.

To my surprise Olga seemed at ease there, introducing me first to Yado, then to the redhead, Rushton's niece, Sarah Rushton. Then, more briefly, to Clinton Maddox, and to the older, blonde woman, Polly, 'one of Mr

Rushton's political friends'. With a brisk nod of self-satisfaction, Olga stepped to one side.

'I handle the media,' Sarah Rushton said. 'Polly's our pollster.'

Anger burned on Yado's face. He looked at his watch, an automatic gesture. 'Where is he?' he asked Sarah.

'Saying goodnight to a few people who have to be said goodnight to,' she said firmly. 'A few stayed on to greet the dawn. The world can't stop because we have a problem.'

'A problem? Christ, Sarah, what planet are you on? The woman's about to lose us everything. Are you too young to remember what Chappaquiddick did to Teddy Kennedy?'

He and Maddox looked from one to another like conspirators as a door to the far right of the fireplace opened and Ben Rushton came into the room. He had changed into a black turtleneck sweater. He stood closing the door slowly behind him. For a moment I didn't know if he was the subject of the conspiracy or the chief conspirator.

He had heard Yado's last words. 'One thing makes it very different from Chappaquiddick,' Rushton said quietly, moving towards the middle of the room. 'As I understand it, there's no Mary Jo Kopechne.' His voice took on a daunting strength. 'Nobody died, Jack.'

'She walked out on the guy in the car. She left him to drown, for Christ's sake.'

'But he didn't.'

'Thanks to Mr Vadim,' Sarah said, looking at me.

'And Stack,' I said. He was standing back against the panelled wall, his clothes hanging wet and shapeless. He looked terrible. I supposed I didn't look much better.

Rushton came over to where I stood. Without speaking he took my upper arm. 'I have you both to thank.' He nodded, more to himself than anything. 'The young guy's OK? You're sure of that?'

'Well enough to run for it as soon as he'd coughed

the water out of his lungs,' I said. 'He's OK, who-ever he is.'

'We have to do something about Katerina's car,' Sarah was saying. 'We can't just get a local garage to have it hauled out of the river. We have to call the police.'

The room went cold.

'If we call the police now, Ben's campaign's finished,' Maddox said in his marked Southern accent. 'But if she were back in her room, sleeping it off, shocked, whatever, *then* we could make the call. A simple accident. She was driving alone. She can make a statement tomorrow morning.'

'But it's not like that,' Yado said. 'You know it's not like that, for Christ's sake. To begin with, we don't know where she's gone.' He turned to me, eyebrows raised. 'What do *you* think?'

'I'd say you have to call them sometime. Delay could cause you worse problems than calling now. Reporting the crash – but saying for the moment you just don't know where she is. Called a friend to pick her up maybe.'

Rushton walked up and down the room, not pacing it, slowly, thinking . . . 'So she's driving about somewhere, maybe making her way back here, sober enough by now to realise what she's done.'

'Shock's exhausting,' I said. 'Not helped by a lot of drink. After what happened she might easily have pulled the Foxbat off the road and be sleeping it off.'

'And the boy,' Rushton said. 'What about him?'

I looked at him. 'I don't know,' I said. I hesitated. 'I don't see why he has to be mentioned.'

Nobody spoke in the room. Yado put his hand through his cropped hair.

'Let's do it,' Sarah said. 'The way Mr Vadim says.'

'OK. As soon as she gets back, I'm to be told,' Rushton said. He was banging the library table with his knuckle, light rapid thumps like a jungle drum.

We all watched him, nobody interrupting.

'OK,' he said again slowly and I could see him weighing, calculating. He had packaged and tucked away the primary question of his wife's safety. Now he would tackle the danger the night posed for himself. 'What sort of a place is the club, the Pirate? Some sort of sex and drugs joint, is that right?'

'More or less.' I didn't want to be standing there telling a man that his wife was there for one of them. Maybe both.

'Now . . .' Yado said, as if lining me up in a courtroom. 'What chance was there of somebody recognising her there?'

I looked at Yado and slowly turned to Rushton. 'You mind if I pour myself a drink? I feel the need of some warmth here.'

'Of course,' Rushton agreed. 'Jesus, we haven't even given you time to change,' he said, as if they had all just this moment registered that I was standing on the polished boards in a puddle leaking slowly from my drenched clothes.

Sarah jumped up, poured a good thumb of malt whisky and I nodded my thanks. I turned back to Yado. 'What was to stop someone recognising her? Ridiculously, guests are required to wear a cardboard cut-out. A pirate's beard, a three-cornered hat, a big eyepatch, that sort of thing.'

'Katerina was wearing a hat?' Rushton said.

'And an eyepatch.' Nobody smiled at the thought.

'What were *you* wearing?' Sarah asked.

'A cardboard parrot on my shoulder.'

She smiled. It was quick but genuine. The first smile I'd seen since I got back to Observatory Point.

'You're saying,' Ben Rushton said slowly, 'that unless anybody knew her before, she was unlikely to be recognised.'

'With luck.'

'Mr Vadim is new to our company,' Rushton said. 'But

he is, of course, Olga's brother. More than that, we know from the way he took care of things in Moscow that he's a man to be trusted.' He came over and shook my hand. 'I'm really grateful,' he said, 'for what you did for Katerina over there. And what you did tonight.'

I was faintly embarrassed. It seemed a late moment in the night's events to be shaking my hand. 'It was just good luck that I was passing through Moscow on my way here,' I said.

'The Virgin Mary,' Olga said from beside a towering bookcase.

'If you like.' I looked at Olga. 'But having said that,' I turned back to Rushton, 'I'm not sure exactly what the Virgin Mary has in mind for me now. I'd like to think it's something to do with a shower and a warm bed.'

'Here, take off that wet coat,' Rushton said, coming forward. He peeled off his sweater and handed it to me. The man had a presence, there was no doubt about it. You could almost feel it. Why exactly he was directing so much of his magnetism my way was something I didn't yet understand.

'Don't get me wrong, Vadim,' Rushton continued. 'I'm not here as the aggrieved husband. I know more about Katerina's tastes in vodka and young men than anybody in the room . . .'

Sarah's head came up. The red hair twitched angrily. 'For God's sake, Ben. Must you be so fucking *under-standing*?'

'OK, Sarah, you see it differently,' Rushton said. 'Just for the moment, keep it to yourself . . .'

Sarah Rushton puffed air through pouted lips, but her head dropped. Rich hair hanging, so thick I could no longer see her face.

'I owe my political career to Katerina.' He let his eyes move round the room. 'That means we *all* do in the Unity Party. I don't think we should forget that.' He paused.

'It's also true that what she does could bring our, my, political edifice crashing down. Caesar's wife, Vadim, must be above suspicion, right?'

'So the Roman people thought.'

'And so the American people think today,' Rushton said. 'So far I've had a lot of luck.'

'But understand this,' Yado broke in. 'Everything changed a few hours ago. The Bernheimer poll made sure of that. It was a triumph.' His mouth was working. 'A triumph we had fought tigers for.' You could see the furious emotion bursting to get out.

'I don't have to tell you we're in trouble,' Rushton spoke slowly, direct to me. 'But I think you can help.'

Sarah stood suddenly. She was no more than a few inches over five feet, a shapely hourglass figure. There was an energy in her manner that I liked. 'Let's get down to cases,' she said. 'Ben's offering you a job. The question to you, Mr Vadim, is straightforward.'

'Is it?'

She nodded crisply. 'Will you take it?'

I didn't need to ask *what* job. Personal assistant to the candidate's wife. Later, maybe, even to the president's wife. Minder. Bodyman, as they call them in Moscow. I looked at Rushton and he nodded.

Then at Yado. 'We're not going to find anybody else,' he said.

I only glanced towards Maddox, the party chairman, to guess the dollar figure he had already pasted on my lapel . . . then I turned to Sarah. She met my glance. 'What do *you* think, Miss Rushton?'

She took a breath, lifting her deep bosom in the scooped black dress. I almost asked the question again.

'I think Ben should get a divorce,' she said.

That put the cat among the pigeons. Rushton glared at her. Clinton Maddox shook his head impatiently.

'Forget it,' Yado said roughly. 'We've got a fucking moral majority out there. People are comparing the 2020s with the 1820s. We could be right on the doorstep of a revival of Victorian morality.'

'It should have been done last year,' Sarah said angrily. 'By now the American public would have forgotten Ben was even married.'

'It was already too late,' Yado snapped. 'I have to remind you that a year ago Katerina was the source of approximately ninety-five per cent of our party funds.'

'That's enough, Jack!' Rushton stood in the middle of the room. 'Sarah . . . take Mr Vadim into the study. He needs to know where we really stand.'

Was this to be the full story I'd been promised?

12

Wet, smelling of river water, I carried my glass into Ben Rushton's study. There was a big fire burning in the ornate grate – but again, air conditioning kept the room suitably cool. Too cool for me. On the huge wall screen an old *Mission Impossible* episode broke to bring up a commercial which featured Ben Rushton's Republican opponent. In hair and features not unlike turn-of-the-century President Clinton, Governor Colson was in his early fifties. Out riding, splashing through flowing streams, looking across to snow-topped mountains . . . He had a certain lazy, action-man charm about him. The VO with just a touch of John Wayne in the voice said: '*In four years Jeff Colson gave Californians cleaner rivers and a cleaner land. He's cleaning organised crime out of Los Angeles and corruption out of Sacramento. In the next four years he could be serving you in every state of the Union. Vote Colson in November for a cleaner America. It's your choice.*'

Was this what we were here to see? I turned to Sarah but her hand went out and snapped off the TV. A disc was already loaded on the player on the low table in front of her. She punched Play.

We picked up after a break on WBB-Y local radio. We were returning to the *Married Life Show*. The host, someone named Marty Lackman, told us he had a particularly harrowing story coming up for us next. The story of a woman, a mother of a young child from Stamford, Connecticut, fighting to preserve her marriage in cruel and unusual circumstances. Lackman led the applause for Carole, describing her as she came into the studio, a young woman, dark-haired, pretty. My eyes were on

Sarah's tense expression, as she poured a drink from the tray on the low table in front of me. I pushed my own glass towards her.

'OK Carole,' Lackman said smoothly. 'You have a story to tell of a young husband, just twenty-five this week I believe, Luke his name is. And you've been married . . . ?'

'Three years,' she said in a voice with, I think, an accent somewhere well south of New York.

'And one child, is that right?' Lackman was saying.

'Yes. We have just the one. But we plan another to keep him company. Luke and I planned starting a second child this year.' You could imagine her moving forward to the edge of her seat. 'A child costs money. Much as you love them, children cost money.'

'They most certainly do, Carole. So let's ask here and now what your husband does for a living.'

'He's a waiter. A contract waiter.'

'And what does that mean exactly?'

'He works when companies have big receptions, serving the food and stuff . . .'

'Companies, right? Or maybe even when rich people have their friends in for lobster and champagne, is that right?'

'That's right.' There was a tightness about the way she spoke now.

Lackman's friendly voice took on an exaggeratedly baffled tone. 'Now Carole, I'm going to tell you I noticed a little change back there. Small but perhaps significant. One moment you were telling us you and your husband Luke *plan* another child. Next, you're saying you and Luke *planned* another child. Now that's what we call the past tense. That's as if it's something that isn't going to happen any more. As if something happened in the meantime.'

'It did.'

'Oh?' Surprise. Sympathy. 'What exactly was that, Carole? Do you mind telling us?'

'That's why I'm here,' the girl said. 'What happened in the meantime is that my husband met another woman.'

A pause. Lackman's voice dropped. 'And when was that, Carole?'

'Not sure. Maybe a few weeks. I only just found out.'

'OK, that's when. Now just tell us Carole, *where* that was. Where did your husband meet her? Where did your husband meet this other woman? At a bar, maybe down in East Stamford . . .'

'At her home.'

'At her home? I see. Could that be while he was doing his job?'

'Yes.'

'While he was serving at one of these big parties his company handles for people around these parts.'

'Yes.'

'So this lady, we can assume, is *wealthy*?'

'Big house up there in back-country Greenwich.'

'A lady his own age?'

'Older'n him. Older than Luke by twenty-five years.'

'Twenty-five years?' Marty Lackman's voice expressed complete astonishment. 'Now let's try and understand this, Carole. You're a very attractive young woman. And twenty-five years older is quarter of a century older. This is a really strange story. Unless . . .' He let it hang in the air a moment, the complete professional. 'Unless there's money somewhere in this story.'

'She gives him presents, sure. But it's more than that.'

'What do you think it is then, Carole? What's the attraction there? Because you won't mind me telling our listeners you're an awful attractive girl yourself. I can't imagine . . . So what is it that draws Luke . . . ?'

'She's well-known. Leastways she's going to be soon. And one thing Luke hankers for, it's the limelight.'

Sarah stood up and switched off the disc.

'By the end of the show,' I asked her, 'had she given Katerina's name?'

'No.'

'Anything concrete?'

'No. But plenty of pointers if somebody wanted to follow up. And they will . . .'

I didn't really understand too well how these things work. 'What's she doing?' I asked Sarah. 'Is she leaving the way open for a cash compensation or a newspaper to buy her story?'

'Probably. *Married Life Show* is just small local-radio stuff, you understand. The way it usually works is that the cuckoo in the nest is named and they get a roasting from the local media. At that point they're invited onto the show to say how deeply penitent they are. And, Jesus, believe it or not they usually come and say just that. It's a shotgun reconciliation. The newly reconciled couple embrace, everybody weeps a few tears and they wrap it there.'

'But this is different.'

'This is very different. Lackman has never had anything this big before, so we can't guess how he'll want to play it. Or what this young woman's lawyers see in it for her – or for Luke and her if they're in it together.'

Behind us the door opened. We turned to see Ben Rushton standing, leaning against the door jamb. He was holding a coffee cup, no saucer and looking haggard. It was after five in the morning. 'So now you're up to speed, Vadim. You can see how we could all be congregating on the deck of the *Titanic*. What do you think?'

I stood up. What was I to say? 'Seems to me a great deal depends on where Mrs Rushton is now, who she's with, if anyone, and what Carole . . .' I pointed to the disc player behind me . . . 'has in mind.'

'In the meantime,' he said, 'we need to find my wife.'

He seemed to change demeanour, posture even. For a moment he stood there, head down, like a tennis star preparing for match point. 'There's much more involved than Katerina here, Vadim,' he said slowly. 'To me politics is a means of getting things done.' His head came up. His strong green eyes fixed mine. 'Opening Ellis Island is a nineteenth-century answer to a twenty-first century problem. The answer has to be found there, not here. Russia has to be stabilised.'

He moved across the room and put down his cup. There was a compelling decisiveness about his movements. He turned back to face the room. 'Unless America creates a humane, balanced aid and immigration policy,' he said, 'we're going to manufacture the greatest tragedy of this century, a sick, anarchic, dangerously resentful Russia with rusting nuclear weapons.'

I stood without speaking, feeling the waves of real emotion given off by this man. But feeling something more too – the flush of bitter shame that it was my country we were talking about, my country that had proved itself so miserably ungovernable since the Soviet Union.

'All this will be a huge task for the next administration,' Rushton said. 'And unless I'm leading that administration I'll say frankly that I don't even think the task will be begun.' He turned to me with a directness that was almost mesmeric. 'I'm asking you, Vadim . . .' He paused. 'Obviously I'm not saying I'm asking you to make that possible – but I *am* asking you to fulfil a vital role in getting me to the White House, the only place these issues will be finally faced.'

Let me admit it, brothers, I wasn't cool, detached, cynical, about all this. I was as excited as hell. The man who could be the future president of the United States was asking for my help. I wasn't thinking any longer about a green card work permit, salary . . . perks . . . the car with the job . . .

'Well?' Rushton said.

In the fire the logs shifted in the last long moment of silence. What was I doing here? I had to tell myself. It was not like the days of the Cold War. I was not defecting. I was accepting a foreign posting.

What I was doing, I was doing for Russia.

'It's an honour,' I said. 'Count me in.'

13

I drifted through the comfortable rumbling of the clock-radio set for seven o'clock by the last occupant of the room. The warm-voiced announcer told me it was average 78 degrees Fahrenheit in New York City and that cloud would surely clear during the morning to give sunshine periods and a bright afternoon. Observatory Point was already being referred to with the familiarity of Hyannis Port or Kennebunkport: 'The view from Observatory Point this morning where Ben Rushton and his campaign team have barely finished celebrating their sensational Bernheimer result . . .'

In my half-sleep, images of the celebrations merged and wavered ectoplasmically. Dozens of well-dressed people were dancing waist-deep in the river. Champagne glasses were held aloft. Orgies of kissing between soaking men and the sodden women draped round them . . . while I dived and swam with a grace I certainly didn't possess between their legs, calling Katerina's name.

I got some sleep. An hour and a half perhaps, before Stack awoke me. I pulled myself up in bed and looked at the room for what seemed to me the first time, a big square bedroom in the tower below the observatory, comfortably furnished with a shower off it. I had fallen into bed earlier this morning with barely a glance at my surroundings.

'The police just called to see if she's back,' Stack said, giving me a mug of coffee. 'They'll want to see you as soon as they've talked to Mr Rushton.'

'*Is* she back?'

'No. No sign of her. I think Yado's taken leave of his senses. He's told the cops that she's here, in bed. Sleeping off the effects of last night. He says any scandal at this moment could kill the campaign stone dead.'

I got up and put on the robe hanging on the shower door. 'And what about the man she was with, Luke? What about the black hood I found?'

He took a deep breath. 'The boyfriend's being wiped off the slate. He didn't happen.'

'Yado's out of his mind. Isn't he worried about that hood?'

'He says it's a shoe bag. Nothing more.'

I got out of bed and wrapped a towel round me. 'I have to speak to Rushton. Where is he?'

'He's on the tennis court.'

'He's playing *tennis*?'

Stack gave me one of his hard looks. 'According to the Yado version of events,' he said, 'Mr Rushton has got no reason to be worried about his wife. She's supposed to be tucked up safe in bed, remember?'

I nodded, bleary-eyed. Stories like this fall apart in your hands. A good lie should be as close to the truth as possible. I saw this as a measure of Yado's panic. I couldn't believe the story would last out the day.

'Here . . .' Stack jerked his head towards the window. 'You've got a grandstand view.'

He went over and pulled open the curtains. The tower room had views down on most sides of the house. As I came up on his shoulder I saw below a young woman in her late twenties playing about the clumsiest game of tennis I'd ever witnessed. Rushton was her opponent. Perhaps her style was not helped by the overlong tennis dress she wore. I was about to say something when I registered that there was something odd about the racquets they were using. Each had, I could see even from up here, a bigger than usual paddle. And the ball, sailing across the net from Rushton, was bigger and slower than anything ever used at Wimbledon.

I turned to Stack. 'Is that what I think it is? I was expecting a child of ten or eleven. That's Alexandra? Katerina's sister?'

'Every morning he's at home he plays tennis with her. I've known him drive out for the game when he's been staying overnight in the city.'

I watched the couple below me. Rushton kept the game at a snail's pace. Most times she missed the shot by yards. Sometimes the big ball hit the wood of the racquet and went flying upwards. But sometimes, just enough times I suppose to make it all fun, she centred the ball and gave a squeal of unfeigned pleasure as it went floating over the net. At which Olga, sitting on a bench near the changing hut, would clap enthusiastically and shout encouragement in Russian.

'Was she blind from birth?'

He shook his head. 'She was a girl of seven or eight when it happened. A bomb in Moscow – intended for some banker.'

I watched, nodding to myself. Katerina had told me in Moscow that when the grenade exploded she was standing on the church steps with her *daughter*. So was Alexandra her sister or her daughter? Or was this just another example of Katerina's devious plaiting of truth and fiction? Perhaps a daughter in her late twenties didn't fit Katerina's self-image.

I nodded towards the girl on the court. 'And she's been like this ever since?'

'She was worse until last year when she had her fourth or fifth operation here at Johns Hopkins.'

'And is that it?' I pointed to the tennis court. 'Is that as good as it gets?'

'Maybe not,' he said. 'She's got one more shot later this month. She goes to a place called the Nevetsky Clinic in Moscow. There's a doctor there . . .'

'Professor Nevetsky. The best there is.'

Stack was sombre-faced. The black eyes glittered momentarily. 'Maybe. Her American doctors are very cool about her going.'

'You mean she could lose what sight she has if the operations don't work out.'

'That's what I mean.' He took a pouch of tobacco and began to roll a cigarette.

As they'd finished their game below, Alexandra walked to the net to shake hands. I saw the way she used the racquet as an unobtrusive white stick, coming to a stop as it touched the net. For a few minutes they stood laughing together, she demonstrating shots just missed or just achieved. I was at a distance but I could see her well enough, tall, blonde, her hair pulled back tightly, emphasising the natural proportions of her face, giving it the coolly sculptured look of a Renaissance head. I watched Rushton kiss her on the cheek and begin to walk back to the house.

Alexandra turned and walked in a direct line across the court towards Olga who was holding out a white cardigan to her. Although I couldn't understand from this distance I could see that Olga kept up a stream of words to guide her.

'My sister's job with the Rushtons is to look after Alexandra, is that it?'

'That's it,' Stack said, his eyes on Olga. 'And a great job she does. When Alex went to college, Olga went with her as live-in maid. When she went on to law school, she was there too. Olga's done as much to give her a full life as Mr Rushton has himself.'

I didn't like the clothes she probably chose for her charge, but perhaps I was going to have to think again about my elder sister.

I came down the main staircase and took a corridor right for the garden. I was extending my hand to the handle when the door opened. Olga and Alexandra were coming in from the garden.

Olga acted as if she'd just found me with my hand in the till. Barely pausing, she made the most perfunctory introduction to Alexandra, giving my name only.

'I'm Olga's brother,' I added.

'You were with Katerina last night.' Alexandra stopped, took heavy dark glasses from her pocket and fitted them on her nose, then bent forward to peer at me, inches away. With the old-fashioned clothes, it all gave the odd impression of a youthful maiden aunt.

'I'm pleased to meet you, Alexandra Ivanova,' I said, deliberately using the old Russian form of address.

She smiled at that. *Was* she a handsome young woman? Or really rather plain? Her heavy dark glasses were firmly in place now; I had difficulty deciding – maybe for the first time in my life. Her eyebrows just above the glasses were faintly scarred but it wasn't that that forced the question into my mind. It was, I think, the really unusual proportions of her face that left me baffled. A beauty or a plain Jane? Maybe I'd be able to decide when I knew her better . . .

'Alexandra,' she said, 'will be enough. And I will call you Constantin.' She turned to my sister, authority rather than imperiousness in her voice. 'Olga, I have to speak with Constantin. Please go ahead. I'll follow in a couple of minutes.'

Olga opened her mouth to object, then, to my surprise, changed her mind and muttered agreement. But she was glaring hard at me.

I spread my hands wide. 'If Alexandra wants to speak to me, I'll bring her to you . . .' I said to Olga.

'There's no need for anyone to bring me anywhere,' Alexandra said sharply. 'I've lived in this house a long time. I'm sure I know my way about a good deal better than you.'

Olga liked that. 'I'll make some tea in the apartment,'

she said to Alexandra as she left us. 'I have some of those cookies from Moscow that you like.'

I could see, through the half-open window at the end of the hall, two cars pull down the drive, a blue and white following an unmarked Chevrolet. Alexandra heard them and half-turned.

'The local police,' I said, 'they want to talk to me about last night.'

'So do I. How was she? When you left her?'

'She was OK,' I said carefully. 'Shocked maybe. It's something to run off a bridge like that. But you've no cause to worry. Shock can cause a dozen reactions.'

'Constantin. I don't need a lecture on the effects of shock.'

'My apologies . . .'

The eyes watched me. How much she saw I couldn't guess. I found it deeply disturbing. 'I mean you don't have to worry that she was hurt in the accident. I saw her afterwards and she was . . . unharmed.'

I found I was asking myself how much she knew about the detail of last night, when she told me: 'I know about the young man,' she said. It was eerie, as if she could read my mind. 'Ben told me the whole story first thing this morning. He told me we have no need to worry.'

The police cars had pulled up outside.

'I guess that's right,' I said. 'But we need to hand the police the same account.'

'Of course,' she agreed. 'Katerina came back here early this morning. She's upstairs asleep. Nothing to worry about. Isn't that the story?'

'That's the story.'

She walked a half-circle round me. 'Except that I don't understand why you aren't out looking for her?'

'Because, to be frank, I don't know where to begin.'

You deal with a woman who can't see and you fall into the error of thinking all sorts of other aspects of her are limited. With a woman like this you soon learn you're wrong.

'You mean it all depends whether we believe she really was struggling with him in the car at the time they went over the bridge. *Do* you believe that particular story, Inspector Constantin?'

I wanted to contact her some way, as we do by glancing at someone, by looking into their eyes. But there was nothing I could do. 'I don't know,' I said. 'There *was* a bag – but as Jack Yado says, looked at one way, it's a simple shoe bag.'

She nodded slowly. 'Looked at one way . . .'

Two uniformed officers got out of their car and stood around leaning on the doors trying to look as though they were not intimidated by the size of the house. A couple of minutes later two plain clothes officers, one very young, the other somewhere in his forties, got out of the other vehicle and walked across the wide area of gravel towards the front door. I could see that Alexandra was following the sound of their footsteps through the open window.

'I must have looked very foolish blundering around the tennis court,' she said suddenly.

'Foolish? Not at all.'

'Isn't that why you offered to guide me back to my room?'

'The clumsiness was mine,' I said.

She ignored that. 'What else were you thinking?'

'Nothing else.'

'You were wondering why I wear these clothes, perhaps?'

Christ, was the girl psychic?

'You were wondering why I didn't ask Katerina to buy me clothes. Why I was prepared to accept Olga's idea of fashionable tennis wear.'

'This is not what you wanted to talk to me about,' I said, but she was determined to answer her own questions.

'I've no interest in clothes, Constantin. When you stand

in front of a mirror and you can't see them, or no more than an outline, no more than a colour sketched in, then I think Olga might as well choose them as anybody else. Doesn't that make sense?'

She spoke without the faintest trace of self-pity. 'Of course, when I go into the city to deliver a lecture then I make sure I'm wearing the clothes expected of me. A skirt suit. Heels.'

A lecture? A law lecture?

She took off her glasses. I could now see the faint scars more clearly as they criss-crossed both eyebrows. Her eyes were on my face, large grey eyes. 'I want to ask you something about Katerina.' The sightless eyes held me prisoner. 'Did she speak to you of a threat?'

I hesitated. 'Yes.'

'But like all the other things you were uncertain whether you should believe her.'

'I suppose so, yes.' I didn't want to lecture her about her sister or mother – or whatever the relationship really was. 'Alexandra,' I said carefully. 'Sometimes she craves attention. I'm no psychiatrist but there are people like that. They create stories . . .'

'And that's what you think is happening here.'

I stood uncomfortably before her.

'Well, Inspector?'

'I'm no longer an inspector,' I said slowly. 'But, always supposing there was a threat, I learnt that it was unwise to take anything like this lightly. And the higher up the ladder, the richer, more famous you are, the less wise it is.'

'All right,' she said. 'Then I know I must ask you directly. Do you believe she's in danger?'

I hesitated.

'Constantin . . . ?'

I nodded. 'If she's not back here in the next few hours, I'd say my answer was yes.'

'You'd be in favour of informing the police of the whole

story straightaway? You'd be in favour . . .' I could see she was getting angrier . . . 'of abandoning Jack Yado's absurd story of her being asleep upstairs?'

I was silent. Rushton was my employer, Katerina's husband. He had agreed to the story. It was, as they say over here, Ben Rushton's call.

But Alexandra didn't like it.

We sat in the library. Rushton in his tennis shorts, myself in shirt and slacks – and two detectives from Greenwich in lightweight, crumpled suits of slightly different shades of pale blue.

Detective Hanratty was the elder and the more senior. Detective Thompson carried the notebook.

Big, his excess weight showing in his jowls and shirt bulging over his plaited leather belt, Hanratty was a man who asked to be recognised as an American police stereotype. His name alone proclaimed an Irish ancestry. With kinked reddish hair and a pale red fuzz on the back of his large hands, he was a man, I'm sure, who would have been delighted to play the suspicious, scoffing interrogator of TV cop drama, had he been free to do so. But that's not the way you treat a man who might easily be the next president of the United States.

'So as I understand the situation, sir,' he was saying, leaning forward respectfully, 'Mrs Rushton left the party early, to go for a drive.'

'That's so,' Rushton said.

'Does she do that often?'

Rushton began to collect up papers from a side table next to him. 'Yes, I suppose she does. When English isn't your first language, these political parties can be tiring.' He smiled. 'They're not relaxing occasions for anyone.'

Slowly, Hanratty nodded his understanding. Thompson scribbled a note. When he'd finished he tugged at the elastic holding down the page in his notebook. It clacked in the silence of the big room.

'Left the party early,' Hanratty counted off the events of the night on his thick, powerful fingers. 'Was involved in the accident at the bridge at approximately one o'clock. Saved by Mr Vadim here. Elected to stay at the lodge for the remainder of the night. And returned here this morning at eight.' Hanratty lifted his eyes to Rushton's face. 'You spoke to her this morning, sir? Before she went up to her room? You were able to see she was OK?'

'She was lucky,' Rushton said, avoiding the question. 'No physical harm. Naturally a little shocked.'

I was astounded at the smooth delivery, the implication that he had seen her, without an actual confirmation that he had. It would have been impossible to believe that Mrs Rushton was not upstairs in her bedroom recovering from last night's accident. But he had not actually admitted seeing her. Was this a skill honed as a director of the World Bank?

'OK and at about eight . . .'

'Eight-ten,' Thompson said. 'Somebody called in at eight-ten. Mr John Yado.'

'At eight-ten Mr Yado phoned from here reporting the incident. That was on your instructions?'

Rushton nodded. 'Yes, yes it was.'

'Do you mind if I ask why you didn't give instructions earlier for the police to be called, sir? When you first heard from Mr Vadim here that your wife had had an accident.'

Rushton made a relaxed movement of his shoulders. 'I suppose I might have done. But, frankly, there seemed no need to call your colleagues to the bridge in the middle of the night. No-one had been hurt. My wife was safe at the lodge. What point *would* there have been in getting everybody out there before morning?'

'Did you call a doctor when she came back, sir?' Thompson was asking.

'No. It didn't seem necessary. She was shocked, of course, but . . .' He looked in my direction. 'Mr Vadim was on the scene within seconds of her car crashing over the bridge barrier. Dangerous as it might have been . . .' He shook his head, all politician. 'It turned out to be no more than a severe ducking.' He stood up decisively. 'You've heard all I can tell you, Detective . . . I'm sure you understand this is a very busy time for me.'

The two detectives stood up.

'Get the rest of the story from Mr Vadim. OK? And thanks.' He shook hands with both of them and left the library by his book-lined door beside the fireplace.

Hanratty sat. He was watching the door close behind Rushton. He pursed his lips. 'You know, that's the nearest I'll ever be to the president of the United States.'

'He's not president yet,' Detective Thompson said. A small but precise mind.

'It's still the closest I'm likely to get.' Hanratty turned to me. 'Big party here last night?'

I nodded.

'Party that big has to be catered for.'

'It does.'

His eyes roamed the room. 'Marty Lackman show mean anything to you?'

'No.'

'Local-radio stuff. Girl telling how her husband's running around with an older woman . . .'

'Lot of older women about.'

'Sure. Except a couple things she said could just have pointed in this direction.'

I said nothing, watching him.

He dropped his voice. 'Listen, Mrs Rushton has a certain local reputation. That's all I'm saying. I'm not here to make trouble.'

'No,' I said.

'I'm asking if you figure there's a connection with her car diving over the bridge. I mean did she leave the party just after the broadcast was aired? Did she rush off all upset, is what I'm asking?'

'I can't help you there, Detective. I was at a soccer match.'

'OK, let's talk about the incident, then. So you reached the scene within seconds of the crash?' He allowed a pause. 'Was that just good luck?'

'The Virgin Mary,' I said.

Hanratty grinned, yellow-toothed. He had more leeway now for his natural disbelief. 'So on the first evening you were employed as bodyguard . . . ? Minder . . . ?'

'Whatever,' I said.

'Yuh, whatever. On the first evening of your employ, you certainly earned your pay.'

'The labourer should be worthy of his hire.'

Hanratty nodded. 'I recognise the lip. You're ex-cop. Right?' When I nodded he kissed his fingertips in self-congratulation. 'OK, let's hear why exactly you went out after her? Are we saying the lady wasn't *allowed* to go out alone? Is there any way we're saying that?'

'Last night,' I said, 'things changed for the Rushton family.'

'You're talking about the Bernheimer result.'

'That's it. Perhaps Mrs Rushton hadn't quite under-stood that it was no longer a wise move to go out driving alone at night.'

'OK. So that's why you were at the bridge. You were looking for her. You were heading for the lodge to check there.'

'I was.' I let him do the work for me.

'Right. You arrive at the bridge, see that part of the railing has broken away, see the Mercedes in the river. So this is it. Only you, Dick Daring, between Mrs Rushton and a watery grave. Dive in. Drag her free. Is that how it was?'

'Except I can't swim so I waded in – and she was more or less free already.'

'OK. Then what? You take her to this lodge she uses to practise music or something.'

'That's it,' I said. 'She was in shock. It was close by.'

'We checked out the place. Since it was only fifty yards down a blind lane, it looked like the place she was heading. So the story checks out so far.'

'Why shouldn't it?'

He looked blankly at me. 'You must have been long enough on the job to know that that's just the way it is. Even good stories don't always check out. It's the fucking leprechauns. They mess with the works.' He stopped. 'You know what leprechauns are?'

'The Leshy in Russia. More or less the same.'

'OK, now help me clear the Leshy off the road. Mr Rushton seemed a little uncertain. Did you personally drive Mrs Rushton back here? Or did she come under her own steam so to speak?'

What had Rushton said? What had he hesitated on? I knew Yado's briefing and I followed on line. 'I left the Foxbat I was driving, at the lodge.'

'So that Mrs Rushton could come back later. And how did you get back?'

'Mr Stack who works here . . .'

'Yuh, I've met him before. Looks like that old movie actor, Jack Palance.'

'That's Stack. I called him. He came over and picked me up. I got back and went straight to bed. What with the party and the accident, I'd lost a big slice of my night.'

'Right. So we got you up?'

'Line of duty,' I said.

'Don't we cops just love to bitch? OK. So when Mrs Rushton returned early this morning, you were dreaming of the onion domes of home?'

'Something like that.'

Hanratty got up. He walked over to the window, easing his belt. 'Only thing bothering me,' he said. 'That's that I don't see the Foxbat anywhere in the drive.'

I stood up. 'In one of the garages, perhaps?'

'No.' He drew out the word. 'Somebody was sweeping

them out as we pulled up. I don't remember seeing no Foxbat.'

I shrugged. 'Maybe one of the staff took it on an errand.'

'You sure Mrs Rushton's still up in bed?'

'You want me to send someone up?'

'No, no. Look, we're talking about someone who could be First Lady. My wife'd never forgive me if I messed our inauguration invite to the White House. It's just that the Foxbat's not there.'

'I suppose it's possible she went out again,' I said carefully.

He cocked his head. 'For another drive?'

'What are you suggesting, Detective?'

He held up his hands in surrender. 'All I have to know is what action to take.'

'Why take any at all?'

He scratched the back of his neck, head angled downwards, not looking at me. 'Listen, Vadim. I'm asking you as her bodyman if there's any chance this whole election business was getting to her. Like the stress was getting to her.'

'I certainly didn't see any sign of that,' I said, blankfaced. 'What are you really saying, Detective?'

He stood up and walked to the window, peeked out as if he were looking hard at something and came back to face me. 'I'm asking you . . . What I'm really asking you is this. With the Marty Lackman show an' all, quite untrue as I'm sure the allegations are, is it possible she drove into that river *deliberately*? And is it now possible she's out driving about on her own again – in the same fucking frame of mind? Suicidal. You follow my drift?'

'I follow.'

'So what I'm wondering here is whether I should be putting a call out to detain this lady for her own safety?'

He was looking troubled. I knew where he was all too well. He needed some help. 'Listen Hanratty,' I said. 'Sins of omission never rate the big black marks . . . like sins of commission. You know what I mean?'

'You're raised in South Boston and your name's Hanratty, you're raised a Catholic. I know what you mean.'

'OK. Perhaps it wasn't someone else in the house who took the Foxbat. Perhaps Mrs Rushton took it. She gets up after a night's sleep, feeling a lot better. She doesn't know you're here wanting to speak to her, so why shouldn't she go out for a drive, see friends, whatever? Maybe she's in the city buying a new outfit.'

He grunted, uncertain.

'It's not going to do you a lot of good if you apprehend the wife of a presidential candidate in her bra and briefs in Bloomingdale's, is it?'

'Very graphic.' He rolled his eyes. 'Very fucking graphic. My point exactly. Thanks pal. I'll look in this afternoon. Keep the streets of Moscow safe for the honest citizen.'

'You've got a sense of humour.'

'In my job . . .'

'Tell me about it,' I said.

14

Katerina had still not returned by the time the motorcade was ready to leave for the city later that morning. Last-minute arrangements had been made for Rushton to take part in a candidates' TV debate this evening. It was the Bernheimer rating that had gained the Unity Party candidate a place at the table, of course, a recognition that Ben Rushton was now a national figure. I went out to the front of the house to see the main group off and was taken aback by the flurry of activity there. From now on there would be TV crews everywhere Rushton went. Journalists would jostle for a one-line comment. He would be flanked by motorcyclists, his own conveyance never less than a limousine.

The man at the centre of all this activity came out of the main door with his private secretary Alison Bryson, a tall, handsome but rather formidable woman in a bright tweed suit. Behind him in the doorway stood Yado, Clint Maddox and several young aides, unknown to me by name. Jack Yado joined Rushton and Miss Bryson dropped back as a half-dozen selected photographers were given their four minutes. Rushton showed himself relaxed and affable and produced a sound bite about tonight's debate, then briskly started out across the drive to the waiting cars.

They formed two small groups as they crossed towards the cars, Rushton, Yado and Clinton Maddox in front. Miss Bryson and two younger political assistants behind. To my surprise Rushton veered off towards where I was standing, making a signal to Yado to stay back. He stopped in front of me.

'They fixed you up a decent room?'

'Luxury,' I said. 'Shower, booze.'

'Good. But first things first. You'll need some scratch. While Maddox fixes you a green card, salary level and bank to pay into, I've had him leave you five thousand dollars cash with Olga.'

'Five thousand?' Jesus.

'Enough to be going on with?'

I nodded. 'More than enough.'

As he stood there, half-turned towards his limousine, there was some sort of reluctance to plunge into the fray.

'I hear tonight's the night,' I said.

He grimaced. 'Tonight's just the beginning. Every night this week we have a ball-breaking schedule. And every week between now and November will be the same.'

Rushton inflated his cheeks, held for a beat and deflated with a hiss of air. It was a mannerism I already recognised. A punctuation. A change of subject. I waited.

'No sign of Katerina,' he said slowly. 'No call from her. Her cellphone's switched off.' He rubbed at the lines in his brow. 'I don't have to tell you that there are two things going on here. One's the straightforward worry about her. Where she is, what she's doing? Is she *safe*? The other is that I'm not denying I'm married to a political time bomb. And I don't mind telling you, Vadim, there are times when my conscience tells me to pull out.'

'To pull out?'

'Of this whole thing. From this week on we'll be spending other people's money on a grand scale. I don't like the idea that they're giving money without fully understanding the risks. The risks that this whole campaign might any time blow up in my face.'

'You have advisers . . .'

'Jack Yado and Clint Maddox are scared out of their wits.'

'But you're not.'

'Of course I am. But I can't afford to show it. I appoint people to the campaign team for their strong, clearly argued opinions. And then suddenly they're discussing my wife. She's a campaign issue. On the team, she's *the* campaign issue. It's not always easy to fight them off.'

I knew what he meant. I'd seen Sarah's outburst about the divorce last night. Maybe I was a little carried away by the fact that I was swapping intimacies with the possible future president of the United States, flattered by what seemed his assumption that I was a trusted ally. I went too far. 'Perhaps something along the lines of what Sarah suggested – even a temporary separation . . .' I said.

He gave me a quick, hard glance. The green eyes were intimidating. 'Sarah's family . . . maybe she gets a little more leeway. But for everybody else, there's a line.' He pointed to the gravel patch at our feet and made the gesture of scoring a line with the toe of his shoe. 'It's invisible but it's there. Katerina is my wife. She remains my wife. That's the basis the campaign team works on. Including you. Is that clear?'

'It's clear,' I said.

He nodded. The reprimand was behind us. He slapped my shoulder. 'Make sure she calls me. The moment she gets back.'

'Of course.' We were about the same height. Did my eyes tell him that I was overwhelmed by the premonition that Katerina *wouldn't* be back? 'I'll make sure she calls,' I said.

'One more thing . . .' He gestured towards the main gate where a small convoy of TV vans lined the road, stretching back out of our line of sight. 'I've done half a dozen interviews so far this morning. None of them have yet raised the Marty Lackman story. That doesn't mean we're going to get away with it. I need someone to talk to this woman Carole. Someone who catches her, and maybe whoever's handling their business affairs, completely off guard.'

'And what does this someone do?'

He made a brief, wry movement of the mouth. 'You're right,' he said. 'I'm talking about you. What I want to know is what's for sale. And what's the price.'

I thought about it for a moment. 'If you're sure,' I said.

He had a way of fixing you with those unusual eyes. 'We're playing high stakes here, Vadim. I don't have to tell you how much rides on you getting it right, however you handle it.'

I said I understood that. We shook hands.

I watched him walk quickly towards the limousine. Immediately he had moved from where we were standing, a dark-suited young man had opened the back door of his car. Another one came forward to take his briefcase. So much had already changed from last night.

Yado passed me next. He was shaking his head. 'Goddam woman.' I thought at first he was talking of the young woman who had appeared on the radio show. But he wasn't. 'Russian slut,' he said. 'She could sink us yet.'

Somewhere further back Clint Maddox was getting into a car, a tall easy figure with a smooth head, improbably bald for someone still in early middle age. Half a dozen assistants climbed into the rear cars. There was no sign of Sarah Rushton. I assumed she'd gone ahead to make arrangements in Manhattan where tonight's TV debate was being staged.

I looked across at Ben Rushton. As he ducked into the back of his car he grimaced and waved. Even at twenty yards I caught a glimpse of those frank green eyes. Suddenly I remembered Katerina at the lodge – and the moment when she seemed to be suggesting that her husband was one of those who wanted her dead.

I shook my head. However desperate he was, I couldn't

and didn't believe Ben Rushton would be threatening his wife. I called across and wished him a final best of luck. I meant it. I really wanted this man to be the next president of the United States.

15

As the last of the convoy swept through the gate, my cellphone rang. I opened it and walked off by myself, turning to the restful façade of the house, the ivy rustling on the Victorian additions as Roy's voice rasped through the ether.

'Got you at last,' he said. 'What are you doing? Watching a game somewhere? Or a porn show? Keep your eyes open for something my station might use.'

'Your station?'

'Didn't I mention it? I bought Kola TV last month. You want to be a director? Trawling cyberspace for hot shows. Hey, what I really like is buck-naked basketball. A real all-girl sport. No room for male chauvinism there. And a TV natural. You come across anything like that, tell me where it is and I'll buy it for our late-night show, *Arctic Blue*.'

'I'll look out for something,' I told him.

'So listen, I have another winner,' he said, all amiability switched on. 'As good, maybe even better than your vek, Lister. Stan McGuinness.'

'Rated by *World of Soccer* at thirty-five out of the top hundred,' I said almost automatically.

'Plays for the Philadelphia Flyers. Number thirty-five? That's crazy. I saw him on TV in practice for tonight's game. A striker you just *have* to check out, Costya, my friend.'

'No,' I said.

'What?'

'I said no, Roy. I can't do it.'

'The money's waiting at Chase Manhattan. You catch

a plane this afternoon,' he said. 'You get your ass down to Philadelphia and watch the game. I paid your way over there. I won't take a no, Costya. Is that clear?'

'It's still no,' I said. 'Listen, Roy. Give me a week and I'll sign you a striker. I promise. You paid my fare over but you didn't buy me, for Christ's sake. I did the job. I checked out Lister. I'll e-mail a full report. Great player. I can see him leading Murmansk to the top of the Euro-league.'

'You checked out Lister? You're telling me you checked out Lister and you didn't even know he had two broken legs for Christ's sake.'

'That last tackle – he broke *both* legs. Like Borleone? It's the Fates.'

'Fuck the Fates!' It sounded as if the regional governor's office had been hit by a bomb. Perhaps it was just Roy hammering on his desk, bawling in my ear. 'You get to that Philadelphia match, Costya. And you get straight back here to report. I'm relying on you to find me a striker for the new season. You understand me?'

'Roy, I've been asked to do a job here with Olga's boss, Ben Rushton. You know who Ben Rushton is?'

'Of course I know who Ben Rushton is. He's the loser who wants to throw a hundred million dollars at a third place in the US election.'

'Maybe. We'll see in November. But right now I'm working for his campaign.'

'What are you doing for him?'

I hesitated. 'I'm looking after his wife.'

'Christ on the Cross, you're standing in for him? You're a fucking gigolo?'

'Looking after her safety,' I said desperately.

He hooted with laughter. 'Costya, friend of my cradle - days, you've become a *bodyman*?'

This was a problem. The bodyman, as we now call all those bull-necked thugs that you employ to walk you down the street in Moscow when you have more than fifty roubles in your briefcase, is a figure of utter contempt in Russia. He has the intelligence of a bullfrog and the morals of a camp guard.

'Costya the bodyman,' Roy chortled. 'Costya working for a woman.'

'That's the way it is, Roy.'

'Don't you believe it.' His voice had dropped to that low hoarse timbre I didn't like to hear. 'You're working for me. And if you don't get down to Philadelphia today, believe me, Costya, I'll have you stood in an ice bucket the moment you land back here in Murmansk.'

I switched off the phone. The ice-bucket threat was not friendly. When Roy was Political Police Chief of Murmansk he had learnt to use the ice bucket, a 500-gallon oil drum that a bound man is placed in up to his neck in warm water. During the Arctic night it cools and *slowly* begins to freeze. It's a race between hypothermia, constriction of the lungs or strangulation by the faster-freezing surface ice. It takes a few hours. The screams, I've heard Roy say, are truly beyond belief.

In Murmansk today the temperature would be beginning to point towards freezing. A dirty, concrete city would be cracking and groaning under the strain. In some warehouse backyard there would be half a dozen ice buckets set up ready for the dawn freeze. Maybe one or two would be occupied by a man screaming hopelessly that he would pay his debt, stay out of the vodka trade, or whatever misdemeanour he was being punished for. There were several ice-bucket teams you could go to if you wanted someone taught a lesson in Murmansk. Had Roy ever used them since his police days? I've no doubt.

I had Stack's Passat. Following Olga's instructions, I picked up the Merrit Parkway until exit 34 and turned off for Stamford. A few miles further on the town surprised me with its business-centre look, its steel and glass office buildings. On slender evidence, I'd come to accept that all Connecticut towns still looked as if the Minutemen had just mustered on the main square.

Atlantic Avenue is different again. The initial sense of prosperity with which Stamford greets you is gone. The area is grim, a mix of project buildings and not always thriving, light industrial. Somewhere here the former contract waiter, the blond boy, Luke, lived with Carole and a baby.

It hadn't been difficult to get his address. The Rego-Santini Catering Company where Luke worked was hoping for a massive increase in functions at Observatory Point and was anxious to be co-operative. The loss of one waiter meant nothing to them against the loss of the Rushton contract.

The apartment was in a decayed part of Stamford, above a Ukrainian restaurant, reached via an open dog-stained doorway and a single flight of cement stairs. I stood there for a moment before the plain, plum-coloured door. Graffiti in thick black felt tip had been obliterated rather than cleaned off the paintwork. For a moment I felt I could have been back in Russia. I even imagined I smelt cabbage.

A young woman opened the door on a chain and I spoke to a half-section of her face. 'If you're Carole Bassenger, I'm here to talk to you,' I said uncompromisingly. 'About your broadcast last night.'

There was a shocked intake of breath from the other side of the door, then her face came back closer to the crack. 'Who are you?' she said, the edge of panic clear enough in her voice.

I leaned closer to the door. 'I'm here on behalf of the lawyers of a lady you made certain allegations about on the Marty Lackman show.'

'Oh Jesus,' she said. 'I didn't mean anything I said last night. Nothing at all.'

'Open the door and we'll talk about it.'

There was a long pause while she thought what to do.

As I stood there I thought I could hear a child somewhere in the background. Then while I stood up close to the door jamb the chain rattled and the plum-coloured door opened.

She was a pretty girl although there was not much evidence she took a lot of care of herself. Wisps of dark chestnut hair straggled from a ponytail and the hand that lifted the cigarette to her mouth had badly gnawed-down fingernails. Down the hall I could hear a child crying clearly now. And smell that milky children smell.

'Come into the kitchen,' she said. 'My sister's looking after the boy.'

We went into the kitchen. It was well enough kept. The dishes were cleared from the central splay-legged table and piled in the sink. Carole Bassenger hadn't given up.

She pulled out a chair for me. 'You want coffee?'

I told her not to worry and she nodded and sat down on the other side of the table. 'Are you Russian?' she said nervously. 'You know, the way you speak.'

'I'm not any sort of enforcer if that's what you're worried about. I just need some answers to a few questions.'

She sat silently. In the next room the child squealed and a woman's voice quietened it.

'Where's Luke?' I said. We would start here.

She shrugged her shoulders. 'Look, I want to say something. Can I say something before you start in on me?'

'Go ahead.'

'OK. I'm sorry, right? I regret ever phoning the guy, Marty Lackman. I'd just found out about Luke and this Mrs Rushton.'

'Found out?'

'That he was seeing her.'

'How was that?'

'There's a club called the Pirate on Sheepshead Road.'

'I know it,' I said.

'My sister saw them last week. Dancing up close. Hard-lucking it's called. That close. Wearing those paper pirate masks, you know? But she recognised Luke all the same. Half an hour later he's getting into a Mercedes with this woman.' She paused. 'I have an aunt in Vehicles. She told me the Merc was registered to this Mrs Rushton. He didn't come home that night. Nan, my sister, didn't want to tell me. Finally changed her mind yesterday over a drink.'

I just bit on my lip and nodded my head.

'I was so mad, so disgusted with him . . . she's twice his age, for Christ's sake . . . I just picked up the phone and called. They have one of those easy-remember numbers, you know?'

'How does it work? Does Lackman take some sort of statement from you?'

'He asked me into his office. Very cool at first. Not super interested. Except in my ass. He managed to tell me that twice in thirty seconds. But when I told him my story he went crazy.'

'You gave him Mrs Rushton's name?'

'I was a fool,' she said. 'I know that.'

My stomach was clenched tight. This sounded like the end for Ben Rushton. 'You put all this on paper?'

She shook her head vigorously. 'He wanted that. I don't think he'd ever had anything like this. He closed the door. Locked it, for Christ's sake, so that we're in there alone.'

'And tried to get you to sign a statement?'

I waited for her reply.

'He went over detail by detail how I'd found out about Luke . . . And I can tell you, all that scared me. I suddenly thought of the great dumper truck of trouble this could bring down on my head. So I signed nothing. I gave him the wrong address. I gave him my unmarried name – Simpson. I figured I could pull out after the show.'

She sat biting on her nails, selectively, one after the other as if it were some considered form of manicure.

'You gave him the name Simpson. That's good,' I

said. 'Does this mean you want nothing more to do with this?'

'I want out. I never wanted in.'

'OK. You won't get trouble from us.'

'You promise.'

'I promise. Let's talk about Luke's side of things. When did you last hear from him?'

'This morning,' she said.

'He was here?'

'No. He called to say he was sorry. He was real upset. He called to say he'd got himself into something too deep. Rich people have power, don't they? They have people like you, who can find out where I live even though I give my name as Simpson and I make up a phoney address.'

There didn't seem any point in denying it. 'You're right, Carole,' I said. 'Rich people have power.'

'And neither Luke nor me want to go up against them. You can tell them that. We're not trying to make money.'

'You mean Luke made nothing from Mrs Rushton?'

'He admitted to me on the phone she gave him presents. But just a few hundred dollars. A new leather jacket. Things like that. Nothing much.'

'Do you know about last night?'

'The car going over the bridge? Yuh, he told me. They were having some sort of argument and he batted her one.'

She frowned and reached for the cigarettes. The movement gave me an angle on the right side of her face. I could see traces of a bruise following the cheekbone. She saw me looking.

'Did Luke do that?'

Her hand went up to the bruise. 'He's not real violent,' she said. 'Sometimes, if he's had a few beers . . . He just can't abide women arguing with him.'

I stood up to go. If what Katerina had called the attempt on her life had been no more than a fight between them, maybe he'd sneaked up to the lodge while I was diving for the black 'hood'. Maybe they took off together in the Foxbat. And the attempted-murder story was no more than a few moments of the fantasy Katerina seemed to need so badly in her life.

'Do you think he's with her now?' I asked Carole.

She thought about that. 'No, I don't. He's too scared.'

'So where is he?'

'He said he was thinking of taking off on a bike somewhere. Drive north, maybe up to Canada.'

'You think he'll be back?'

'He said a week maybe. Give it time for it all to blow over.'

'And you don't think he's gone off with her?'

'No. I told you. He was too scared when he heard about me going on the Marty Lackman. He loves our boy. He's not going to do anything that'll keep him apart from him long.' She refixed her ponytail. 'He might not love me all that, but he loves young Joe. He'll be back when he says. And without no old lady.'

Back at Observatory Point I sat on the bench beside the tennis court and called Yado. The air was warm, the waft of Olga's cake cooking reached me on the breeze. Alexandra was playing Rastinov's haunting *Composition for Piano and Silence*. I tried not to think about the work that I should be doing for Roy.

When Yado came on I told him first to let Ben Rushton know that Mrs Rushton was not back. Second that Carole Bassenger was on hold. Third, that the near certainty was that Mrs Rushton was with Luke Bassenger, travelling in upstate New York or over the border into Canada. Yado's reaction surprised me. He didn't bawl, he didn't explode. In a measured tone, he said, 'OK. I'll pass that on.'

I switched off and sat there for a moment catching my breath, thinking about Katerina on the back of a motorbike, her arms locked round Luke's waist as they raced towards the Canadian border.

Perhaps I was there a few minutes. More deeply pre-occupied than I realised, I didn't at first register that the piano had stopped or that someone was walking behind me. I turned, expecting Alexandra, and saw Sarah Rushton coming towards me. She was wearing a dark green business suit, black heeled pumps and her red hair held back in a French fold. She stood a long moment with pursed lips, looking me over, then broke into a smile. 'Hi,' she said. 'Mind if I join you?'

I stood up. 'Pleasure. Thought you were back in the city.'

'On my way.' She grimaced. 'I just talked to Yado. Right after you. I should tell you that in moments of severe stress I smoke.' She took a pack from her tote bag. 'Cheroots. How about you?'

'Only in moments of severe stress,' I said, taking a long, thin Winterman. 'So you're up to speed with the news?'

She sat on the bench and demonstrably crossed her legs. 'Times like this . . .' she gestured towards the court with her unlit cheroot . . . 'this is the place to be. Have you ever noticed that once the hustle and bustle of a game is over, the tennis court becomes a really Zen place?'

'Thinking that myself just a moment ago,' I said. 'It's the geometry of the lines. An empty tennis court has its own sense of order. We should keep the players off.'

I sat down and she lit my cheroot then drew on her own.

She wasn't thinking about Zen or tennis courts or even the arrangement of her legs now. 'So we're through, are we?' she said. 'And Ben's political future is suddenly non-existent? Is that the way you see it? After all the work we've all done, all the hope everybody's put in, all just pissed away. Just because one fucking woman can't keep her loins out of our lives. Is that it?'

'If Katerina's on her way to Canada with Bassenger, it's hard to see it going any other way,' I said.

She looked at me. 'It's all new to you. Maybe you don't feel like the rest of us about it.'

'How do the rest of you feel?'

'Fucking murderous.'

'I can understand that.'

'Can you? Everybody, including Ben, is working eighteen, nineteen hours a day. We're spending thousands of strangers' money on new ads, posters, radio time. We're ready to hire limousines, offices, secretaries. A 707 for Ben's use, a Learjet for Jack Yado. We've got a whole spring and summer's campaigning to catch up.' She balled her fists. 'We are *killing ourselves* with effort.'

'OK, Sarah . . .'

'Yado's taking it all pretty well so far. He's a pro, trying not to crack. And he won't. Clint Maddox's given up even trying. I think the guy's crazy under that Southern lay-back. He just can't believe she's walked out like this.'

I didn't know quite what to say. High hopes shattered by a woman with a dangerous need for the melodramatic . . . I suppose I didn't blame them all for feeling murderous. But in the context it wasn't really a word I liked to dwell on.

'How will it work with the media?' I asked her.

'It'll take a day or so. They'll pick up on the fact Katerina isn't here – somebody'll connect it to the accident at the bridge – that'll be the excuse for speculation to begin about her, her mental condition, her whereabouts . . . her sex life. It'll all come tumbling out. Then some bright-eyed young journo will walk into a hotel lobby somewhere between Albany and Toronto, straight into the scoop of his life.'

We stood up and began walking slowly along the gravel path towards the house.

'So what really happened between Ben Rushton and

Katerina?' I asked her. 'What put the rocket under the marriage?'

'Katerina's tastes in young men. What else?'

'But until a couple of years back everything was OK?'

We were walking through a burgeoning myrtle grove that flanked the path. 'If you could time and date it I'd say the change was not long after her father died. Maybe all that money gave her a sense of independence. That's when she hit the vodka. That's when she began hitting on the guys half her age. Make sense of that.'

There were small white myrtle flowers all around us, mixed with an imperial purple from a few rooted buddleias. She stopped and took a myrtle branch, pulling it towards her, breathing in the fragrance of the flower. 'Is Murmansk really the hellhole I'm led to believe?' she said.

A defence of my home town leapt to my lips and as quickly died away. 'Don't go visiting,' I said.

'No plans,' she assured me. 'I notice you don't say much about your own intentions.' She spoke to the white myrtle flowers. 'Would you ever think of staying on here?'

The question came as a jolt. I must have showed it.

'What's wrong?' she said, looking up. 'Have I offended you?'

'No . . .' I shook my head. 'No. You've just put into words what I've been brewing for some time.'

She smiled. 'But out in the open it's more shocking. Is that it? Makes you feel what – guilty?'

This woman knew a thing or two about life.

'Perhaps. Mostly just vaguely bad. Like I'm betraying everything Russia ever stood for.'

'And what's that?'

'Oh . . .' I said. 'Anarchy, injustice, cruelty, inhumanity. That kind of stuff.'

She looked at me. 'My poor Constantin,' she said. 'You're a mess.' She flipped her cheroot down onto the gravel and crushed it. 'I have to hit the road. Big night.'

'Tell your uncle, best of luck for the debate.' I was becoming the campaign's official well-wisher.

'He'll need it. If either of the other candidates get as much as a whiff of all that's going down with Katerina, they'll find a way to tear Ben to pieces.'

'She could come back,' I said without conviction.

'Only to cause more trouble. One way or other Katerina's determined to sink Ben's political chances.'

'After spending a fortune building them up?' I said. 'Doesn't make a lot of sense.'

'With respect . . .' she began.

I finished it for her. 'With respect, sense is not a commodity you associate with Russians.' It was easier if I said it.

She shrugged. 'It's hard,' she said. 'One time, two or three years back, I thought Katerina was exactly the sort of woman Ben needed. Somebody to lighten him up . . . You know the sort of thing.'

'Not what you think now.'

Her mouth tightened. It brought a surprising hardness to her face just for a moment, before she relaxed her lips, consciously, as if in a cosmetic exercise.

'Don't lose touch,' I said.

'I don't intend to,' she said levelly.

She turned away, half-turned back and waved. I watched her the length of the gravel path back to the house. The girl had nerve. She walked: she knew I was watching her. She didn't turn round once.

16

I went back to the Pirate. It had a drowsy, lazy-afternoon feel. A few young men necking Cobras. A few girls. One of them asked me out into the parking lot. Economy afternoon rates. It was the girl I'd talked to last night. I bought her a beer and asked her if she knew Luke Bassenger.

She grimaced.

'What does that mean?'

'It means not many people like him a lot down here.'

'Why not?'

'Cheap, sneaky . . . that enough?'

We tipped our Cobras in unison.

'And what he does,' she said. 'Makes his money gigoloing older women. He brings these old ladies down here and lets them make fools of themselves.'

She didn't approve.

'Did you ever meet any of them?'

'I met some but they don't give names. "Call me Tangerine" if that's what the band's playing at that moment. You know the thing.'

'So you never met the woman he was with last night?'

She frowned. 'Just another old crow. Played the trumpet.'

'You never saw her before?'

'I don't know. Maybe yes, maybe no. He's had a lot down here.' She smirked, safe in her eighteen years. 'Your wife one of 'em?'

'Could be,' I said.

I left the Pirate and was cruising the leafy byways of Fairfield County, Connecticut when Hanratty called.

'Where are you?' he asked brusquely.

'Sheepshead Road travelling towards Greenwich.'

'What the fuck you doing there?'

'Sightseeing.'

'Get up to the Merrit Parkway. Keep on going towards the city till exit 27 and turn south. A mile or so along, a small cemetery. Greenhill.'

Dread seized me. Yes, even a term like that has real meaning sometimes. 'What's happening?' I asked him.

'We've found the Foxbat.'

I got to Greenhill without difficulty. I left Stack's Passat near the entrance and walked through the untidy jumble of police cars just inside the gate. Hanratty was leaning against an open car door smoking in the sun. 'Yo . . .' he said.

'Yo . . .' I said back.

He grunted. 'The lieutenant's gone back to headquarters. Instructions are, nobody's to go near the Foxbat until the crime team's finished.'

'How are you treating it? Abandoned stolen vehicle?'

'Not with eighty-five dollars left in the glove compartment. Never yet met a thief who didn't steal.'

We followed a narrow gravel path through box hedges. Four uniforms had taped off an area behind some yew trees. Four or five others in yellow coveralls and plastic boots were engaged in familiar tasks, lifting and bagging minute items of what might turn out to be evidence.

I never was a technical policeman. 'What's it amount to?' I asked Hanratty.

'No blood, no sign of a fight, a struggle. But one thing the lieutenant passed on.' He dipped his head and raised his pale eyebrows to me. 'The vehicle's out of gas. Or very nearly. Running on the warning light for some time.'

'It was low when I was driving it last night.'

'So how does that help us, I wonder?'

He was leaving me to speculate. I'd done it a thousand

times myself in the past. I knew to keep quiet.

'No ideas, then?' he grinned. 'How about they're riding back from Bloomingdale's sometime this afternoon – and hey, suddenly they're running out of gas.'

'They being . . . ?'

'Mrs Rushton and a friend, maybe.'

'OK, she's with a friend. And she's almost out of gasoline.'

'So she pulls off the Merrit Parkway, looking for a place to leave the vehicle. Hits on Greenhill Cemetery. Calls a cab to come out and get her. And her friend.'

'You seem to be pretty sure there *was* a friend.'

'Yuh, I'm pretty sure. And I'd even add that the friend was the retiring type.'

He was dangling something in front of me. 'Stop fooling about, Hanratty,' I said. 'What have you got?'

'Somebody, Mrs Rushton maybe, wiped the steering wheel clean of prints before they baled out.'

We stood looking at each other. 'I don't see why Mrs Rushton would do that.'

'Ergo – that means therefore . . .' Hanratty said evenly. 'There was a friend of a retiring nature in the car with her. Wouldn't you say?'

I lifted my shoulders and let them drop.

'A friend who might have been around, one way or other, for some time. A male friend even . . . ?'

'I only met Mrs Rushton last night,' I said.

'Sure.' He pursed his lips. 'You know we got all these old rules go back hundreds of years about not fucking with the cops.'

'I've heard.'

'That's good. Because I wouldn't like to think you didn't know what you're doing, Chief,' he said.

17

I got back to Observatory Point as the light was fading. I wasn't surprised to find Katerina had still not returned. Worse, I would have been astonished if she had.

Rushton had called twice. I called back and got through to him with a lot of difficulty; the TV debate was scheduled to begin within the hour.

'I know this is a bad time,' I said.

'She's back?'

'No, but the police have found the Foxbat.'

I could hear alarm in his voice. 'Where, for Christ's sake? Not in an accident?'

'Abandoned just off the Merrit Parkway.'

I tried to keep the foreboding out of my voice as I gave him the details.

'What does all this tell us?'

There was no point in holding out baseless hope. He'd see through it quickly enough. 'It doesn't tell us much,' I said. 'But it alerts the police that all this is not the simple story we've been telling.'

'You think?'

'They've been holding off because you're who you are. I don't think they will for much longer.'

Before I managed to get out of the hallway, Yado had called back to say definitely no more calls before the debate. Hanratty had called just to check she wasn't back. Sarah called as I put the phone down on Hanratty.

She was crisp and professional. The challenge in her job, she said, was, when the floodwater broke, not to be carried away by it. So far the dam was holding. So far, she said, the media story remained low-key. The accident at the bridge had appeared in all the lunchtime and afternoon newscasts, a mildly worded account, mostly. But as the evening approached, the story was increasingly being given a sting in the tail: *Mrs Rushton is reported to have escaped uninjured from the accident at the bridge, although this must remain unconfirmed until the Rushton spokesman at Observatory Point is able to establish her precise whereabouts this evening.*

'Like you, like the police, I just don't know what the car in the cemetery means,' Sarah said. 'So I'm taking one thing at a time. For now the Greenwich police are releasing no details until they've finished work on the Foxbat. But right now our biggest time bomb's still the Carole B. public *cri de coeur*. So far nothing from Marty Lackman. So here's the way I see it. I think maybe Carole was right. She covered well enough on the show to make Lackman's lawyers move cautiously on identifying the woman without further confirmation. At this moment they can't trace Carole and they can't trace the woman. So no story. So far.'

That evening, the stay-at-home group, Alex and Olga, Stack and myself, had supper in Olga's small kitchen. One worry lay heavily over another. Top of the present list was whether Katerina's name would be dragged into tonight's debate. Had either of the other candidates been leaked sufficient information? Worse, did either of them know more than Ben Rushton did about his wife's whereabouts?

Over pizza and salad, the talk was tense but desultory. Only Alexandra's visit to Moscow at the end of the month proved anything of a diversion from worries about Katerina and tonight's debate. 'I've decided to go to the Nevetsky Clinic,' she said. 'Stack tells me you know it.'

'I know of Dr Nevetsky. He has a worldwide reputation.'

'And what do you think of him?'

'You can't ask me, Alexandra,' I said. 'I'm not qualified to give an answer.'

'He's developed amazing new techniques for planting a micro-chip deep in the eye.'

I saw Olga flinch.

'I went through a week of tests with him when he was in New York,' she said. 'He concluded he could give me up to another twenty five per cent improved sight in one eye. Sixteen per cent in the other.'

Sitting next to her I could feel for a moment what these bare percentages meant to her. Not seeing landscapes or driving a car, obviously enough. But a crucial difference in her ability to see the expression on the face before her, to catch the body language of someone across the room.

'He's had great successes, that's certain,' I said. 'There are examples all over the world.'

'But many American doctors look on him with suspicion. If you have any opinion, anything you've heard in Moscow, I want you to tell me.'

'I'm not an ophthalmologist, Alex.' I thought about what she was asking for a few moments. 'But over the last three, four years,' I said carefully, 'Dr Nevetsky has worked for the loved ones of some of the most violent men in Russia. And he survives. He prospers.' I put my arm round her shoulder. 'If he'd screwed up, he would have been lying in a Moscow gutter by now.'

She laughed. 'It's a strange way to evaluate a doctor.' She leaned from her chair next to me, reached to kiss my cheek, missed, planted a kiss on my ear. 'Just wait till Dr Nevetsky has done his work,' she said. 'I'll do better. My kisses,' she said, 'will be more accurately planted.'

We left Olga's kitchen and made for the television room, Alex's promise resonating in my mind. 'I'll do better.'

Why did I like the strange, indefinable flutter that small assurance gave me?

Stack switched on Olga's big set, the giant flat-screen allowing Alexandra to just about see the outline of the figures in the debating studio.

She sat down next to me on the sofa. 'Now, Constantin, I'm relying on you to give me any important body language. Just whisper: the governor looks worried – the senator wants to run hide somewhere . . . That sort of thing.'

'OK,' I said. 'Colson in a grey suit, looking pretty cool, no five o'clock shadow. For the Democrats, looking overweight and pretty apprehensive, a man with a lot to lose tonight, Senator Bass . . .'

'I have Judge Brunswick, the arbiter, in the centre there.'

'Behind a high desk,' I said. 'And the presenter, Joe Emden, is sort of floating in between. He's wearing a tuxedo so that nobody confuses him with the main parties.'

'How about Ben?'

'He's not on stage yet. It's part of the deal he only gets to come on *after* the main debate.'

Stack moved silently around the room serving drinks. Vodka for Olga and me. A glass of red wine for Alexandra. Scotch for himself.

The debate began.

The truth is it was a lacklustre affair. You couldn't blame the participants but they had spoken, shouted, whispered, mouthed these ideas since way before the New Hampshire primary. On the economy and healthcare the euphemisms came thick and fast.

'Surprise, surprise,' Alexandra said. 'They both seem to be in favour of a healthy economy.'

The Russian issue caused few sparks. The governor coolly outlined his view of the facts. A massive exodus was taking place. Sweeping across Russia like the disease that inspired it was a sense of hopelessness that things would ever get better in that huge country. And who could say they were wrong? Ill health, corruption, epidemic disease, were what the average Russian had to look forward to. Did we want to import these problems into the US? 'We favour a complete one-year ban on all Russian tourist visas, and a total five-year ban on Russian immigration.'

When Ben Rushton was brought into the studio to the applause of the audience, I was reminded of last night's party when Rushton was asking Katerina to come to the platform. I remember that strange, almost tragic look she gave him that seemed to express a dozen things, bafflement certainly, despair, love, distrust, even fear. All right, I know one look can't do all that. Perhaps what it came down to was turmoil – or maybe just plain misery. Whatever it was, a lot of it had stayed with me.

We settled in for Rushton's segment. Stack, I noticed, on the other sofa, had chosen to sit tight up to Olga. I tried to look at my sister with eyes unclouded by all the jealousies and irritations of childhood. What was she really like? In terms of personality, it was difficult to say. Perhaps there was a certain warmth under that Murmansker hardness. And as a middle-aged woman? Well, with a touch of make-up, like tonight, and her hair cut decently, I suppose not bad. Stack, I was beginning to be aware, thought so too. Catching my eye, if not, God forbid, my thoughts, he lifted his glass of Scotch to me. 'Here's to you,' he said.

I raised my vodka. He laughed, gap-toothed.

I turned my mind from the emasculating thought of Stack and my heavyweight sister testing the bedsprings, and moved my concentration back to the screen.

Ben Rushton looked good. Confident, big, clean-cut without being in the least smooth. The stuff of recent American presidents. He stood at the lectern provided for him, leaned over it slightly and surveyed his two opponents.

'Let's cut away the rhetoric,' he said. 'We don't have a

lot of time and I don't favour politics by sound bite, so let's take just one issue here, the issue that's quite rightly beginning to occupy all Americans. I'm talking of the extent of Russian illegal immigration. And what to do about it. The simple fact is that *nobody*, the Bureau of Immigration, the coastguard, the city authorities, police, social workers . . . *nobody* knows how many Russian citizens have illegally entered our country in the last year. Some have found jobs and slipped into the immigrant economy. The less successful we see in our cities, begging on the streets. The evidence on the streets of New York, of Boston, Baltimore, Philadelphia, Miami . . . the evidence suggests tens of thousands, perhaps even hundreds of thousands.

'They are not all infected. Many have fled to the United States to escape infection. But they are demanding accommodation, care and sometimes treatment.

'What are we to do?

'Of course we can't take the brutal action the two main parties' harebrained planners have commended to their candidates. We are a rich and kindly people. It is the US reputation in the world that has attracted these unfortunates. We must intercept illegal immigrants at the airports. We must land their boats. We must treat their sick – and we must return them to Russia, healthy or at least with a real chance of health, and in a humane and dignified manner.'

He paused and looked out over the silent audience, no longer even recognising the presence of his two opponents.

'I claim the experience to say that the new aid programme must be administered, not by appointees of the Russian government, but by appointees of the people who are supplying the money – in large part the taxpayers of the United States of America.

'We should not be shy about this. Let's say it loud and clear. There'll be nothing here for the Moscow banks and investment houses and financial institutions who have pocketed most of the aid that has flowed into Russia in the past. Instead, we would appoint an Aid Commissioner. *We* would appoint him. A Russian Aid Supremo, an administrator, or politician with a proven, *honest* track record, who will administer funds aimed at the suppression of the tuberculosis epidemic which is sweeping Russia and driving her people from their cities. This man will be responsible to the people who are providing the aid – the taxpayers of the United States.'

He straightened up and his tone softened. 'What is happening in Russia is unique. America must act for Russia and for ourselves. We must act to prevent the total breakdown of this ancient, gifted but benighted people – and to prevent, next year, a new flood of Russian illegal immigrants.

'We must not duck the problem, or pretend it belongs to someone else. We cannot lead with our eyes closed. We must behave as we did at the time of the Marshall Plan with great generosity and hard common sense. We must behave and go on behaving *like Americans.'*

The studio audience applauded, responding to the moral certainties of earlier days. Back at Observatory Point we poured more drinks and drank toasts during the advertisements. I went out into the hall and walked back and forth. I was more keyed up than I had been for years.

When the phone rang I picked up from the hall table. It was Sarah. 'What do you think?' she said. I could hear the suppressed excitement in her voice.

'I think you're shortly to become the niece of the US president.'

'If only.' Her voice was suddenly flat. 'No news?'

I came down to earth. 'Of Katerina? No.'

'I think I could strangle her with my bare hands,' she said.

I grunted. 'Anyway, all's going well there.'

'At the studio they're going crazy. Suddenly, totally against the rules, the walls, staircases, desks, everywhere's covered with Rushton for President posters.'

'You gave them out.'

'Of course. So did the other parties. But they're using ours.' Her voice faded as she turned away from the phone. 'OK,' she said, back into the phone. 'The ads are over. Seconds out. Last round coming up.'

'Will I see you back later?'

'Sure,' she said. A beat. 'Can't wait,' she added.

I put down the phone. Alexandra, silent as ever, was standing in the doorway behind me. 'They're starting,' she said.

We went back into the room and sat down. Alex, I noticed, didn't sit quite so close. Stack and Olga, on the other hand, had eliminated the last millimetres between them.

L'Oréal was running an old successful campaign. 'Because I'm worth it,' the impossibly soignée girl whispered to us.

'And is she?' Alexandra said next to me.

'She might have been, twenty years ago when they first ran these ads.'

Part two of the debate began.

'Senator Bass is standing up,' I whispered to Alexandra. 'Hot and sweaty and very, very angry, I'd say.'

'Your honour,' Bass addressed himself to the judge. 'Now you've heard what Mr Rushton has to say, we see clearly that the rhetoric he was talking about cutting through was his own.'

Not a muscle in Judge Brunswick's face moved.

Bass looked around for a crowd reaction. Got none and continued. 'My question to Mr Rushton is this: should he, by any mischance, actually *win* in November, what part does he envisage his wife playing in a Rushton White House?'

'I don't like this,' Alex said. 'Not at all.' Her Russian

accent, normally almost too faint for me to pick up, was more marked. She shook her head as if caught in a cold blast of air.

Ben Rushton had lifted his eyes very slowly towards the camera. 'Let's see now, Senator, I'm not sure I get the full gist of that question. My wife's Russian of course, which has given me sympathy and maybe a little more understanding of the appalling dilemma Russians find themselves in . . .'

'My question, Mr Rushton, was quite simple: will you expect your wife, Mrs Katerina Rushton, to be performing the normal functions and role of the First Lady of the United States of America?'

Ben Rushton was not comfortable. He took his time, straightening papers on his lectern.

'What's he doing?' Alex was asking in a low voice. 'Why isn't he answering?'

'Because he senses a trap,' I said.

'Well, Mr Rushton?'

'Yes, Senator. Why shouldn't I expect my wife to act as First Lady?' In his nervousness he became uncharacteristically pompous. 'I have to confess to a degree of bafflement as to why you're asking this question.'

It didn't suit him. 'Careful, careful,' Stack said into his Scotch.

'I was only asking for clarification on this,' Bass said.

'Then you have it,' Rushton said shortly.

I could see he was nervous. I think anybody who knew anything of the Katerina story could see it, but, for the mass audience, he succeeded in looking exasperated, irritated at an irrelevant line of questioning.

'All roles and functions, then,' Bass said heavily. He placed his plump hands before him. 'Acting as hostess to visiting heads of state . . . Yes?'

'Yes.'

'Visiting royalty, even?'

'Of course.'

'And delegations of the American people?'

'This is tedious, Senator.'

'Let's say from my own state of Massachusetts. A visit to the White House by the girls of Boston Latin. Would a hypothetical First Lady Rushton be showing them round, amusing them with little anecdotes? That sort of thing?'

'Of course.'

'And would you consider in your heart of hearts, Mr Rushton, that Mrs Rushton would be an entirely appropriate person to conduct such a group of young American girls . . . ?'

Rushton's face had flushed a raw red, as if the studio make-up had suddenly burnt away. 'What are you hinting at, Senator?'

Henry Bass's face was all smug innocence. 'Hinting at . . . ? Why at nothing, at nothing at all, Mr Rushton. Since Hillary Clinton filled that position, the role of First Lady has become more and more important. Just getting that point entirely clear. That the American people not only vote for a chief executive – but a First Lady as well. If you're sure, as of course you are, that Mrs Rushton is fit and proper for the role, then so be it. I put the question to you out of courtesy, Mr Rushton. As we say, the husband's always the first to know.' Bass smiled contentedly and sat back in his chair as the debate was called to a conclusion.

18

The others had gone to bed. I took Stack's Passat and checked out through the new men on the gate and drove over to the Pirate. In less than five minutes I had exchanged a Cobra with my underage hooker for the information that neither Luke Bassenger nor the woman he was with last night had been anywhere near. She remained convinced I was tracking an erring wife. But she was a nice girl. This time she didn't even laugh at my uxoriousness.

From the Pirate I drove down to Katerina's lodge and saw no change there except that the garage or maybe the police had lifted the Mercedes out of the river. My last trip was out to Atlantic Avenue. Carole Bassenger came to the door hoping for news about her husband. She was holding the baby over her shoulder. I could see she had been drinking, not a lot but enough to make her unsteady. I believed her when she said she had seen nothing of Luke.

Back at Observatory Point, I poured myself another thumb of vodka. I didn't like the signs, didn't like the way things were going. I was tempted to get out the cards or run water across a mirror to read my future but I'd vowed to myself to give all that up, so I tipped back the vodka instead. A lot of responsibility was steadily descending on my shoulders, like heavy, rain-filled cloud. But apart from what I'd done already I had no real idea where to look for Katerina. Less than an hour's drive from Manhattan, there were a thousand places she might be. Tucked away in a hotel room with Bassenger . . . cruising the clubs and bars in neighbourhoods of New York City I hadn't even

167

heard of. I felt my stomach clench. The sense of doom hanging over Rushton's campaign was palpable.

The only brighter quarter of the sky was the fact that Sarah would be coming back tonight. Images of her walking, laughing, smoking a cheroot, flickered like an old bioscope through my mind. I paused, glass to lips, suddenly a-blister with lascivious imagery.

Outside there was a sudden crash of maybe pottery on polished wood floor. I was close enough to the open door to hear Alexandra mutter a very fruity Russian curse under her breath.

I walked out into the hall.

'I knocked over a vase,' Alexandra said as she came into the room. 'It infuriates me when I do that.'

'I thought you'd gone to bed.'

I was aware she was looking into the darker corner of the room.

'Were you looking for Olga?' I asked her.

She shook her head. 'Do you have time for a night-cap?' It seemed a strange question coming from this tall virginal figure.

'Sure.' I poured a thumb of vodka and handed it to her.

'Thank you.' She had an impressive dignity about her, long shapeless dress or not. She stood, lifted her glass and tipped it back as if she were toasting someone.

I moved towards the bottle but she shook her head. 'Will you come for a walk with me in the garden?' she asked.

I hesitated only in surprise. 'Of course.'

'At night it comes alive with something almost approaching colour.'

'Colour?'

She laughed, a muted laugh. 'The garden scents,' she said. 'I find I ascribe them all a colour. Many blind people do.'

We walked through the library and let ourselves out.

A security man passed with flashlight and gun and said a polite goodnight to Alex. I took her hand and led her down into the Japanese garden.

'I always wanted to ask,' she said. 'Is Sarah beautiful?'

I thought about it. 'She's certainly very good-looking. Very vivacious. With good looks like Sarah's you don't really ask if she's beautiful.'

'No . . . why?'

'I guess because you don't have time.'

'And she has a good figure?'

'Oh yes,' I said.

We walked on through the garden. She was taking deep breaths, then closing her eyes for a second as if savouring a thought. 'Did you hear the phone?' she asked. 'A few moments ago.'

'In this house I hear nothing but phones. What was special about this call?'

We were walking side by side. 'It was Katerina,' she said coolly.

I stopped too quickly, Alexandra going on half a pace until her hand tugged against mine. 'Katerina? She called here?'

'She wanted to tell me she was all right.'

I glanced at her expecting to get something from her features, but of course there was nothing. Alexandra didn't use facial expression as other people do, as part of the very process of communicating. But her tone had said something.

'All right? But you mean you don't think so?' I said.

'No. No, I don't.'

'How did she sound?'

'She sounded like Katerina. Excited, maybe or nervous. Or even downright scared.'

'You must know.'

'I don't. All I know is what she said. She didn't want Ben to be told that she'd called. She said he'd want the police in. And there was no need.' She paused, thinking.

'No. What she said was getting the police in wouldn't help.'

I frowned. 'She wasn't trying to tell you just the opposite? Telling you to get the police?'

'I don't think so.'

I nodded, put the idea aside for a moment. 'Then what? After saying she didn't want Ben to know? Did you ask her where she was?'

'Yes. She said.' Alex took a breath. 'She said . . . in a not very nice place.'

I don't know why but the sense of understatement there caught at my throat. 'In a not very nice place.'

'I asked her if she was with someone and she said yes.'

'Luke Bassenger?'

'She wouldn't say. I asked her but she wouldn't say. She avoided an answer.'

'Nothing else?'

'Just . . . Hope to be home soon, darling. She called me darling.'

'She doesn't often?'

'I hardly remember the last time. Hope to be home soon, she said. But the way she said it . . . it's not what she meant.' Alexandra shook her head.

'Then what?'

'She switched off.'

We stood there in the scented night air. I was still holding her hand.

'She was saying goodbye, Constantin.'

'You're sure of that?'

'In her way – she was saying goodbye.'

I squeezed her hand and she responded with an answering tightening of her fingers.

I knew she was going to tell me something important to her by the way she looked down, as if she could see the bronze leaves of the acer waving across the path. 'She's my mother, you know,' she said. 'Not my sister.'

I didn't tell her that it hadn't been difficult to guess.

She looked up and gave me a brief smile. As it faded, she said, 'It was our secret when I was a child. Nobody else knew. Nobody else at all.'

I think she meant it didn't matter any longer.

19

I cornered Rushton as soon as he got back and told him that Katerina had called. He puffed his cheeks in relief. When I told him the rest he nodded. 'OK, she's playing games.'

'Alex thinks she sounded scared.'

He made an exasperated movement of his hands. 'Maybe that's part of the game? God knows. Yado's advice is we call in the medical men ... start taking guidance on her mental health now. Then we're all ready if Bass's allegations blow to the surface.' He guided me through the library. 'Sit in on the meeting,' he said. 'You're part of this now.'

There were Yado, Maddox, Sarah and two male assistants I hadn't seen before. Miss Bryson, in formal shirt and tweed suit, sat with her notebook ready on her knee. Polly Seagram, the lanky, hack-cut blonde, the campaign pollster I had briefly met last night, roamed the far end of the room whispering into her cellphone.

Maddox in an armchair, long legs tucked back, his body jackknifed forward, was talking. 'We've had a good day and a lousy evening,' he said to Yado. 'Cash commitments have been pouring in all day. But commitments are not conversions. The question is will this debate make the difference? Will they be converted to cash tomorrow? That's the question I keep coming back to.' The intensity, ferocity even, in his expression was unmissable. 'The big question: how much damage has she already done us?'

No-one was listening.

Sarah stood at a side table dropping ice into a tumbler. The sound clattered round the room. She added Scotch.

'Hold on,' Jack Yado said to everybody and nobody. 'Just hang in there until we get some sort of real figures coming through.' He nodded towards Polly.

Sarah lit a cheroot. Looking into her tumbler of Scotch, she shook her head with incredulity. 'Henry Bass,' she muttered to herself. 'Gentleman senator from Massachusetts . . .'

Rushton was standing at the window, back to the room. In spite of the clear moonlight, I doubt if he was seeing anything. He turned round slowly. 'It's going to be an hour or two before debate scores are in. Anybody wants to go to bed, I won't feel deserted.'

Everybody shook their heads. I was beginning to learn that a good night's sleep was the first casualty in an American election.

Polly Seagram had been out and back into the room five or six times at least. A quick rap on the door brought her back in. Two paces across the room she stopped dead. The thick, hack-cut hair was awful. But there was a real sense in which she was a fine-looking woman. She carried several sheets of paper in her raised right hand and all eyes were drawn towards them. 'First past the post ratings,' she said. She waved the papers again. 'Do I give them to you?'

'Let's have them,' Ben Rushton said. I could hear the dread in his voice. 'What are they like?'

'Well . . . uh . . . I wouldn't say they were wall-to-wall good news, boss. But not *that* bad either,' she said. 'Mostly phone polls.'

Rushton nodded.

'My young people picked up phone-ins from twenty-three cities including New York and Chicago but not LA or San Francisco.' Her voice rattled like wind through dry papers. A heavy smoker's voice. 'Here's what they tell us about tonight's debate. OK?' She shuffled papers. 'Of the twenty-three results examined, five cities gave you as winner. Eleven gave either Colson or Bass. In the case of Chicago, you hardly took a rating. The remaining seven cities, including New York, gave all three candidates pretty much level pegging.'

Yado nodded. 'Not as bad as it might have been . . .'

'So far,' Polly rasped. 'OK, let's get the worst over. Monaghan's *Late, Late Night*. They went for the jugular: *Most certainly Rushton's performance raises the question whether he has the public self-control necessary for high office*,' Polly read.

'Wow,' Sarah muttered.

'Most are better,' Polly said quickly. '*The Latest Show* was positive. Balance that against probably the biggest and maybe most reliable poll of the night so far, conducted by AM Polls of Boston which shows Bass taking the debate 44–39–22, us trailing. Not as bad as it looks because it's Henry Bass's home town.'

'So how do you read the evening on what you've got?' Sarah asked her.

Polly turned to Ben Rushton. 'The way I think it's going to work is this. We haven't stalled. But we haven't rushed them either. That's straight from the hip. I think we're holding our own or just below for the moment. But one real blow to the body and it won't look like this at all.'

Rushton nodded slowly. The room went quiet. 'Katerina called tonight,' he said.

Everybody drew breath.

'She spoke to Alex. She says she's fine.' He paused. 'She says she's with someone.'

'Is she planning on coming back?' Polly asked.

'I don't know,' Rushton said. 'I don't know if, when, or in what circumstances. Katerina's often enough asked me in the last several months to get out of politics. But I don't think she'd have the spite, the venom in her if you like, to kill me dead.' He paused. 'But let's not fool ourselves, any of us. She could.'

*   *   *

'Walk me up to my room,' Sarah said as we left the meeting. It was well after two o'clock. We walked up the main stairs in silence. At the landing I glanced at her. Her face was set in a way I'd just glimpsed this afternoon, the lips thinner, the eyes narrowed in anger. 'That whore is going to ruin everything for him,' she said deliberately. 'I know he's my uncle, but that doesn't stop me believing this country desperately needs him in office. Colson would never dream of putting anything or anybody before his own advantage. And Henry Bass is a self-satisfied political coward. It's the way the system works, Costya. Some election years just offer the American people a straight choice between two types of mediocrity. This year we've got Ben to break that gridlock. Except that bitch could be back any time with half the New York media in tow.'

I didn't want to mention Alex's intuition that Katerina in some way was saying goodbye. With this crisp American girl it seemed too fey, too Russian maybe.

'Listen, until we know where she's been, and who with, we have no idea of the damage done. Maybe none at all. Maybe she's been staying with some friends we don't have on the list.'

'Olga was calling round all afternoon,' she said. 'If she's with friends it's certainly not the sort of friends she ever brought back here.' She stopped in the middle of the landing as if the idea had just occurred. 'You know, you try too hard,' she said angrily.

'I'm just trying to pull you down to ground level. The chances are she'll be back tomorrow morning. Thirty-six hours, that's average for a Russian drunk.'

'That's how you see her, is it, just another Russian drunk?'

'For Christ's sake,' I said. 'Nobody's just another Russian drunk. Life's lived under different stresses there. Pressures that ordinary people can do nothing whatever about. It's why tens of thousands are moving out every month. They want to be like you. They want to live in a country where you make your own mistakes. They don't want to come from a country where you go out shopping for a new dress and someone throws a bomb that explodes in your kid sister or daughter's face.'

'OK,' she said, her face white. 'But that was below the belt.'

'Probably.'

We continued walking. 'Not just another Russian drunk then,' she said quietly. 'But a drunk all the same. Can I say that?'

'You can say that.'

'So this whole story of stalkers, threats to her life, black hoods . . . what is it? All fantasy from step one? Maybe she and the boy had a fight in the car. Maybe he smacked her. Maybe that's all there was to it.'

I had to admit it all made more sense than black hoods and threats.

'So it's a simple enough story, Costya. She's been screwing him for the last month or more. He knew who he was fooling with. Lot of fun and maybe some nice pillow presents until he ends up in a car underwater and the chance of taking a beating from you and Stack. He ran.'

'And later they meet up? Go off to some motel?'

'And she calls Alex. Alex is the only one of us she gives a damn about.'

'Maybe.' I drew out the word. Stubbornly perhaps. But still some of the things she'd told me didn't smack of total fantasy. In that church in Moscow, an impression I'd taken in, more than words spoken. In the music lodge.

'You're not saying a lot,' Sarah said.

I wasn't saying anything. I walked along the corridor beside her, not talking.

We reached a door and she stopped outside. 'This is mine,' she said.

'I think she spends a lot of time living fantasies,' I said. 'Drink, *stoke* . . . none of it helps. But the fantasies come from inside her head. Under pressure to get out.

I don't think she knows when she's entered this other world.'

Sarah's head came up. 'What I'm not happy about,' she said, 'is the idea that, at heart, you like the slut. Is that because she's Russian?'

'God knows,' I said. 'But you're right. The two or three times we've met haven't been in anything like normal circumstances. But there's something about her . . .'

'Does it make no difference to you that she's humiliating Ben, threatening everything he wants to do? Things like instituting the only sane immigration policy on offer at the moment? Doesn't that make a difference to you?'

I felt a burn of anger rise in me. 'Of course it does,' I said. 'But you don't get anywhere towards solving the problem by thinking of her as a slut or bitch or whatever term you favour. I don't think her life is all fantasy. I think some of what she has to say has more reality than you're willing to see. I saw that boy she was with, remember. I saw his face.'

'Now who's running the fantasy?'

I took a deep breath. 'OK, enough about Katerina,' I said.

'More than enough.' She paused. 'Let's think about something else. What do you say?'

Silent seconds passed. She leaned against the door jamb, her arms folded across her chest. She leaned down and turned the handle, letting the door swing slowly open. I sort of pretended not to notice.

'I don't want to make a big thing of it,' she said, 'but I'm asking you, do you want to come in?'

I held out for a long moment.

'The clock ticks faster during an election campaign,' she said.

Still I didn't move. I wasn't sure what was holding me back. I knew I had to answer. 'Maybe not a good time, Sarah,' I said. 'You're too angry, too worked up about Katerina.' I couldn't believe I was saying no.

She pursed her lips, nodding. 'Suit yourself,' she said. She stepped back into the darkened room. The light falling on her face from the corridor showed the tense, angry lines on either side of her beautiful mouth. But by then I wasn't sure if the anger was directed more at Katerina or at me.

20

This, brothers, is a house of a hundred phones. Every room, every office seems to have its own private line. In the public rooms, as Olga tells me I should call them, the library, the television room, the conservatory, the vast tiled entrance hall, there are still more phones, but, if I understand right, they're public – the house phones, to be answered by anybody who happens to be passing. Ben Rushton and his team never answer them. Mostly it's Olga, Stack, Alex and today, me.

It's Hanratty on the line.

'My Russian friend,' he says. Does he mean that? It's possible I suppose.

I'm more guarded. 'Good morning, Detective,' I greet him. 'No further news from this end.'

'Did I expect any?' he says gruffly. 'You tell me.'

I don't like his tone. It's not unfriendly. But it's heavy, perhaps with bad news. This sixth sense again, that I might or might not have. 'Has anything happened your end?' I ask him.

'You should ask. This sleepy little Connecticut cop shop got a shake-up call at seven this morning. You're familiar with smart cops, the guys in suits?'

'The FBI?'

'The New York field office called our chief here with an offer of assistance.'

'What does that mean?'

'It means it's an offer he can't refuse. You've seen the movie?'

'And read the book,' I tell him. 'What grounds?'

'They can always find grounds when a presidential candidate's involved.'

'So we can expect a visit. Will you be with them?'

'I'll be there. It's the way they work. At first they'll allow me to tag along. Within a day or two I'll be squeezed out. Effectively off the case. So what, I'm at the end of the line anyway. Retirement's giving me the high five.'

I stand in the hall, the sunlight shafting over the Victorian tiles. I am picking up, I swear, what Americans used to call bad vibes. 'What's this all about, Hanratty?' I ask him cautiously. 'There's something you haven't told me.'

'You're right,' he says. 'But can't. This is just half a tip-off call. Because you're a cop with a run-of-the-mill street background like myself. But this is as far as I go towards getting myself half-pickled in brine. I've told you nothing, right?'

'You've told me nothing.'

'Good. I'll be along with the guys in suits in twenty minutes. Let Mr Rushton know.' He coughs, throaty, close to hawking. 'Listen Vadim. Prepare him for the idea we may have less than good news for him, OK?'

By now Observatory Point had a Fort Knox level of protection. At what point the federal government supplies protection for candidates, I just don't know. I know that everybody living in the house, including myself, had been issued with an ID card, and a lapel card was to be worn on the property at all times. The commercial security men who had guarded the gate on my first night here had passed on and a different breed had taken over. They were first and most obviously different in that they wore civilian clothes. The senior men wore suits. Those who actually checked passes and examined the back seat of cars wore short-sleeve shirts and tan slacks. All the front men carried guns under lightweight Kevlar bullet-proof vests.

I stood in the hall with Stack and watched, through the Gothic window, the convoy pass through the gate. Every pass was examined in the two leading cars, well-polished fleet-hire Fords, and in Hanratty's dusty Chevrolet. Thompson was in the passenger seat.

Within moments Ben Rushton appeared behind me, flanked by Yado and Sarah. They paused for a while in the hall, watching the convoy pull up in front of the main door. All three were casually dressed, Sarah in jeans and tasselled loafers and a yellow sweater. She glanced at me and turned her head away.

I was about to leave but Rushton made a quick gesture with one hand. 'I want you here, Vadim. Sit in on whatever they have to say.'

What Special Agent in Charge Randal and Special Agent DeLane had to say took nearly an hour. It was, I'm bound to admit, a rigorous form of questioning that neither Ben Rushton nor I had suffered from Hanratty. Worse, the major part of my interview and Ben Rushton's were conducted in separate rooms.

Mine was a basically restrained but harsh grilling by DeLane. He was a tall thin-shouldered man with a narrow face and dark smudges under dark eyes. A sharp widow's peak made inroads into his flat black hair. What was immediately apparent about him was the nervous vigour of his movements. He took his long frame across a room at a pace just short of a run. His head moved from one speaker to another with the sharp movement of an anxious bird. He drummed his fingers, but more about that later.

A young assistant agent, present throughout the interview in the TV room, handled the recorder. From time to time DeLane stopped the recording and left without explanation. At the end I expected to be asked to sign a statement, but DeLane simply thanked me and said, 'I'm not going to ask you to sign any document at this moment in time, Mr Vadim. The reason is simple. I'm aware that your statement is inaccurate in several details . . .' I went to protest but he held up his hand . . . 'and I believe you might want to revise certain elements in your story when Mr Rushton has had a further opportunity to talk to you.'

These men *were* different. Or I was in greater trouble than I realised.

When we reassembled in the library I glanced across at Ben Rushton. He was looking, how else can I put it, thoughtful. The two special agents and their assistants, neither of whose names I clearly heard on introduction, were as polite, as deferential, to Rushton as when they arrived but a subtle change had taken place in Randal and DeLane. Both had a studied, imperturbable look on their faces which suggested to me that they had already won some sort of victory.

Rushton indicated I should sit down. 'Vadim,' he said carefully. 'First I want to thank you for your support through all this. I fully accept that your account had been modified at my request – and my request only.'

Hanratty and Thompson exchanged glances. Thompson wrote in his notebook.

'I've informed Special Agents Randal and DeLane of the full circumstances of the night of the party . . .' Rushton stopped and moistened his lips as if he were delivering a political speech, which I suppose in a sense he was. 'I've made it clear that my wife, Mrs Rushton, never returned to this house after the accident. And that the Foxbat in which she was last believed to be driving was taken from the lodge while you had gone back to dive at the bridge.'

In other words, he had come clean. But had he mentioned Luke Bassenger – and Carole's broadcast?

Yes he had. 'I've also informed the Special Agents,' he said, 'of the radio show *Married Life* and of the steps you took to question Mrs Bassenger yesterday.'

I was struggling not to draw a deep breath. The FBI might well take an understanding view of the distorted account of the events of the party night from a presidential candidate. I very much doubted if they would take the same view with me.

So clearly did Hanratty. In the background, unseen by the others, he grinned and wagged an admonitory finger at me.

Randal nodded confirmation and leaned forward in his chair. 'I've had an opportunity to discuss this matter with senior levels,' he said. He was mid-height, mid-weight, mid-bald. But, like his taller partner, DeLane, he had sharp eyes. 'Essentially, I am instructed that no action need be taken.' He pursed his lips. 'We can see how the confusion might have occurred.' He looked at me and shot his eyebrows.

'Very easily,' I said. 'It was a highly confused night.'

'Indeed.'

Then suddenly, with that politician's ability he had, Ben Rushton brusquely seized back the initiative. 'Something has arisen, Vadim, which might just have a connection with Katerina.' He stopped, glanced at the two FBI men and corrected himself: 'Which might *well* have a connection with Katerina.'

He was doing a strange breathing thing, an attempt to control the facial muscles that suggested strain or maybe worse. Grief perhaps?

They'd found her. That's what had happened. Or rather they'd found a woman who could be her.

Randal leaned forward. 'There are obvious media problems about Mr Rushton going to the site.'

The site.

Rushton stood up. He was moving across towards the door beside the bookshelves. 'With the agreement of Special Agents Randal and DeLane, I'm going to ask you to take care of this for me, Vadim. I'm going to ask you to go with Detective Hanratty . . .'

He paused at the door. I saw two tremors pass through his body which he only partly concealed by fumbling for the door handle. His voice, I noticed, was not affected. 'Special Agents Randal and DeLane will explain,' he said before he nodded towards the Bureau men and left the room.

I looked from one to another, at their hard eyes. No, they weren't planning to explain anything.

I drove with Hanratty, sitting next to him, with Thompson in the back. As soon as we had cleared the gate, Hanratty laughed out loud. 'I knew that story about her being tucked up in bed was bullshit.'

'You didn't say anything.'

'Am I going to be saying anything to a presidential candidate? No. You know, Vadim,' he said, offering me a cigarette, 'this is a great democracy and all that. Men are born equal and that's terrific. But my captain would still kick my ass if I crossed Mr Rushton or anybody up at the Point. And kicking ass, in my case, could *just* affect my pension status.'

'You're riding home, Hanratty. How long?'

'One month from casting in my badge. But I can still be useful. I checked out young Luke Bassenger.'

'And?'

'Charges run from debt to violence . . .'

'Against women?'

'Men and women were involved. Mostly seemed to be drunken flailing-about if I read between the lines. Then two arrests, one charge of theft. For twenty-five years old he's gathered some experience. He's no stranger to the penitentiary.'

'But nothing to suggest potential for murder?'

'Luke Bassenger's just a kid. Twenty-five years old. Any violent kid of twenty-five has got potential for murder.'

For a moment Hanratty's eyes followed the road. 'Of course no need to mention I checked him out.'

'No,' I said. 'Thanks. But . . .' I used my eyes to indicate Thompson in the back.

'Thompson?' Hanratty reached dangerously over the back of his seat and whacked his colleague on the knee. 'No need to worry about Tommy. If he hasn't recorded it in his notebook, it didn't happen. Is that right, Tommy?'

There was a grunt of assent from behind us and Hanratty concentrated again on the road.

I pointed ahead. 'So, is this her?' I asked. 'Is this Mrs Rushton?'

'We're going to the cemetery,' he said. 'Let's leave it there.'

'The cemetery. Where the Foxbat was found?'

He gave one brisk nod.

'And a woman's been found nearby?'

'Help me out here, Vadim,' he said. 'If I say anything more, I'll have to eke out a living selling doughnuts on the beach.'

I hadn't taken in too much of my surroundings yesterday. Now I saw that the cemetery was well-kept, with swept gravel paths and white monumental masonry and several gardeners in sight. Not at all like a rambling, overgrown Russian country cemetery.

DeLane was the only senior Bureau man who had driven over although two of the younger members from the field office were somewhere behind. By the way DeLane walked in close, shoulder to frequently bumping shoulder, I began to get the impression that he was my man. By that I mean that I was *his* man, despite the apparent immunity that had been granted so smoothly in the library. I had, after all, been the man who had found the Mercedes in the river. It was my story, un-supported by anybody else, that Katerina had driven away from me in the Foxbat. Then last but certainly not least, I had lied in my statement. Or I had supported a lie by telling Hanratty that Katerina was upstairs sleeping when he called.

Hanratty was a different case, willing to forgive and forget. He knew people added a protective gloss to their statements to him all the time. The sharp-eyed Mr DeLane knew it, too. But I didn't feel he was the forgiving kind. In fact, he might go a lot further than that and feel he had good and proper grounds for suspecting my whole story.

We were walking down a well-kept narrow asphalt path, DeLane and myself, Hanratty and Thompson behind us. Every time Hanratty laughed, most probably at one of his own jokes, DeLane frowned. It's what elitism is all about I suppose, that removal of yourself from the ordinary people of this world, the over-heavy drinkers, the smokers, the makers of bad jokes, people like Hanratty and me. Problem is, a lot of people like DeLane come to believe in themselves. They believe their clean-cut looks are reflected in their clean-cut lives. And then they find they have a teenage daughter who buys drugs with her takings from blowing local boys in the church porch.

We stopped in a small grove of trees. So lost was I in my own less than elevating thoughts that I hadn't noticed there were at least six people, three of them uniformed, standing about. There were more police cars about too. White local cars and blue Fords marked State Police. They were in from Litchfield, Hanratty told me, where the State Police Major Crime Squad came from.

I crossed to stand beside DeLane. 'Perhaps you could just tell me what's going on?' I said as a kind of courtesy to Mr Rushton.

He knew there was no good reason not to. There hadn't been all along. But being tight about information is a way of exercising power. He chewed his lip for a moment, wondering how he could phrase it to give me the least possible information. 'One of the grave-diggers,' he said slowly, 'finished a grave yesterday morning for a funeral today . . . Then came in this morning and found the grave had been filled in.'

'And that's it,' I said. 'That's why we came running down here? Because a couple of shovelfuls of earth had been thrown into a grave during the night.'

He looked at me sourly. 'No,' he said. It was as far as he was going to go. 'There were a couple of other things. You'll see.'

One of the plain clothes officers came forward from the group in front of us and introduced herself. 'Lieutenant Miriam Cohen,' she said. 'State Police, Litchfield.' She was a mature, overweight woman who wore a grey trouser suit and Reeboks. It was the only thing I had to hold against her. We shook hands. DeLane gave a crisp nod of the head and offered his rank and name as Special Agent Frank DeLane. She already knew where he came from.

'I understand there's a vehicle that might be connected,' DeLane said. 'A Foxbat.'

'They weren't able to book a recovery vehicle yesterday. Major accident on the Post Road. It's being removed now.' She turned and pointed through the trees. A Greenwich Police Department recovery vehicle was lifting the Foxbat into the air. I watched while it swung round and was placed expertly on the back of the recovery flatbed.

'Found yesterday afternoon,' the lieutenant said to DeLane.

'What time?'

'Three-thirty. By one of the Greenwich guys taking a leak. Men have their uses.' She turned away from the swinging Foxbat.

She walked ahead with DeLane. I took the other side of her.

'It's looking more and more likely that there's something in the box,' she said. '*Someone* in the box.'

Box? What box?

'If this *is* a crime scene, we've held it for you for absolutely as long as we can.' She nodded hello to Hanratty as she spoke to DeLane. 'The situation is this. We want to move the coffin . . . Correction. We are *going* to move the coffin. In the next twenty minutes, OK? My scene of crime people have finished here, pictures have been taken, enough to fill a dozen family albums. So we're through. Take your twenty minutes as you will, Mr DeLane,' she said. 'It's hot, it's humid and it's high time we got out of this place and ascertained whether we have something or nothing.'

I looked at Hanratty. 'Coffin?' I said. 'What's going on?'

He rolled his eyes.

Lieutenant Cohen stepped back and waved her people away. As they moved to one side I saw a simple grave, newly dug. It was an odd shape. Imagine a newly filled-in grave. A six-foot-long hump of earth. Now see the middle section carefully dug out and the earth placed upon two orange police-recovery blankets. From where I stood I could just see the exposed lid of a shallowly buried coffin. There was a small brass plate, unengraved.

'The initial digging-out is our doing,' Lieutenant Cohen said. 'We needed to check there was a box there at all.'

I stepped back. There was nothing else around the grave. There were no flowers – just a plain wooden cross. It was that that I was staring at.

'Crazy cross,' one of the uniformed officers next to me said. 'Mean anything to you?'

I didn't answer. A slanting crossbar had been nailed to the upright at the head of the grave. It was a Russian Orthodox cross.

'The grave was reserved to a George Martin Liston whose body is as of now residing in the Rummel Funeral Home up the road in Glenville.' Miriam Cohen stood in front of the mound facing the small group as if she were the priest and we the mourners. 'The funeral was to have taken place this morning. But when the party got here there was a half-hour of confusion. Looked as though the cemetery management had fucked up. Someone else was occupying Mr Liston's grave.'

'Yo,' I muttered to Hanratty.

'At least,' the lieutenant continued, 'that's what we think's happening. We've removed some earth, as you can see. The George Martin Liston grave was three-quarters refilled before this present coffin was placed here. Mr Rummel over there, the mortician . . .' she dropped her voice . . . 'he's been tapping the exposed part of the coffin. In his opinion it's . . .' She pulled a face. 'Occupied.'

The heat rose around us. In Murmansk at this time of the year, the bitter chill of autumn would already have been back. In the more expensive apartment blocks and certainly in Roy's tower-block regional government offices, the heating would have been switched on weeks earlier. Some places are more favoured.

Special Agent Frank DeLane asked for everybody to be moved back from the grave and he and Lieutenant Cohen circled it. He was plying her with questions and speaking a summary of her answers into a recorder which he had clipped to his suit lapel. Hanratty rolled over to me, hands deep in his trouser pockets. 'You ever have one of these in Moscow? A grave like this.'

'In Russia, we've never been short of the unmarked grave.'

'Is that so?' he said.

I grimaced at him. 'It's her, you know it,' I said.

He nodded, serious now. 'I guess the Foxbat clinches it.'

'And the Russian Orthodox cross.'

'Oh boy,' he said. 'It's Russian, uh? I missed that one.'

'There's plenty I missed, Hanratty,' I said.

'Don't lose sleep over it,' he said. 'Only the great American public believes cops can be perfect.' He laughed at that one too.

'It looks as though I was wrong about her story,' I said. 'I didn't believe she'd been struggling for her life in that Mercedes. I didn't believe she'd pointed it over the bridge and driven into the river as a deliberate act. If I had I wouldn't have left her alone in the music lodge.'

He shoved his hands into his pockets and looked at the coffin. Dust was drifting across his toecaps. 'You can't blame yourself, Vadim. That way lies madness.'

Miriam Cohen waited twenty minutes for DeLane to prowl the crime scene. I understood there was overlapping jurisdiction here but I decided not to try to work it out. To reinforce her authority the lieutenant checked her watch at exactly twenty minutes and ordered two officers with spades to start digging out the grave.

'In America you can exhume a body without a warrant?' I asked Hanratty.

Miriam Cohen heard me and came over, shaking hands. 'You're Mr Rushton's man, Mr Vadim, is that right?'

'Constantin,' I said.

'Ex-cop.'

I nodded.

'Point is, Constantin,' she said easily, 'this isn't officially an exhumation of a body because we don't know yet whether or not we've got a body. The body that fits that grave is George Martin Liston and he's lying comfortably, or at least coolly, on a slab in Mr Rummel's basement at Greenwich. What we're doing here is investigating circumstances which could lead to the discovery of a homicide. All clear?'

'You really think you have a body?'

She looked sombre. 'I think. We'll know in a few minutes.'

Hanratty drifted towards the grave. Lieutenant Cohen and I stood together. 'Jesus,' she said softly. 'This could be my big one.'

I knew what she was saying. 'Candidate's wife,' I said. 'Eyes of the world and all that . . .'

She lifted her head and eyed DeLane. He was obviously her competition. 'Do you have Feds, in Russia?'

'Of course. We call them the secret police.'

She laughed. 'So do we. Anybody ever tell you you speak English like a Brit?'

'Everybody. Except the British. They tell me I speak like an American.'

'Everybody has their angle, uh?'

I nodded. 'You haven't got to Luke Bassenger yet?'

'Spoken to Carole. She claims she hasn't seen him since the night of the Rushton party. Could be telling the truth. Neighbours didn't see him around yesterday.' She glanced down at the shovelful of earth that scattered at our feet. 'If this turns out like I think it will, I'll want to do more than just speak to young Luke.'

The two uniformed men sweltered in their coveralls but the earth was loose and came out easily. They had some reluctance about actually standing on the coffin but no real choice. When they climbed out they had attached thick lifting tapes to the four carrying handles.

Lieutenant Cohen signalled a Police Department van up from the gate, then nodded to the men holding the lifting tapes.

The talk stopped. Graveyards demand a certain air of reverence. The odd circumstances of our gathering here reinforced that. The two men took the strain, a tape wrapped round each wrist. We watched their faces flush with effort. The coffin wasn't empty, we could see that. Every extra effort necessary increased the chances that it contained more than a few stones or shovels of earth.

Two other men came forward. Between them they distributed the tapes until they held one each. The leader nodded. Dust and small stones trickled into the grave and bounced on the lid. Somebody was muttering some sort of prayer behind me.

I watched the coffin rise in the grave, oddly spooky even in bright sunlight. The foot of the box was rising above the head. The four cops, sweat pouring off them, adjusted the pull, overcompensated until the head of the coffin rose quickly, shockingly, to produce a muted gasp from some of the watchers.

Other hands came forward to guide the coffin to a flat space beside the grave.

'What now?' I said to the lieutenant.

'We open up, I guess.' She looked around uneasily. 'Except I don't want to lever the top off while we all stand around to gawp inside . . .'

'How about taking it to Mr Rummel's place?'

'We'll do that,' she said.

This is the serious part. The coffin stands on a high gurney in a dun-coloured, air-conditioned room. But no air-conditioning unit can remove the sinister odour of lilies that seems to impregnate the carpet, the upholstery, the thick drapes that try to disguise the fact there is no window behind.

Miriam Cohen, her plain clothes sergeant, Hanratty and myself have squeezed next to Mr Rummel into the cramped elevator that takes us down into the tiny basement. Others, including Frank DeLane, are still waiting upstairs.

'The coffin,' I say, standing close to the lieutenant. 'I suppose it is one Rummel might recognise?'

'It's a good thought,' she acknowledges.

We cross to Rummel, small, thin-necked, balding grey hair and very agitated. 'The Liston family are waiting upstairs,' he says. 'Can we get on with this please?'

'A question first,' Miriam says. 'Do you recognise the coffin? Is it local? One of your competitors perhaps?'

Mr Rummel looks sick. 'One of mine,' he says.

'OK. Open the box,' Miriam Cohen wants to move things along. 'After that we'll decide whether we're talking homicide or someone's idea of a cemetery joke.' She nods to Rummel. Frank DeLane, I see, has just arrived in the elevator and is self-importantly easing his way past Thompson and two or three others I don't recognise, into the crowded room. It is getting hotter, even down here.

Rummel comes forward. He carries two large screw-drivers. 'We buy this casket in without fittings,' he says, brushing off the last remnant of graveyard dust. 'We sell it as the Windsor Castle. The least expensive end of the range. Nine hundred and fifty dollars.'

'Just open it up, please,' Lieutenant Cohen tells him.

The air conditioning rumbles. Nobody speaks. We all stand in silence while the small man with the scrawny neck lowers the gurney and bends over it. Very deliberately he removes his black jacket and rolls up his sleeves to his fore-arms. There is a sharp squeak. Nearly twenty people in a room twelve by twelve stare as the screwdriver scratches across the screw heads. 'In the laying-out room, of course,' Rummel says, 'we would have electric screwdrivers.'

'Of *course* you would,' murmurs Hanratty.

Rummel's wrists and forearms turn and twist. The head of the coffin is loosening. A strange musty smell, not really unpleasant, seems to ease from the quarter-inch gap.

There are six screws on either side. Another two at the head and foot. Without the electric screwdriver it proves a long job.

When the last screw has been removed Rummel nods to Hanratty who stands near the foot of the coffin. 'If you would, Detective,' he says in his funereal voice.

Hanratty moistens his lips and takes the edge of the casket lid. At a nod from Rummel they both lift.

Inside the casket, the body of Katerina Rushton lies in a pale grey dress. She is barefoot. A single strand of twine is tied round the skirt just above knee height. Her tongue is swollen, her face discoloured by asphyxiation. Two dabs of grey candle wax seal her eyes.

21

Most people had been cleared out of the basement room. The coffin sat on the gurney in the centre. The air conditioning hummed. In white shirt, the sleeves now rolled down, Mr Rummel was required to go through his evidence several times. For a man who had seen and dealt with many thousands of bodies, I found it odd the way he kept glancing towards the coffin, even leaning forward to take a closer look, before pulling a large black silk handkerchief from his breast pocket and applying it to his forehead.

The first fact that emerged was going to be the most difficult to absorb into the pattern of events we knew so far. A man had come into the showroom ten days ago. He had asked to buy a simple burial casket. This one.

Ten days ago? Long before Katerina Rushton had driven off in the Foxbat? Even before her trip to Moscow where I'd met her? Documentation was produced. Sales slips, computer records. Mr Rummel's organisation was efficient. There could be no doubt that the sale took place ten days ago.

DeLane and the lieutenant conducted the questioning. Hanratty and, surprisingly, myself, were the only others allowed in the funeral director's office.

'We'll get to the description of the man in a moment,' Miriam Cohen said. 'Just tell us what he asked for.'

'He asked for a casket. A simple, no frills casket. He said this was important to his community who were Quakers and did not approve of funereal pomp.'

'Is that how he phrased it?' I asked.

DeLane looked up irritably. The lieutenant nodded for Rummel to answer the question.

'No. No, that was my impression of what he said. In fact he was a very simple young man himself. Possibly not a college type. But earnest, I'd say. At least that's how he came over.'

'How did he pay you for the casket?'

'In cash. He said the Quakers preferred to use greenbacks.' He nodded to himself. 'Yes, he actually said greenbacks.'

'And how did he explain not using your services? Your other services? The whole funeral process?' DeLane asked.

'He said their community dealt with all that themselves. Perfectly legally. He asked if I was familiar with the Quakers' Graveyard at New Canaan. I said no, I'd never heard of it.' He paused. 'But frankly I'd dealt with several Quaker families before and this issue never arose. I began to suspect something to tell you the truth, Lieutenant Cohen. I began to suspect he might want the casket for some other purpose.'

'What sort of other purpose?'

'Caskets are frequently used in satanic services, I'm sad to say. Or for many sexually perverted purposes. As responsible funeral directors we have to be aware of the often bizarre uses death becomes associated with in some minds.'

I looked at Rummel in surprise. DeLane, I could see, was speculating on what uses Katerina's death might be associated with.

Miriam Cohen nodded briskly, as if yes, she'd seen all that in her time. She wanted to move onto firmer ground. 'What did he look like?' she asked.

'Let's see now . . .' Rummel counted off points on his fingers. I barely listened past young, blond hair, not a bad-looking young man . . .

Miriam Cohen looked towards me. 'Can't really be

anybody else, can it?' She turned back to Rummel. 'What happened then? Did you arrange to deliver the casket somewhere?'

'He asked one of my assistants to help him carry it out. As it happened there wasn't an assistant available, so I helped carry it out myself.'

'He had a vehicle there? A van of some sort?'

'A Foxbat. New. Dark blue.'

I swallowed hard.

'We loaded the casket and they drove off right away.'

'They?' I couldn't help interrupting. '*They* drove off.'

'We all caught the plural pronoun, Vadim,' DeLane said.

'There was a woman driving the Foxbat,' Rummel said. His large Adam's apple was appearing and disappearing from behind his pearl grey funeral director's tie.

A woman. Carole perhaps . . . or . . .

'It's not easy to tell, the condition the face is in.' Rummel was pointing down. 'But I'd swear it was the corpse.'

I found a phone upstairs in the mortician's office and called the Observatory Point number. I only had the number for the main line and I waited long, sawing seconds until someone picked up. It was Alex.

'Olga told me you left with the detectives this morning,' she said. 'Ben says you've just gone with the FBI to check something out. It's so obvious he's keeping something from me. What's happening, Constantin?'

I really didn't want this. I wanted to get back and tell her face to face that her sister, or her mother, as I now knew her to be, was dead. That, however much of Katerina's stories might have been fantasy, this one part certainly wasn't.

'Alex,' I said. 'I'm down at Greenwich . . .'

'What is it, Constantin?' she said. 'Your voice sounds strange.'

I'd forgotten that odd sixth sense she seemed to have. A blind person's compensation, perhaps. I stumbled on, trying to break the unbreakable news. 'There was a report, Alex. A report of a sighting.'

'You've found Katerina?'

'Yes,' I said.

'And she's dead,' Alex said.

'They found her this morning.'

'Not an accident? Murdered?'

I was silent, handling this like a schoolboy. I hadn't realised myself how anxious I was to protect Alexandra from hurt. 'Not an accident, no. We're at a funeral director's.'

'What happened?'

'Listen, Alex, nobody's really sure yet. But I'm coming back to the house now.'

'Good,' she said.

'Is Olga with you?'

'Olga's here. She's standing beside me.'

'Will you put me through to Mr Rushton? I have to tell him.'

'I'll tell Ben,' she said. 'But don't hang up. He'll want to speak to you.'

I waited a few moments but it was Yado's voice, not Rushton's that came on the line. 'Vadim,' his voice was hoarse. Perhaps he was keeping it low so that someone not far away would not hear. 'Alex tells me you found her. Murdered?'

'Yes.'

'Are there any media there?'

'Not yet.'

'You're at a funeral home now, is that right? The body's been taken there? Not the morgue?'

'Listen,' I said. 'It's weirder than it sounds. The body was taken to the mortician's because it was found in a cemetery.'

He absorbed this a moment. 'OK . . . OK. Then we have

to get our own spokesmen there straight away. Sarah can handle it. Tell Agent DeLane to keep all media at bay. Tell him there'll be a statement shortly. Tell him this is as important as keeping the crime scene clean.'

'Mr Yado,' I said. 'I'm not telling DeLane anything. Partly at least because he wouldn't listen anyway – and for that I wouldn't blame him. If you want to call him here, the company is Rummel at Greenwich. Now I have to talk to Mr Rushton. Will you please put him on.'

'Listen to me, Vadim. Your days are numbered in this job. Hasn't it occurred to you – no Mrs Rushton, no you.'

This time it was a much longer wait until Ben Rushton's voice came on the line. It was controlled, unusually deliberate. 'Vadim, Alex told me.' There was a long pause.

'There's not much to add at the moment,' I said. 'But, I'm sorry to say there's no room for doubt. She *is* dead. And it *is* a homicide.'

'I should have gone with you.' His voice was little more than a low mutter. 'Where was she found?'

'It's all sort of weird, sir.'

'Just tell me. Where was she found?'

'In the grave itself.'

'She was buried?'

'In someone else's grave.'

I'd done this a hundred times in Russia – but not usually with people I knew. It was always hard. A certain formality helps keep you on the track, helps keep the emotive words at bay. 'She was found in a coffin which seems to have been bought over a week ago for the purpose.'

'You mean before the party, before she disappeared?'

'Long before.'

He thought about that for a moment. 'How did she die?' His voice was thick and low.

'She was asphyxiated,' I said carefully.

'You mean lack of air in the coffin?'

'I don't know what I mean yet, sir. I'm still finding out.'

He seemed not to have heard me. 'Lack of air in the coffin? Or strangled?'

'There was some sort of ligature,' I said reluctantly. 'The marks of some sort of ligature.' The line went dead. I had this image of him standing alone in the Japanese garden, staring shocked at the phone.

At Greenwich police station I was led by a uniformed officer through a large room with desks arranged in pods, then into a smaller room marked Homicide on the door.

I saw immediately by the seating arrangements that this might have been Lieutenant Cohen's domain but Frank DeLane was now running the show. He nodded me into a seat opposite him. Miriam Cohen sat to one side, her sergeant to the other. She opened the recording with a list of those present.

DeLane got out of his chair, walked the length of the room in a few strides and leaned over the desk towards me. 'You don't need me to tell you the position you're in,' he said.

I returned his stare.

'I don't like the way you weave in and out of this story, Vadim. It disturbs me.'

'I'm sorry to hear it.'

He sat down again and stared at me across the table. 'Yet it doesn't seem to disturb you. I find in general that the laid-back, *un*disturbed personality is quite capable of harbouring violent intentions towards women.'

'Are you going to ask me questions, Special Agent? Or shall I let you just ramble on?' I said.

'I'm giving you a warning, Vadim . . .' He got up and moved towards the door. 'You've already lied once about the whereabouts of Mrs Rushton . . . You admit it?'

This was clever stuff. He knew, on record, I would not point out that Ben Rushton had required me to lie. 'I admit I made a number of misleading statements,' I said. 'Although there were mitigating circumstances.'

'What I'm saying, Vadim, is that Lieutenant Cohen and her colleague are about to ask you for a statement. This time, we want the truth.' He pulled at the door. 'Special Agent DeLane is leaving the room,' he snapped to the microphone.

Miriam Cohen smiled and took over DeLane's chair. 'OK, Constantin. Say you give me a complete account of your movements since you arrived at Observatory Point. And I'll interject questions where I think the detail needs filling out. What Special Agent DeLane says has some validity . . .' She put a careful, faint emphasis on 'some'. 'You do weave in and out of the story of Mrs Rushton's last days. Of course, there's a reason for that. Mr Rushton employed you for his wife's security.'

'I didn't do much of a job.'

She shrugged sympathetically. 'OK, let's go.'

I drove back to Observatory Point with Hanratty. Now that the talking was over, it was hard to know what I was feeling apart from an uneasy nausea. I had not spent more than a few hours with Katerina Rushton. Mostly her fantasies (although they were looking more real by the moment) had been irritating, but there had still been something in her that had really touched me. Something I responded to, as a Russian.

'Makes you feel bad, uh?' Hanratty said next to me. 'Seeing that done to someone you know.'

'Makes me feel bad seeing that done to anyone,' I said shortly. 'The next step must be to find Bassenger.'

'Lieutenant Cohen, with a couple of young FBI agents, is on her way over to the Bassengers' apartment now. He won't be there waiting for her, but it can only be a matter of time before he's picked up. Young guys kill women all the time; but you have to be something else to go for all this fancy footwork. I ask you, what was the mad fuck doing, buying a coffin?'

I shook my head.

'Because she wanted him to is my guess. What is it, Vadim? Hey, hey – one of your Russian sex games?'

'For Christ's sake, Hanratty,' I said.

'We'll find out soon enough. By this afternoon, Bassenger's face will be on every newscast in the country. He'd need immediate plastic surgery to buy a cheeseburger.'

'That's what's troubling me,' I said. 'He's got a son he's devoted to – and he virtually signs his name to a homicide. Something's astray here.'

'Don't brood on it, pal. You're looking for good-sense actions where there's none to be found,' he said.

I sat silent for a while, a discontent prickling my collar. It seemed to me that whatever Luke Bassenger's involvement, it wasn't as the killer. 'What happens now, Hanratty?' I asked him as we climbed the hill towards Observatory Point. 'The FBI takes over?'

'Things aren't that simple,' he said. 'I'd say you have a mix of jurisdictions here. The FBI will run it. But now they have a murder on their hands they're in need of someone local like the lieutenant. She's seen two dozen homicide investigations when she was NYPD, working out of North Manhattan. And after seven years here, she knows something about the local lowlife. Like your Mr Luke Bassenger.'

'What about you, Hanratty? Will you still be around?'

He scowled. 'If they put me on the investigative task force, it'll be to buy the breakfast bakery and pour coffee. But hell! Why should I worry, retirement's round the corner.'

We showed our passes to the Secret Service men at the gate and Hanratty dropped me at the door. 'Listen,' he said. 'The atmosphere's going to be dark in the house, there. Any time you want to drink a beer together, call me.' He slid a card through the open window.

'I appreciate the thought,' I said. That's what Americans

say when they want to be polite but are probably not going to take you up on the offer.

'Fuck you too, Vadim,' he said amiably. 'The Broken Bottle. It's a tavern in Greenwich, right along from police headquarters. Quiet, tasteful. I've a season ticket for the corner barstool.'

22

Alex was standing alone in the garden. An English Edwardian picture. A girl in a long dress on the edge of a myrtle grove. She was waiting for me. I walked over towards her and at some point she seemed to know it was me because her expression changed and she came forward into my arms. I stood with her like that a long moment, not embarrassed, just feeling the fit of her. Liking the feeling.

'Ben's told me how she was found,' she said.

'Anything I can do,' I said awkwardly. 'I don't know what. But any time you want to talk . . .'

'No . . . I don't want to talk about it,' she said quietly. 'Not just now. I want to stay like this a minute. Is that all right?'

'That's all right,' I said.

She didn't cry or shudder or do any of those things that might have expressed grief but I could absorb those pressures and emanations from her body that told me almost as much as words. When I released her she stood away, looking at me, I would say, if she could look, then we walked through the big arch into the courtyard. It was natural somehow to hold her hand.

That afternoon the house was like an overexcited art gallery. Police and politicals moved from room to room, interviewing or discussing events in tight cliques. Hammering echoed through the house as a team of carpenters converted the TV room into a television studio.

I ate a sandwich and drank a cup of coffee standing in the kitchen with Polly and Sarah who had just come back from Greenwich. PAs, political assistants, burbled around us, the murder adding a new dimension of excitement to everything that was happening around them.

'How did the press statement go?' I was making a mild overture to Sarah.

'OK,' she said. 'Ben will have to go before the cameras, of course, but I bought him a couple of hours to compose himself.'

Polly chewed her sandwich and shoved her free hand through her hair. 'She was a poor sad woman,' she said. 'She gave us a lot of trouble but she didn't deserve this.'

'She spent her life asking for trouble,' Sarah said. 'Finally it came to town.'

'And that's it?' Polly exploded. 'That's her obituary from you?'

'What did I say, Polly?' Sarah looked at her, baffled.

'What didn't you say? She was Ben's wife. She was a pretty crazy, difficult woman. But she had some warmth and care for some other human beings. That's what counts, Sarah. That's what counts for me, anyway.' She activated the lid of the trash can with her foot and dropped in her sandwich and styrofoam coffee beaker. Looking up from the trash can, she gave Sarah a quick, deliberately artificial smile. 'OK. I've said my word. Now let's get back to business. Katerina will be item one, story one, front page, everywhere. Question is, how will it run with the public? I'll let you know as soon as I get the first puff of smoke.' And she was gone.

Sarah stood looking after her. 'Katerina stirred up more support in the camp than I realised. Next we'll have Jack Yado telling us what a great girl she was.' She too dropped the remains of her sandwich in the trash can. Her silk jacket rustled. 'What about if I call up to your room for a drink early evening?' she said. 'You won't be holding a meeting?'

'No chance,' I said. 'But I may be packing my bags.'

'You're not leaving?'

I liked the alarm in her features. 'At some point the police or FBI are going to want to talk to me again. After that, who knows?'

'We'll see,' she said firmly and carried her styrofoam coffee to her office.

In every corridor in the house someone was asking for Ben Rushton. Everyone claimed an urgent need to consult, but there was no sign of him. In Olga's apartment, I stopped by to watch a brief TV statement by Rushton on his wife's death. Stack told me that after recording it he had apparently gone up to Katerina's room and locked himself in. So far he hadn't come out.

Around three or four in the afternoon I was called for by DeLane and Miriam Cohen. The library door was slightly ajar when I arrived and I could hear them arguing inside. My name seemed to be mentioned with uncomfortable frequency.

'I just plan to get his view on all this,' Lieutenant Cohen was saying. 'He's in deep in this household. Rushton trusts him. More than that, he might have a Russian point of view.'

'Jesus Christ,' DeLane said. 'You're inviting a time-server from some hayseed militia to help? I'm not sitting here being lectured by some provincial Russian cluck.'

I pushed the door. Both of them looked startled. 'It'll be a different point of view at least,' I said to DeLane.

The session began with them inviting me to give another full account of events since I had arrived at Observatory Point and an equally full account of my connection with the Rushtons.

'So you'd never met either of the Rushtons before you came out to Observatory Point to borrow some money from your sister?' DeLane asked me.

I hesitated for a good few moments, then I retraced my

steps and told the story of Katerina in Moscow. DeLane took it without so much as a raised eyebrow. Perhaps the FBI knew already.

'And, at Station 13 in Moscow, that was your very first meeting with Katerina Rushton,' DeLane said.

'My very first.'

DeLane sat back and scratched his dark chin. 'I think you had an affair with her.'

'You don't.'

'I think the two of you had had something going for some time.'

I gave him a weary shake of the head.

'Your own sister admits you've got something of a reputation.'

'Compared to hers maybe. In any case I come from a long way from Moscow. I don't know how well you know your Russian geography, Mr DeLane, but I come from the far north-west.'

'So did Katerina Rushton.'

'Ah well, a lot of us live up there. St Petersburg, Archangel, Murmansk, Belomorsk, Povonets, Petrozavodsk . . .'

'For Christ's sake,' he said, flat-toned.

'Believe me, DeLane, I never set eyes on Katerina Rushton until my sister asked me to help her out in Moscow. I'd also like to point out that she's . . . was twelve, fifteen years older than me. So no affair. OK?'

'OK,' he said suddenly. 'Just brushing up the crumbs. Thanks for your time.'

I stood to go, slightly bemused by the swift termination of our interview. I found myself no more taken by the dark-eyed DeLane than when I started.

'Before you go,' Miriam Cohen said. 'Very briefly, what's your take on this morning's events?'

I smiled at DeLane. She was asking for the Russian cluck's opinion. Leaning back against the door jamb, I thought for a moment.

'Do you have any ideas about motive?'

I had none. Or very few. 'What's the preliminary report on the cause of death?'

'Definitely strangulation by ligature. A thick rope left almost incised marks on the flesh of the neck.'

'I saw the mark.' I flinched. 'You can't rule out sex games. Hanging games.'

'Maybe not,' DeLane said. 'But my guess would be, if it was a sex game, death was still the player's object.'

I didn't argue with that. 'Did you learn anything from the Foxbat?'

'A dozen different sets of fingerprints,' the lieutenant said. 'We're checking them. We'll need yours to eliminate.'

'You find anything else?'

She nodded. 'The FBI found traces of oakum.'

'What's oakum?'

'Strands of hemp,' she said. 'From the rope he used to strangle her, I'd guess.'

I stood for a moment, thinking about that.

'Any sexual interference?'

'Recent sex but no sign of force. They're running the semen at the DNA lab now. Hundred dollars says it's Luke the lad.'

'Does he have that sort of background?'

Miriam Cohen took out a cigarette, gazed at it and put it away again. 'Not really,' she said. 'I guess Hanratty's already passed it on to you. Some casual violence with women. Of the bully-boy tradition rather than seriously unbalanced. OK, we all know it's the sort of violence that can get out of hand . . .'

'But it doesn't usually get dressed up in Victorian clothes,' I said.

DeLane looked up sharply. 'Victorian clothes?'

'Let's think about the simple story. The raunchy wife of a leading politician trawls the clubs and bars, living life on the dangerous edge. Finally she meets one young guy too many. This one's maybe even trawling the bars himself. Looking for someone like Katerina Rushton.'

DeLane rapped his fingertips on the table. From index finger to pinkie. I think that's supposed to indicate you're a psychotic but I wasn't about to say so because that's the way I tapped tables myself.

'You have a Behavioural Science section at Quantico,' I said. 'If you asked them to describe the man who killed Katerina Rushton would they come up with a Luke Bassenger?'

'Why not?' He raised a black eyebrow.

'Because it *is* a simple story.'

'I don't understand you,' the lieutenant said.

'He's saying it's too simple,' DeLane put in.

'Count off the points,' I said. 'A man whose connection with the victim is established. He worked at her house. Ten days before he killed her, he went with her to buy the coffin her body was finally put in. He was seen by me at the Pirate.' I shook my head. 'Charlie Chan would have nailed him in the opening reel.'

'There's plenty of evidence that if the frenzy's hot enough, the killer doesn't give a thought to capture,' DeLane said.

'*During* the act, perhaps. But not *before*. Not *after*.'

'Maybe.' Very reluctant.

'Look, where did he bury her, for Christ's sake? Not on a scrap of wasteland. Not even somewhere on the edge of the cemetery. He buried her where he knew she'd be found and exhumed or recovered or whatever you call it. The plot was marked for someone else. It was bound to be dug up. That's not Luke Bassenger, a man that, whatever his plentiful faults, is at least devoted to his son. Not unless he's moving in another dimension.' I looked from one to the other.

'So who is it?' DeLane said. 'You give us the profile.'

'I'm not so good at that sort of thing,' I said. 'I'd just say that there's a ritual element here. A hemp rope is hard to manipulate. A poor choice to strangle someone. Unless something in the killer's make-up makes it necessary.

Think about it. It's almost like setting yourself a challenge. Or being set a challenge.'

'Go on,' DeLane said.

'Why not use a knife? Or if he had to strangle her, why not use nylon cord? What I'm saying is, like the other elements, the hemp is a Victorian touch. Along with the wax and twine.'

Miriam Cohen frowned. 'What does the twine give us?'

'When a woman was taken to the scaffold twine was used to tie round her knees. So that, as she plunged, as the neck cracked, the governor and visiting worthies were not shocked by the immodesty of flying skirts. It's early days to take a guess. But I think what we're looking at here, Lieutenant, is something along the lines of a re-enacted Victorian hanging.'

23

The noise level in the house was prodigious. Television sets were placed in corners and on landings and watched by groups of people who might equally have been police or political staff. Moving along the corridors, I must have watched at least a dozen more broadcasts of Ben Rushton's statement. It was short, dignified, and gave out no information that Lieutenant Cohen had not already supplied in her initial briefing.

Other broadcasts hit you in the face. Confused, excited comment came from a host of on-the-spot reporters haunting the main gate, desperate to weave something from nothing. Drugs received several vague mentions, along with the inevitable suggestion that all was not well with the Rushton marriage. This was backed by the story of the appearance of a young woman making allegations on a local New York radio show hosted by Marty Lackman. Could Mrs Rushton have been the older woman referred to? Then, as if unconnected with any of the foregoing, a picture of Luke Bassenger was screened and he or anybody who had had contact with him in the last few days was asked to get in touch with Lieutenant Miriam Cohen, Major Crime Squad, Litchfield.

On the electoral front, there were a thousand versions of the same question, addressed back and forth by reporters and anchorpersons: what, they asked each other, will all this do to the polls? Most respondents gave some version of the same answer: we just don't know. I stopped on the big landing on the way to my room and leaned on the banister to look down on yet another anchorman as he set his face for the summary. '*Whether this undoubted tragedy for Ben Rushton the man, will prove equally tragic for Ben Rushton the candidate, is something we don't yet know. What we do know is that today's events in a small cemetery outside Greenwich, Connecticut have shaken to the core this whole nation and the course of the presidential campaign.'*

I heard an indraw of breath. 'Christ.' The voice next to me was Jack Yado's. 'It's balanced on a fucking knife edge,' he said. 'A fucking knife edge. Have you seen Ben yet?'

'Not yet.'

'He's been locked in Katerina's room all afternoon. He's only just back in his office. He's asking for you.'

'Maybe – but I can't get in past the praetorian guard on his door.'

He took me by the arm and drew me into a blind arch that was one of the Gothic architectural features of this strange house. It was as close as anyone could get to privacy. Our faces were a foot or so apart. His sallow skin carried a heavy flush beneath it. His eyes had a watery look, as if he were close to tears. I'd seen fear, horror, disgust but I'd never seen plain executive stress on a man's features like this. 'He's breaking up,' he hissed at me. 'You've got to go in there and talk up his morale. You've got to go in there and tell him the game's far from lost. The fucking game's just started, for Christ's sake.'

I held his upper arm and squeezed tight. The pain diverted the hysteria building in him. He pulled his arm away and rubbed at it.

'Get in and do it, Vadim. Sarah's tried, I've tried, Clint Maddox has tried. But it's a blank so far.'

'What are you talking about?' I said.

'Goddam it, he wants to withdraw his candidacy. *That*'s what I'm talking about.'

Movement in this house was like a film where in any given minute a few frames were cut from the sequence.

Suddenly Polly Seagram was standing with us in the Gothic arch.

'What you got?' Yado snarled.

'Phone-ins show eighty per cent don't knows. Don't know what the killing makes them feel, don't know how they feel about Ben running. Just don't know.' She took a deep breath. 'Scuttlebutt on the net is different. As you'd expect it to be. A free airway.' She whistled.

'What are *they* saying?' Yado asked nervously.

'Almost everything. Sympathy for Ben. Not much sympathy for her. But most sinister development is that some bastards are suggesting Katerina's death was something that had to be.'

'I don't understand you,' Yado looked wildly at her. 'Had to be?'

'They're saying the reputation she was getting was going to sink the Rushton for president campaign. So she had to be killed.'

'Conspiracy theory,' Yado said dismissively. 'Who are they fingering for the killer? Me?' He laughed, a hoot of derision and hysteria.

'No, not you, Jack,' Polly said.

He got there very quickly. 'Christ no.'

She nodded. 'You've got it. They're saying that a contract was taken out on her by Ben himself.'

'He knows that's what they're saying?'

'He knows.'

I thought Yado was about to collapse. 'Get in and see him, Vadim,' he whispered. 'Talk to him. Tell him these guys who put this stuff about are vicious crazies, nerds, geeks, depraved anoraks, whatever. Anonymous wreckers. They *love* this conspiracy stuff. Tell him that to withdraw now is just what the scumbags are after.' His voice rose. 'Or wait a minute. Tell him this. Tell him it's some dirty tricks department of Colson's or Bass behind it. Tell Ben we've got to fight, fight and go on fighting. We still believe in what he believes in, don't we . . . ?'

Suddenly tears were streaming down his cheeks. 'Don't we, for Christ's sake?'

'I'll tell him,' I said, backing out of the archway. 'Polly, why don't you take Mr Yado for a drink somewhere quiet on the other side of the house?'

'OK,' she said. 'But you'll speak to Ben? He thinks you're separate from all this. He'll listen to you.'

I promised. Suddenly I was Sir Galahad.

Ben Rushton sat alone in the corner of his office. On the arm of his armchair was a glass with, I imagined, Scotch in it. As he picked it up I heard the Japanese chimes of ice against the glass. My first impression was that he looked composed, in tan slacks and a dark blue polo shirt. There was a pair of deck shoes beside the chair. He stretched his legs, bare-footed, wriggling his toes on the carpet.

But as I crossed the big room I seemed to see other things in his face. A sort of desperation that had momentarily wrecked his good looks. I saw the redness of his eyes. I saw the need, every few seconds, to exercise the muscles of the jaw. I saw the signs of grief.

'I imagine you've had too many condolences for one afternoon,' I said, 'so I'll keep quiet. Except to say I genuinely liked her. Didn't understand her. But liked her.'

'Thanks, Vadim,' he said. 'Pour yourself a drink.'

Maybe for the first time in my life I declined.

He sipped his Scotch. 'I'm withdrawing, Vadim. Did they tell you that?'

'Jack Yado told me you were thinking about it. He thinks you should wait.'

'He thinks I should fight on to the end. I don't need telling what Yado thinks.' He made his facial gesture that announced a change of subject. 'I've been going over it in my mind. I feel the need to know what we're dealing with here. Was it some sociopath she's been dating?'

'Perhaps,' I said cautiously.

'There's talk of a hitman. Do you think that's a possibility?'

'Nobody on your campaign team, the inner team, needed telling Katerina was a threat to your chances.'

'So what are we talking about? A lunatic? Or a hitman?'

I took my time. I didn't want to seem too glib. 'What I saw,' I said. 'The burial and Mrs Rushton herself, was definitely the work of a psychopath. And full-blown psychopaths aren't normally the stuff of contract killers. They don't have the discipline, the patience, the plain stability, to accept a contract, plan it and carry it out.'

'That's pretty much what the police and FBI say.'

'Except,' I said carefully, 'I have a different feeling about Mrs Rushton's murder.'

A deep silence fell in the room. He was frowning, looking down at his drink. He glanced up. 'You think it might have been made to look like a lunatic but was a contract killing, after all?'

'We can't forget the threats she talked about.'

He got up and walked to the window. 'Did Polly tell you?' He turned round. 'What the anoraks are saying on the net?' He dropped his head and blew air from closed lips like a man emerging from the water. 'How sick can these kids get?'

I stood up. 'If you listen to all the slime that's going to float out into space in the next few days, you'll go mad.'

'It still hurts.'

'It's meant to,' I said. 'It's meant to hurt you and titillate others. So if it *is* a contract and it isn't you, who else could it be?'

'You mean who placed the contract?' He shook his head. 'I'm not even going to discuss Yado, Sarah, Clint Maddox. No. They've all put a huge commitment behind this, Vadim. But their desire to see me win falls far short of murder. Even murder by proxy.'

'What about your financial supporters? People who've already sunk millions into your campaign?'

He made a half-laugh. 'My foremost supporter was Katerina herself. More of her money has been spent than anybody's. We have very strict federal law about donations . . .'

'She was obviously pretty keen on you making it.'

'I suppose she was ambitious. But she also felt the way I did about doing something for Russia. An aid structure that did more than line the pockets of the rich.'

I listened to him in silence. 'And you don't mind putting all that aside now.'

He gave me a sharp look. Not unfriendly, but sharp. 'After all the money Katerina put into my candidature, you mean.'

I shrugged. 'I don't really mean anything,' I said. 'I know nothing about American politics.'

He smiled. 'You know enough to put a calculated bite on an old hand like myself.'

'I'm pretty keen on the new Russian aid policy too.'

'So you'd go on? Is that what you're saying? For Katerina's sake?'

'Yes. I'd go on.'

'And what about all these hints and innuendoes?'

'One announcement only. You wife's death is a private matter for her family to grieve and the police to investigate.'

He stood up. 'You're saying that you'd wait for the polls to decide. Having come this far, you'd stick it out.'

'At least until they were howling for my blood.'

With Yado and Polly I was a hero, although in Yado's case I knew his gratitude would be brief. It wasn't hard to see everything about me rubbed him the wrong way. He still wanted to see me on my way home.

Minutes after I left Rushton's office he had called in his key people and told them that he had changed his mind. He would stay in the race until there was a clear signal from the polls that American voters wanted him out. There would be no further announcements from him on the murder. A dignified silence – and an equally dignified withdrawal if the polls turned against him.

I didn't feel a hero. I went straight to my room and downed three huge mouthfuls of vodka. Sitting on the side of the bed I necked it from the bottle. Where did I go from here? Home, I guessed. I was clearly finished here. The bodyman who loses his charge on the first day of hiring can't rate highly in anybody's opinion. Somehow, even if I told myself she'd disappeared that night of the party *before* I was hired, it didn't help a lot.

I had just poured myself another thumb of vodka when there was a knock on the door and Sarah came in, looking sleek in a cream dress that curved over her hips and a green Hermès silk scarf chosen for her eyes. 'Hi,' she said. 'D'you mind if I come in?'

'Not as long as you need a drink as much as I do.' She came in and closed the door.

I poured Scotch for Sarah and vodka for myself. I carried her drink over to her as she took the big reading armchair under the window. I collected my drink and sat across from her on the edge of the bed.

'It's a madhouse down there,' she said.

I agreed and settled back on the bed and let the vodka course lazily through me.

'I upset Polly,' she said.

I nodded into my drink.

'But what do I say?' she said. 'I didn't like Katerina. I thought she was a screwball. I thought she was destroying a potential president this country desperately needs.'

'But . . .'

'But I didn't wish on her anything like this. I mean that.'

We sat for a few moments in silence. 'Yado tells me you pulled it off single-handed,' she said. 'He's never going to like you – but he admits it was you who persuaded Ben not to withdraw.'

I was about to deny it. I was about to say I'd done no more than nod vigorous agreement to his own decisions, but I was learning this was not the American way. Take credit. Take any credit offered you. Don't hang back.

'I told him if Katerina had spent her fortune on his candidature, he surely wasn't going to withdraw now.'

'Smart.'

'I meant it.'

She laughed. 'I have to admit there's something about you, Costya,' she said. 'How do you do it? You've got Yado singing your song. And Polly. And Alex and Stack.'

'But not Olga. She took me aside this afternoon and told me it was time I was on my way. She's not keen on me being around. She thinks I'm challenging her for faithful family retainer of the year.'

'Maybe. But for Yado you've performed miracles. He's just been through one hell of a crisis. Now he's like a pig in shit.'

'You mean he's going ahead with planning the campaign?'

'Full steam. You don't have to like Yado to admit the man's an organisational genius. In the last two months he's achieved a miracle. He's built local staffs in every state in the Union for a party without an acknowledged candidate-leader. Now that Ben's out of the closet, the whole operation moves this week to the big new headquarters he's taken in the Bartram Building in Washington. TV ads are going to have to be remade, obviously, but Clint Maddox says we're getting the money . . .' She got up and crossed to refill her glass.

'Sarah,' I said, as gently as I could. 'Ben's wife has just been murdered. Isn't that going to slow things down?'

'That's the danger. Which is why we must move at the speed of light. This mustn't be allowed to go negative.'

'When's a murder been anything else?' I sat up on the bed.

She flushed angrily. 'Don't play Polly's game with me, Costya. I'm not taking sanctity of human life stuff from a Russian.'

She had me. We both knew Russia had probably notched up around fifty million murders in the twentieth century. I could perhaps have argued that it all started with one murder, the first. But philosophy is a world away. We know, in the end, it's numbers that count.

I got off the bed. We were standing toe to toe, her nose about a foot below mine. But it was her mouth I was looking at. I'd noticed before, she had a powerful magnetism in anger.

'How about we kiss and make up?' I said.

'I'm not in a kissing mood, Costya.'

'Does it help if I tell you I'm sorry for last night?'

'It was my doing,' she said shortly. 'I was running ahead of myself.'

'I mean really sorry.'

She looked up and nodded slowly. 'That helps. That helps quite a lot. Listen,' she said. 'You've had a grim time, today.' She reached up and just briefly slid a hand round the back of my neck. It was a signal that declining her hospitality last night was more or less being put behind us. 'I shouldn't have stayed this long. I have to get down to a strategy meeting. I came up to tell you thanks for what you did.'

'Nothing,' I said.

'From here on,' she said, 'everything's going to start whirling like a prairie tornado. I hope we get the chance to see something of each other.'

'I hope,' I said.

She walked to the window, glanced out and turned towards me. 'There's a future for you here in the United States,' she said slowly. 'I can almost feel it for you. Ben doesn't really trust too many people. But he trusts you. If

Ben comes through, and I think he will, your place will be around the White House for the next four years. Even the next eight. That's to say the place will be waiting there if you choose.' Very slightly she jutted her hip. In that one small movement she seemed to be including herself in the deal. 'Do you?'

'God knows,' I said.

'Think about it, will you?'

'An hour ago I was thinking of seeing my last American soccer match and booking my plane. Staying on would involve a big, big choice.'

The green eyes hit me squarely. 'And maybe not just for you.'

She turned and we walked together to the door. She put an arm round my waist and I did the same to her. I wondered if she was in a kissing mood now.

But she wasn't. She detached encircling arms and turned to open the door. 'We're different, Costya, you and I. Different backgrounds, different worlds even. But every time we meet we come closer together. You feel that too, don't you?'

I said I did.

24

Days stuttered past in media chaos. All of us at Observatory Point became uncertain whether we were living real life or being portrayed in some wide-screen TV drama. The house began to resemble one of those World War II British grand houses newly taken over by an American Army headquarters. Folding chairs and tables had appeared overnight. Dozens of stencilled Day-Glo notices announced, in black on pink, this way to Rest Rooms, the Commissary, the Communications Rooms, the Press Room, the Press Rest Room, the Morning Briefing Room . . . and a dozen other sites and rooms . . .

The main players had all left for Washington. Alex received a phone call each morning from Ben Rushton to see how she was and she would pass news along from the front. One morning he would be in Seattle, the next in San Francisco, then a jump to Chicago and another down to Houston. We would pick him up on the main evening news programmes delivering his message again and again: there would be no world stability without a stable Russia. Channelled Aid became his slogan. And the theme: America was world leader not just in wealth and power. In humanity too. For the Russians still pouring into the US illegally, firm but humane arrangements must be made for treatment and immediate repatriation to Russia. The way he put it over, the policy became a crusading appeal to the good sense, the good heart of America.

Katerina's murder still occupied a prime rating in every newscast and Luke Bassenger became a household name. His wife Carole, I learnt from Lieutenant Cohen, had left her apartment, probably to stay with her family down south. Tracking her down became as important a journalistic object as tracing her husband was for the police.

Meanwhile inside the house, television screens rattled off news and views, people ran through corridors waving pieces of paper, phones rang, voices shouted for Jim or Georgie or Sue or Betty Anne, or begged and pleaded for silence or for that high-octane Muddy Waters to be damped down while I talk, for God's sake.

If we were an art gallery that first afternoon, now we were a medieval castle: scowling leathered messengers carrying helmets shouldered their way past, like hard-riding knights. Girls in particoloured tabards looked more like serving wenches than liaison assistants wearing high fashion tee shirts. As I searched for a kitchen that wasn't full of people mixing milk shakes, I expected tumblers to come somersaulting across the tiles or the king's fool to run screeching prophecies through the corridors.

While Alexandra, accompanied by Olga and driven by Stack, spent most of her days in the city where she was delivering a course of lectures in international law, I found I spent time in the *Broken Bottle* in Greenwich where Hanratty, his quarter-century with various police forces drawing to an end, was usually to be found.

Over a club sandwich and a beer, Katerina's death was, not surprisingly, our main subject of conversation. More specifically, Luke Bassenger's part in Katerina's death.

I didn't for a moment believe he was the murderer. But there was a lot of solid indication: the coffin, the black hood, the fact that he had known where Katerina would have gone after she had rescued herself from the submerged Mercedes.

To a former detective, that should have pointed to Luke Bassenger, fair and square. It did for Hanratty. But not for me. I'm a bunched nerve mass of guesswork and intuition. Beyond that I once had a young son. A boy named Mischa.

I couldn't believe that any father who loved his boy as Carole insisted Luke did, would not only murder, but would murder *and display* in such a way that it was virtually certain the police would be onto him.

No. I thought of Luke as a patsy. Whose patsy? That one I *couldn't* answer.

In a minor key, I suppose, the call I got early that evening was one of the most surprising in my life. It was Special Agent DeLane and he was inviting me to accompany him to the Microsoft Stadium to see tonight's Manhattan Islanders game against the New England Patriot All-Stars.

Now, why would the saturnine Mr DeLane want me to accompany him to a soccer match? I had told him the original purpose of my coming to New York had been to view a striker for Murmansk Dynamo – no point in keeping it secret now that Lister, the poor vek, was lying in traction with two broken legs – but DeLane had certainly not confessed an equal enthusiasm for the game. He'd even, as we rode into the city, made a few comments about the superior qualities of the home-grown brand of football.

But I didn't hold that against him. He produced a show of amiability with the tickets at the turnstile and we took the elevator to Level H-East. 'My first soccer match,' he said, as we emerged high above the brightly lit electric blue AstroTurf. The yellow touchlines and the penalty boxes sparkled with a special magnetic glitter they fed into the paint, enabling an electronic line-judge below the stand to communicate immediately with the referee. Different from your average Russian stadium with its balding, bumpy grass pitch and concrete step seats. But even while colonising football the Americans weren't going to rest until they had given it a transatlantic gloss, an extra bit of razzamatazz.

The truth is, I liked it.

Hardly had the two teams come out of the tunnel, and I had vocally registered my delight that Paxton, the Islanders' huge black goalkeeper, was playing, than DeLane began to talk. He had asked me tonight, he said, for a purpose.

'Not to watch the football?' I said, something sinking in my stomach.

'Not to watch a soccer match, no.' He drew closer to me. 'I'm beginning to learn,' he said, 'that you have connections.'

'I'm here to watch football,' I told him. 'I am congenitally incapable of hearing anything else when watching a match.'

'Vadim.'

I refused to turn my head. I could hear the heavy breathing close to my ear.

'We'll watch half the match, then. Then we'll talk. A deal?'

Half a match? I looked at him as if he were mad. What degree of restraint would a normal human need to watch *half* a match?

I love this game. I am bemused with pleasure. The teams are lined up. The Manhattan Islanders in red shirt and white shorts, the New England Patriots in yellow and black. They are also (I swear to you, brothers, because they *are* Americans) each wearing a black tricorne hat. You get it, I'm sure. This is to underline the Patriot theme, the yeomen Yankee farmers who fought the British to a standstill to snatch independence from a world empire.

In a disciplined display they all remove their hats at once and toss them to a team assistant carrying a great fish net. The referee checks everybody is in place. Paxton the Magnificent prowls his goal. The whistle blows. The game begins.

My mouth is dry, my pulse throbbing. I am on my feet.

'You really go for this game?' DeLane asks. I look down

and see he is glancing at a copy of the *Wall Street Journal* and at that point I *know* he's not totally sane.

He pulls me down into my seat as if he wants to snuggle up and read me choice items from the *Journal*. But I am ready for the greatest, the only game on earth. I sit down, but leaning forward on the edge of the seat. I'm already an Islander fan. DeLane taps me on the shoulder. 'Couldn't we talk business while you watch?' he says.

'You're a sadist,' I tell him. 'Watch this movement down the wing. It's a feint. Catch the real attack building down the centre. Paxton's seen it coming. He's waiting for the cross. Just look at Paxton's positioning!'

'The FBI prides itself on being a watertight organisation,' DeLane is telling me. 'We have a tendency not to think very highly of other law-enforcement agencies.'

I say it's very often the case with elite groups, and he looks at me suspiciously, as if I'm planning to undermine the constitution.

'Which is why,' he says, 'I was surprised to see the degree of support you have in Washington. At FBI head-quarters.'

It's half-time. My attention is cut between DeLane and the long-legged majorettes out there on the blue grass. I confess the first ten minutes have been taken up by the two Patriot supporters behind me. They have found it necessary to tell me in detail why Paxton is a lesser ornament to the game than their own goalkeeper. I have found it equally necessary to make a detailed riposte.

DeLane is not happy. He knows we're now minutes from the restart of the game. He plays his ace. 'In the Bureau, Abby Cunningham is a very senior figure these days. She asks to be remembered to you.'

Now he has my attention. Abby Cunningham is a woman I worked with – and a little more – in Murmansk, two or three years ago. In other circumstances, things might have worked out very differently. Herself a senior

FBI agent, she married an even more senior figure in the Bureau early this year.

'Abby knows I'm in America?'

'She intervened in a check we were running on you. I sort of hoped it was to pour manure on your head. It turned out it was to heap praise.'

'A disappointment for you. Give her my love. Tell her I hope to get down to Washington as soon as the present fog clears in New York.'

They are out on the pitch again. The tricorne hats have been doffed to the crowd and tossed into the fish nets. The Manhattan Islanders are now all wearing facial war paint and are executing a minatory war dance. Miraculously, these boys can fool around and play soccer with equal verve. The score is a tense 1–1.

'Listen to me,' DeLane says. 'We have to talk.'

'Later,' I tell him.

He is about to try again, but I round on him. 'D'you mind if we watch the game?'

The Patriots are fast and fearless. They move the ball well and take any space Manhattan leaves them. Half an hour into the second half they build beautifully, swinging the ball to a striker's foot at just the perfectly timed moment. When the shot comes it is low and strong. But Paxton's great hand reaches for the ball in the air. Stops it dead, his fingers halfway round the circumference. He is *holding* it there, a big slow smile on his features. *Gotcha*, the smile says.

'Just look at that,' I say to DeLane. '*Just look at that.*'

'I can see this was a mistake,' he says sourly. He takes me by the arm. 'Special Agent Cunningham suggested, given our somewhat differing personalities, I might need to do a little male bonding. To get you on message. Let's get ourselves a cup of coffee.'

'Are you really serious?'

'There's a viewing panel up in the restaurant. When you

find it unbearable at the lunch counter you can go over sneak a look at the action.'

He isn't saying all this with a smile on his face. His mouth is turned down. His eyes are darkly contemptuous.

I've held out for almost the full second half. The Islanders are well ahead now at 3–1. The game, even I admit, is as good as over.

We sat at the counter with coffee and a turkey sandwich, our backs to the big TV set which was showing the closing minutes. On the far side of the long room where the fortunate sat at tables and ate dinner and drank wine, was a long glass panel overlooking the game. Even catching the reflection in the polished hot-water urn in front of me gave nothing more than a wavy glimpse of Level H-West seats on the other side of the stadium.

I capitulated. This way I might even catch the very end of the game. 'OK,' I said to DeLane. 'I'm listening.'

'Abby Cunningham's report on you suggests one of your law-enforcement strengths is that at times you can get very close to becoming one of these guys yourself.'

'Close to becoming a murderer!' I said incredulously.

'A mild psychotic. Fairly mild.' He was enjoying this part. Who wouldn't?

'Abby's an old friend,' I said. 'We swap jokes.'

'Not in official reports, you don't.'

'I'll take that up with her when I next see her.' I bit into my turkey sandwich. 'OK,' I said, sneaking a glance over my shoulder at the big screen. 'What would be the point of all this bonding?'

'We've fed the details of Mrs Rushton's murder into the VICAP computer,' he said. 'We hold a very full description of murders round the world. Wherever we can get full co-operation from local law enforcement.'

'Rare in Russia, you're saying.'

He nodded slowly, with some satisfaction, I thought.

'Rare but it happens. What the analysis reveals is disturbing.' He stared at me.

'You've got something shocking to tell me.'

He inclined his head gravely. 'The murder of Katerina Rushton doesn't stand alone.'

I'm not sure why, but I didn't want to ask how many more killings there had been.

'It joins seven others. All similar.'

'Hangings,' I said. 'All hangings of one sort or another?'

'You've got it.'

All hangings. What sad and vicious human had done this to seven other people? In the end, the act describes the mind. One of the reasons I left police work was to avoid sloshing around in minds like this one.

'All seven suffered strangulation by hemp ligature,' DeLane said. 'All women.'

All women. Why did that seem to increase the brutality of what the man had done?

DeLane delved into his inside pocket and brought out a paper which he pushed, still folded, along the counter. I opened it. A list of women's names, numbered 1–7. Katerina's name was scribbled in pencil as number eight. But what riveted my attention was the professional eminence of each of the women.

1. Baroness Crawford (59 years) – British – High Court Judge. Found London, England. April 2003.

2. Helga Falk (38 years) – German – Member of the European Parliament. Found Sutton Place, NYC. June 2010.

3. Señora Marina Burgos (42 years) – Argentinian – Justice Minister. Found Massachusetts Ave, Cambridge, Mass. September 2014

4. Mrs Leonora Broker (51 years) – American – Corporation CEO. Found Tom's River, New Jersey. October 2016.

5. Dr Françoise Marcelle (37 years) – French. Research scientist. Found Seattle, Washington. December 2018.

The last two were both killed in Moscow: an American, Luce Carey and Moscow theatre-celebrity Ludmilla Simenova. Both were names I remembered from the Russian press and television. The first, an aggressively successful banker in her fifties. The Russian woman an actress. Hanged in an empty theatre in Moscow last year.

'What links these women?' I said. 'They're all prominent women, I can see that ... You say they were all strangled by ligature – *hanged*?'

'Tied skirts like Katerina Rushton's and sometimes, not always, a dab of sealing wax or plain candle grease in each eye socket.'

'You don't have DNA evidence that points to one man?'

'No. But the VICAP computer sees enough points in method and victimology to make it positive.'

'Has it ever been wrong?'

'No.'

'OK,' I said. 'So we obviously aren't talking about Luke Bassenger, whatever part he had to play in the events leading to Katerina's death.'

His mouth twitched. 'We still need to talk to him.'

'Of course.' I lifted the list. 'Can I keep this?'

'No.'

I slowly refolded the paper and pushed it back to DeLane. 'Hanging is the common factor. And background.'

'It must be the same man,' he said.

'A traveller? London, Moscow, New York? Not impossible but unusual. Serial killers usually like to stick to the territory they know.'

'You understand none of this is for dissemination, don't you? You understand what passes between us is for your eyes only.'

'As I understand it you're cutting me in because you hope to get something out of the *aperçus* that flow from my own unbalanced mind.'

'Don't take offence, Vadim. It's unprofessional.'

'I'll remember that. Now if I put what you've told me together we're not only talking about a serial killer. These victims are all eminent women. Killing them in his own style – by hanging. He gets off on their celebrity. That's a possibility. But there's another possibility.'

'Yes, there is.'

'The possibility that we're talking about a *contract* killer.'

He stretched his lips back across his teeth. Don't doubt me, this face seriously lacked charm. 'British judges,' he said, 'South American ministers, members of the European Parliament, an internationally known French medical researcher, yes, we most certainly could be talking about a contract killer.'

'But we have a problem. We all know the profile of the contract killer is about as far apart from a serial murderer as you can get.'

We sat silent for a moment. I didn't even turn to the screen behind me for the final whistle. 'When did the killings start? I don't have the list, DeLane. When did he set up shop?'

DeLane's mouth twisted. 'He set up shop, as you put it, on April 7, 2003. That's the night he killed the British woman judge. She was found hanging from a street lamp just down from a pub called the Cheshire Cheese. A favourite of Dr Johnson. He was an English writer. You've heard of Dr Johnson?'

'Thanks to Boswell,' I said.

'OK. The Cheshire Cheese is a writers' and lawyers' tavern. A few dozen yards down from the Royal Law Courts in London. The tavern's down a narrow alley that leads to an old courtyard, a place called Red Lion Yard, you know the stuff, York stone and iron lamp brackets. Her Honour was found hanging from one of the brackets.'

'In her everyday clothes?'

'Her court robe and the wig British judges wear were on the flagstones below her feet. The second murder was in 2010, the third and fourth murders were September 2014 and October 2016.' He tapped his fingers on the counter, index to pinkie. The crazy man.

'So he was gaining confidence,' I said. 'Drumming up more business as his reputation grew.'

'Each killing was by hanging. With or without the high Victorian touches. Several of the deaths were taken for suicides when they were first found. We've only just assembled this dossier bringing all these killings together. There may even be others.' He paused. 'So what strikes you, Vadim? You're a professional. What's your take?'

'I don't believe he's a serial killer at all in the usual sense. The motivation for the *style* of killing may well be his own functional psychosis. But I think the status of the victims suggests he's also taking money.'

'Not bad . . .' DeLane said, mouth turned down. 'All right, not bad at all.'

'We've become all too familiar with the contract in Russia over the last few years. It's not unusual for the hitman to begin as the professional, killing by different methods, knife, strangulation, shooting . . . Sometimes a little sex added to throw us off the scent. Or robbery maybe. But in the end the pure sadistic act gets to them. They begin to collect trophies. Or leave a trademark. Maybe just for themselves. Maybe for others in the business. Finally, they love what they're doing. They become dependent on it. Some of them can't live without it.'

Silently he pursed his lips.

'Militia friends in Moscow tell it this way. There are usually three perpetrators involved: the man who places the contract. The middleman who accepts it. And the killer who executes it. No clue to who issued any of the contracts?'

'No,' he said. 'But if a middleman was used in each case to hire the hitter, it was probably the same middleman.'

'In Moscow, locating the middleman has proved the most profitable investigatory path – so they tell me.'

'Another brick wall,' he said. 'Or so it seemed. Until,' he said, smiling that unlovely smile, 'about a month ago we heard an angry shout from an asylum for the criminally insane.'

'Here in America?'

He nodded. 'Fleetwood, Connecticut. It's a federal facility, privately run. A very sick man there.'

'Sick in the head?'

'No doubt about that. He's a Russian. Volodya Rinsky. But with heart problems too. Serious problems. He's not too long for this planet.'

'And why is he shouting?'

'He's been betrayed.'

'Do we know who by?'

'Rinsky was put away by one of our contacts. The FBI maintains a unique range of informants.'

'As did the KGB.'

'For a different purpose, Vadim. Plus the fact that we don't blackmail people into giving us information. We pay. You understand we were not, at this stage, buying information on the contract killings. Our informant was simply selling us names of men who had committed various crimes in the city. We mostly passed them straight on to NYPD.'

'Who were you paying here? Who was the informant?'

'A Russian we deal with. All our informants operate under code names of course. Frequently we don't know their real names.'

'And in this case?'

'We know nothing about him. He's a professional salesman, a salesman of information on criminals. He gets good results.' He sniffed, embarrassed. 'We call him Mr Wonderful.'

'*Mr Wonderful*?' I smiled.

'OK,' he said irritably. 'It's just an FBI code name. I didn't choose it.'

'Of course not.'

'Two years ago this man . . . this informant, Mr Wonderful, sold us the name of one of his associates, Volodya Rinsky. He was a rapist the NYPD had been after over a ten-year period. Volodya Rinsky had worked for the Russian mafia in New York. Rinsky had just had a second massive heart attack. He was unconscious. Wonderful obviously thought he was selling us damaged goods, thought Volodya would never survive. He was selling us a corpse. But Volodya made it through to trial.'

'Is he still alive?'

'Just.'

'How long do the doctors give him?'

'No time at all. Healthwise, he's in almost permanent heart failure. He recently agreed to hypnosis, ostensibly to reduce his breathing problems. But by the end of the first session, it was clear that Volodya's criminal past ran wider and deeper than we thought.'

'What did you get?'

'Some of his sexual gabblings under hypnosis were strong stuff.'

'So would yours be, DeLane.'

'I'll ignore that. Of course we were looking for Mr Wonderful's name.'

'But he wouldn't give it?'

'No.'

'So what was the connection between Volodya and the contract killings?'

'Substantial. Under hypnosis certain references were pretty clearly to the British judge. There was enough information there to indicate Volodya had not been present at the crime. But there was also enough to tell us that this man knew details the public didn't. Enough to tell us that Mr Wonderful did more than sell names to the FBI. From Volodya's ramblings we became convinced

that Wonderful had other lines, too. One of them was
contract killings.'

'You think that Mr Wonderful was the middleman in
these killings?'

'We do. But at that point we lost contact with him.
He's an old man. Maybe he died. Maybe he went to live
in Moscow. Maybe he just found out we had Volodya
under a hypnotism programme.'

'But you never got all Volodya has to give?'

'We don't think so. Which is why we want you to
see Volodya,' he said. 'You're Russian. You understand
a mind like his.'

'You mean you've had people in there . . .'

'And no luck,' he said.

'So how will I do better?'

'Volodya has only ever had one visitor, an old uncle
who visited him recently. Let's say he's just died, aged
seventy-eight, in Moscow. You'll be the man who brings
him the news.' He gave me that vulpine smile. 'We need to
know the identity of Mr Wonderful. He's almost certainly
the middleman in these contract killings. He receives the
contract and hands out the victim-details to the killer.
Bring us back something on Mr Wonderful, Vadim. Bring
us back the goods and you can stay on here in the US
for ever.'

'You assume I want to.'

'A Russian who wants to stay in Russia, I never heard
of . . . Naturalisation, the lot.' He spread his hands gen-
erously. 'You have the Bureau's word on it.'

25

It was still not much after nine when DeLane dropped me back at Observatory Point. My mind was churning and I needed someone to talk to. I thought first of calling Hanratty, but then another idea came to me.

I found Alexandra at home in her apartment and she looked at me with surprise and slow delight. Perhaps it was the first time in her life she'd been asked out for a drink. She was pleased, more than anything else, I think, by the ordinary casualness of the invitation. She asked for ten minutes to get ready. Olga, muttering, gave me the devil's eye and went after her. To warn her, no doubt, of the ways of man.

I wandered round the sitting room as I waited. The shelves were lined with an impressive collection of Braille volumes of international law. On her desk was dictating equipment I guessed she used to write her lectures.

I was still poking around when Alexandra came back into the room. She wore jeans and a linen shirt and carried a tote bag. Looking at her, nobody could have guessed she couldn't see across the room.

Ten minutes later, in Stack's Passat, we were driving down to a wine bar he had suggested on the outskirts of Greenwich. On the way I ignored all promises of confidentiality and told her most of what DeLane had told me. I told her, without details, that the FBI believed they had matched Katerina's death with the deaths of other women in the US, England, and Russia. But this, I emphasised, was not simply a travelling serial killer. The status of the victims suggested this was unlikely. More likely, I said cautiously, was the idea that Katerina was the victim of a contract killer.

'Somebody *hired* a killer to murder Katerina?'

I could hear the shock in her voice. 'Somebody who knew her? Somebody who stands to gain from her being dead?'

She sat back in her seat, deeply shocked. 'Somebody who knew her,' she repeated.

'It's possible.'

'Someone *I* know, even.'

There was nothing I could say to diminish the shock. I could hear her breath pass through clenched teeth.

The bar was quiet and more or less as Stack had described. As we settled down in a corner booth, Chippie Hill playing on the jukebox, and cold beers in front of us, I could see the agitation in her expression. Never having seen her face in the mirror since she was eight years old, perhaps she had no real idea how fleetingly transparent her emotions could sometimes be. 'Tell me what you think, Constantin,' she said. 'Tell me what you really think.'

'About Katerina's death?'

'About *who*. About who might have put out a contract.' The intensity was direct and very disturbing. You'd say she was looking at me, except the eyes had closed; her features set. Like a Roman bust almost, the upright head, the marble whiteness of the face, the blank, white-lidded eyes. Intimidating.

'I've just come into all this,' I said. 'How could I know all Katerina's friends?'

'It might not be necessary,' she said. 'It might be someone at the house.'

We sat, locked in silence.

'You're asking the question, *cui bono*?' I said cautiously. 'Who benefits from what's happened?'

She nodded. 'Who benefits first, in the immediate family? Well, of course, I do. Katerina was rich. I stand to inherit what remains of her fortune.' She raised her eyebrows. The thin scars reddened. 'But *I* did not hire her killer.'

She knew something. Or suspected something. I rattled my fingernails on the table, heard the sound like galloping horses and stopped abruptly. 'You have someone in mind.'

'I have to have, don't I?'

I didn't press her to tell me. The answer loomed too large, too obviously perhaps. But she was wrong, I was sure of it.

At our table, in our corner booth there was complete silence. Perhaps in the rest of the tavern the clatter of cutlery on plates, the thump of dishes of seafood on hard polished tables, the sound of talk and music, continued. But as I paid the bill and organised her coat and we walked towards the door, a silence seemed to surround the two of us.

'Before she died,' Alex said abruptly, 'Katerina told me she knew who it was threatening her on the phone. Doesn't that have to be our starting point?'

We left the bar and crossed the parking lot to Stack's Passat. 'She told me, too,' I said. 'But she wouldn't say who it was. I still think she was playing with me.'

'Even after what's happened?' she said. There was a bitter edge to her voice. Could I blame her?

I guided her forward and opened the car door. 'She didn't tell you who it was either.'

'No.'

'Ah . . .' I said. It was out before I could bite it back, revealing in one syllable all my doubts about Katerina.

Her face flushed with anger. 'No, not ah . . . like that, Constantin. Telling me would have *included* me. You must see that. That's not fantasy, for God's sake. If I'd known, I'd have been in as much danger as herself.'

I closed the door, walked round to the driver's side and

got in. 'Listen, Alex,' I said carefully. 'We have to think about this.'

'You mean I could make a bad mistake. You mean just because it points to one man, I could make a bad mistake believing it's him.'

'Yes. That's what I mean. I've made mistakes like this. I've accused innocent people. Perhaps all investigators have at one time or another. But it's not easy. It stays with you. Accusing an innocent man can haunt you for life.'

'Accusing an innocent man? I'm accusing no-one.'

I left a long silence. 'I know who you have in mind, Alex.'

'Yes,' she said quietly.

I glanced at her and saw her cheeks running with tears. 'I'm in agony, Constantin,' she said. 'It can't be him. Surely it can't be.'

I didn't want to mention Rushton's name. It doesn't always help, as the psychologists insist, to bring things out in the open. To say his name now would make the accusation more solid, more real.

We drove back slowly. I didn't feel good about her sitting alone in the dark like that. I could well imagine how ideas, how suspicions would grow. Fester is what I really meant. After five minutes I knew I couldn't avoid talking any longer. It had to come out into the open.

'When you think about Ben Rushton,' I said, 'can you really imagine him seeking out a contract killer? Paying him, probably with Katerina's money, giving him the crucial details of her life that would enable the man to do it? Looked at like that, it's crazy, Alex.'

She gave the faintest movement of her shoulders.

'OK,' I said. 'True enough that Ben knew that if she didn't stop what she was doing, the media would be on to her. He knew that his chances in the election would be ruined. I don't deny that. But there were others too. Yado's shot at the vice-presidency would go down with Ben's withdrawal. The whole team's chances of political careers would disappear down the same rat-hole.' I drew a breath. 'You can't concentrate suspicion on just one.'

'No,' she said.

'And we still don't know for sure it was a contract. The police and FBI are still looking for Luke Bassenger. *He* certainly isn't a contract killer. He would have been seventeen when the first homicide took place in London. He doesn't even have a passport. This could be a stand-alone murder. Luke Bassenger could still be our man. In which case we're wasting our time speculating about who took out the contract. Because there was no contract.'

'All right,' she said.

I felt deeply for her in that darkness. What I'd said about Luke Bassenger was not what I believed. I didn't like the idea that I was leading her away from what was likely to be the truth.

We passed through the gate security at the house and I took the car up to the front door. I went in with her, past two more security men, and walked her to her apartment, thinking to come back and park the car afterwards.

At her front door she stopped. She stood opposite me for a moment, her hands in her coat pockets. 'It'd break my heart if Ben were behind this. The last thing in the world I want to do is believe he's responsible. But it's not something I'm going to duck.' She stopped. 'You know what I mean. I'm not letting this go. I'm not letting this go, Constantin, just because it's something I shouldn't be thinking.'

She rubbed tears from her eyes with the back of each hand in turn. It was a gesture that, I'm not sure why, affected me strongly.

I was reeling. 'Do you have any vodka?' I asked her.

'Sure.' She opened her door and walked into the apartment ahead of me. We crossed a narrow hall into her sitting room. It was furnished unlike the rest of the house. Here there was a minimalist feel, uncluttered surfaces of furniture pushed back against the walls. A room she could cross freely without running into obstacles. She poured vodka competently, a good thumb of pepper for each of us.

I took the glass and watched her almost float across the familiar room to what was clearly her favourite chair. For a second or two I had a glimpse of what she might have been like with sight. But at that moment, a more disturbing thought came to me. Physically, the similarities between Katerina and Alex were, of course, striking. But I was Russian myself. I knew enough about Russians to know that the denials and distortions of our history have caused deep and perhaps even permanent damage to every one of us. Fed with lies for over a century, we have become uncertain judges of cause and effect, of likely and unlikely hypotheses. Face the fact that's rising before your eyes, I told myself. The question, rather. Is it possible that Alex, law lecturer she might be, lives as much by fantasy as Katerina did? She would, after all, have so much more excuse.

She sat opposite me and I got my breathing back into order.

'Are you angry with me?' she said. 'For thinking the unthinkable. For saying it.'

'No,' I said. 'I'm not angry.'

'You have every right to be angry with me, you know. Among friends, blindness rates no special consideration.'

'OK, maybe just a bit angry.'

She smiled. A brief smile.

I had to ask now.

'Is there anything else?' I said. 'Anything you haven't told me?'

She thought for a long moment, her lip on the rim of her glass, as if she were watching me. At this distance, ten or more feet, I guessed I blurred into the furniture. 'There's something Katerina said. Something she said when she told me she knew who had made the threats to her on the phone.'

I waited.

'She told me she'd bought herself a small phone-recorder. So that she could record her calls.' Alex hesitated as if reluctant to let loose this last dart at Ben Rushton. 'That's what she said.'

I crossed the room towards her, bottle in hand. She held out her glass.

'This recording, if it exists, where would it be?'

'I don't know, Constantin.'

'Did you ask her?'

'She laughed and said it was a military secret.'

'Wherever, it would be somewhere private to her,' I said.

'The lodge perhaps? Her room?'

My stomach turned. I remembered suddenly, that day we had found Katerina at the cemetery, how it was impossible for anyone to speak to Rushton – because he'd been in his wife's room all afternoon. Was it just another of those things that might mean something, but more likely meant just what it seemed? That the man was shattered by the murder of his wife. A wayward wife, certainly, but one he still felt a lot for. So he had sat the afternoon out in her room. Maybe looking at pictures, reading old letters.

Or was he searching for a recording which, as a deliberate counter threat, she had perhaps told him existed?

I knew now I couldn't leave it there. Alex's fears had hooked me. I still didn't believe Ben Rushton had done this unspeakable thing. But I was no longer as sure as I would like to be.

26

The house was quiet at last. Or at least pretty quiet. Coming from the wing where Polly had set up her army of young shock troops were the distant sounds of heavy beat – or the occasional yelled cuss words that were the mating calls of the very young.

We stood before Katerina's door. Alexandra stretched a hand to turn the heavy brass handle. It half-turned and locked. The police or FBI had ordered the room sealed. Normal enough.

'Are you ready to try the lodge?' she asked.

'You think that's where she might have hidden it?'

'The lodge was her place. She went there alone for hours, sometimes days. She played her music there – and I suppose in later years had lovers. It was recognised that nobody ever went there without an invitation. And they were rare. If Katerina had something to hide it would be there.'

We went out into the front drive where I had left Stack's car. Showing ID cards that had been checked twenty minutes before, we passed through the front gate and took the road for the music lodge.

There was no police officer on guard but the tapes and seals of the state police barred doors and windows.

Yet there was no problem breaking in. Someone had done it before us. The back door had been crudely forced. The pine slats were split in all directions around the area of the lock. I told Alex what had happened and opened the door.

It was eerie being back there. Alex chose to concentrate

on a bureau and a large tallboy in the bedroom, putting aside possible objects for me to examine. I took a slow look round the place first, checking picture and furniture positions.

'Whoever broke in,' I said, 'gave the place a thorough but unprofessional search.'

'You're sure of that?'

'You can see by the dust marks that every piece of furniture has been moved, but not pushed back into quite the same position. Every picture too, I'd guess. This is not Lieutenant Cohen. Or the FBI.'

'How do you know that?'

'The police have been here. They wouldn't have been looking for anything specific, so they conducted a different type of search.'

'But the person who broke in the back door knew what to look for.'

'I think so.'

'It was a woman,' she said calmly. 'Perhaps a man and a woman together, I don't know. Perhaps a woman by herself.'

'How do you know that?'

'I can smell a trace of her perfume on the air. Not Katerina's.'

'A stranger?'

'I'm not sure,' she said. 'A sense of smell isn't like sight. It's more elusive. You have to work harder.' She nodded to herself. 'I'll have to think about it. But a woman has definitely been here in the last two days or so.' She pushed closed the drawers in the bureau. 'Are we wasting our time?'

'I don't think so.'

'Despite the fact that the FBI and at least one stranger have searched the place.'

'You'd be surprised,' I said.

'I would.'

She sat down and I restarted work. 'Just think of

Katerina,' I said. 'Just think where she might have hidden this recording. Try and guess how she was feeling when she hid it. Angry, frightened . . . bitter, if you're right.'

I worked for another half an hour. I had meticulously, I thought, searched the whole place.

I sat back on the sofa and let my eyes travel the room. Of course it was fifty/fifty that Katerina had left the disc in her room at Observatory Point. In which case more than fifty/fifty that Ben Rushton had found it – and said nothing. I didn't like to think about that. Alex poured us a drink and for one last time I scanned the room. The piano I'd searched, the bookcases, under the carpet. I'd tapped and listened at the walls, checked the high shelves and unscrewed the collection of matrioshki, Russian wooden dolls. I was running my eyes along the shelf when the thought struck me. *A military secret*, Katerina had said.

The dolls were six or seven inches high, each hollowed out to contain other carved dolls. In Russia you can buy junk manufactured dolls at fairs, badly carved, badly painted. Or you can buy quality matrioshki, carved by eighteenth- or nineteenth-century village craftsmen. Some of the best modern matrioshki will last as antiques. These were not quite on that level but they were all nice, customised examples, well enough carved for Alex to run her fingers across the faces and recognise the most famous.

Katerina was a collector. Some dolls went back to early Soviet days, Lenin inside Stalin, Marx inside Lenin. Later Soviet times had produced the figure of Gorbachev with purple birthmark on his forehead, and inside him Chernenko, then Andropov and finally a tiny plump Brezhnev. She had tsars and priests and Russian writers and musicians, twenty or more carved dolls altogether. I had unscrewed them all and examined their interiors. There was nothing but the carvings they were meant to contain.

When I had checked them, I had upended each separate

doll in turn and shaken it before sliding it back into position.

I sat staring at the shelf. 'The dolls,' I said. 'The military secret.'

Alexandra got to her feet. 'I never thought,' she said. 'Politicians, tsars, writers, musicians and *soldiers*. Guide me to it, Constantin.'

I took her hand and guided it to the high shelf. She took down the doll that I'd already checked. The figure of Stalin. Of Marshal Stalin. Stalin the *military* not the political figure. And inside, more military men. The great Russian World War II marshals, Zhukov himself, conqueror of Berlin, then inside him, Koniev and inside him Rokossovsky and finally Timoshenko.

She unscrewed Zhukov at his waist and drew out the bald Marshal Koniev. Her fingers caressed the base of the rounded figure. A circle of gummed paper covered the bottom. And underneath that was the faint outline of the recorder's disc.

There was a player in the lodge. For a moment I hesitated.

'Play it,' she said.

I loaded the disc. Switched on and placed the player on the top of the bureau. I stood staring down at it. Alex's bare arm looped out to rest her hand on my shoulder.

There was a long silence, so long I thought the disc was blank. Then a phone rang. It continued for a moment or two then someone picked up and a young man's voice said, 'Joel and Manda Wilson are out at the moment. Working their asses off, if that's the boss calling. Otherwise goofing off and having lots of great sex. Leave a message.'

A woman's voice, Katerina by the accent, said, 'Wrong number. Fuck it.' We heard the slow punching of buttons. The phone ringing again. And Ben Rushton's voice. 'Rushton speaking.'

From the beginning it was clear from Katerina's slurred

tones that she had been drinking heavily. The first words were almost incomprehensible. 'How's your woman?' it sounded like. Then again, clearer. 'I said how's your woman? Is she there in the hotel room with you?'

I felt the shock register up through Alex's arm to the hand on my shoulder.

'Katerina,' Ben's anxious voice said. 'Let's talk later when I get back. Please. There is no woman.'

'You're lying. I can see her now, as sharp as if I were in the room with you.'

Alex's head dropped. I stared at the disc in dismay.

'Later, Katerina, for God's sake. I have a meeting. An important meeting.'

'No, talk now,' Katerina said. 'Tell me all the details. I want to hear everything. Everything, Ben, you hear me? Have you had her on this trip? Once, twice. Perhaps even more. She's along with you isn't she?'

'I'm hanging up.'

'Don't!' Her voice was a peremptory screech. 'Sorry Ben . . . Sorry.' Suddenly all apologetic and fluttery. 'Didn't mean to scream at you like that, but I've got to talk. Got to talk to you. Not when you get back. Now. It's important, Ben. Very important.'

You could hear his breath whistle through pursed lips. 'What is it, Katerina? Alex is OK, is she?'

'Your first thought always. Has Alex slipped or tripped or walked into something . . . Well, we both love Alex. And Alex is all right, Ben. No worries there. This is about me.'

I looked at Alex. She was biting her lower lip, tears welling in her eyes.

'The woman, Ben. I want to hear about the woman.'

In a voice that was not as unkind as the words uttered, Ben Rushton said, 'You're drinking too much, Katerina. You've been drinking all afternoon, right?'

'Does that matter?'

'It could. Look, sleep for a while. I won't be late. I'm taking the ten o'clock flight.'

'Just time for a quick screw before you leave.'

'I don't want to talk this way, Katerina. It's insulting.'

'Insulting, who to? I don't keep silent about my paramours, Ben. Why don't you tell me about your women. Or is it just one? Is she someone I know?'

He was silent.

'Then what is it you want?' Katerina picked up on him. 'You want me to kill *myself*? How about that, Ben? It'd solve all your problems.'

'Katerina . . . Get control of yourself, for God's sake. I'll be back soon.'

'What good will that do? I want to know now. Who is she? Is it Alison Bryson? She's with you all the time. Does she service you, Ben? I've seen her eyes following you around the room. Did you know that . . . ?'

'I'm coming back, Katerina. We'll talk.'

'Tell me one thing – just to prove you're sincere.'

'What's that?'

'Are you in bed with her? Now. This minute?'

There was too long a pause. 'No,' he said. 'No, I'm not.'

'You're lying,' she said wearily. 'Ben, listen. If you give up politics . . .'

'Give up now . . . ? You *are* crazy.'

'If you become a man again, the man I first met, we could rebuild everything. Block by block.'

'It's too late, Katerina.' His voice was firm, undeviating. Each word seemed to be underlined.

Then he – or she – switched off.

We sat down on the sofa. I took Alexandra's hand. It was a gesture equivalent to looking at her. No more significant than that.

'He was lying,' she said heavily. 'He had a woman with him.'

'You don't know that.'

'I do, Constantin. I could hear it in his voice. There's a way people speak when there are others in the room with them. The woman was with him in that room – probably in the bed beside him – as Katerina said.'

'If you're right it tells us he's begun to look somewhere else,' I said. 'No more.'

'No! It tells us he's been lying for a long time.'

'People lie about matters of sex, Alex. That's the way of the world. It's so close and potentially explosive that even truthful people know they must lie.'

'Play it again,' she said.

As the recording played I poured two thumbs of vodka and handed her one.

'Stop it there,' she said.

I stopped it and played the last words back. *If you become a man again, the man I first met, we could rebuild everything. Block by block.*

'What can that mean?' Alexandra said.

I lifted my shoulders. 'God knows.'

She was, I could see, deeply moved.

'So what do we do now, Constantin? What do we do with this disc?'

I was good at this. Anybody who had been in the Russian militia for sixteen years knew a thing or two about covering his backside. 'What we do now,' I said, 'is take this disc into Ben first thing tomorrow morning and let *him* hand it to the FBI.'

'All right.'

'But not before we've made ourselves a recording,' I added.

27

I slept three or four hours of thick, deep, satisfying sleep in the last heat of the Indian summer. At some time I dreamed a dream of great significance if only I could work out the meaning. The scene was a battle royal. Twelve boxers, in shorts and gloves, were led blindfold into a ring. Three were placed at each corner. A bell announced the struggle. Each of us, yes I was one of them, launched ourselves forward swinging and punching and flailing. As it can be in dreams, I could see – and not see. Men went down and scrambled to their feet. Men went down and stayed down.

The simple objective was to be the last man standing. When I pulled off the blindfold, my opponents unconscious at my feet, I was presented with the winner's trophy. It was Sarah on a golden dais in a diaphanous Roman toga. A bright light on her piled hair. Mine to carry away.

The stadium was empty now, but for us. I reached out to her.

The tap on the door that wakened me was probably not the first of the series. I got up, wrapping the sheet round me. Passing the open window I glanced down at a two-man patrol with a Dobermann on a lead, their flashlights poking into bushes and the deep arched doorways of the house.

Bleary-eyed, I opened the door. Alex, her hair loose, wearing a towelling robe, stood there. 'I'm sorry, Constantin. There's a call for you.'

'Who is it?'

'I don't know. A woman.'

'At this hour,' an unmistakable voice said. I peered into the shadow beside her. Olga was standing there in a dark red housecoat. Above the closely drawn collar I could see Mickey Mouse reproduced a hundredfold on her pyjamas.

'What does she want?'

'She wants to talk to a tall, dark-haired Russian,' Alex said. 'Doesn't know his name. About forty. Good-looking man, is what she said.' She turned to Olga. 'Now, could that be Constantin, I asked Olga?'

Olga looked angrily at me. 'You should not have your women calling you here. Not in the middle of the night,' she said. 'Not at any time.'

'Didn't she give a name?' I asked Alex.

'No, but she wants to talk to you urgently. She's on the line.'

I wrapped the sheet round me like a toga and went down to the phone in the hall.

I recognised the faint southern accent with her first sentence. 'I'm sorry, I couldn't remember your name,' she said. 'Do you recognise my voice?'

'Of course.'

'Then tell me who this is,' she said.

'Carole,' I said. 'It's me, Constantin Vadim. You remember the name now.'

There was a pause and the blunt hiss of cigarette smoke being exhaled. 'But some old lady kept putting me off. I've been trying to reach you all night.'

'How did you get the number?'

'It was in a pair of Luke's jeans. Will you meet me?' she said. 'I have things to say to you.'

'That you don't want to say on the phone?'

'Absolutely.' She dropped her voice. 'It's like a deal I want to make.'

'Where are you? Not at your apartment?'

'I'm at a pay phone in an all-night drug store. Listen.' She gave me the details of a place to meet. 'I'm driving

Nancy's car – my sister's car. It's a 2012 Honda Civic. Pretty beat up, but it was once silvery grey.'

I told her I'd be there in fifteen minutes.

I took Stack's Passat and drove it out through the gate guard, checking in my rear mirror that it was not part of their mission statement to follow me wherever I went. After a few minutes along Observatory Road, I made a stop without lights for three minutes just over the brow of a low hill. Nothing passed me.

Confident I was alone, I drove down to the Sound at Greenwich Point and parked just off the road. To be candid I don't like these meetings in the middle of the night. Even less when they're beside a restless sea where the wind whistles and animals rustle through the marsh grasses.

Approaching in the lee of the dyke, I saw the old Honda Civic parked tight up against a wind-roughened wooden fence. Cigarette smoke trailed from the open driver's window.

I stopped a few yards back off the road and called her name. With some relief I saw it was Carole who got out of the car and began walking towards me, throwing the cigarette down on the gravel road. She was looking past me, I noticed, into the shadows behind us.

'I'm alone,' I said.

'Where's your car?'

'Parked off the road.'

She was wearing a thick sweater and jeans but she still shivered in the dawn breeze that came off the bay. 'I've heard from Luke.'

'He called you?'

'He called Nancy's husband at work. Left a number for me to call him.'

'And you did?'

She offered me a cigarette and I shook my head. For a moment she struggled with her lighter in the wind, turning this way and that, her hair flying. I watched her. Eighteen or nineteen years old, with a child, a man with violence convictions and now almost certainly much worse to come . . . America's troubles may not be on the scale of our own, but the United States isn't without its own problems.

'Yeah, I called him,' she said. 'Course I called him. Luke was so scared he could only just talk. He's in tears. I'm in tears. He's telling me there, on the phone, he had nothing to do with it.'

'He's lying, Carole.'

'He's *not* lying. Not this time. I know Luke. When he's this scared, I tell you he ain't lying.'

'He was seeing Mrs Rushton.'

'Yes.' Reluctantly.

'For a month or more.'

'A month maybe.'

'You can see how it looks for him, Carole. He was with her that night. And you know about the coffin?'

'He didn't buy it for himself. Some guy he met playing pool gave him a hundred dollars for himself to go and pick it up.'

'And he took Mrs Rushton? Used her Foxbat?'

'I didn't know that,' she said quietly.

'Wake up, Carole,' I said. 'He was with the woman the night she disappeared. He'd already bought the coffin, but you say he didn't kill her and he didn't put her in it? Who did, then?'

'I don't know. But not Luke. The guy he met playing pool.'

I zipped my leather jacket against the wind and walked beside her, without speaking, back past the Honda.

'Did Luke say what he looked like?'

'Well-dressed, that's all he said. Suit and tie.'

'Does this pool player exist?'

'You heard what I said,' Carole said. 'Luke didn't do it. He just didn't do it. If you don't believe that, who will?'

'Do the police know where to find you?' I asked her.

'They know where I'm staying. They grill me every day. A woman cop who's all right, I guess. And a big smart-dressed dude from the FBI.' She shuddered. 'DeLane, he calls himself.'

From where we stood the path descended rapidly now towards the waterline. Across the waters of Long Island Sound the headlights of cars passed, bright pinpricks along the Long Island coast road to Oyster Bay. We stopped against a piece of low solid fencing. 'Let's get down to talking,' I said. 'Why exactly did you bring me out tonight?'

'I may be through with Luke, I suppose I don't really know that yet. Haven't had time to make up my mind. But what I do know is he's been set up. You see that, don't you?'

I shrugged. I didn't see it that way at all, but I didn't want to say anything that would set her off again protesting her husband's doubtful innocence.

'And it's Murder One. That right?' She was white-faced. 'My boy's daddy's up for Murder One.'

'I don't know that much about American law. But it's murder. There's no doubt about what happened to Mrs Rushton.'

'You saw her in the coffin?' she asked quietly.

'What pictures don't tell you, movies or TV, however realistic, is what a bad shock it is. Even when that's what you've been expecting.'

She took out her cigarettes again and this time I accepted one.

'Look,' she said. 'Luke's not all bad.' She looked at me defiantly. 'He let Mrs Rushton make that call to her daughter, didn't he?'

She was breathing heavily, uncertain whether she should have said that. Whether it made the case against her husband better or worse.

'Luke had Mrs Rushton with him when she called? He was holding her against her will?'

'He was holding her for the pool player,' she said. 'That was the deal. That Luke should get to know her. Then take her to a place he had . . .'

'A place Luke has?'

'In Manhattan. A dump. The pool player paid for it, a couple of months ago. He was pretending to partner Luke in a motorcycle business. It was only later that he asked Luke to get to know Mrs Rushton.'

'So Luke took her there – and what?'

She looked at me, a tense, furtive look. 'He did what he was told. He locked her in a room there. He was supposed to wait for the guy, the pool player, to turn up – but he couldn't take her crying in there. So he left.'

'Where did he go?'

'To a friend's place over in Jersey. Getting drunk every hour of the day and night as he watched his own face on TV. Trying to work out some deal to save his ass.'

'And now he thinks he has?'

'He's in possession of valuable information, right? Valuable information about this guy.'

'Does Luke have his name?'

'Not that I know.'

'You've never met him?'

'No.'

'Carole . . .'

'That's the truth. God's truth.'

The wind had dropped a little and her gas lighter worked. I watched the smoke whipped from Carole's mouth and disappear into the darkness across her shoulder. When she was sure she was alight, she lit mine.

'So what are we doing out here, Carole?'

'I'm not having my boy brought up as the son of a murderer,' she said. 'Where I was raised people pointed all the time, boys mostly, she's the stripper's daughter, they said, because my mom worked in a dance club in town. Girls pointed too – and stripping's not even against the law. What d'you think it'd feel like if your boy was pointed out all through school as the son of a murderer? Listen, what's your name again?'

'Constantin.'

'OK, listen, Constantin. Luke's willing to make a deal with the cops.'

I could have cried at the innocent naivety written on her face.

'What's Luke got to offer?'

'A description of the guy who gave him the money to buy the coffin. The pool player.'

'He really exists?'

'Of course he exists.'

It struck me then. Eight hundred dollars for what Rummel called the casket. Luke Bassenger had never had eight hundred dollars to spare in his life. Certainly not on some funereal sex fantasy. And the FBI had checked Katerina's account. There had been no thousand-dollar withdrawals ten days before her disappearance. Perhaps there really was a pool player.

So was it conceivable that Luke had something of real importance to sell? Did he really know the identity of the man who had killed Katerina?

'He wants to see you,' Carole said. 'He's not going to deal with the cops. Sure as hell not with the FBI. But he'll talk to you.'

I was surprised after our meeting in the Pirate. But it *was* true I'd hauled him out of the submerged Mercedes. And been slack enough to give him the opportunity to make a run for it. I suppose that stood in my favour.

'Where is he?'

'Luke's on his way there now. I'll take you there. But for the last few minutes you cover your eyes. Is that a deal?'

I put my arm round her shoulder and we walked back up the gravel path like a pair of lovers thinking of warmer

254

things than the salt tang in the air coming in from Long Island Sound.

I was moved suddenly by how young she was. How she was handling all this. 'What about your parents?' I said. 'Where are they?'

'Not far enough away,' she said. 'Never will be.'

Pert nose, bruised eye, teenage pouty lips. 'Carole,' I said. 'When you talk to the police, tell them you knew nothing. Nothing at all. Until earlier tonight when Luke called you for the first time. You know what an accessory is?'

'I think.'

'Or you could just cut loose of all this,' I said. 'You could just get on the phone and give Luke's address to the cops, move yourself and your boy back down south and start a new life. Innocent or guilty, I doubt if Luke is worth looking forward to.'

'I wouldn't do that, man,' she said. 'Tell you the truth, Luke feeling as he does about the boy, I wouldn't consider that honourable.'

I was put in my place. I got into the Honda beside her. 'So what sort of deal's he hoping for?' I asked her.

'I don't think you understand me. In law, Luke ain't done anything wrong. He screwed around with some big man's wife. And one morning he went out, bought himself a coffin. No law against that, is there?'

'And one night he abducted a woman and held her against her will until she was murdered by persons unknown. There's sure as hell a law against that, Carole.'

It was that half-light, that pre-dawn light beloved of Russian World War II commanders as a time to hurl another million men across the steppe at the entrenched German positions. In New York City it was more half-dark than half-light. Buildings spawned fuzzy shadow across the streets. Sometimes, at the end of a long avenue, I saw streaks of grey light in the east.

The city streetlights were still on, their ardour dimmed by the promise of dawn. There was activity but without the crowds of daytime. All-night diners were being cleaned up and swept out for breakfast; produce and delivery trucks manoeuvred across roads to back into alleys.

I had no real idea which part of the city we were in. North Manhattan somewhere. A few minutes later she pulled over. 'I don't want you to see where we're going from here on. How we going to arrange that, Constantin?' She pronounced my name with a heavy emphasis on the middle syllable.

'I could just duck down,' I said.

'Sure.' She fumbled in her tote bag. 'But this is better. Get your head back.'

I slid down the seat and pushed my head back. She placed a beige six-inch plastic-backed cover over each eye. With some soft, satiny material, a scarf perhaps, she bound them in position.

'OK?'

'Dark as the womb of moist Mother Earth.'

She punched my shoulder. 'How you talk, Constantin.'

We were moving forward. Stopping, moving again. Minutes later I smelt spices, pungent and penetrating, and heard the shouts of men, drivers trying to push their vans between obstructions that I imagined as great banks and crates of exotic produce.

'Keep your head down, for God's sake. They'll think I'm kidnapping you.' She giggled and then was unable to stop. Laughing tears. On what? Booze, coke? Or worry?

We were going very slowly now through an early morning market. I could hear Spanish voices, shouting, bantering, cursing all around us . . . Somehow, enclosed as I was, in the darkness of my blindfold, I touched for a moment Alex's world, where sound and smell shaped everything.

Very slowly, we moved forward. It was a long narrow market, perhaps even several blocks in length. Powerful smells of spices or meat cooking would dominate for a few moments, then give way in rotation to the penetrating softness of fruit or vegetables. There, in my own darkness, I began to exercise an unexercised sense of smell. Accompanying the tang of vegetables, I discovered, was an earthy freshness, less sharp than the other smells, but somehow more persistent. In the packaged and plastic world of much food in the United States, there was something warming about the idea that *earth* was the base smell of this market.

To a Russian, earth has that atavistic import. The oddest rites of old Russia had all to do with earth. As a defence or preventative against disease, Mother Earth has been summoned up throughout Russian history. Now that plague and cholera have given way to the great tuberculosis epidemic, the old ways have come back. From hundreds of villages in the deep countryside there have been reports of the strangest rite of all. Aimed at the destruction of disease in the village, it begins at midnight. As the Russian bell strikes, old women begin to perambulate the village, lightly tapping on windows to call forth other women, so that the men, deep in the arms of vodka, will hear nothing. At a moonlight assembly on the village square the old women choose nine virgins and three young widows. In the woods they will be undressed down to their shifts. Then, while the summer breeze or autumn winds whip the thin shifts round their bodies, one of the young widows will be chosen by lot. She will be strapped, by force, to drag the plough. Then the procession assembles, the virgins take scythes and the other women brandish terrifying objects like skulls and bleeding wolves' heads. They are led by two widows holding aloft oil lamps on long bending alder sticks. Forming up, they escort the plough back to the village, shrieking and howling to the spirits to allow the plough blade, as it cuts into the sandy road surface, to release the lurking germs of cholera yesterday, and today, tuberculosis, the Dog Plague.

Men of the village cower in their beds. Any travelling stranger, any man, that is, who meets the procession on its way is struck down without mercy.

God knows, personally, how far I am from all this, brothers. I know that too much of that Russian past floats constantly in some level of my consciousness. Strangely, I both treasure it and long to be free of these primitive fancies. Too many times I lie awake at night, in ecstasy and disgust. Like the helpless lover of a truly wicked woman.

We came to a stop and Carole got out and opened some gates, iron . . . screeching in their rusting gullies. She got back into the car, drove it forward, got out again and closed the gates.

'OK,' she said. 'Let's take it off.'

I pulled at the knot in the scarf and it fell around my neck. Two panty wings fell from my eyes. She picked them out of my lap, one in each hand and flapped them in front of me. Not laughing, smiling awkwardly.

I loosened the scarf round my neck, handed it to her and got out of the Honda. We were in a small yard with dark brick walls and barred windows rising two floors above us. Above the single wide door there was a framed board with something, perhaps a company name and trade painted, originally gold on green but now too faded, the board itself too cracked to read. A date was legible: Established 1902.

Carole went forward and hammered with the flat of her hand on the door.

'You're sure he's here?' I said after a pause and another bout of hammering.

'He's here,' she said. 'He has nowhere else to go. What puzzles me is I don't hear Sally barking her head off.'

'His dog?'

'German shepherd. Long-haired. Stay back, she doesn't like strangers.'

'I'll stay back,' I said. I looked over the façade 'What *is* this?' I asked.

'A while back Luke set up repairing bikes. He needed a yard to work in. When the pool player came up with his offer, Luke rented this place. The top floors are derelict, used to be a soup kitchen. On the ground floor there's a couple of offices. A yard through on the other side used to be a loading station for a brewery. Bigger'n this. Not bad for a biking business. Except the business didn't come in.'

We were still waiting. She hammered on the door again and stood back. There was a little more light in the sky now, but cold, sunless. 'This is a guy who could sleep through Christmas,' she said. 'And his dog's no different.'

I leaned past her and turned the door handle. 'It's just worth trying.' It felt greasy but it turned. The door creaked open. I let her go first.

The narrow passageway smelt damp. The hall was painted Chinese red, peeling to cream decorated with roses. At handlebar height the plaster was scored deep by the motorcycles he'd brought in for repair.

There was an office on either side. Cautiously, I looked in one, an unused room with a net hanging at the barred window. I came back into the hall and saw Carole had already gone into the other room. The window was dark with grime and a torn curtain. But there was enough light to make out a desk with a few oil-stained repair manuals and a couple of kitchen chairs. One wall was covered with tear-outs from men's magazines. Yamahas competed with pink nipples. Sometimes the naked girls rode the bikes.

A sofa under the window had once been green but was blackened with grease. A pillow and a neatly folded blanket lay on the sofa arm. Four or five peanut or pickle lids and a few beer cans piled with cigarette butts and roaches were scattered on the floor.

'He sleeps here sometimes,' Carole said, stepping across

the lids to reach the window. Strap heels among the dust and beer cans. Leaning across the sofa, not touching it, she pushed aside the curtain. A little light came into the room. I saw her flinch, as if at a blow. 'Oh my good God,' she said and turned and ran past me to the door.

She turned into the narrow passage and threw herself forward, bursting through the door. I don't think she screamed. Or perhaps she was screaming already.

I came into the yard as she stumbled forward. I caught her round the waist. Her arms flailed. She was screaming now.

Blind walls towered around us. On one side, to the east, the broken windows of abandoned tenements looked down. It was a small loading yard from the days of the horse and cart. A wooden board platform stood at shoulder height on thick timber stilts against one wall. A pulley on an arm above held the rope. On the end of the rope, half-dangling into the access trap, the dog hung, unmoving. Next to it, sprawled across the bare boards, Luke Bassenger lay with his throat gaping.

I fought Carole back into the narrow red hall. I held her against the wall. 'Listen,' I told her. 'I'll go out and look at him. Just in case. Sit in the car.'

I dragged her out to the Honda and got her into it. I went back to the yard to see what I could do about Luke. I wasn't going to bring him back to life. His throat had been cut; he had been stabbed several times. In the face, the shoulder and twice in the chest. There was blood but no pulse.

I stood up. The dog glared at me. Eyes, grey and cloudy like a dead fish; the tongue, big as an ox tongue; the knot under her left ear, a truly massive twist of hempen rope. A professional's knot. A hangman's knot.

The car door was open when I came out into the alley. Carole was hanging out of it, retching air.

'Carole,' I said. I got my hand under her chin and lifted her head. 'Swallow. And breathe deeply.'

She let her head fall back against the headrest and breathed in and out steadily.

'Where are we?' I said. 'I have to call the police.'

She opened her mouth a couple of times, then shook her head, retching. She felt for a pen in her tote bag and searched around in the rubbish on the rubber floor. Coming up with a piece of coloured card she wrote on it and passed it to me. Print side up, it was a piece torn from a Veneziana pizza packet. It had a series of harlequin figures, almond-eyed and sinister, crowding the narrow alleys of Venice on their way to a masked ball.

28

The weather had broken. It was raining hard, the clouds brown and drifting low like smoke from a chemical plant on fire. There were coroners' vans, crime-scene vans, the micro-forest of TV vans. I stood with a bottle of vodka in a doorway out of the rain and watched it all happen as an outsider. Carole had been taken away, suffering from shock. I had given my story three times to a hard-faced NYPD detective from the local precinct whose name I hadn't caught. Only DeLane's arrival from the New York FBI field office had saved me from being taken down to the station. But it meant another grinding hour in DeLane's car. It was nine o'clock before I was finally free to go.

This area was known as El Barrio. Spanish Harlem to some, it appeared. What was going on around me was La Marqueta, a great, jostling Latin-American market. Except I wasn't in the mood for tourism. Lack of sleep and probably shock were taking their toll. That and the bottle of vodka I'd bought from the corner liquor store as soon as it opened. I was so tired I was rocking forward on the balls of my feet. I sat down on the step of the empty doorway. The smell of vegetables was thick on the air; produce trucks hooted, drivers leaned out and swore at each other. The buyers, the people of the neighbourhood, under-chefs from big restaurants and hotels, when they weren't shouting to each other, glanced across and registered me as just another homeless man. Around nine-thirty I dragged myself to my feet and walked down to 114th Street before I found a cab to take me to Grand Central.

*   *   *

Back at Observatory Point, I showered away the smell of spices and death, climbed into bed and slept for two hours. Then I got up and made myself coffee. I could hear the wind howling in off Long Island Sound, a pleasure, I supposed, for yachtsmen whose distant white sails I had seen tracking across the water most days since I occupied the tower room.

But it's not a sport for me. I took my coffee and turned on the TV. I flicked through a dozen cartoons and last-century cult reruns. Glossy Ben Rushton ads were playing on channel after channel. I sped past them and something that might have been news and clicked back for it. The death of Luke Bassenger had already been media-packaged. There was film from the market. Smartly dressed young women gave stand-alone pieces from under multicoloured umbrellas, and in one or two shots I even picked up a drenched figure with a bottle of vodka swinging from limp fingers as he rocked backwards and forwards in the doorway of a long-closed building that announced Soup Kitchen for the Jewish Poor in art nouveau tiling across the terracotta fascia.

The stories had a good deal less to tell than I already knew. I switched to another news channel and the screen resolved itself into a scatter of TV vans on a hillside. It took me a moment to recognise the gravel alleyway crammed with people. I was watching a funeral, the funeral of George Martin Liston, the man whose grave at Greenhill cemetery had been used to bury Katerina's body. The harassed Liston family stood under black umbrellas, crowded into the middle of what must have been almost a hundred press photographers. Strobe lights flickered like lightning through the sheets of rain.

The news commentary was not about George Martin Liston. It was a rerun for the hundredth time of yesterday's shocking events at this cemetery. Tacked onto it was the story of the death of Luke Bassenger who had become 'the man who bought the coffin'.

Back in the TV studio an anchorman interviewed two professional commentators on how this dramatic turn of events might impact upon the coming election.

The Washington professionals, a man and a woman, were notably more frank than yesterday. Against footage of Carole Bassenger leaving the motorbike shop where her husband had been murdered, they ran her voice on the Marty Lackman show. Regulars in the Pirate had been questioned and were now prepared to swear they had recognised Katerina as the cornet player on the night before her death.

All these elements enabled the professionals to talk of Ben Rushton's problem with an 'erratic' wife, to assume a stance which suggested Washington insiders like themselves had known of Katerina's predilections for some time. Did this mean Ben Rushton was finished as a candidate? Probably, the male pundit said.

'Not necessarily,' the woman disagreed. 'Mr Rushton is, in the eyes of many Americans, deserving of sympathy. He maintained a marriage which many of us in Washington knew to be extremely difficult for him. He maintained the relationship, under duress, with grace and dignity. One could say, in the circumstances, with humanity.'

'In the circumstances?' The anchorperson smelt a coming revelation.

I felt the influence of Yado and Sarah's spin in the answer. Mrs Rushton's problem, the commentator said authoritatively, was alcohol against which she fought a losing battle. Pressures on the wives of leading male politicians simply don't get enough publicity – and thus public sympathy. 'I personally don't see Americans,' the Washington commentator said, 'particularly the women of America, turning against an outstanding candidate in his moment of need. OK Ben Rushton is fighting for his life. But I think he's winning.'

I switched off, showered and dressed in jeans and a Yale

sweatshirt which I guessed belonged to Ben Rushton, and, late as it was, went downstairs to hit another extraordinary day.

My first hit was Polly, running across the big hall. She skidded to a halt when she saw me. 'Ben tells me you were with Carole Bassenger when she found her husband.'

'Luke was going to propose a deal, give us a name or description. Our man was there first.'

'It's certain whoever killed Katerina, killed Bassenger?'

'Certain.'

'So he's still around.'

'Not far away,' I said. 'And even more dangerous because we don't know his agenda.' I leaned on the big carved newel post. 'So what's all this doing to the Rushton chances?'

'There's a lot of baffled people out there,' she said. 'But there's definitely a wave of sympathy.' I noticed how just talking about the election immediately put her on another plane, released her energy. 'Yup. Something is telling them Ben deserves a break.' She jumped from Nike to Nike. 'Wouldn't call it a flood yet. Certainly wouldn't think in terms of a tidal wave. But it's building. We are getting more phone calls than we can handle. This is true for all the separate offices – even Chicago. The demand for stickers, posters and Rushton buttons exploded this morning. We're not going to be able to keep up. So – what's new with you, Constantin?'

'My job's finished,' I said. 'Obviously enough. I'm just waiting for Katerina's funeral. I'd like to make it before I go back to Russia.'

She looked at me. 'You crazy or what?' she said. 'You're part of this team. Nobody's going to let you go.'

'Ask Jack Yado.'

'It's not Jack's call.' She looked serious. 'Need you around, Constantin. Ben needs you. Alex needs you. Fuck it, we all do.' She went to move on, skidded round again.

'One thing. You're not beginning to cuddle up to Sarah, are you? Olga thinks you might be.'

I didn't answer.

'Said the wrong thing?'

I came down the last steps. 'You know Olga,' I said. 'She thinks her brother can't wait to cuddle up to every woman he meets. What are you saying – with Sarah it'd be a wrong move?'

'That's what I'm saying.'

'Why?' She was already crossing the corridor towards her office. At the door, in place of an answer, she half-turned, waved, a sober smile on her face, and disappeared inside.

Shredding flowers from the myrtle grove in its downdraught, the black and yellow campaign helicopter landed on the lawn at Observatory Point a few minutes after midday. Right after a pair of Secret Service agents, Ben Rushton ducked out first with Alison Bryson holding her hair in place just behind him. Behind Rushton and his secretary, Clint Maddox emerged, his light double-breasted jacket billowing in the wind, his ever-wary eyes sweeping the area ahead of him. Yado was campaigning in California.

I watched the party, augmented by two political assistants, cross the lawn towards the house. Rushton was looking sombrely distinguished in a very dark suit and black tie. Alison Bryson, once clear of the helicopter downdraught, had recovered her composure by the time they reached the gravel path. I thought about her for a few moments. Very New England. Tall and looking formally shapely in her black suit. Not young but one of those women who will be poised on the edge of middle age for many years. I suppose I was looking for signs of intimacy with Rushton. Signs that this woman, divorced several years back, was the woman with him when he had answered that recorded call from Katerina. The woman in bed with him.

I turned from the window I was standing at and saw Alex behind me. 'Ben will see us straightaway,' she said. 'Give him a few moments to settle in.' She joined me at the window, looking out as if she could see, her hand on my shoulder, rhythmically rubbing small circles with the flat of her hand.

In the last days I had developed a strange intimacy with Alex. Like nothing so much as the intimacy of schoolfriends, not unconscious of our differing sexes, but somehow barriered against giving the difference any special significance.

She could put her arm round my waist as we walked, or, as we sat talking, she might casually run her fingers through the hair on the back of my neck. I felt it, like her hand on my shoulder today, as some additional assurance she was asking that I was there, the images conveyed by her eyes alone being insufficient.

In return, I never touched her, except to guide her somewhere by the hand. It had crossed my mind that she was perhaps the only attractive woman I had never responded to in some way, at least. The truth is I think I would have felt as if I were taking an unacceptable advantage of her, even to have thought about it.

But there was something else too. I could feel us drawing closer together, into a friendship that was unique in my experience. After all, I was suffering myself. Three years ago my wife had been killed in Murmansk. Murdered. Something like that leaves a scar that only heals in a raw, knitted-up way. Physical relations with a woman are possible but anything more is precluded. Growing closer to a woman whose physical limitations represented a barrier in so many ways, was perhaps some sort of unconscious compromise on my part.

I watched the helicopter party reach the corner of the building and disappear. 'What do you know about Alison Bryson?' I asked her.

She shrugged. 'She became Ben's PA at the World

Bank a few years ago. She's the super-efficient American assistant. Super-efficient, super-loyal . . .'

'Do you like her?'

'I do.'

'She's what some people call a very handsome woman.'

'I only know what I hear. She's very Philadelphia, very Katharine Hepburn, but I think she has a warm heart.' She leaned towards me, the flat of her hand still making circles on my shoulder. 'I have a secret for you. I think she's always been in love with Ben.'

She straightened up, realising what she had said. 'That was childish,' she said. 'Forget it, Constantin, will you?'

'Forgotten,' I said.

For a moment we stood in silence. She had removed her hand. 'I played the recording again this morning,' she said. 'I'm beginning to think I got carried away when I heard it last night. Having an affair is a long way from hiring a killer.' She shuddered.

'A hell of a long way,' I said.

'Let's go and talk to Ben,' she said.

29

Alison Bryson was in Ben's office when I entered with Alex ten minutes later. She was busying herself at a desk to the side of the massive colonial ebony desk he used. She looked up with a quick smile and continued sorting through papers as Rushton came forward and hugged Alexandra. 'How are you?' he asked. 'How are you getting through all this?'

She shrugged in his arms.

'Aren't these just the most horrible days,' he said soberly. 'And now we hear this young guy, Bassenger, has been murdered . . .' He stood, shaking his head. 'The worst of it, Alex, is I know I should be spending them with you. That's what I should be doing. That's what I'd sooner be doing.'

She didn't respond. I could see it had not escaped him.

'But what I want to be doing doesn't count any more. The campaign rolls on inexorably. Even in these circumstances, I'm owned by the party.' He released her, and looked at her, concern in his expression, sensing some lack of response. 'Vadim's taking care of you, isn't he?'

She nodded. 'He's taking care of me.'

Again the tone caused a faint shadow to flicker across his features. 'I got your message,' he said. 'It sounded grim.'

'Important,' she said, turning her head towards Miss Bryson. Unseeing she may have been, but that did nothing to reduce a touch of imperiousness in her glance when she wanted to convey it.

Alison Bryson understood. 'I have some things to do

upstairs,' she said easily. 'Not least of all to get myself a change of clothes.'

She gathered up papers, her briefcase and left quickly. Ben led Alexandra to a chair and gestured to me to sit down. 'We've a lot of things to talk about, you and me, Alex,' he said. He put his hand to his head. 'But this life . . . This morning we did a fund-raising breakfast in Washington, a ceremony at Arlington, and an immigration seminar in Philadelphia.'

I saw him look at Alex's face and again registered her expression. He changed tack quickly. 'So, Alex . . .'

'I'd like to play you this,' she said abruptly. She held up a disc.

'What is it?'

'We found it in the lodge. It's a recording of a call between you and Katerina.'

There was a long silence. His eyes stayed on her. I could read nothing on his face. 'I knew it existed,' he said slowly. 'Katerina told me she had recorded that call.'

If a room could be said to have wings, I stood in the wings. It was almost as if a spotlight picked them out centre stage.

'Did you search Katerina's room the day she died?' Alex asked him.

'I did.'

'And you searched the lodge? Or more likely had someone search the lodge.'

'That's true,' he said. 'It was necessary to break in. The police and FBI had finished there. They'd made no mention of finding the disc. Although, to be fair, they'd no reason to believe it existed.'

'You'd not told them.'

He looked at her. 'For a politician that'd be beyond the call of duty. I remembered enough of my call that night with Katerina to know it was dynamite. Now you've heard the recording, Alex. You can see what damage it could do.'

'The reference to another woman.'

'Of course,' he said.

I sat regretting that I'd agreed to come with her. Potential presidents shouldn't be having to admit such things to me. Even if I had already heard the recording.

Alexandra felt no such qualms. 'I think I should ask you, Ben – is there another woman?'

'I don't think I have to answer that question,' he said slowly.

'For me, you do, Ben. You know it isn't the simple question: do you have a mistress? Too many other things hang on it. There are too many possible implications.'

'Implications?'

'You know what I mean.'

'I never thought we'd come to this, Alex,' he said. He had a tone of voice that could face down anybody. I stood there wondering what it would do to Alex.

Suddenly her face changed. Tears were running down her cheeks. 'It pulls me apart to do this, Ben. Not to trust you like this. But, for Katerina's sake, I have to ask. I'm *going* to ask.'

'OK,' he said.

She stretched a hand towards him and he came round and sat on the arm of her chair. 'Let's take a deep breath,' he said. 'We're both in pain.'

She nodded. I watched this very American exchange, unsure whether I was impressed by it, or thought it just too much. He was being accused of complicity in murder. Or at least he was being told that he was suspect. What was he doing sitting on the arm of her chair, stroking her hair? In Russia he would be striding the room shouting denials.

But he didn't. 'OK.' He got up decisively. 'First we play the disc. Then we dig out the questions, one by one. Then we answer them. How's that?'

I found it hard not to admire him. It sounded fine to me.

It sounded fine to Alex too. I could see her expression change. Nodding agreement, she wiped her cheeks.

Rushton picked up the phone. 'For the next half-hour, I want to speak to nobody. Campaign, FBI, police . . . Nobody. After that it's business as usual.'

I fervently hoped it would be. But it was only as I watched him, calm and confident on the phone, that I realised he still hadn't answered the question.

The disc was running. Politicians are actors, we've heard that enough times. And perhaps Ben Rushton was acting. But if he was it was the performance of his life. I could *feel* the pain. Or thought I could as he flinched and grimaced at his own words.

The machine switched itself off. We sat in silence.

'Your question,' Rushton said.

Alex nodded slowly. 'Was there a woman, Ben? You haven't said either way.'

He allowed a long pause. 'What you heard on that recording was repeated a dozen, two dozen times over the last months. The more Katerina wandered herself, the more she became convinced I was doing the same. Maybe even, the more she hoped I was.' He stood, trailing his hand across his desk. 'I don't come over well on that call, Alex. I don't come over as sympathetic . . . But there was no woman with me.'

Her face was turned towards him.

'There's no love affair, Alex. Katerina thought there was. Was convinced there was. You can imagine . . . she wouldn't let it go.'

Alex was nodding her head each time he made a point. 'OK Ben, thank you.'

He smiled.

'But there's just one other thing on the recording that I must ask you about,' she said. 'Katerina asking you to give up politics . . .'

'Yes . . .' he said. 'That was strange.'

'You didn't understand what she meant?'

'You heard yourself on the recording . . .'

I could see he was evading something. Could Alex divine it?

'And the reference to you becoming . . .'

'A man again. Yes,' he said, shaking his head. 'Just don't know what that meant. Although you must know it wasn't unusual for Katerina to make these direct sexual barbs. Perhaps this was one. Sexually, things hadn't been good for us – for me particularly – at around the time she started drinking. Politics can sap your sex drive. I don't know – maybe that's what she was talking about.' He looked down at her and although she wouldn't have been able to see it, he made a small apologetic shrug. 'Doesn't seem that important now.'

Her face was turned up to Rushton, pale, her eyes wider than I had ever seen them, aching to see his expression, to make a decision as other people make decisions, on what they see as well as what they hear. I knew the all-important question was coming. So, I think, did Rushton.

He got there first. 'Question is,' he said. 'What do we do with the recording?'

'Will you hand it over to the FBI?' she asked him.

There was a long pause. 'If you insist, yes. Is that what you want?'

'I don't know,' she said.

'If that's what you decided, I'd like to ask you to talk it over with Vadim first.'

'No,' she said, a real touch of asperity in her voice. 'It's something I can decide for myself, Ben.'

'OK.' He stood very still. 'But I can't honestly see,' he said slowly, 'how this recording can in any way advance their investigation. What will it tell them? Nothing more than that Katerina was accusing me of having an affair with another woman. You were a policeman, Vadim. Do you see that as a factor in the investigation?'

'I don't know the lines they're pursuing.'

'True enough. But they never knew Katerina. My guess is that any cop, any Bureau agent, would most likely believe from that recording that there *was* another woman in that hotel room. And however much I deny it, there's always the danger of a leak to the media.' He snapped his fingers. 'Or, maybe suspicion of an affair might marginally persuade the FBI that I have an additional motive, although God knows, if every man having an affair were to be suspected of organising the death of his wife, the police would have a busy time on their hands.'

He came and rested against his desk facing Alex, looking down at her. 'What's in this disc, Alex, has no importance to the terrible thing that has just happened to Katerina, except in one circumstance only. That is if you still believe there was a woman with me the night Katerina called. In which case you might, just *might*, go on to believe I am brute enough to solve the problems I admit I had with Katerina by hiring a twisted maniac as a contract killer.' He paused. 'Is that what you believe?'

The tip of her tongue snaked out and wet her lips.

'Do you believe that, Alex?'

She hesitated just one fraction of a second longer, then shook her head. 'No,' she said. 'No, Ben. I can't believe it. Of course I can't.'

He stepped forward and raised her up and hugged her. His arms were tight around her waist. I think her arms were equally tight around his chest. 'The recording will be in my safe,' he said. 'If ever you feel you need it, this is the number.' He went round the desk and scribbled a number on a piece of paper. Then handed it across to me.

'Perhaps Alex should keep it,' I said. 'I think my time's up here.'

His head turned sharply. 'Not at all, Vadim. I have an important job for you to do. Is it your idea to leave?'

'No.'

'Then who said your time's up?'

'I got that idea last time I spoke to Mr Yado.'

'You're on my team, Vadim. Not Jack's. His problem is he doesn't like independence in the people he hires.' He smiled grimly. 'I can't claim I *always* do.' He looked down at the recording on the desk. 'But it's mostly a whole lot better than bootlickers.'

We all three walked towards the door, he with an arm round Alexandra's shoulder. 'I have to talk to you about Katerina's will, Alex,' he said.

'I'll leave,' I said, reaching for the door handle.

'Before you do, Vadim, I've something to ask you. In a way this concerns you too.'

'Something to ask me about Katerina's will?'

'Yes. The original full version, both the financial and personal aspects, is with her lawyers of course.' He kept his arm tight round Alex's shoulders. 'I hold a paraphrase of the non-financial aspects of the will. I should tell you now that Katerina has left an instruction in it which might not be easy on any of us. But isn't all that surprising.' He looked down at the carpet for a moment. 'It's certainly one we're bound to comply with.' He paused again. 'She asks that her body be returned to Russia. She wants to be buried back home.'

Alex nodded slowly.

Rushton turned to me. 'The job I mentioned just now . . .'

I saw it coming of course. 'The funeral . . .'

'I can't think of anyone better qualified. With Alex's agreement, I'm going to ask you to go on ahead and make the advance arrangements in Russia.'

30

We stood together in the Japanese garden.

'Are you OK?' I asked her. 'Are you OK about that?'

She was silent a long time, touching the plants with the tips of her fingers. 'I have to be,' she said after a moment. 'I have to believe what Ben said was the truth. Katerina was paranoically jealous. There *was* no other woman.'

I could see she was forcing herself to believe it.

'Ben wouldn't lie to cover a simple affair. Why should he? No need to hide it from me. He could trust me with that secret, for God's sake.'

'What are you saying?'

'I'm saying . . .' she said slowly, 'if he's lying, it means much more than a simple attempt to cover up an affair. I'm saying if he's lying, it's to cover up something much more serious, Constantin.' She walked on a few paces. 'And the implications of that I can't handle at all. Don't want to. Don't believe I have to. So I'm OK with what he told us. I think – I pray – he must be telling the truth.'

I left Alex with Olga and headed for my room. Did I think Ben Rushton was lying? No . . . but I still wasn't entirely sure he'd told Alex the *whole* truth. Maybe that was what Alex had been trying to say in the Japanese garden. I was a few steps from the door, a few steps from that soothing thumb or two of lemon vodka when my cellphone rang.

I left it for a moment. Was it Rushton with further explanations, Alex with further reservations . . . ? I waited until I could leave it no longer, then pressed the button and said, without thinking, 'Observatory Point.'

Except for the fact the voice spoke with a powerful

Russian accent, I don't think I would have recognised it. 'I wish to speak to Constantin Vadim,' the hoarse voice said. 'If you'll be so kind.'

'Vadim speaking.'

'Fuck your mother, it's you, Costya,' Roy said, his voice a whisper. 'What's happening over there?'

'Everything,' I said. 'Have you been gelded in my absence? I didn't recognise the controlled polite tones.'

'A death,' he said, 'in the home of a presidential candidate. You don't go bawling about like a camp guard, naturally you don't.'

Roy's images never failed to reflect his chequered past.

'The story's getting coverage in Russia?'

'Moscow, I don't know. But up here it's getting first place on *Polar News* every hour. You're surrounded by history, Costya. Now here's what I want you to do.'

'No football, Roy.'

'I'm not talking about football. That's on hold. More important things.'

'Such as?'

'Christ on the Cross, Costya. You're still talking about football when *I'm* talking about nothing less than the salvation of Russia. The country's falling to pieces under my eyes. The armed forces are disintegrating. The roads are crammed with refugees heading West. Moscow and Leningrad . . .'

'St Petersburg.'

'Correct. St Petersburg. Both seized up with people with false vaccination certificates fighting to get onto flights to the US. For the moment the Interior Ministry forces are showing enough discipline to remain in place. But it won't last.'

'Listen Roy,' I said. 'I'll be back in Moscow in a couple of days. I can catch up then.'

He ignored me. 'Costya,' he said. 'We have to look at the broader perspective. We can't reform Russia alone.

Russia *needs* this man Rushton to lead us out of this hellhole. What sort of a man is he?'

'I think he's honest, intelligent certainly . . .'

'Stop there. That's more than twice as much as we've had from any Russian national leader since Ruric the Glorious. What about this assassination of his wife? Will it bring out the sympathy vote?'

I leaned into one of the arched alcoves that decorated the long passage. 'Roy, what's all this about? Why are you so interested in who makes president in November?'

'I'm planning to give Rushton my backing.'

I almost choked. 'Somehow I think you might have exaggerated how impressed he'll be. What do you really want, Roy?'

'This idea of Rushton's . . . the Russian Aid Supremo. This is statesmanship, Costya. This is statesmanship of the very first quality. I have to admit I'm impressed.'

'And what do you want out of it?'

'I'm saying it's brilliant. It's the only workable approach for the chaotic Russian scene. I'm completely convinced by it.'

'And . . .'

'I'm out for the job of Health Aid Supremo. I think most people who know me would agree it would suit my talents and experience.'

I took a deep breath. 'I'm hanging up,' I said.

'Not before you've told me how I can contact Rushton's Number Two.'

'You mean Yado.'

'Yado, Jack,' he said. 'That's it. He gets a good press here. Confidentially, I've decided to make my pitch for Health Aid Supremo through him.'

'Roy,' I said slowly. 'I think you're out of your mind. Did you hear me say that? I'll say it again. Out of your mind. Things don't work the same way over here. You can't just ring Jack Yado and offer him a million dollars, or his own troupe of showgirls or a dacha in the Catskill mountains. It doesn't work like that.'

'Don't lecture me on politics, bratkin,' he said. That dangerous edge had entered his voice. 'If I don't get an introduction to the Rushton camp through you, I'll do it some other way. But you owe me a favour there in the US. Make contact with Yado for me. Tell him about me. Paint a picture . . .' I shuddered at the thought. 'Do this and we'll be quits, Costya. Pass up on it, and I'll remember it as a black mark. You won't spend your whole life among the Yankees, Costya. Or hanging around the bright lights of Moscow. You'll be back in Murmansk sometime – and I'd like to feel you've come back as a friend.'

The line went dead. I leaned back into the alcove. Roy and Rushton were unimaginable in the same room even. But Roy's nose was acute. He had read the reports of the Bernheimer poll. He had sniffed dollars. He was a regional governor with a totally undeserved reputation for reasonable honesty. And he had an old friend, me, in the Rushton camp. One who, as he saw it, owed him a favour.

Perhaps this is what always happens when a man begins his rise to presidential power. Perhaps Roy was just the first of the grasping parasites Ben Rushton was going to have to fight off.

I was lost in thought, slumped in the alcove, my eyes shut, when I breathed in deeply and realised, from the perfume, that a woman was standing in front of me. Fingers covered my eyes. I felt the pressure of her mouth on my lips and as I opened my eyes I was being pressed back into the alcove.

Her tongue slipped between my lips and rippled my teeth before she drew her head back. 'Just too tempting to pass up,' she said. Sarah removed her hands. 'Who did you think it was?'

'Olga,' I said. 'In incestuous mood.' I straightened up, catching my breath.

'I need to talk to you, Costya.'

'OK.'

'It's about Alex.' She led me along the landing and down a back stair that I hadn't noticed before. 'What's going on?' she said. 'As I understand it, Alex is suggesting Ben could have had something to do with Katerina's death.'

'How did you hear that?'

'Yado.'

'For two people who hate each other you have a pretty regular exchange of confidences.'

'Politics, Costya. We exchange when it suits. So, what's Alex up to? Is she really saying Ben's got some connection with Katerina's death?'

'Listen Sarah ... it's over. There were some things Katerina had said ...'

'That's grotesque. Worse than that it's as dangerous a piece of scuttlebutt as I can imagine. The woman's as mad as her sister, mother, whatever the relationship really was.'

I was stuck. I wasn't going to tell Sarah about Katerina's accusation on the recording, but I felt the need to defend Alex. 'It's not really like that,' I said.

We walked out to her Jaguar in the stableyard.

'What's it really like then?' I picked up the sharp tone of voice.

We stood beside the sleek black Jaguar. I struggled for an answer.

'It was a bitch of a thing to do,' she said. 'To accuse him of hiring a contract killer ... Jesus, it takes the breath away. What is it with Russian women?'

'Russian men,' I said. 'Mostly.'

'Talk sense. This dust gets out to the media, Ben'll be crushed underfoot. Does the fucking woman understand that?'

She looked up at me. She was quick enough to see we were going into a rerun of our fight over Katerina. 'OK, I know she's different. Her sight's seriously impaired. She's led a sheltered life and all that. But for Christ's sake, Ben's been the next thing to a father to her. What makes her think it's even a possibility?'

I ran my hand across the polished top of the car. 'As I said, there were some things Katerina told her before she died,' I said. 'Alex went in to see Ben as soon as he got back. They straightened it out between them. That's all there was to it.'

She knew it was an unsatisfactory answer. A half-answer at best. She opened the door to the car. 'You're close to Alex. She trusts you, I can see that. And you're a man, for Christ's sake. Try and talk some sense into her. If a report like that got out . . . Jesus, I know she's nearly my age but she's like a kid. Let her know it's time to grow up.'

I nodded.

'I'm out of here,' she said. 'To pick up Yado at JFK. We'll get time to talk about Ben's revised campaign programme on the drive back. Under five weeks to polling day and a funeral in Moscow to fit in slap bang in the middle.' She put her foot on the rim of the door and pulled her skirt high on her knee. Swinging easily behind the wheel she looked up at me, her hand on the open door. 'Do I have to apologise for that moment of stolen osculation up there in the corridor?' she said.

'Not to me.'

'Maybe we could begin to feel our way forward from there.'

'What a way you have with words,' I said.

She pulled the door closed and the car seemed to leap away from me. Osculation. I liked it.

31

After perhaps an hour, as the light began to fade, we broke away from the ribbon of tail lights ahead of us and turned off the highway onto smaller roads that slid and twisted between the mist-covered woodlands. Hanratty smoked the best part of half a pack of cigarettes and kept up a running complaint about the ill-signed Connecticut byways. I had answered his earlier questions as we drove north towards Hartford, filling in all I could from DeLane's brief report on Volodya Rinsky.

Mostly he had just expanded what he had told me at the Microsoft Stadium. Rinsky was what some New Yorkers call an old Russian. He had transferred to the United States as soon as the Soviet Union began to collapse. In 1991 the reason was clear enough. As a KGB inter-rogation officer he had tortured and beaten confessions out of hundreds in his career. Some prisoners had died. In 1991 nobody in the KGB knew if a democratic legal system would bring the *boxers*, as the torturers called themselves, to trial. Of course it didn't happen. In Russia nobody was brought to trial for Soviet crimes. They all received pensions. But people like Volodya did not know that in 1991. He fled to America.

But he was not a gifted man. Even the inevitable drift into New York crime was unsuccessful. He had hung around on the fringe of Russian crime in the city as the century turned and picked up a reputation for being prepared to muscle for anybody. But a heart attack quickly reduces the muscle available.

It was now that the beasts of the jungle turned on him. Or one beast. The FBI's Mr Wonderful saw the chance to make a final pay day out of Volodya Rinsky. While he was unconscious, believed to be dying, from his second heart attack, Mr Wonderful sold his name as a serial rapist the NYPD had been searching for several years back. While Rinsky recovered, he was in a prison hospital awaiting trial. He never knew where the information came from. A year later, no longer dying but still a very sick man, he was sentenced as the rapist who'd operated all over Manhattan, haunting the parking lots of hospitals, late-night bars or convenience stores, anywhere women left work late. His last assault was an attempt on a nurse coming off duty at the Lincoln Mental Health Centre, a few dozen yards from where he lived in the Bronx. In all, between his other criminal activities, he had raped seven and severely injured one woman.

Hanratty was peering at road signs. 'And this is the man, according to DeLane, who knew more about the murder of this British judge than had appeared in broadcast and newsprint.'

'This is the man,' I said.

'How does DeLane believe he knew about the British judge? He thinks Rinsky killed her?'

'No. Some of the hangings took place while Rinsky was in jail.'

'So . . .'

'Rinsky worked for every Russian thug in New York City in his time. DeLane thinks he knows a lot more than the FBI have got out of him. It began to leak during the hypnosis sessions that Volodya's having to improve his breathing.'

'So what are we looking at – the name of the hitman?'

'I don't think so. But maybe something on the man who takes the contracts.'

'OK. Looks good. Go get him, Chief.'

We drove on in silence until I heard Hanratty grunt beside me as he swerved the car to squint awkwardly at a whitewood road sign. 'Missed it,' he said, pulling at the wheel to straighten us up again. Then: 'OK, we don't need a road sign from here on.'

He seemed to gesture with his chin. I looked about me. There was, I was suddenly aware, something strange in the air. The dark, rolling Connecticut countryside, a moment ago speckled with friendly yellow lights from houses and farms, was dying away around us. Even the car headlights were fading before the blue-white haze ahead. Powerful spotlights, somewhere beyond the next ridge, lifted the grey mist, creating the impression of the underside of a great dome.

'In America,' Hanratty said, crushing out a last cigarette, 'the stockholders have even taken over the prisons.' As we passed, he gestured up to a roadside board inscribed: Fleetwood – Federal Private Hospital Facility.

The dome of light grew brighter. We breasted the last rise and immediately Fleetwood announced itself as a modern but no less grim place for the detention of human beings, a custom-built asylum for the criminally insane.

A floodlit rectangle of chain-link fencing marked out the ground. Red and green lights flashed alternately at the gates. There were buildings within the wire rectangle, each set arranged in the shape of a wheel. A central two-storey administration block formed the hub, its spokes the armour-glass corridors which linked it to six single-storey accommodation blocks. Intense, stark lighting shone into the empty corridors.

We came down a hill towards this desolate place by a long approach road, on the side of which sensors set in cement blocks flashed blue as we passed. At the wire-mesh doors a recorded voice politely asked us to get out of the car and place the ID cards DeLane had provided in the slot of a machine that photographed them. When they rolled out again we were automatically thanked, got back in the car and the gates creaked slowly open for us.

It was two gates on before we were faced by our first human being, a large friendly man in a khaki uniform and brown rain slicker who was waiting for us in a small concrete guardroom. 'We've lost the summer,' he said, as he shook hands. 'I've lived here all my life. You wouldn't believe it – but I can feel winter in these winds.'

Hanratty said he wouldn't. I was more interested in the map that covered one wall. Each arrangement of central building and dependencies was known as a Spider. Presidential names had been assigned to each group of buildings. Our man was held somewhere in the Lyndon B. Johnson Spider. Hanratty had not been given permission to accompany me and he was left in the guardhouse with a copy of *Playboy*, the *National Enquirer* and the *Daily News* while another guard was called to take care of me.

Any place without the smell of armpits and cabbage, I'm reluctant to recognise as a prison. But these long glass spider legs that we walked had their own depressing ethos. The last prison I visited as a militia officer was in Novocherkassk. This is a penitentiary near Rostov on Don where that sense of foreboding is achieved by filth and neglect. The dark green of the cells is stained even darker around the base of walls where urine combines chemically with the paint to turn it black. The floors are lined with broken multicoloured tiles, the shattered rejects of a tile factory down the street. Chikatilo, the first Rostov mass murderer, was there, I remind myself as we reach the end of this glittering corridor of glass and show IDs at the entrance to Lyndon B. Johnson Station 1.

Here, there's polished linoleum on the floor. The walls are unscratched. Only the twenty or thirty radios all playing different stations, different kinds of music, tell you this impeccable hellhole is occupied. The guard salutes. He asks me if I wish to be accompanied in Mr Rinsky's cell. I tell him no and he informs me that he will be watching, but not listening to the interview taking place. He pauses before he opens the cell door. 'You'll observe a white line running across the floor, sir. You may not cross to the detainee's side. He must not cross to yours. Mr Rinsky is informed of this fact. If either side crosses the line the guard is entitled, as a matter of fact, *required*, to intervene immediately.'

He touches his cap again, swings open the door and says, 'Mr Rinsky. The visitor you've been informed about. Mr Constantin Vadim.' There is something almost eighteenth-century in the formality. I expect the guard to bow. And I think of Novocherkassk again.

I step inside and see the broad white line immediately. For no good reason I'm surprised it runs diagonally across the grey polished linoleum. There is a single chair on my side. Under the steel-barred ceiling light a man sits on the other side of the line writing at a small plain table. Like an important executive, he doesn't look up straightaway.

I have a moment or two to examine the cell. It has a bookcase above the grey-blanketed bunk. It has a lavatory bowl in the corner, stainless steel and free of smell. And a small white tin cupboard. But that is all.

I look down at the writer. He has longish brown hair and a bald pate. I am reminded of the First Folio picture of William Shakespeare.

'Volodya . . . You've done better for yourself here than in Novocherkassk,' I say in Russian. 'What do you have to say about the tentacles of American capitalism now?'

He finishes his sentence and looks up. 'I never did time in Novocherkassk. And for all the spit and polish here, I'd sooner be in a Russian prison.'

'Spoken as a Russian,' I say.

It is a coarse face. Not at all like Shakespeare's. Big-lipped and round-cheeked. Two or three front teeth have been capped with a poor colour match. But his eyes don't fit the rest of his features. They are a bright baby blue. And there's something else about his features that exists independently of these bright blue eyes. There's a greyness that seems almost to have weight, that drags heavily on his jowls. It's more than the familiar grey prison look of lack of sunlight and exercise. The purple rim to the lips, the tongue and corners of the mouth tell us something else. Cyanosis comes from a severe malfunction of the heart muscle. This man is seriously sick. He has to make an effort to organise his breathing, a moment before he can speak words: 'I read terrible things in the American press. Everybody's fighting to get to America. At home, are there still people who believe in Russia?' he asks.

'All true Russians,' I confirm.

His breathing is hard. He pushes back his locks. 'Who are you?'

'I have a message for you, Volodya.'

He accepts the familiarity, used to it in prison.

'A message from Moscow,' I say.

'From my uncle?'

I shake my head. 'There'll be no more messages from your uncle, brother,' I say to him. I hand him a cutting from a Moscow veterans bulletin that DeLane has provided me with, the details true or not, I don't know.

He glances at it and looks up at me. His eyes are misting over, but he holds me in their rheumy stare. Challenging me to speak the next words.

'Your uncle, Boris Sergeivich, died on Monday morning. Your family's weakness. A heart attack . . . It was quick. He had time for a few words. A message to his daughter, Nadia . . .'

He sits shaking his head, like an old, old lady remembering the golden past. 'And for me? Was there a message for me?'

'He was happy, he said, to have had that last chance to talk to you here.'

I see Volodya's face change. There is a new furtiveness in the movement of his shoulders. Now from this point it's no more than a shot in the dark. DeLane believes that the uncle brought Volodya the news that it was Mr Wonderful who sold him to the FBI. I try to rub home the point. 'Your uncle was happy to have given you that last message.'

Volodya nods slowly. His hand, I see, has risen to his heart. 'Give me the box there,' he points to the shelf. 'The tablets.'

I glance down at the white line that divides us and shrug my apologies. He grimaces, in pain now, and reaches up for the shelf, fumbling a tiny glyceryl trinitrate tablet from the box into his mouth and under his tongue. He is straightening to relieve the pain in his back and chest. 'The last message, you say?'

'That you'd been betrayed, fingered to the FBI. Put you in here for the rest of your life.'

He is breathing hard, a low whistle from deep in his lungs.

'When he died your uncle left money to settle scores.'

'I don't understand.'

'Money to settle with this scum.'

'You know his name?'

I shake my head. 'But you do.'

His hands spread wide. A long pause, leaning forward to relieve the pain. 'I worked for him from the time I first arrived in the US. Courier, that was my job. I gave him loyalty, brother, as Russians can. But he never allowed me his name.'

'And in the end he handed you over.'

'He threw me to the lions. The cops were desperate to get me, the guy who'd done over these women. They paid well.'

He makes no attempt to deny the rapes, no claim of innocence.

'Tell me how I find him,' I urge him. 'We'll make sure he regrets it.'

'Perhaps,' he says. 'Perhaps he's dead already. He was old. Too old to carry out the contracts.' He looks at me for a few seconds.

'You could pay him back for what he did to you,

Volodya. He's wanted for running a hitman. You know that.'

'He's wanted for a dozen things.'

'The hitman who only deals in women.'

He nods, glassy-eyed.

'So he was the one who took the commissions,' I say, 'but who actually did the job?'

'Killed them? Hanged them? The old man had someone.'

'Just give me something,' I say. 'Anything that will lead me to them. Did the old man work with other people?'

'Just the one,' he says. 'Dangerous-looking type. You wouldn't want to cross him.'

'Christ – you met him?'

'Listen.' He recognises my need. But he wants to use his breath to talk about the past. 'Once, the old man sent me up to the Adirondacks, right up around Saranac Lake. It's wild up there. North Creek. I was to deliver the name of a woman, a German woman, I remember.'

'Helga Falk,' I say. 'A member of the European Parliament.'

He smiles grimly. The thought even seems to improve his colour. 'Helga Falk. Right,' he says. 'You know what we're talking about. It was a wooden hut, not much more. A wildlife place in the woods. This young fellow was living there alone. I expected targets set up. You know, for practice. Maybe even hear gunshots as I got closer. You see that film: *Day of the Jackal*?'

'But nothing like that?'

'Nothing. Instead, outside the hut, a sort of long pole slung between two trees. And all sorts of ropes and wires hanging from them. Dusk, it was. He had camp lights.' He pulls a face. Disgust. 'And hanging from the ropes and wires, he had these dogs. Five or six. Dead, most of them. One or two still just alive. He was practising all right. But he wasn't a shooter. He was practising the drop. He was the hangman.'

'What did he look like?'

'I gave him his target, Helga Falk. He was nothing much of anything to describe. This was a few years back. He was late thirties. Jeans, a plaid shirt. Hunting cap. I don't mind telling you, there with his hanging dogs, he scared the hell out of me.'

'The hut . . . did he continue to use it?'

He shakes his head. 'The old man told me it'd be burnt down that same night when the vek left to do his job on the German woman. Caught up with her in Sutton Place. I remember.'

The pain comes back in waves. He is nodding to himself, grey again now, breath labouring, flinching . . . He is in urgent need of a doctor, I can see that. But he's also on the brink of telling me something. Some tiny grain of information that could lead to Katerina's killer . . . And, for this man, the doctor can wait.

Volodya is rocking back and forth with pain. Two trinitrate tablets have done nothing to relieve it. The greyness has gone to white. Yet sweat begins to drip from his chin. 'You're afraid, Volodya,' I tell him. 'I think, even after all he's done to you, you won't give us the old man's name. You're afraid his arm stretches even inside these walls.'

He mutters inaudibly. He is distressed by the accusation, probably because it's true.

'You say you don't know his name – but I think you do. Give it to me,' I say. 'We have friends who will deal with him. Here or in Moscow.'

'Listen.' He is groaning. 'I need a doctor.'

'Betrayal,' I remind him. 'You want revenge. Who is he? Who betrayed you?'

For a moment or two more he is silent. I think he is going to fall to the ground, but he pulls up his head. 'Please, now,' he says, 'call the doctor now.'

'His name. Where does he live? Still in New York?'

'Back in Moscow now. Get me a doctor. For mercy's sake.'

I stare down at him, unrelenting. He's made other people suffer enough. His time has come. 'Not,' I say slowly, 'until you tell me.'

'What are you doing to me? A doctor. I need him now.'

And I need the name. Too late for Katerina. But the lives of other women depend upon it. 'You're a coward,' I tell him. 'Like every KGB *boxer* I ever met. You preferred to hit a man with an iron bar when he was strapped to the wall . . .'

His eyes seem to sink in pain.

'The man who betrayed you . . .' I urge him, unable to cross the painted line to get at him. 'Give me his name, fuck your mother!'

His voice is thin and reedy. 'Who are you?' he says. 'You're not from my uncle . . .'

'It doesn't matter who I'm from. I want that name. There's no doctor for you until I get that name.'

'I don't know it anyway, he changed names. The FBI helped him.'

The words stop me dead. *The FBI helped him? How?*

'The FBI helped him to change names?' I ask him.

'He was a defector, fuck your mother. He came to New York in Soviet times. Sometime in the Eighties. Afraid someday his victims' families would turn on him. So he traded Soviet secrets. Here, the FBI looked after him. CIA perhaps. Gave him protection, papers, a false name. That's the way it was in Cold War days. If you knew how to play the game . . .'

He stops. I watch another phase of pain come back. His face stills. His lips draw back from his old teeth. 'Now please . . . I'm begging you. All right. I'm begging. A doctor . . . For God's sake.'

I lean over the bell for assistance. I allow my forefinger

to linger. The blue eyes look bizarre, young and healthy in the white sweating face. Young and healthy but pleading too. His arms are wrapped round his chest. He is no longer able to speak. He is not going to give me the name. I know the pain is excruciating. He croaks something. I am the *boxer*, the torturer. But I lack the skill he once had.

I hold it, three, four, five seconds . . .

Finally, as I see him slipping, I push the bell.

Hanratty is on his feet. 'What the fuck's happening?' he says. There are blue lights flashing across faces, walls, windows. 'Has there been an escape?'

'Volodya's having a heart attack.'

Hanratty looks at me, genuine concern on his face. 'You dumb fuck – you didn't try to beat the name out of him?'

'I didn't get a name.'

'Right.'

'But I got something almost as good. The middleman operated for years out of New York.'

'Didn't we know that?'

'We guessed it. But we didn't know why. In the early days he operated out of New York because Moscow was banned to him. The vek was an old-time Soviet defector to the West.'

'A defector.' Hanratty hikes his shoulders and eyebrows in one movement. 'Hell,' he says, 'it's something. Could help.'

But I am excited. I am also trying to justify the pain I have just inflicted. 'Don't you see, Hanratty? Volodya's narrowed the choice for us to a few dozen at the most.'

I can hear the echoing yell of *Cardiac arrest!* at the end of one of the glass corridors. In the bright lights a group in green coveralls appears, moving at speed towards us. Within seconds, the gurney is run past us by four medics. Two, three other khaki-uniformed men follow.

I have a chance to glance down at the white face

of Volodya. 'I think he was dead before I rang the alarm.'

Hanratty is following the gurney with a movement of his head. 'Is that so?' he says conversationally. He grins. 'Hey, let's go find ourselves a couple of drinks. Somewhere to drown our tears.'

32

I met DeLane at the state police barracks, a two-storey cement building opposite McLeavy Hall in Bridgeport. He was even less impressed by the information I had forced from Volodya than Hanratty. He stayed just long enough to let me know I'd brought him back a severe headache from my trip to the federal penitentiary. Did I have any idea of the number of defectors from the Soviet Union there had been in the years we were dealing with, say from 1978 to 1990?

I told him no and he told me hundreds. As a Russian, of course, I really didn't know. DeLane almost discovered good humour as he explained it wasn't only the United States which had received defectors. Large numbers of Soviet citizens had defected to the United Kingdom. There were also well over a hundred who had defected to West Germany, France or Italy, Switzerland, Canada or Australia. My parting with DeLane was without warmth. His manner reproached me for letting Volodya die before he could give us at least one more detail to use as a cross-check.

I left the barracks with State Police Lieutenant Miriam Cohen walking me to the big parking lot. Some warmth had returned to the air. But with October under way I could feel that coolness as the sun lost height, a coolness I knew well. Except, of course, in Murmansk the same coolness appeared well before the end of August.

'When do you plan to go back?' Miriam Cohen asked me, setting her big hip against the side of Stack's Passat.

'As soon as you release Katerina's body for burial,' I said.

'OK. I'm informing the family that I estimate the body will be released for burial in two days' time.'

'And Luke Bassenger?'

'I'm releasing *his* body to Carole tomorrow morning. I don't think he had any idea what he was involved in. The way Luke saw it, he was probably being paid twice for the same service. Once by Katerina – and once by her killer who gave Luke the job of getting her to the brewery yard. And keeping her there.'

'There's no doubt that's where Katerina was hanged?'

'All the forensic evidence points to it.'

'Why wasn't he hanged too? When the guy finally got him.'

She shivered. 'I think we have enough to know our killer's only interested in hanging females.'

'Women or dogs.'

She nodded. 'Here on the ground, we're talking about a murderous lunatic. I only use official terminology when I have to. It gives them status they don't deserve. To me the guy's a madman, intelligent enough to do the job he gets paid for, but crazy enough to enjoy hanging women. So, he doesn't even bother to hang Luke Bassenger. Not enough kick in that. He doesn't do this entirely for the pay-check. One way or another, that's going to be his downfall.'

We shook hands.

'It's been good knowing you,' she said.

'You too.'

'See you at Hanratty's retirement party. We're giving him a send-off at the Broken Bottle on Saturday night. Like me, he's pretty new to Greenwich but he's made his mark with the other guys. Even the captain's agreed to come along.'

'Hanratty asked me,' I said. 'I'd like to get there. But something tells me I'll be on my way back to Moscow this weekend.'

*   *   *

At Observatory Point I was called to the library as soon as I got back. The lawyers had been and left. Alex and Rushton were sitting alone together on the leather sofa between the two long windows. There was a sense of something about them, a formality that had not existed the few times I had seen them together before the night we found the recording Katerina had made.

Coloured folders were piled on the low table in front of them. Rushton, I guessed, had been reading documents to Alex. But it was Alex, perhaps because she was a lawyer by profession, not Rushton, who took charge. 'We've seen Katerina's lawyers,' she said. 'We know the outline of Katerina's will and the US financial arrangements. But apparently we'll have to deal with her notaries in Moscow for her instructions on the funeral. The two lawyers here today suggested that those instructions are likely to be unusual.'

'There was also a pretty broad hint that the instructions might not be that easy to carry out,' Rushton added. 'We've had a document drawn up giving you a limited power of attorney to receive details of Katerina's wishes. If the Russian notaries accept the document you can go ahead making the preliminary arrangements for the funeral.'

'Will you do that, Constantin?' Alex asked.

I nodded. 'Of course,' I said.

'I would like to ask you to take Katerina's body back with you,' she said, her face turned towards me.

I nodded, wondered if she could detect the movement, and said I would.

'There's an early United flight from JFK. You'd be going alone. Stack and Olga will bring me a few days later.'

I hesitated. 'Do you still intend to go ahead with the operation?'

'I'm going ahead,' she said briskly.

She was, I thought not for the first time, a strong-willed girl. A critical and immensely risky eye operation and her mother's funeral in the same week were some undertaking. I wanted to step forward and put my arm round her. Tell her I knew what she was taking on, but with Rushton there it didn't seem the thing for an employee to do at just this moment. 'I'll do what I can to help,' was all I said.

After Alex left I stayed on with Ben Rushton. We had to face the fact, he said, that his presence in Moscow just weeks before the election would cause an explosion of press interest. Nobody on his political team had any experience of dealing with the Russian press and they would be hiring people in Moscow, as well as an outfit in Washington to escort American journalists.

The real area of ignorance was how to handle the Moscow militia. Personal feelings apart, it would be politically disastrous if any mafia-inspired demonstrations against his Russian policies were mishandled. Did I know anyone in the Moscow militia who could help?

Yes. I knew Ilya Dronsky.

Neither Alex nor Rushton had mentioned Yado or Sarah being present at the funeral and I assumed they would be left in charge of the team running the election back here in the US. There'd be no bitter tears coursing down my cheeks if I missed saying my goodbyes to Yado – but Sarah was different. I felt we had unfinished business. But first I had to contact her.

Polly's office seemed to be the best chance.

'Sarah,' Polly said, 'will be back from Washington this evening. Ben's called a team meeting here to assess the impact of Katerina's death – and settle our approach on the funeral.' She looked up at me from the long planking desk she had had herself built. 'I know it sounds callous,' she said. 'But we all agree on this, don't we? Whatever's happened we mustn't let Ben's candidacy slip.'

'Is that what's happening?'

'It's a completely unknown situation, Costya. The American public have had presidents and candidates who've broken into offices, screwed showgirls and stolen party funds. Lefrank even got away with a homosexual relationship that was, I quote, "non-sexual". But what do we all think about a candidate whose wife has just been horribly murdered? A candidate who, the most vicious scuttlebutt says, might have had something to do with organising it himself. The polls are all over the place. The *LA Times* polled the same areas three times over five days. On the first day – the day Katerina's death was announced – they got an estimated twenty per cent sympathy vote for Ben, taking him clear into the lead over the other candidates. On day three the sympathy had vanished as the net took up the rumour-mongering. Then on day five a backlash for Ben recovered eleven per cent of his sympathy vote to take him just back in the lead over Colson – and a good eight points above Henry Bass.' She threw her pencil down on her desk. 'Make what you can of that.'

I waggled my head from side to side. 'In the end – is he going to win?'

What were they, tears, making her eyes gleam? 'You betcha,' she said.

She came round her desk. 'You look after that man in Moscow,' she said.

'What man? You mean Ben?'

'I mean Ben. He's smart. But he's not street-smart. Damn man never has been.'

I hung about in my room waiting for the big meeting to finish downstairs. Or rather waiting for Sarah to pay me a visit afterwards.

Dusk arrived already, it seemed to me, earlier than when I first came to Observatory Point. I stood at the window, a long thumb of vodka in my hand, looking out over the Sound. Coloured navigation lights pricked the gloom in ten or twenty different places out at sea as boats from Oyster Bay and Cold Spring Harbour, and Greenwich and Bridgeport on the Connecticut side of the Sound, made their way back to their moorings. As I stood there staring out I again experienced that closeness to Jay Gatsby, a fictional figure, almost a hundred years ago now, but still powerfully present for me. Like him I was an outsider here. Like him I had spent half a lifetime chasing a dream of America that only half-existed.

Gatsby had succumbed. His sweetheart Daisy had led him to create a false world around himself, one bound to collapse under its own contradictions. Was that what was happening to me? Was the girl downstairs, who I hoped would be joining me tonight, drawing me into another unreal dream of America? Urging me to stay, to put down new roots here. I had days left to decide whether I was playing with a dream. Whether there was any more substance in my dream than there had been in Jay Gatsby's.

My cellphone rang. Sarah's voice was warm. 'We're about through down here,' she said.

From my tower window I could see down into a good part of the library. I saw her in a corner of the room, the others talking on, polls, policies, politics . . . And Sarah, her cellphone held in the crook of her neck, her red hair spilling across it.

'Then what's keeping you?' I said.

33

She was wearing a black tailored skirt, a fine-woven dark green cashmere sweater. She carried her jacket over one shoulder and a briefcase in her free hand. The red hair was loosely ponytailed. She looked, I thought, very, very good.

I pulled wider the door and reached down to take her briefcase but she dipped her head and intercepted my mouth with hers. It was a nice easy movement, bringing our heads up until we stood tight together just inside the doorway. I removed one hand from under her sweater and pushed the door closed.

I felt the briefcase drop, the jacket slide from her shoulder. Our mouths moved apart as I brought the cashmere sweater over her head. Then reconnected as she did that thing that women do to unhook her bra and slide it off her shoulders.

There are no such similar erotic movements for a man. I pulled off my shirt and got out of my jeans. By the time she reached one side of the bed, naked, tanned, very rounded at the hips and shoulders, breasts bouncing as she dragged back the duvet, I was already kneeling across towards her. This time there was to be no coy male hesitation.

For five minutes, maybe more, we kissed. No talking, no long eye contact, just a satisfying of that spontaneous hunger for each other that two people can generate.

In the first moment in which neither was engaged frenziedly osculating parts of each other's body, Sarah lay half across my chest and smiled down at me. 'Just so that I know this is going to be more than a one-shot stand,' she said, 'I need to ask.'

'Go ahead.'

'You *will* be coming back to the US after Katerina's funeral?'

In bed, you should never talk about anything else but the glorious proportions of the beloved. The wise lover sticks to the rises and dips, the hills and dales, the promontories or crevices of the warm companionate body. Any other talk, I've found, can lead in dangerously detumescent directions.

'It's a big question,' I said. Then felt the need to expand my answer. 'Very big.'

Was she already sliding off me? 'No compelling reason to stay?'

'One at least,' I said.

Her eyebrows rose expectantly. If rule one is stick to talk of sex, rule two is never, never banter. 'And that is?'

'In America, I drink a lot less.'

She had pulled back to put perhaps a foot between us. Certainly no parts were touching. 'Have you ever been to bed with an American woman before?' she said.

'To bed? Just once.'

'Was she passionate?'

'I never really decided. I think she killed in cold blood.'

She raised her eyes to the ceiling and sat up, not bothering to pull the duvet up with her. 'How about you pour me a stiff vodka?'

'What about . . . ?' I made an all-encompassing gesture.

'That's going to have to wait until afterwards.'

'After what?' I got up and went, self-consciously naked, to the drinks table. 'I can offer you Uzbek honey vodka,' I said. 'On the whole women like it.'

She was still sitting up. Her face was more pink now than tan and her red hair was spread against the piled pale green lawn cotton pillows. 'I can't really make up my mind about you, Costya,' she said. 'Maybe it makes most sense if I just think about you as a not entirely competent adventurer.'

'With a soul,' I added.

She sighed exasperation. 'Let me have the Uzbek special,' she said. 'Do you have a robe?'

I handed her a yellow bathrobe which Stack had provided. She put it on, rolled up the sleeves and took the honey vodka from me. 'You better put something on,' she said. 'Like that you disturb me, and I have things to say.'

I pulled on a pair of jeans.

'We have to talk,' she said. The yellow robe, short on me, trailed the carpet quite becomingly as she paced the room. 'Yado's asked me to marry him,' she said.

'To marry you,' I gurgled vacuously. 'Yado? You despise Yado.'

'As a matter of fact, I admire Yado. I just don't happen to like him.' The tie of her robe had slipped. She glanced down, then looked at me in a not entirely friendly way. 'I'd hoped to say all this after we'd consummated our friendship,' she said.

I tapped my lips. 'My fault. Big mouth. I should stick to essentials.' I poured myself some vodka. 'Listen, I can't keep up with you, Sarah. Have you agreed to marry *Yado*?'

'Yes,' she said slowly. 'I've agreed.'

'And yet . . . you're here.'

She grimaced.

'OK. Tell me why.'

She tipped back her vodka and handed me the glass. 'I sometimes think,' she said, 'that you've no idea of the stakes we're all playing for.'

'Maybe not.'

'Right. There are a lot of ways of seeing this. Let's take them slowly, one at a time. Scenario one. The big one. The one we're all praying for. Ben wins the election. Now no criticism of my uncle, but we all know – he'd tell you himself – he'll be a one-track president. He's completely absorbed in the Russian problem. He regards its solution as the United States' number one priority. Essentially his first term – up until the point he has to throw himself into the next election – will be taken up by Russia. So someone's going to have to look after the shop.'

I began to nod some understanding of where she was going.

Her chin came up. 'This situation offers Yado the chance to be the most powerful vice-president the US has ever had.'

'So *you* think the time has come to tie up with Yado? And you can't tie up closer than marriage.'

'Right.'

'One thing I don't understand. In a couple of months, if things go right, Yado can have his choice of any Monica in the White House. So why should he tie up with you?'

'You put your point very directly.'

'So?'

'In a Rushton White House I can have everything I want, darling. I'll have *power*. But I need Jack to front for me. As VP he's the perfect front.'

'Am I beginning to understand this? It's not so much Jack Yado will be the most powerful vice-president in history. More that Sarah Yado will be the most powerful woman in the White House since Hillary Clinton.'

'Listen, Costya,' she said. 'As I told you once before. This is politics. I don't give a fuck for your disapproval. I want you on my side, so I'll keep talking. There's a great deal here for all of us. You listening?'

'I'm listening. What do you and Jack have in mind for me?'

'This part's my plan. Not Jack's. Nothing to do with Yado.' She smiled, gave me her glass again and I filled it. And filled one for myself.

'Marrying into the Rushton clan works for Yado. It seals the Rushton alliance. Yado has agreed that you and I will be free to seal our own alliance whenever and wherever and as often as we choose. As long as we do it in absolute secrecy. You're getting the shape of things?'

'I think I am.'

'I couldn't touch the man, Costya. I couldn't have him touch me. This political life is tough. First it requires that holders of high office have consorts. Then it doesn't allow for getting found out tomcatting around, or the female equivalent. If I make the deal with Yado without you around, it's four years' celibacy. The devoted wife.'

'And that's where I come in? Enter the Russian paramour?'

'This is serious, Costya,' she said, leaning forward. 'You and I get along. I've felt that over and over again since we met. Like most couples we still have a few personality rough edges to smooth out maybe. That's what makes for something like this fiasco a few minutes ago. But we're cast from similar moulds, Costya. We're adventurers. Think about it. You get a smooth political post. An office and mini-staff in the White House. Advising Yado on something. Anything Russian'll work fine. For this you get a big, big pay-check. And you get me.'

'It's got a nice romantic ring, I must admit.'

She threw herself petulantly back on the bed. 'Romance is fine. It can even last a few months if you're lucky.'

'But you're a realist.'

'I really like you, Costya, but I'm not in this for romance.'

'You've made that clear. You're in it for a Friday-night fuck.'

'And you find that such an intolerable idea?'

I crossed the room, picking up her clothes. 'No. What I find intolerable is the idea that I'm being bought.' I had a skirt and briefs in one hand, a bra in the other, when, without a warning knock, the door opened behind me and a Russian greeting announced Olga. I whirled round. She stood in the doorway looking shocked at Sarah whose open robe, loose hair and vodka glass in hand added up to a classic post-coital pose.

'Oh my God,' she said in English. The door slammed behind me. I heard Olga's heavy step go fast down the corridor. I must have looked stricken.

Sarah was laughing. 'Forget it,' she said. 'Just make sure she doesn't start talking about this.'

I dropped her clothes on the bed. 'Best get dressed,' I said.

She held me in a bright-eyed, emerald stare, suddenly aware. 'Does this mean what I think it means?' she asked slowly.

'I'm sorry, Sarah. Yes it means what you think it means.'

Her lips tightened. Contempt that anybody in my lowly Russian émigré position could turn down her offer. 'Turn your back,' she said.

I faced away from her.

'Make damn sure that sister of yours doesn't start talking,' she repeated as she got dressed.

'Talking? Who to?'

'Hasn't it occurred to you the press are running laps round Observatory Point trying to talk to *anybody* from this house?'

But Olga talking to the press wasn't what was worrying me at the moment. Strangely, Olga talking to Alex was something that had much more effect on my churning stomach.

34

I took the almost full bottle of Uzbek honey vodka and went down to Polly's office. In the last day or so I had stopped by now and again, and we managed an easy, companionable air while I drank a few thumbs and she smoked her weed. Not for the first time in my life, brothers, I was a seriously confused man. Underlying everything, I couldn't understand the ill-at-ease feeling I had about Olga telling Alex that she had seen Sarah and me frolicking in my room. Perhaps, I thought, Polly's common sense would help sort things out.

But there were no lights on in her office when I got downstairs. I pushed the half-open door and went in. Light shafted from the security lamps in the garden outside, making the room deep-shadowed, a comfortable place to drink alone, the piles of documents, reports and poll printouts merging with the dark shapes of desks and chairs. I sat down in the one comfortable seat behind her desk, put up my feet and necked the bottle of Uzbek.

Turning down Sarah's offer had been no problem at all. Turning down Sarah hardly less. But the whole proposition had brought to the surface another question altogether. I would be back in Moscow in a couple of days. I would then have a choice to make. Would I return to the US after Katerina's funeral? Would I try to carve myself out a new life here, perhaps even on the periphery of a Rushton White House? Or should I stay in Russia, seek out another career in Moscow or Petersburg perhaps, but above all remain Russian? Did I owe that much to Russia? Did I owe *anything* to Russia?

Somewhere in the dark passage outside a couple of

murmuring youngsters had found themselves a private nook, an alcove, all that was available to them as a place to be together in this house of non-stop activity. I listened for a moment to the snuffle of the girl and the muted huffing of the man – and felt envious.

For ten or fifteen minutes I sat there, getting drunker, and trying to unravel the problem.

The remains of the Uzbek honey was sloshing round in a rapidly emptying bottle. From the time I was a teenager, I had been caught between the pull of two cultures. One, though I had only known it through books and films, nevertheless exerted a powerful draw. But so too did the messy, undisciplined, Russian world, a looser, more dangerous, but oddly, a sometimes even freer society in which to live. A place where there were few pretences to be kept up. Where consistency wasn't demanded of you, a place of passion, of danger and love/hate.

Nostalgia and the clear bottle took me back to the bitter cold of my northern Russian home town. By now the Arctic night has fallen on Murmansk; ice and a thin layer of wind-borne snow coat the low hills. The slightly warmer water from the northern ocean steams mist along the fish quays while, inland, the freshwater lakes freeze solid. Any day now, Roy Rolkin, as governor of Kola Province, will be opening the ice fair on Lake Poltava. But no ordinary ice fair. The Poltava Fair is not known as Sin City for nothing.

Each year, as the ice thickens on the lake, two kilometres long and half as much wide, an army of gypsies and travellers arrives to build a vast jumble of garish wooden structures. Within a week or two, a main ice-road traverses the lake, electric cables are strung, lights blaze and beckon over timber casinos and whorehouses in the shape of rickety onion-domed churches or miniature Kremlins. There are fortune-telling booths, vodka stalls and restaurants billowing the smells of sizzling reindeer sausages from their great open grills. The permanent militia unit, of which I was once an officer, struggles to suppress the more open violence, gang fights, assaults and muggings. Pickpockets are mostly tolerated.

For the moment, America drifted away. I envied Roy Rolkin for just being there. I had picked up one of Polly's phones and was holding it in a shaft of borrowed light from the garden to call Roy's number to make my peace with him, when I heard again the movements of the young couple outside. I listened.

'See you tomorrow,' the girl said. Girl? Woman rather. A voice too raspy for a twenty-year-old girl.

There was a muffled male reply. I could hear the shuffle and movement of what seemed like bodies being pressed together. Then I registered. Jesus, it was Polly's voice. Guiltily I put down the phone and pulled my feet off her desk.

Outside there was silence.

'Get some sleep,' she said.

'You too, Pol,' Ben Rushton's voice whispered. ''Night.'

I wanted to duck under the desk. She stood in the open doorway, her hand on the light switch, as his footsteps faded down the corridor. She turned. I was silhouetted against the light in the garden. 'Who the hell . . . ?' she said. Turned on the light. And stood staring at me.

'Polly,' I half-rose and sat back. 'I'm sorry. Came down for a drink and a chat . . .'

She walked slowly into the room, pulling down her tee shirt.

I handed her the bottle. 'Uzbek honey vodka,' I said. 'Highly prized.'

'By Uzbeks?' She took the bottle and necked the remaining half-inch. She sat down in the director's chair in front of the desk, her eyes on me. 'I don't owe you an explanation,' she said.

'The reverse.'

'But I think I'd like to take the chance to tell a friend.'

'A drunk friend. Why not stay quiet and hope I've

forgotten everything by tomorrow. I promise you I will have.'

She smiled.

'Play it as you feel,' I said.

'It wasn't me.'

'In bed with Ben when Katerina called?'

'No.' She shifted a hip to one side in the chair to take from her jeans pocket tobacco and papers. 'I'm not denying I'd have liked it to have been.'

'But you know about the phone call. He told you about Katerina's recording, all the same.'

'He has to have a few friends he can trust.'

'Everybody does.'

'Ben knows I've been in love with him since he taught me at Yale. But that's as far as it went. As far as it goes.'

'OK, Polly . . .'

'If you're really asking who was it in bed with Ben . . .'

'I'm not.'

'Good, because I'm not about to tell you.'

I stumbled to my feet and she helped me to the door. 'As somebody told me tonight, American politics is a tough business.'

'Stay with it,' she said. 'Greatest show on earth.'

I thought of Sin City as I blew her a kiss goodnight. 'I'm trying to decide whether I believe it.'

I walked back to my room. From the downstairs corridor I could see across the courtyard to the apartment occupied by Alex and Olga. Olga's sitting room was curtained, dark. Alex's sitting room was brightly lit. She was standing in the middle of it listening perhaps to music I couldn't hear. Her body was swaying slightly, rhythmically.

At this distance of perhaps fifty feet, the detail of her rather old-fashioned dress was lost. Her blonde hair hung down her back. I watched her raise her arms and begin to circle the centre space of the room. She was dancing the *gopak*, the village dance of Ukraine and Russia. I could have stayed watching but voices were approaching from further down the corridor.

I stood for a last second looking across the courtyard at her. Ben Rushton had lied to her. Katerina had been right. There was another woman. OK, that didn't make him the man who had hired a contract killer. But the lie was the first serious crack in Rushton's façade. Would there be others? I looked across at Alex in her window and decided there was no point in telling her.

35

Word of the disturbances in Manhattan reached Observatory Point while I was still sleeping.

Vodka usually provides me with a seamless oblivion but perhaps there's something about Uzbek that I don't quite get along with. I slept heavily but fitfully. At one time I awoke thinking of Katerina's murder . . . spent ten minutes hopelessly worrying at the detail, wondering how far DeLane had got in tracing Mr Wonderful . . . and fell back to sleep again. The eerie blue glow of my bedside clock showed another hour's sleep had intervened before I woke again. This time I was thinking, or perhaps still half-dreaming, of Alex. She was moving round me in a slow dance movement, arms held high, smiling . . . Had Olga said anything yet about Sarah?

The phone was ringing when I woke next. It was three a.m. The hour of the wolf we call it in our wolf-infested corner of Russia. Stack's voice grated down the line. 'Get yourself dressed in something warm, Vadim. There's been some trouble in the city. Mr Rushton wants you to go in with him.'

'What sort of trouble?'

'Just meet him down in the main hall in five minutes. He'll brief you then.'

I pulled on jeans, a sweater and a leather jacket. A pair of rubber-soled work boots seemed appropriate footwear.

In the hall there were two or three groups of people. Ben Rushton had not yet arrived. I heard someone say Sarah had gone back to her apartment in the city. Stack was standing with a group of security men. He detached himself quickly and came across to meet me.

'The Secret Service don't want the boss to go,' he said. 'They're dead against it.'

'Hold on. Go where?'

'There's rioting in Manhattan.'

'The Hitler's Name crazies,' Ben Rushton's voice said. He was crossing towards us in a dark green trenchcoat over a dark open-neck shirt. 'Do you know what Crystal Night was, Vadim?'

'The pogrom in Berlin after Hitler came to power?'

'That's it. Murderous anti-Jewish riots. Small businesses attacked and their shop windows spread across the sidewalk.'

'Thus Crystal Night,' I said. 'Is that what the Hitler's Name people are doing in Manhattan?'

'This is probably just a practice run, the opening of their Reclaim New York programme. Police reports say they're staging up to a dozen torchlight rallies against Russian immigrants – St Nicholas cathedral, Columbus Circle, Times Square, down on Brighton Beach and others. In several places they've attacked and beaten Russians. An attempt to burn down the Orthodox cathedral at about two o'clock failed but they've firebombed half a dozen small hotels off Broadway that take in Russians.'

The broken glass was all over the street when we got there, glittering red, white and blue from stutter lights. Police cars, ambulances, fire tenders and TV vans lined the sidewalks. A bitter odour of smoke caught my nostrils as our convoy pulled up somewhere off Broadway. From a small hotel twenty yards down, steam or dying smoke rose around thick black smudge marks above its shattered windows. A shallow stream of black water poured through its front doors and down the steps. I could see flashlights moving about inside and the hulking shapes of firefighters in their slickers and huge helmets.

People were gathered in groups staring at the hotel, or over the rooftops to where flames and sparks kept shooting up as the firefighters tried to douse an established fire. I heard a small grizzled man in a parka say, 'I don't much go for Russians. But, as a Jew, I don't care for this stuff, either.'

About twenty people on the sidewalk stood in topcoats over pyjamas. Some of them had hastily packed bags beside them. You could see items of clothing peeking out. I could hear Russian spoken.

'Over here,' Rushton said.

His Russian was simple but OK. Occasionally he called on me for a word or phrase. With some of the stronger accents he was lost, but his manner was friendly and his condemnation of the people who had thrown the Molotov cocktails into the hotel hallway left no doubt about how strongly he felt. Did it matter that he had lied to Alex about another woman – especially if it was a casual one-night stand? Or even, come to that, if it was a more serious affair with someone like Alison Bryson? With the smoke and shouts and sobbing of children and older women around us, what Ben Rushton chose to do while his wife was running wild seemed barely relevant to the real world.

While the police guided the Russians into vans Rushton made a statement to several of the TV journalists jostling around him. I dropped back and Stack came up beside me. 'The cops have arrested fifty or sixty marchers apparently. But proving they actually torched these hotels is going to be a whole lot more difficult.'

'How many hotels were attacked?'

'The TV people say there were three down here. Nearly two dozen altogether. Mostly north of 150th Street.'

In all the noise and confusion, the first sniper fire went barely noticed except by the Secret Service men around Rushton. Then as a burst crackled down the street and police shouted through loudhailers, people scrambled for cover. I crouched with Rushton and the Agents and five or six others, mostly camera crew, in a deep doorway. I could see the rounds kicking up the tarmac.

People raced across the street – to left or right depending on where they thought the firing was coming from.

Then suddenly the noise, the movement, died away. There's a passage where Henry Miller imagines a moment in New York when everything stops, cars, pedestrians . . . it was a bit like that. But the pedestrians were pressed into doorways, white-faced, anxious-eyed.

I was scanning the face of the brick warehouse building opposite, Victorian Gothic windows painted with an old obscure advertisement, when the next burst of shots came. Four or five sparks from a broken window. A SWAT team must have been already in position in a doorway a few yards from the warehouse. I saw men hurling themselves into the darkness of the entrance, heard the thunderous detonation of acoustic grenades. The Secret Service men were helping Rushton to his feet.

'Constantin Vadim.' I heard a voice in the doorway behind me. I turned and saw, kneeling a yard or two back, a slender figure in a huge black motorcyclist's helmet. She was carrying a baseball bat.

'It's Rosalie,' she said. 'From Ellis Island. Remember me?' She scrambled forward.

'Rosalie,' I said. 'What are you doing here? What are you doing . . .' I pointed to the baseball bat.

'I'm part of a Local Protection Squad.' She pointed to a yellow and black LPS armlet on her right arm. 'We patrol vulnerable districts at night,' she said proudly. 'We were the first to warn the police that a firebomb unit of the Hitler Boys was heading this way.'

Hitler Boys, Stalin Boys. I hated them all. I even, I admit, didn't entirely trust what Rosalie's Local Protection Squads would turn into in a few months.

Across the road the SWAT squad were bringing out a man with his hands cuffed behind him. He was in his early twenties, wearing camouflage, blood running freely from his nose. Some people cheered. A hero.

'Will you introduce me?' Rosalie said, her helmet lifted off now.

Rushton was gracious and flattering to Rosalie about what the LPS had done tonight. 'But make sure you always remember which side of the line you're on,' he added meaningfully.

Dawn was edging cautiously through the smoking streets. As everyone began to move out of the doorway my phone rang. It was Sarah.

'Listen,' she said. 'I hear there's trouble.'

'For some.' I told her briefly what was happening here. She grunted her understanding. The TV was on in the background and I could hear excited commentary, presumably from one of the news teams around me.

'Look,' Sarah said. 'You're leaving for Moscow soon, uh?'

'If today's started – which I guess it has – tomorrow morning,' I said. 'And if Katerina's body is released by Lieutenant Cohen by then.'

'Yuh . . .' She sounded thoughtful. 'I'm in Chicago tonight. Ben's speaking there to business leaders. Organised and paid for by the Lake Michigan Insurance Group. I wondered if you felt like dropping in here on the way back. Sort of kiss and make up.'

'Sarah,' I began.

'Listen,' she said. 'We're not talking politics, long term or anything else. It's too long since I've had a man – and my guess is for you it's too long since you had a woman. I'm talking about something real. The sort of thing we have going for us.'

'As soon as I can get away,' I said, 'I'll come round for a drink.'

'Whatever you choose to call it. Let's just get together, for an hour. For God's sake.'

*   *   *

Ben Rushton stayed until it got light. It was great publicity but I swear he wasn't there for publicity alone. He sat on the curb and talked to people awaiting ambulances, he walked uninjured but badly shocked people away from the hissing smoke. When he left at dawn he slipped away without a final word to the camera.

I saw him into the back of his car. With his thumb and forefinger he was rubbing his eyes. 'When I was a young man,' he said, 'I was in Germany when a neo-Nazi mob burnt down a Turkish guest-workers' hostel. Year or so later, I watched a French *Front National* mob in Marseilles attacking Arab cafés.' He pushed his head back but kept his eyes closed. 'I never expected to see this sort of thing in Manhattan. It's made me think more about what we're planning to do with aid to Russia. I'm more and more convinced we're taking the right road, Vadim. Tonight could be just the beginning . . .'

He sat staring out at the early morning streets around him. Had I really ever entertained the idea this man had commissioned the brutal murder of his wife?

And of course, I had. Maybe not as strongly as Alex, but it'd certainly been more than a thought, fleetingly considered.

'I've a duty to win this election, Vadim. I've a duty to pass a Russian Health Aid measure through Congress. Russia's too big, too dangerous to fool around with. We've got to wrench your country onto the straight and narrow,' he said. 'Whoever and however much it hurts.'

36

I took a cab to Sarah's building on the Upper West Side. I sat in the back and listened to the news. The driver wasn't talkative. At somewhere past 86th Street I was aware of him leaning forward, peering ahead.

'We got trouble there,' he said and began to brake.

For a second I thought we'd run into another demonstration, although only rich Russians lived in this neighbourhood. Then I saw police cars, stutter lights and, as we got closer, a small crowd of men and women, mostly uniformed, clustered round an ambulance.

I stopped the cab and paid off the driver. The address I'd given him, he told me, was about where the police black and whites had gathered. I walked forward, apprehensively. My last few days had been tinged with murder in a way I hadn't realised.

In that New York street, as I walked towards the little cluster of cars and uniformed people, the word *murder* passed through my mind a dozen times. I could see the entrance of the apartment block now and I knew by the number on the striped awning that it was Sarah's.

When a voice yelled 'Vadim', I nearly jumped a foot in the air. Clint Maddox was running across the road towards me. He clasped my arm. *Murder* the voice in my head said. Murder. Murder. Murder . . .

I forced myself to listen to Maddox. 'They got the number of my mobile from her apartment,' he said. 'They rang me five minutes ago.' Murder, that voice said.

'What happened? What happened to Sarah?'

'It's as horrible as it gets,' he said. 'She has the old turn-of-the-century loft up there. Superb apartment. They

317

found her in the middle of the carpet. Neck broken. All sorts of terrible things done to her. But even the uniformed officers who broke in could see she'd been hanged. From the old wooden beam that she'd left exposed, right across the living area.'

The FBI were firmly in charge. Somebody from Washington had stepped in and negotiated the use of the club room in a local golf club just across the New York state line from Westchester County Airport and the VICAP liaison team from Quantico were able to fly in with no more than a couple of miles drive to the meeting.

I have to admit I am not accustomed to having access to human resources on this scale. There were probably close to thirty men and women in the room. Many of course were Connecticut State police and some were no doubt NYPD Homicide detectives since Sarah had been murdered on their patch. But the FBI was making the agenda. Special Agent in Charge Randall took his seat at the head of the long table. A woman in an FBI suit was assigning places. DeLane, who was responsible for me being here at all, pointed to a chair next to him and I took it. I was clearly in the Bureau section of the table. Hanratty, ambling past to his seat near the door, bent towards me and nodded to the FBI presence. 'So they signed you up, uh.' He lifted his eyebrows and moved on.

The meeting began at midday with résumés of witness statements on the circumstances surrounding the finding of Sarah's body, my statement included. Clint Maddox's statement was incoherent, even in résumé. He seemed to be worried that the police might think he was having an affair with Sarah because he had called her at six o'clock that morning. Fighting elections, he had pointed out earnestly, was a twenty-four-hour business. Sarah had to be on a plane to Chicago later that morning. And since he was only a block or two away . . .

After witness statements came preliminary medical reports. A young woman who identified herself as an assistant medical examiner read a clear account of what had been established so far. Death by hanging, with red wax sealing the eyes. Signs of violence to the victim *before* she died – and signs of considerable sexual interference. Further medical examination would be needed to confirm rape. But it would in any case be, as many rapes now were, rape with a condom.

Forensic evidence was thin. But the laboratory at Quantico was working on a number of foreign hairs and fibres (foreign, I gathered, meaning not originating in the apartment) on Sarah's body. Hemp fibres had already been identified on the crossbeam from which she was hanged.

'OK, so far so good,' Randall said. 'What I want to add, before I call on the VICAP liaison team, is that the dominant factor in our thinking so far is that we have absolutely no motive that goes beyond a sexual assault on a woman. We are all aware that political motives might well have been involved in Katerina Rushton's death. Indeed we have decided to put full weight behind that approach. But that does not go for Sarah Rushton. So far . . .' he checked his watch . . . 'some four to five hours after her death, nobody has produced other than a sexual motive.'

Hanratty pulled a grotesquely disbelieving face.

Randall had paused, head down, then lifted his eyes to a middle-aged woman with short greying hair. 'OK, Jane.'

Assessments from the VICAP computer formed the core of the meeting. VICAP, standing for Violent Criminal Apprehension Programme, had helped to analyse violent crimes for over thirty years. The programme's fame had even spread to Russia. A liaison team special agent, Jane Barlow, outlined the areas of discussion. The VICAP computer had identified a series of hanging murders of successful women in the United States and had linked them with the murder of the British judge and two similar killings in Moscow. Major cross-reference, her position as a presidential candidate's wife and her death by hanging had linked Katerina Rushton to the same series. But in the murder of Sarah Rushton we were reduced to one factor only. The hanging. The fact that Sarah was the niece of Mr Rushton did not make her a figure of importance or eminence as VICAP had previously defined the term. There was also the question of the considerable violence used before hanging and the sexual assault which had not before been an element in the series.

SAC Randall leaned forward. 'So what are you suggesting, Jane? That the murder of Sarah Rushton does not fit our grid?'

'Exactly that.'

'It's a hanging,' someone said. 'A rare murder method anywhere. It also has eyes sealed with wax, a distinguishing factor in the Katerina Rushton murder and some of the others . . .'

'That's true,' Jane Barlow agreed. 'But I don't accept that it clinches the case for adding Sarah Rushton to our list. We'll develop and, I think, explain these similarities in just a moment. But allow for now the assumption that this was a sexually, rather than a politically, motivated murder.'

Randall: 'You mean Sarah Rushton was sexually targeted. By a stalker, for instance.'

'I believe so.' She looked across the table. 'Would you like to take over, Liam.'

A narrow-faced agent opposite Jane Barlow nodded. 'Liam McEvoy,' he introduced himself. 'What we're looking at is that almost certainly the killer knew Sarah's connection with Katerina Rushton. As Media Relations Director of Ben Rushton's campaign his niece has had a lot of recent TV exposure. We're positing a perpetrator who was reacting to the Mrs Rushton murder.'

'Sexually?' Randall said.

'Sexually,' Jane Barlow confirmed. 'Purely sexually.'

'We're saying,' Agent McEvoy said, 'that the TV exposure made Sarah a target. I don't want to get into these things, but most men here would agree she projected sexuality on screen.'

There was a shuffle of guilty agreement from the men round the table.

'So put the two together,' Jane Barlow came back centre stage, 'and you have the pathology. This man was excited by the *method* used to kill Katerina Rushton. He was also sexually *responsive* to Sarah.'

'You're proposing another killer,' Randall said. 'Is that right?'

'We're proposing just that. That the contract series that we developed began with the British judge and ended, so far, with Katerina Rushton. Sarah Rushton was not a contract killing. This was killing for pleasure. We're proposing the concept that these are two separate cases.'

When we left I stood in the parking lot of the golf club with Hanratty while he lit a cigarette. 'Bullshit, uh? The fucking computers have got their own turf war going, Chief. They want to divide up the murders so there's enough to go round. And we have half a hundred FBI agents gathered in a golf club to tell us the story. Hey, I'm not sorry I'm getting out.'

DeLane joined us. 'What do you think?' he said, dark-faced, leaning forward. 'Is Sarah ours, or someone else's?'

'Ours,' I said instinctively.

'What about the sex, the violence against the body?'

'I think our man might not be the cool contractor that he used to be. Maybe she gave him a struggle. Maybe he had to wrestle very close to subdue her. Your Bureau colleague was right. Sarah was a very attractive woman. Sexually very potent. If our vek's going to kill her he's not going to have moral scruples about rape. So have you got onto tracing that defector, DeLane? His name is what we need.'

He frowned. 'It's not easy,' he said. 'We have cross-agency problems with the CIA. I am working on it. I promise.'

I tried to scowl. Hanratty did better.

'So you think the meeting was a waste of time?'

'Yes,' I said. 'But not too serious, unless it diverts us from what Volodya had to tell us about an old defector and a young guy who just loved hanging. Katerina and Sarah were done by the same man.'

DeLane bit his lip.

'Don't let it get to you,' I said. 'Big organisations have to have meetings. Meetings are what make the developed world go round.'

His face darkened further. Agents and cops were climbing into cars all around us. 'You know, Vadim,' he said with a certain fervour, 'I only wish I agreed with you much less often than I do.'

It was delivered with a dark grimace – but with a graciousness all the same.

Hanratty and I walked towards his old Chevrolet. DeLane had moved off towards his car.

'Fall's early this year,' Hanratty said. It was a cold, still day, the thin mist hugging the lower bushes and hanging in tattered shreds among the taller pines. Hanratty drew deep on his cigarette. 'What gets to me is this,' he said. 'End of the day, the VICAP data could be right or wrong. I think it's pointing wrong but I got to admit they have a pretty terrific record there. What troubles me is that two separate theories – contract killer or sociopath – are going to tear this investigation apart. Resources going in two different directions, one team holding back information from the other.' He looked glum. 'Not your problem though, pal. Nor mine, I guess, after next week.'

'I'm staying with it, Hanratty.'

'Once a cop always a cop, uh?' I think his eyes were misting. He sniffed in the cold air.

I was looking across his shoulder as he fumbled for his car keys. The headlights of a long line of vehicles were riding down the gentle slope towards the club. For the moment I thought they were golfers, hell-bent on a round in the mist. But a moment later I spotted the first dish on the roof of the first van. The first van of perhaps thirty or forty bearing down on us, with their escorting helicopter gunships swooping down from above.

They broke on us like a tidal wave, vans and reporters' cars pushing into the club parking lot. In seconds it was a storm of thrust microphones and shouted questions. Why were we here? What were we discussing? Is it true that . . . ? Can you confirm that . . . ?

I saw DeLane struggling with a determined girl in a well-cut parka and incongruous short skirt and heels. I saw Randall fighting off two cameras and a reporter who had him pinned to his car. They rushed Hanratty and me spouting questions, too many to even begin to answer.

'And who are you, sir? Can I have a name,' a reporter was urging Hanratty through the open window of the car.

'A name? Well, it ain't Santa Claus and this ain't Christmas. So fuck off while I'm still in a giving mood,' he said.

'You do realise, sir, that your words are being recorded.'

'For posterity?' Hanratty put one hand on the reporter's chest and pushed him aside. 'Send me a recording.' He winked at me. 'My wife'd love to have it.'

While Hanratty handled, manhandled, reporters on his flank, I took my cue from him and flat-handed three or four newspapermen out of our path until we reached Hanratty's car.

Even so, getting out of the parking lot was not easy. Horns blared, sirens whooped, headlights flashed, police stutter lights winked red, white, blue into the mist. Over-head the three gunships circled . . . filming.

I was packing to leave at the crack of dawn the next day. I felt as if I'd never lose the habit of staying tuned to a news channel whatever I was doing. Masses of comment on Sarah's murder, of course. And already, miraculously or maybe a lot less than miraculously, the commentators had stitched into a disagreement among the investigating officers, State police and FBI, about whether Katerina and Sarah were killed by the same man – or whether Sarah's death was copycat in pathology.

I was coming out of the shower when I heard the knock on the door. My first, water-befuddled thought was that it was Sarah.

I called out for whoever to come in and was really surprised to see Polly. This was the first time she had been up to the room. I put on a robe and offered her a drink.

She shook her head. 'I have to talk to you, Constantin,' she said.

'OK. Why don't you sit down?'

'Sitting in place is not for me,' she said. 'I'm too nervous, het up, Christ knows what.'

'What is it you want to say?'

'I'm looking for advice. I want to ask you whether I should go to the cops. And if I should, who to. Lieutenant Cohen, DeLane . . . Both together.'

'We could talk about that,' I said slowly, 'once you've told me what you think you might need to go to the police about.'

'OK.'

She glanced up at me and ran both hands through her hair, then linking fingers at the back of her head, she stared down at her knees.

'What is it, Polly?' I said. 'Something about Ben?'

She nodded, still looking down.

'Something about you and Ben after all?'

'No, wrong track, Constantin. Ben really wasn't touching me up in the corridor.'

'Just old friends.'

'That's all we've ever been. I'd love to tell you different but . . . that's all we've ever been,' she said again.

'OK, Polly. I don't need convincing.'

'You do. Because it means I *wasn't* the woman in Ben's bed when Katerina recorded the phone call.'

'Maybe there wasn't a woman. Maybe Katerina got it wrong.'

'There was,' Polly said slowly. 'There was a woman with him.'

She was going to tell me who it was. I wasn't going to be able to stop her this time.

'It was Sarah.'

'Oh Christ,' I said. 'Are you sure?'

'It was Sarah,' she said, bitterness for the first time in her expression. 'I worked it out. It wasn't really that difficult. Sarah's hatred for Katerina, her ambition, her opportunity, always on the road with Ben.'

'Alison Bryson had the same opportunity.'

'Alison runs a discreet one-on-one relationship with a woman of her own age and interests in Westport. Alison is definitely not a secretary/mistress.'

'You spoke to Ben?'

'He admitted it. It wasn't an affair. He and Sarah had slept together twice. That was all. That was all it was going to be, according to Ben.'

'Jesus,' I said. 'He must be crazy.'

'That's what I told him. You know what he said. He said she'd made up her mind. She wasn't going to be refused. Goddam men,' she exploded.

For a long time we held each other's stare.

'His niece,' I said. 'Incest? No. Consanguinity at least.'

'Forget consanguinity,' she said. 'As a citizen you may or may not have a right to marry your niece. But as a politician in America today, you sure as hell don't have the right to fuck her.'

I had advised Polly to go straight to DeLane. I think she hoped I'd come up with some compromise. But I don't think there was one.

When she left I walked through the house and into the Japanese garden in a daze. It was cold outside but I didn't really feel it. I was thinking of Sarah, killed by her raging ambition. When Ben Rushton had made it clear there was no place for her in his life, at least in his bed, she had moved on to Yado – with me as back-up. But it was her few nights with Rushton that had killed her.

And if the media ever got the story that Ben Rushton was sleeping with his brother's daughter, that would be as destructive of his chances for the White House as Katerina's wild nights on the town. Maybe even more so.

So the motive for killing Sarah could quite easily be the same as the motive for killing Katerina.

And in both cases the finger could, quite convincingly, point back to Ben Franklin Rushton.

37

A brief call from Polly had told me Rushton wanted to see me. I was to stay where I was and he would come to me. I waited in the Japanese garden as it got darker overhead.

I had been sitting for half an hour with a bottle I'd fetched from the library when I heard a sound behind me. I looked up to see Rushton on the top step closing the French doors to the library, checking, I think, that we were alone. He was wearing a skiing sweater and jeans and looked like a college professor on the weekend. But as he moved closer to one of the hanging lanterns I saw how haggard his face was.

I stood up as a mark of respect I didn't entirely feel. I'm not usually condemnatory of others' mild sexual excesses. But this time I couldn't be sure that it ended there.

'I've just been talking to Poll,' he said.

I sat down again.

He shoved his hands in his jeans pockets and paced back and forth between the small water gardens. 'You obviously think me a complete idiot . . .'

I poured vodka. 'It doesn't matter what I think, Mr Rushton.'

'Oh it does,' he said. 'It matters very much to Polly what you think.' He came round to face me and I refilled the glass and offered it to him. He took it and I drank from the bottle.

'You know what seduction's about, don't you, Vadim?'

I looked at him over the open neck of the bottle.

'You've had women in your life deliberately set out to get you into bed.'

I grunted. The bottle echoed the sound.

'I think I can say this to you without seeming totally weak and helpless. It's after all what almost every attractive woman knows: if she wants to get some man into bed she can do it.'

'You're saying Sarah . . .'

He nodded before I finished. 'There was one shockingly intimate moment. It only lasted a second. We were sitting at a fund-raising drinks and under the tablecloth she quite deliberately took my hand and pushed it down on her thigh. Then pressed her legs together, holding my hand there for a second or two. That was all it took. She said nothing. She didn't even look at me. But the next day was charged, for me anyway. I couldn't stop looking at her. A thirty-year asexual view of her had shattered like glass. That evening I went to her room.'

'I don't need the details, Mr Rushton. I'm only here because Polly said you wanted to see me.'

'I do,' he said crisply. The guilty manner, the shoulders hunched, the throwaway gestures with the left hand, were suddenly all gone. It was what I'd seen before, when Alex had confronted him with the tape recording. A few moments' penitence – and then a reseizure of control. 'Your advice to Polly was . . .'

'That she should go to the cops. Randall or DeLane. Or preferably you should go. This is material evidence whichever country you come from.'

'I don't see how it can possibly affect the investigation.'

I didn't believe that. It was the first statement Ben Rushton had made that I didn't actually believe – and it set me back.

'The investigation,' I said slowly, 'is split at this moment, perfectly reasonably, between police officers and agents who believe that our vek is a contract killer who started with the British judge and ended with Mrs Rushton and Sarah.'

He was silent.

'The other persuasion, police officers and Bureau agents again, are inclined to believe that Sarah was killed by a sociopath who had seen her on TV, responded to her magnetism in his own way, and has stalked and finally murdered her. They see a copycat element here from the method of Mrs Rushton's murder, strangulation by hanging.'

'So . . .'

'So if we're to stop the police and FBI chasing all over after a second killer who doesn't exist, you have to give them the information which tells them they're still fully on track with the one, single contract killer. A madman who hangs women for pleasure – but a professional contract killer all the same. You've got to give them the motive for Sarah's murder.'

'You believe,' he said quietly, 'that my liaison . . . You believe someone was determined to stop that liaison?'

'I believe Katerina and Sarah died for the same reason. They were threats to your otherwise excellent chances of getting to the White House.'

He handed me back the glass. 'You don't pull punches . . . You are accusing either me – or perhaps any one of six or eight of my closest advisers of taking out a contract first against Katerina, then against Sarah.'

'And you're still paying my salary. You're right, it's time I resigned.'

He reached out and put his hand on my arm. 'Carry on with your job, Vadim. Go to Moscow tomorrow. Make all the necessary arrangements. You see, in the middle of an election, the brain gets addled with tiredness, with the sheer effort of keeping one thing, victory, and one thing only, in sharp focus. Even when dreadful events occur around the campaign, you're still trying to retain that focus.'

'What are you saying?'

'I was wrong not to tell DeLane this morning,' he said. 'I'll call him now, right away. And I'll make sure he knows how I came to be doing this.'

He turned to go – then stopped at the top of the steps. 'Alex,' he said. 'Do you have to tell her?'

'I don't,' I said. '*You* do.' Very faintly, he dipped his head before he passed back into the library.

I took my bottle to Olga's apartment. Olga and Stack were with Alex as I expected, big TV on. We watched newscasts, sickened by the endless repetition but staying with it like addicts. There was always the chance of an additional minute item.

Half an hour later, Polly came to tell Alexandra that Ben wanted to see her. She was gone no more than ten minutes, coming back into the room and taking her seat as if nothing had happened. The newscasts rattled on interminably.

Several times I looked at her but there was nothing to be learnt from her expression.

I left well before midnight with an early start before me the next morning. I said goodnight to Olga and Stack, and Alex walked with me to the door. 'I'm sorry about Sarah,' she said in a low voice as I opened the door.

'We all are . . .' I knew what she meant.

'I mean I'm sorry for you.'

'I'm as sorry as anyone else, no more no less. Sarah was not anyone special to me,' I said. 'Despite what Olga might have told you.'

She inclined her head, neither accepting nor rejecting the assurance.

'Have you talked to Ben?'

'Yes,' she said. 'He came down to my apartment. He told me everything.'

There was something in her tone.

'Everything?' I said.

She gave a half-laugh. There was a bitter quality to it that I found painful.

'When I recover my sight, Constantin,' she said, 'I think I have a great deal of growing up to do.'

38

The dawn release of Katerina's body from the Bridgeport State Police mortuary was skilfully organised by Miriam Cohen. While the media remained camped opposite, in front of McLeavy Hall, the coffin and its gurney were manhandled across the back fence into a yard where an unmarked van was waiting to receive it.

Hanratty and myself were in the only following car, trailing the grey van along the Post Road, then crossing the East River to Flushing before picking up the Van Wyck Expressway south across Long Island to the huge freight area of JFK.

'In one week's time,' Hanratty said, 'you realise I won't be a cop any more.'

'You're going to take your pension and run, you told me.'

'Orlando, Florida. I've got a place down there. Sun, golf, a girl when I need one.'

'A girl when you need one? I thought you had a wife?'

He grinned. 'I talk up the wife – but she doesn't really exist. We've been separated fifteen years or more. But in police work if you mention a wife everybody thinks you're a safer pair of hands with women and kids.'

'I suppose.'

'The feeling is, married men can't be perverts – you and me know the charge books tell a different story. So like I said, it's a Florida life of sea, sun and sex. And a little over for travel when I get antsy.'

'Lucky man. You should treat yourself to a flight over to Murmansk some time. You'll never want to leave Florida again.'

'I'll think about it,' he said. 'Too bad we didn't get further on the case.'

'Leave that to the FBI,' I said. 'One of the most difficult things about retiring is to remember you're an *ex*-cop.'

'I take your word.'

There were huge tailplanes of cargo aircraft rising above the buildings all around us. We ran down between two brick and cement warehouses and Hanratty pulled his car over. He offered his hand. 'See you in Murmansk, *maybe*.' He grinned. 'Best of luck, Chief.'

I got out of the car.

A group of people stood forlornly outside No. 51 warehouse building, a halogen wall light illuminating the glint of rain falling on their shoulders. The tall figure of Alexandra stood slightly apart from Olga, Stack and Polly. It had been agreed that it would attract too much media attention for Rushton to come himself.

Standing by the van, all of us awkward in the banal presence of the dead, I was next to Alexandra. She turned with a quick smile of recognition. 'In a few hours,' she said, 'you'll be back in Moscow.'

'Do you remember the city?' I asked her.

She reached forward and held both my hands. 'I remember the noises and the smells and the grumbling,' she said. 'But I've no picture of the city. The last time I *saw* it was twenty years ago. Really saw it.' She smiled. An effort. 'But in a few days, a week, it'll all be different again.'

I found it difficult to bear the thought that she'd be disappointed. 'Nevetsky's a brilliant surgeon . . .' I said.

'But he doesn't always succeed? I know that, Constantin. I've spent this last year getting myself ready for it.'

This was not an easy woman to understand, I knew that. Underneath that air of dependence she was much tougher than I had at first realised. She stood for a moment as if making a decision. 'I had a phone call just before we left the house,' she said. There was a determination about the way she spoke that sent a chill up my back.

She had turned slightly away from me, her head lifted as if she were reading the black letters on a red and white background: JFK Cargo point 3. 'A Russian voice . . . a man.' She took a deep breath. 'He said he was offering me some advice.' She paused. 'He said I should not go to the Nevetsky Clinic.'

'Not go to the clinic? What did he mean?'

'He said Nevetsky was a charlatan. Worse even.'

I took a step towards her and turned her shoulders to me. 'Who was this man? A doctor?'

'I doubt.'

'So what does he know about Nevetsky? What was he calling for anyway?'

'He said,' her voice was controlled, full of tension. 'He said that Nevetsky was a sadist. He had a thousand failed operations behind him. He would . . .' Her voice bubbled up. 'He said in one operation this man knew of, Nevetsky had cut a woman's eyes out. Because it gave him pleasure.'

I held her arm. 'I don't know how he got through. All calls are supposed to be screened. Tell Hanratty about this. Ask him to see how it could have happened.'

She stood there, nodding her head. 'OK.'

'And listen,' I said urgently. 'There's been unbelievable publicity since Katerina's death. Olga hasn't read them to you but magazines and newspapers have run stories on your operation. And on Nevetsky. This is just a crazy. A sadist himself. He should never have been able to get past screening. Talk to Hanratty.'

'OK,' she said again. 'I feel better just telling you about it. It was a shock, especially hearing it in Russian.'

I looked at my watch. I had to get across the airport to go through boarding. 'You mustn't let this get to you,' I said, then realised how dumb and banal that sounded.

She did too. She smiled. 'Shall we say goodbye here?'

'We'll be seeing each other in Moscow in a couple of days.'

'All the same . . . I still want to say goodbye.' She lifted her face towards me.

I bent forward and kissed her on the forehead, hesitated, then kissed her on the lips. For a second I felt the quick, warm point of her tongue. 'Henry Miller,' she said. 'He says it's a very nice thing to do.'

From the corner of my eye I saw the deeply disapproving movement of Olga's head. 'Henry knew a lot about these things,' I said.

Alex smiled. She was holding my upper arms. For a moment she tightened her grip. 'You'll be there when I go to the Nevetsky Clinic,' she said.

'I'll be there,' I assured her.

'OK.' She forced a smile. 'See you in Moscow then.'

Technical problems with our Ilyushin jet meant a longer stopover in London than I had expected. It was early evening when the Air Russia flight landed at Sheremetevo–2. With real relief I saw the short figure of Dronsky, his thick eyebrows, dark roll-neck sweater and black raincoat giving him a forbidding air as he waited next to the closed information booth.

We shook hands. 'Lot to tell you,' he said. 'I finally got the criminal record of your lady.'

'Katerina Rushton.'

'Katerina Borisova before she married.' He looked up the metal staircase to the green-glassed offices on the floor above. 'But first let's cut our way through the bureaucracy.'

Two hours of negotiation is probably a record for cargo release at Sheremetevo–2. For the cargo release of a dead body, two hours must be close to a miracle. Officials nodded and muttered 'fast-track' and then called other officials. Armed customs officers examined Dronsky's militia papers and faxed requests and examined the papers again. I stayed in the background. We had agreed that things would probably move faster if it were Dronsky rather than me who took receipt of Katerina's body. That way would also enable us to lodge it, until the funeral, in the Station 13 morgue, more reliable than any of the public mortuaries.

In the waiting periods between the examination of papers we drank coffee and watched through the green glass the winding lines of people below. The rumour, Dronsky said, had seized Moscow that the US was closing its doors to Russian visitors, even those with genuine vaccination certificates. At the same time a counter-rumour was running which claimed the Russian government was about to ban all tourist flights to the United States until the tuberculosis epidemic had been brought under control.

'Why should the Kremlin be so friendly to Washington?'

'To keep things as they are,' he said. 'To keep any aid flowing in coming *their* way. Your candidate Rushton's direct-aid policy is frightening some of our leaders. They know that if he's successful in applying American aid where it's needed, like a Dog Death treatment programme, there'll be nothing left for our rulers.'

A customs officer with the rank of colonel finally signed off our papers. Provided with the necessary clearances we were escorted by a sergeant down a cement fire-escape stairway and came out into an enclosed courtyard. A biting wind swept across it. October Moscow is usually too early for snow but the temperature was already dropping fast. The old truck waiting for us was off-white with *Militia* transferred in blue along its side. It sat with its engine running, shaking every few moments as if shivering with cold. A militia driver sat smoking, reading a newspaper by the cab light. When he saw Dronsky, he got down, cigarette held between his lips, banging his gloved hands together. 'I can squeeze you both in front there, Captain,' he said. 'Don't suppose anybody wants to travel with the corpse.'

'We'll take the back,' Dronsky said. He turned and signalled to the customs sergeant to open the wire gate. 'OK,' he said to the driver. 'Take it easy over the potholes.'

The back of the truck had been modified to take a stack of riot barriers held by brackets on either side. The coffin occupied the central position, plain metal with simple toggle handles at each end. Dronsky and I sat on sour-smelling brown blankets on either side of the coffin.

'You've a lot to tell me, you said.'

'I have, Chief.' He handed me a cigarette across the coffin, took one himself and lit them both with an old American Zippo lighter. Then from inside his trenchcoat he drew a flat half-litre bottle and passed it to me.

Bumping along in the back of an old militia truck, sitting across a coffin from my old friend, smoking chest-rasping cigarettes and unscrewing the cap of a bottle of Dronsky's favourite Kuban vodka – I was back home, back in Russia again.

'You know, Chief,' he said conversationally. 'Nearly ninety-nine per cent of my time as a Moscow militia station commander is spent with minor burglary, causing an affray, bodily harm . . .'

'Traffic,' I threw in.

'Yes, traffic. But then you turn up and suddenly I'm bumping down Leningrad Prospekt with a coffin full of trouble between us.' He lifted his heavy eyebrows, inhaled his cigarette. 'I never learn.'

'Thank God.' I shifted to get more comfortable. 'You said you've got a lot to tell me. Where did you start?'

'As I said, I started with Katerina's record. This is her Moscow record, you understand.'

'What does it tell us?' I necked the bottle and passed it to him.

He took it but didn't drink for a moment. 'It tells us she started off being run out of a few hotels for soliciting. There's a note on her record that she's seen moving around among the top *racketiry*.'

'That sounds dangerous.'

'It was all under orders. The note tells us that in her early thirties she became a prize girl – you know what that means in Moscow, Chief?'

I shook my head. The truck bumped over the potholes in the old Leningrad Prospekt and I held the back of my neck.

'When two Moscow gangsters make a serious deal – a temporary alliance usually – they exchange favourite girlfriends for a month as evidence of good faith. I once read the old Romans did something like that. Isn't that right, Chief?'

'I think they sometimes handed over their wives or daughters if the deal was big enough.'

'We don't know who she was prizing for, but at one point a deal went wrong. The offended gangster arranged for a grenade to be thrown at her in a church off Tverskaya Street. Missed her, but blinded her eight-year-old daughter.'

'I see,' I said.

He looked up, from under those eyebrows, but asked nothing.

'After the bombing, Katerina disappears from view for a good many years. Maybe went back to Budapest where she'd once been on the game. I've seen a medical record on the daughter that shows three major operations in Paris. So that's probably where she . . .' He tapped the coffin to make sure I didn't confuse mother and daughter. 'Probably where she moved on to – doing what? Society hooker to earn the money for her daughter's operations? Maybe.'

'The way we live now,' I said. 'When did she come back to Moscow?'

'Just a year or two before she met Candidate Rushton. By then she spoke fluent French and English and had set up a small language school, staying away from the hotel trade.'

I took a taste of vodka, let it run round my mouth and slowly down my throat. I was looking at the coffin jumping under the flat of my hand with every particularly vicious bump. Katerina Borisova had left the high life for her daughter's sake. I didn't really doubt that.

'So she was not poor but not rich either when she met Ben Rushton.'

'That's the way it looks, Chief.'

'Although, of course, her father might have been giving her money. He had plenty.'

'Katerina was *left* plenty,' Dronsky said deliberately. 'He didn't have plenty when he was alive.'

I almost stubbed my cigarette on the coffin, instead crushed it on the floor. 'He wasn't a millionaire?'

Dronsky shook his head. 'Maybe we can find out more when we visit the notary tomorrow. But all my information is that he was a drunk who used to hang around the Belorussian Station in his last years. Finally fell down on the embankment with a bottle of vodka inside him and was frozen stiff by the morning. Perhaps he was one of these old men who live in rags and hoard millions. But somehow I doubt it.'

'Are you saying he became rich *after* his death?'

'Don't know what I'm saying, Chief. We're going to have to find out. But old Borisov was a Belorussian drunk right up until the time he died.'

The wheels hit a deeper than usual pothole. The coffin jumped between us.

I stayed in the truck in the parking lot of Station 13 while Dronsky went in to arrange for a gurney to take Katerina's body into the mortuary.

I waited until the van door swung shut. Furtively I clambered to my feet and rested one knee on the end of the coffin, kneeling forward. From time immemorial

Russians, some Russians I should say, have believed that a traveller should sit, reflectively, on his bundles of luggage for a few minutes before setting out. The object is to be granted a peaceful journey. In my part of Russia, the dead are thought of as travellers. A relative substitutes for the shade of the deceased and rests a knee for a moment or two on the coffin.

You could say it was a mark of respect. Of hope for a journey less frantic than life had been. Dronsky, of course, doesn't believe in these things. In fact I think he sees them in me as a sign of prematurely failing powers. 'An old woman's superstitions,' he calls them. 'Yesterday's fears.'

I stood like that, one knee resting on the coffin for a minute or two, thinking how frenetic Katerina's life had been, wishing her well on her journey. When I heard Dronsky returning and the squeaking wheels of the path-lab assistants' gurney, I straightened up, pushed open the door and jumped out. Reaching inside for my duffel, I pulled it out and swung it onto my shoulder with what I hoped had just a touch of the devil-may-care about it.

Dronsky looked at me, suppressed a smile and raised his thick eyebrows in one of those knowing expressions even good friends can rarely fathom.

Moscow has a system of ring roads enclosing the centre of the city. The big wall map in Station 13 reception showed the Nevetsky Institute off Pokrovka Street between the Garden and Boulevard Ring. On Dronsky's advice I took the longer than necessary route round the Garden Ring. Most of the refugee trouble was concentrated round the main railway stations and the militia had orders to keep the Garden Ring clear for the movement of riot police or the military.

Driving a militia car I was waved through the road-blocks and half a dozen kilometres later I had reached

Pokrovka Street and turned off to park outside the superb art nouveau iron railings of the Institute. The building beyond the railings was less grand than its courtyard, a Seventies pink/red concrete block squatting on low stilts with two long rows of black-framed, mean-looking windows, most of them lighted but all glazed with frosted glass.

I passed through the gates and crossed the wide courtyard. From the days of the original building, the architect had left by intention, or the builders by neglect, the columns of a miniature classical temple still standing there. Within were the bases of two broken statues which had perhaps once been of unclothed, sportive girls, one with Chastity incised in the stone; the other making a bare-breasted claim to Innocence. Sculpture was, of course, the public soft porn of its day.

The entrance was by a short concrete stairway. I pressed the bell beside the double ochre-painted doors. Through the portholes in them I could see a highly polished hall and a receptionist in white crossing to open the door for me.

Moscow people in positions of even minor authority, especially if there's a uniform provided, tend towards the arrogant and unhelpful. This wasn't the case here. I explained that I had called an hour ago for an appointment with Dr Nevetsky and she took me straight up a floor to a large square room with three frosted glass windows.

Dr Nevetsky was a small, broad-shouldered man in his late fifties, bald and with a cheerful, friendly manner which inspired immediate confidence. As we shook hands, I glanced down. The file on his desk was marked Alexandra Borisova.

'I saw Alexandra . . .' He tapped the file. 'In New York. She had received excellent treatment, both in Paris and later in America. My belief, Mr Vadim, is that we are now able to take the results obtained a significant step forward.' He paused. 'If we are lucky.'

'Lucky?'

'Why not? Luck is an element in all surgery of this delicacy. I explained that fully to Alexandra. I explained to her that the depressant effect of an unsuccessful operation is not something to be dismissed. She's a young woman of great courage. In my profession you see something of courage, Mr Vadim. And Alexandra is as well equipped to handle failure as anybody I've met. As the man she's going to marry, you are entitled to know that she might easily undergo the surgery here without any significant improvement to her sight. Even with a slight degradation.'

As the man she's going to marry? I was about to correct him when the meaning of his last sentence distracted me. 'Do you mean there's a risk she won't even be able to see as well as she does now?'

'Yes.'

'Jesus.'

'If you didn't know that before, I'm doubly glad you came in to see me. Now if you'll look at these charts on the wall behind me . . .' He touched buttons to illumine back-lit charts and photographs of dead eyes that had been sectioned by surgery. The mass of vein and tissue meant nothing to me but I felt, for Alexandra's sake, I had to listen. Carpenters and plumbers love to explain to you the detail of their work, the difficulties of access, the neatness of the discovered solution. Doctors are no different. With charts, diagrams and the most horrendous photographs I've seen outside the autopsy file, Dr Nevetsky illustrated exactly what the problem was, the risks that would have to be taken, the outcome within our grasp.

As a militia officer I had developed a technique for listening to autopsy reports and ignoring the illustrative material. On those occasions when I had known the victim in life I'd achieved some sort of separation from her (it was usually her) and the ghastliness I saw before me in photograph or on the autopsy table.

It was what I did now. Exhausted by my flight, New York–London, London–Moscow, I lapsed visually and tried to select the salient points as Nevetsky described them.

This was not state-of-the-art surgery. This was something five, six, seven years ahead of that. Therein lay the risk. In a sighted person's eye the retina is covered with a layer of tissue that acts as photoelectric cells. The signals which the cells transmit are relayed via ganglions to the optic nerve which is the assembly point for delivery of the messages to the brain.

But the explosion in front of the eight-year-old Alex had destroyed most of the minute rods and cones in the retina. Nevetsky was planning an extraordinary piece of surgery. I swallowed as I listened. He planned to open the eye and place a microchip inside which would transmit light signals to the brain.

'Has this never been done before?' I asked, shocked at the thought.

'Hundreds of times,' he said. 'In the United States Johns Hopkins were doing this before the millennium. This series of experiments was ground-breaking but produced only relatively crude images. Since then we've all moved forward.' He paused, hands down on his desk. 'I've just moved forward faster than others. I'm a risk-taker on my patients' behalf, I know that. But I think it's what they want.'

'You've had great successes . . .'

'And failures,' Nevetsky said. 'All the ophthalmology will depend upon a pair of perfectly normal-looking spectacles which will in fact carry a minute camera device which will send the image, in coded form, into the eye and thence into the brain.'

I was no longer trying not to listen. I watched the man in front of me, saw the way his hands moved in sheer excitement at the thought of what he was about to do – and decided he was the man to do it.

343

He made it crystal clear. At very best he was aiming at an improvement of twenty per cent in the right eye; fifteen per cent in the left. It would make a dramatic difference, he assured me, if we achieved those figures. It would not restore Alex's eyesight to what it was before the bomb exploded twenty years ago. But it would reclassify her as sighted, rather than blind.

Nevetsky leaned forward, his big brown eyes staring hard at me. 'You understand *sighted, blind*, these are not terms we use in ophthalmology. But they are terms people with damaged or part-functioning eyesight use about *themselves*. There's a great opportunity here for this beautiful young woman. So we take it?'

I sat back in surprise. 'Of course,' I said. 'If you can do that . . .'

'If . . .' He lifted a finger in the air. 'And if not. If we achieve a miserable zero to three/four per cent improvement? Worse, if we fail, what then?'

I was silent.

He nodded gravely. 'Her mother has just been murdered. I have spoken to Alexandra on the telephone in New York. She is determined to take this opportunity. But the combination of surmounting her mother's death and the prospect of the operation itself . . .' His voice dropped. 'It's a challenge we can't appreciate.'

'No.' I was deeply shocked. Not because I had just learnt there were risks – I already knew that. But to hear this competent, sympathetic man put them to me from the depths of his knowledge. That brought me to the edge.

I was, cravenly, asking for myself now, as much as for Alex. 'I have to ask you,' I said. 'You have enormous experience. You've examined her.' I paused. 'What do you think?'

Suddenly he smiled. Broadly. Almost broke into a laugh. For a second I was startled by the change. 'I think we'll do it, Vadim.'

'Constantin,' I said.

'Constantin it'll be. We'll do it. I'm sure as I can be. I've told you the risks. Now let's not even think about them.' He stood up, shaking my hand. A short stocky man with dark eyes that glittered with enthusiasm. 'We'll do it, Constantin,' he said. 'We'll do it boldly. And we'll *succeed*.'

39

Dronsky had left for home by the time I got back to Station 13. V. I. Lenin was sitting in the far corner of the room as I entered. Suspiciously amiable, he raised a paw in salute. The reason for this display of conciliatory behaviour wasn't difficult to see. Dronsky had left me a quarter-litre of Kuban and a paper bag that smelled, in very general terms, of food. I lifted the greasy brown bag and saw the side had been ripped apart. The hamburger had been prised open and chewed furiously.

Junk food is one of the few things I have to hold against Dronsky as a superior human being. His love of cats, and V. I. Lenin in particular, is another. But tonight I felt an edge of gratitude rise in me. After all, the brown bag might have contained his all-time junk favourite, the local salt-cod fishburger. And that, believe me brothers, is truly a delicacy to be avoided.

I settled down with a good thumb of pepper vodka and thought about that line of Dr Nevetsky's which had floated close to my conscious level ever since he had spoken it. *As the man she's going to marry.* Had the good doctor made a mistake? Had Alexandra just told him that to make access easier for me when she was in the clinic? Had she actually *meant it*? I looked up. V. I. Lenin, I swear, was nodding.

I poured another thumb of Kuban. She couldn't possibly have meant it. And how did I feel about it if she had? Well, not offended, of course. Not really even too shocked. Olga would be, there was no doubt about that. But too bad. I was not Olga's business. I looked at the bottle. The liquid level was not much more than a centimetre or two from the bottom. I blamed Olga – I had drunk most of the quarter-litre of Kuban vodka sitting here.

I fell backward on the narrow bed. The hamburger would wait until morning. One more small thumb might give me the same number of calories. Surprisingly clumsily, I poured . . . She couldn't possibly have meant it. I looked again towards V. I. Lenin, taking his ease on the filing cabinet. He closed one eye conspiratorially.

I awoke with all those familiar sensations. Welcome back to Russia, said my spinning head. I looked at the hamburger which the mice had been at and my stomach churned.

It was one of those mornings when starting the day requires a special gearing, an unusual, almost heroic effort. Something to do, perhaps, with being back in Russia. I disposed of the hamburger. I took clean clothes from my duffel. Downstairs in the basement where Katerina had been held that morning I first met her, I used the prisoners' shower with its cracked tiles and leaking green copper piping. Back upstairs again I shaved and cleaned my teeth. With a glass of tea and the last dribble of Dronsky's vodka, I felt set up to face the day.

It began with a nightmare drive through Moscow traffic with me following Dronsky's militia vehicle in an unmarked. Dronsky was being driven by one of the more skilled Station 13 drivers and was no doubt periodically assured I was close behind. I was because I had to be. While some traffic will give way to a militia car, none will give way to a common or garden Renault Economy. To keep the militia car in sight I was forced to jump lights and overtake with a reckless verve that just isn't in my nature.

I finally caught up with them as they turned off the back street we were running along, onto a spur of waste-land that had once held light industrial buildings. Bumping over the uneven ground I pulled up alongside the militia car. Dronsky was already leaning against the bonnet rolling a cigarette. 'I'd no idea you were such a nifty driver, Chief,' he said. 'Young Petrov there told me you were up his tail all the way.'

I grunted and accepted his rolled cigarette.

'What do you think?' He waved his hand to take in an area which formed a saucer of land, about a hundred metres in diameter, between the curve of a raised rail line on one side and a canal embankment on the other. Bombed or shelled in the Civil War, in all probability, the bottom of the saucer sloped down to hold a vast puddle of unguessable depth. Signboards stood out of the water announcing that swimming was forbidden. Danger to life was possible from the high chemical content of the water. The signs were posted by the International Red Cross.

'This is it?' I was astounded. I took a light from Dronsky, drew in deeply, and looked at him. 'This is it? This is the piece of land that was sold to provide a thirty-million-dollar fortune for Katerina? It can't be, Dronsky. You or your Formula One driver have made a mistake.'

He shook his head. 'Don't doubt it, Chief. *This* is the piece of land that the InMos Bank paid old Borisov's estate thirty million dollars for.'

I walked away from the cars and stood by myself looking out over the dead land. Was it my imagination that the surface of the pond glinted green whenever the cloud thinned sufficiently to allow a pale ray of sunlight through? Probably not. Thirty million dollars was a hundred times the price the land was worth – unless someone were laundering money through Borisov's estate.

Katerina? Ben Rushton?

And, I wondered, does this thirty million have any bearing on Katerina's murder? Is the money, in some way, the reason Katerina Rushton is now lying in a coffin on a mortuary tray at Station 13 morgue?

'You want me to go with you?' Dronsky asked. 'It's a bad area.'

'Dronsky. They're a firm of lawyers, for Christ's sake,' I said. 'They handled a thirty-million-dollar land sale, whatever the shady purpose behind it. They're not going to be lodged at the top of an ILU.'

Improved Living Units, the government term for the project housing in the ageing New Districts of Moscow where high-rise apartment blocks, damaged during the Civil War, have been hastily and sometimes dangerously patched up.

'All the same, Chief, the Babushkin neighbourhood is a mess. I could act as a back-up if that'd help you feel better about driving there alone.'

It was Dronsky who felt bad about me driving there alone, not me. I thanked him and told him I felt fine about going to Babushkin. It was daylight, nothing untoward was going to happen on a visit to a notary's office.

Just after the end of Russia's Civil War, when I was working in Moscow, I don't recall there were any lawyers at all. So I had little in the way of expectations as I drove up the Prospekt Mira. Once I had turned off the Prospekt, the shells of sixteen-storey blocks closed around me like the canyons of New York. Except that the sides of these canyons were walls of gaping holes torn by shellfire. Some of the blocks seemed to lean, others had lost their top four or five storeys and ended in a crumpled battlement of rubble and twisted steelwork. The whole area looked as much Grozny as Moscow.

But at street level there were signs of life. The roads had been cleared of debris and there were a few cars and lurching vans to be seen. In many buildings where living on the second or third floor might court death from falling masonry, shops had opened at street level, their ceilings reinforced by timber struts.

The bureau of notaries Barbarovsky & Lawson was a

brightly lit shopfront of newly fitted armour-plated glass. As I crossed the sidewalk I could see the receptionist seated at an elegant modern desk inside. Slightly disconcertingly, he was a bearded, shaved-bald blockhouse of a man in camouflage with a light machine gun lying next to the phone and surveillance screen.

A cleared area beside the offices provided a parking lot. I left the car and walked round to the front door. The receptionist was already on his feet, the machine gun under one arm as he approached the glass door. I held my ID up to the glass and he swung open the door, as close as he could get to a welcoming smile on his face.

'I'm here to see Vassily Barbarovsky,' I said. 'I called this morning. Constantin Vadim.'

He rolled menacingly towards me. 'You won't object, Mr Vadim . . .'

'Of course not.' You get used to being searched for concealed weapons doing business in today's Russia. I held my arms up like a penguin.

One-handed, his finger hooked into the trigger guard of his assault rifle, he frisked me skilfully.

'Thank you,' he said and straightened up. 'Mr Barbarovsky is ready to see you right away,' he said. 'May I offer you tea, coffee, a thumb of vodka?'

'Kuban, if you've got it.'

'We've a wide range of beverages, sir. Our clients come from all parts of the world and their tastes vary greatly.'

Words that might easily have come from a coiffed blonde girl in a miniskirt sat oddly on this shambling brute. I nodded. 'I'm sure they do,' I said vaguely.

He led me into a modern office furnished with chrome and black leather furniture. Two young men in Italian suits rose from behind two smoked-glass-topped desks. The dark-haired man came forward. The fair-haired companion hung back with a polite smile.

'Mr Constantin Vadim,' the receptionist said, smacking his trigger guard. 'Checked and clear.'

'Vassily Barbarovsky,' the dark-haired notary said. We shook hands. 'And this is my English partner, George Lawson.'

'Very enchanted to meeting you,' Lawson said in English rendered almost incomprehensible by his Russian accent.

'You're English?' I said incredulously.

'From Surrey County.'

'Perhaps you speak English yourself?' Barbarovsky intervened.

'I do.'

'Ah. Yes. Then you'll know that Mr Lawson only *looks* English. Sadly, compared to ourselves, English and American lawyers have a reputation for integrity. It seemed to us Barbarovsky & Lawson conveyed the right impression.'

'Of course.'

'Conveyed correct illusion of honesty,' Lawson said, again in English.

'Perhaps we should stick to Russian,' I said. 'Among Russians.'

'And get down to business.' Barbarovsky gestured me to a comfortable, leather-covered chair at the conference table at the far end of the room. Before each of the eight chairs there was a water glass upturned on a red napkin, a bottle of Perrier water and a small dish of cakes. I found it hard to believe this room was in the middle of an area of windowless, half-collapsing buildings. Until the receptionist came in with a tray of vodka and glasses in one hand and his assault rifle in the other.

'Help yourself to vodka,' Barbarovsky said. 'George will handle the coffee.'

Lawson was already at a small silver-fronted Gaggia machine scooping grounds into the filter.

I poured myself a thumb of vodka and took a seed cake from the dish in front of me. 'Allow me to ask,' I said, 'why you locate yourself here in Babushkin.'

'It's not a prime Moscow site,' Barbarovsky conceded smoothly. I thought of the collapsing buildings and the armed receptionist. 'But many of our clients started out in this neighbourhood. They appreciate us locating here. Isn't that so George?'

'They certainly do,' George said, back towards us, working to the hiss and aroma of the Gaggia.

'So how did you come to handle Katerina's affairs?' I asked Barbarovsky.

'The connection came through my father. He was with a firm of notaries working from the Arbat. He used to handle the investments for all the business girls.' His eyes met mine. 'I mean, of course, for many of the single young women living in the neighbourhood. When the daughter, Alexandra, was injured, Katerina entrusted her savings to my father to invest for Alex. It was not a large sum, by the later standards of her wealth, but it was significant. A hundred and fifty thousand dollars.'

'Does your firm still handle the original sum?'

'No, that was merged with the rest of her holdings, the much larger sum that came from her father's estate, and transferred to lawyers in New York.' He paused. 'So all I now handle is her private testament. Her special request for interment principally.'

'Before we go into that,' I said, pouring myself a little more vodka and watching George carry two overfull cups of espresso to Barbarovsky and himself, 'before we go any further, perhaps I could ask you about Katerina's father's estate?'

For the first time Barbarovsky looked less than comfortable. 'Yes?'

'What were you responsible for, exactly?'

'We were responsible for the sale of his property. The funds were then forwarded to Chase Manhattan in New York. Isn't that what happened, George?'

'Exactly so,' George said. Again in English.

I looked from one to the other, then up the wall behind

their heads. A certificate with the crest of England's Cambridge University announced that George had a Bachelor's and Master's in Law from *Pembrok* College. The final *e*, mysteriously missing, made the word look more Russian than English. Barbarovsky's degree might well have been genuine. He had graduated from Moscow University with honours in History and Law.

'Katerina told me,' I lied, 'that the final sum came as a great surprise.'

'I believe,' George said.

'So Borisov's ownership of the piece of land was only established at the last minute. She had no idea her father was so . . . wealthy.'

'That was probably the case,' George said.

Barbarovsky's dark eyes had not left me.

'Who purchased the land?'

Barbarovsky leaned forward and selected a small cake. 'Why are you asking these questions, Mr Vadim? The sale extracted the maximum amount possible for the land, I'd say.'

'Who bought it?'

'InMos Bank. You don't know Moscow, I understand, but on the site once owned by Mr Borisov, an American company has erected sixty prime quality American houses. It was one of those happy good deals for everybody.'

'I'd say so,' George said. 'Quite so.'

Barbarovsky glared at him. 'Speak Russian or stay quiet,' he snapped. 'Now what is your problem, Mr Vadim?'

'I'm not sure it's a problem,' I said. 'But I was down at Noginska this morning to look at the land.'

Both men ceased all movement, Barbarovsky with his coffee cup at his lips. His eyes lifted towards mine.

'I'd say InMos Bank had not really started on its American building project. And never will.'

'That, of course, is entirely possible, old chap,' George said amiably.

'Why is that, George?' I asked him.

'InMos Bank went into liquidation a number of years ago. Exceptionally sad.'

'That's enough,' Barbarovsky said. He stood up. 'I think we should bring this meeting to an end.'

'I'm happy to stay on and chat about things,' I said.

'You're leaving. Let me show you the door, Mr Vadim.'

I stood too. 'You still haven't given me the details of Katerina Rushton's last wishes.'

'No . . .' He went back to his desk and picked up a long envelope. I could see he had regained his composure once we were back on the subject of Katerina's burial.

'Her wish was to be buried in the city of her birth,' he said. 'The details are what you might think of as a little eccentric, but they're all there.'

'The city of her birth?' I was dismayed. I knew she wasn't born in Moscow. That could mean a substantial journey. Not attractive at this time of the year. 'She was born in Northern Russia somewhere.'

'Far north-west,' he said. He handed me the envelope. 'Her last wish was to be buried in her home town, the city of Murmansk.'

Murmansk! I'm not quite sure why it struck me as so odd, even faintly eerie, that Katerina should have come from my own home town. In a strange way I felt that I should have known her, although when Katerina was born, Murmansk claimed a population of nearly half a million people. It was a centre for the nickel industry, a great fishing port and the base for the powerful Soviet western fleet.

Today, the city is in decline. The fleet's submarines and their nuclear power plants rust and (local rumour has it) glow blue at night, uncared for, unmaintained. More than fear of radiation, it's the cold, bleak life within the Arctic Circle that has driven the population away. In Soviet times those who were here were obliged to stay, and newcomers were tempted by cheap fuel and a better than average range of food supplies to keep them coming. Roy Rolkin, governor of the province of Kola and Murmansk's ruling figure in his gubernatorial office tower has, I admit, made great efforts in the last three years to entice a skilled population back. But people coming to the crumbling concrete workers' apartment blocks, the forty-degree-below cold and the Arctic darkness from October to the end of January, seldom stay long.

So, even in today's Murmansk, a city with a rapidly decreasing population, it was absurd to think that, just because I had served as a militia officer in most areas of the city, I should have heard of the Borisov family. Unless what was really troubling me was not that I *hadn't* heard of Katerina Borisova. But that I *had*.

I got into Dronsky's unmarked and drove back to the Prospekt Mira. Katerina Borisova . . . Katerina Borisova . . . Was I making it up, or did that name really ring a distant Russian bell?

I had used the notaries' phone before I left to call the Washington headquarters of the American Unity Party. I had been given a code word that took me fairly quickly through the tiers of operators. Barbarovsky and his Wodehousean partner were impressed when I got onto Jack Yado in under five minutes.

'I'm at the lawyers' office now,' I said. 'The news isn't good. Katerina's testamentary request is to be buried in her home city, Murmansk.'

I could hear the horror in his voice. 'Jesus, that woman. She's going to drag her husband in the last few days of a presidential election up to Murmansk? How far is it from Moscow?'

'About fifteen hundred kilometres north.'

'In *miles*.'

'Say nine hundred.'

'Change in St Petersburg?'

'Or Moscow if you prefer.'

'It's still going to take five days out of the campaign. This is a catastrophe. He can't go.'

'I think we both know he has to.'

'Yeah,' he said. 'You're right. He can't not go.'

'I didn't have a chance to say it before I left,' I said. 'Given your plans for both of you, I'm sorry about Sarah.'

He grunted.

'Nothing new on the investigation?'

'Stop riding me, Vadim. Ben's told the FBI about him and Sarah. They've dropped the lone raving lunatic theory. They're all over us. Everybody in the campaign team's now a suspect for handing out the contract. Thanks to you. I won't forget. I owe you one.'

I found a quiet bar. I took my cellphone and sat at a corner table. I signalled the old waiter. He shuffled unhurriedly over. He had, I noticed, the top of all the fingers missing from his right hand – frostbite, labour camp? Or drunken collapse on his own frozen doorstep? No time to ask. I ordered bread and sausage and a coffee-vodka. I needed a clear head to make this call.

I was passed through two men to a light woman's voice. I explained I was an old friend of the regional governor and would appreciate it if she'd put me through.

'It's Constantin Vadim, isn't it?' the woman said. 'I recognise your voice. This is Marya.'

All Roy's secretaries have a high degree of physicality. Marya had enough to project over a cellphone connection from a city nearly a thousand miles from Moscow.

'Marya!' I affected delight and flirted with her for a few moments before asking if Roy was in town. 'He's in his office,' she said.

'So he can't be busy.'

She laughed. 'Not usually. But let me tell you this place has just gone mad.'

'Just?'

'Well,' she corrected, 'we're all mad in Murmansk. You know that, Costya.'

'I do. It's the unbearable excitement of eight months of Arctic winter. Listen, Marya, what's going on there?'

'It's the American visit. Roy's just heard.'

'Which American visit?'

'One of the American candidates for president. Mr Rushton. His wife was killed and she left a will saying she wanted to be buried in her home town – Murmansk.'

I sat back, stunned. How in God's name did she know that? How did *Roy* know that? As the official emissary of the husband and daughter of the deceased, *I* had only just heard. 'Put me through to Roy. This is important.'

'I hope he thinks so too,' she said.

There were a few clicks and then Roy's voice. 'What the fuck? I'm busy, Costya.'

'How did you find out that Katerina Rushton wanted to be buried in Murmansk?'

He chuckled. All good humour suddenly. 'I'm regional Governor here, remember. I have a right and a duty to know everything.'

'So you say. But how the devil did you know this?'

'I can tell you it's no thanks to you. When your old friend called you in America and asked for help, your old friend who'd paid your way to New York ... when he asked for help, a little oil to smooth the wheels, a little introduction to Jack Yado – you turned me down, fuck your mother. So I had to build bridges alone.'

'You're saying Jack Yado called you. Immediately after I called him.'

'I'd laugh, Costya, if I wasn't planning to drop you in an ice barrel the moment you get back here.'

'I don't like jokes like that, Roy. Did Yado call you?'

'That's what I'm saying. Whatever a Rushton presidency does about Russia – Jack Yado will have a voice.

He's already talking to Rushton about me for the Health Supremo for North-West Russia, that's St Petersburg, Archangel, Murmansk . . .'

'I know what North-West Russia is, for Christ's sake. When did all this happen?'

'A couple of days ago. Jack and I had a very fruitful lunch meeting. No thanks to you.'

'You were in the United States?'

'Flew into Washington and out the same day. It was a gesture trip. Establishes rapport. So naturally when he discovered the funeral's to take place in Murmansk – he calls me straight away to let me know a presidential candidate will be visiting my bailiwick. Listen,' he said, without a pause, 'in Washington, I caught the White Housers against the Manhattan Islanders. That new striker Manhattan has is rubbish.'

'But Paxton, the goalkeeper . . .'

'We don't need a goalkeeper.'

'What was last night's score?' I said.

'Murmansk lost 7–1. To Anchorage, Alaska.'

'So the referee couldn't count or somebody else let the goals through. You're an idiot, Roy. We need a goalkeeper. Even before we need a new striker.'

There was a long silence at the other end. 'I'll think about it,' Roy said, a surly concession. 'But your man Paxton's *black* for Christ's sake. I've promised the fans a local team. Local recruitment of local boys. I could have claimed Russian ancestry for Lister. But after a lifetime up here it's struck most people, if not you, that we don't have many black faces around. How am I going to get round that?'

'You will, Roy, if the spirit moves you. See you in Murmansk.'

'I have an ice barrel waiting for you.' His voice had moved back to that hard-joke tone. Difficult even for me, an old friend, to be sure of.

I put the phone down. I could feel my lips were pursed.

He didn't mean it of course. But what was always frightening about Roy was that you knew he was capable of it – if he ever decided he meant it. He had, as I've said, done it many times before.

40

Evening in the Bullfrog, an alley chattering with girls and reeking of burnt mutton from dozens of shashlik bars. Country boys, soldiers on leave from the Chechen front wandered the length of the narrow alley bumping shoulders as they gazed into the strip-bars and tableaux joints.

'So Rushton and his retinue are all going to be in Murmansk for the funeral, Chief?' Dronsky asked, acknowledging, as we walked, thieves and hookers and perhaps even a few ordinary citizens who knew him as head of the local militia station.

'I haven't told you the worst yet,' I said. 'Let's get ourselves a beer and I'll show you Katerina's testament.'

We settled in a narrow shashlik bar and decided to forgo the beer in favour of a quarter-litre. Waving away the two girls who immediately tried to join us, I pulled out the document I had been given by Barbarovsky & Lawson. 'She had it drawn up when she was in Moscow that last time,' I said. 'When she was arrested.'

Dronsky took the document and unfolded the thick paper. 'Instruction for my burial at Sin City, Murmansk, Region of Kola,' Dronsky read under his breath. His head came up. 'Sin City? That's that huge whores' camp outside Murmansk, the Ice Fair, isn't it?'

'Read on. There's a lot of missing biography there. You'll find Katerina worked in Sin City as a teenager . . .'

'Worked?'

'It was work, believe me.'

'I believe you.' He read on, sat for a moment staring at the document, then, refolding it, slowly pushed it back across the marble-topped table towards me. 'Some funeral,' he said. 'Some funeral to ask the man who's possibly the next American president to attend. Is it craziness or just malice?'

'Maybe neither,' I said. 'Perhaps it's her way of explaining to American voters the way things are over here.'

Dronsky's eyes met mine. The thick eyebrows rose. 'I have a snippet for you. Could be useful.' He swallowed his vodka. 'I was looking at the cases of the murdered women you sent me. Last week I dropped in on the investigator who covered the Simenova murder here in Moscow. He talked to a lot of people at the time. One thing he said was her killer was probably American but spoke faultless Russian.'

I sat back in alarm. When Alex had received the call in Russian at Observatory Point crudely warning her against Dr Nevetsky's skills as a surgeon, we'd both assumed it was a crank. Someone who'd broken through the phone barrier by sheer chance.

Now I had to wonder. Do more than wonder. Was it possible the man or men who had handed out the contract to murder Katerina and Sarah were also interested in Alex? Interested anyway in her not regaining her sight?

I sat there for a moment staring at Dronsky. He's the sort of friend who doesn't push you with questions. He sat silently.

'The investigator on the Simenova case. Can I talk to him?'

'Why not. Vassily Balkhin, Station 4. I'll call him. He appreciates a drink.'

Balkhin was fat and greedy. While we all exchanged cop talk he demolished the best part of a half dozen skewers of shashlik and a dish of pelmeni dumplings, all washed down by a quarter-litre. 'We found her in the

Little Pushkin Theatre,' he said. 'Centre stage, hanging by the neck.'

'Fully clothed?' Dronsky's eyebrows rose.

'She'd been playing the part of a countess in her latest play. Some French farce. She was wearing jewellery and a long black evening gown, cut to show everything she had. The make-up was expert. You know, stage make-up, curling eyelashes, everything. Looked very strange with her face blown up like a football.'

'Nothing unusual about the dress?' I said, fishing.

'One thing,' he finished his glass, took the neck of the empty vodka bottle between finger and thumb and waggled it for a replacement.

Dronsky signalled the waiter.

'The skirt,' he said, 'was tied with string. Just above the knees. We never did work that one out.'

There didn't seem any point in enlightening him. 'You never had a lead on who would want her dead?'

'Oh yes,' Balkhin said. 'We knew from the beginning. Her lover was an old goat who'd arranged a lot of good parts for her. At the time of her death he was already over eighty and she'd told him, in public the week before, that it was all over. Trouble was the old goat had very good connections. Kremlin . . . secret services . . . we checked them all.'

'Weren't they too old?'

'To do the job themselves maybe. Not too old to put their hands on a hitman when he was wanted. The old man covered himself with the perfect alibi: at the opera. Seen by a hundred witnesses. Then at the officers' club where he passed out in an armchair and slept in full sight of a dozen carousers until dawn. She was alive when he was seen at the opera and dead by the time he left the officers' club. The question was which old friend had helped him out with the name of a younger man.'

'Was there anyone specially he'd worked with? Anyone he felt he could trust?'

Balkhin tore the last piece of lamb from a skewer. 'Too many to be of use to us. We concentrated on the killer. We found a stagehand we're pretty sure talked to the killer in the theatre.'

'You got a description?'

'Too dark for that. But the stagehand said he could tell the man was an American. Clothes, accent maybe. But his Russian was near perfect.'

I thought of Volodya's visit to the Adirondacks. About the man in the woods. The travelling hangman. 'At this stage we're thinking it might be easier to find the middle man than the killer.'

'Could be.' Balkhin wiped a piece of bread round his plate. 'Yes, could be . . .'

'Do me a list,' I said. 'The old goat's KGB friends.' I pushed the folded testament of Katerina in front of him. 'Go ahead.'

'You want a lot for a thumb or two of vodka,' Balkhin grumbled. But he took out a chewed pencil, licked it like a man to whom writing was almost an unnatural act, and began to scribble. 'This'll take hours,' he said. 'In addition to which, it's very thirsty work, citizen.'

When the waiter brought the next quarter-litre, I poured a generous thumb for Balkhin.

'The list means nothing to me,' Dronsky said when Balkhin had waddled away. 'All this was a long time ago, Chief. And as the fat man said, Simenova wasn't hanged by an eighty-year-old.'

'True enough. But I feel it in the bones, Dronsky. Our lead is still going to come from this list.'

'What are we hoping to do here, Chief?'

There are times, I know, when Dronsky worries I'm going off on the wrong tack. The truth is he's seen it happen. But this was different. 'What we're hoping to do here, Ilya,' I said, 'is to find that one of these names defected just before the Soviet Union crashed, went to

New York for a spell and then returned to Moscow. We need an expert on KGB defections. A Russian expert. Can you do that for me?'

Dronsky pursed his lips. 'I think so. Yes, I think I can manage that, Chief.'

On the southern approach to Moscow, the Voronov monastery has stood within a protective swallowtail rampart wall since the fifteenth century. A collection of cloistered stone buildings stands around a brilliantly red and gold painted seventeenth-century wooden church, the Church of Dimitry of the Blood, commemorating the murder of the Tsarevich, the son of Ivan the Terrible.

The priest who met us at the main gatehouse wasn't immediately recognisable as Dronsky's brother. But once I got past the beard, and the black robes of Orthodoxy, I could see the same squirrel cheeks and thick black eyebrows, the same lugubrious good-humoured smile.

'This is good of you, Father Nicolai,' I said as Dronsky introduced us.

He shook his head, the beard brushing his broad chest. 'We have been archivists here for six hundred years, Constantin. It's what we do.'

'Even during Stalin's time? You were archivists even then?'

He shook his head. 'You're right, of course. During Stalin's time all the archival material from our Great Library was buried in barrels lined with copper and goat skins. The priest-archivists were scattered throughout the Soviet Union and the monastery here became a private pleasure house for the KGB.' His dark eyebrows shot up, as Dronsky's did when making a point. 'But the archive survived. More than survived in fact because of a peculiar circumstance Ilya might not have recounted.'

I looked at Dronsky who shrugged. 'I left the grand tour to you, Kolya,' he said to his brother. 'You enjoy it.'

The priest smiled. 'It's true. I enjoy the irony of it. What happened was this. In their Lubyanka head-quarters, certain KGB records were marked *To Be Preserved For Ever*. They were personal records of defectors and their families and friends of their families. Thousands, in the paranoia of the times. When the Secret Police began to run out of archive space at the Lubyanka headquarters, they looked around them, and thought of their play palace here at the Voronov monastery. It had ample space. A tradition of storage of records, Church records of course. And now its shelves were empty. It was the ideal spot for torturers to transfer their dirty secrets. So by happy chance, an important part of the KGB archive was moved by truck here. And we, archivists as we've always been, inherited it all when we returned at the time of the Soviet collapse.'

'Good fortune,' I said.

'A small victory,' the priest said, 'in the bigger struggle for Russia's soul.'

'My brother likes to phrase it in these terms,' Dronsky said.

'I'm not alone, Ilya,' Nicolai said. 'Many people see Russia as a country culturally split between West and East. There are many who see we might have been a western country based on Novgorod or later St Peters-burg, a western country that was suppressed by an alien, Asiatic Moscow.' He shrugged. 'The struggle for a western Russia, which was lost to Ivan the Terrible with his massacre of the independent priests and burgers of Novgorod in the sixteenth century, has been fought and lost right up through Stalin's days into the present. Novgorod was the standard-bearer of a Western Russia.' We were walking through an alley of what might have been medieval shopfronts. Inside priests with aprons and rolled sleeves were beating copper for church ornaments, making pots and ecclesiastical dishes, painting simple ikons, carving furniture, weaving tapestries . . .

'East or West,' Dronsky said, 'will winning or losing these arguments make a difference to the ordinary Russian?'

'I really believe so,' his brother said. 'I'm an Orthodox priest, but I still think winning or losing this argument is *life and death* to the ordinary Russian.'

We stopped for a moment or two while Nicolai greeted one or other of the worker-monks. Then as we walked on, Nicolai turned to his younger brother. 'So what is it you want exactly, bratkin? On the phone you were playing the policeman.'

'I was in my office,' Dronsky said. 'With half a dozen pairs of ears wagging. Even now it's not wise to talk about defectors. The KGB may be long gone. But, as you well know, Kolya, its old friends and members keep a careful eye out for each other.'

The priest led us through another archway, a sort of inner rampart. The Church of Dimitry of the Blood rose red-walled and gold-domed, preposterous almost, above us. To the right, three sides of a square were made up by ancient two-storey stone buildings.

'The Great Library,' Nicolai said, with evident pride. 'The oldest manuscript we have is a twelfth-century copy of *The Bestiary of Isidore of Seville*. The latest is the private notes of the man in charge of the English spy, Kim Philby. They show what a traitor like Philby was *really* responsible for. Not the romantic view of the E. M. Forsters and Graham Greenes.'

Dronsky shot a glance at me that said: I hope you understand what he's talking about. I don't.

A last vicious blast of cold wind struck us as we entered the main doors of the library. Inside it was neither warm nor cold, a still even temperature maintained, I saw, by an arrangement of heated pipes that ran along the walls down at the level of the stone floor. Three long oak tables stood in line in the centre of the room. The shelving was all, I saw to my surprise, in stone, the filing cabinets below the shelves probably made in the carpentry shops

I had passed earlier. Would I be able to track down here one defector among the thousands who had fled West, one man that I knew little or nothing about, except that he was old . . . that he'd lived in New York City and had returned to Moscow – probably to die? True, we had Balkhin's list. Almost fifty names, for what they were worth.

We sat down at a long table and I explained the background of Katerina's murder, which the priest had, of course, heard about. I outlined the FBI information on the other women who had been similarly murdered by a contract killer and told him about my visit to the prison for the criminally insane in Connecticut. Then, summing up, I said, 'We have the information from Volodya Rinsky, just before he died, that the man who accepted the orders to kill these women was Russian, lived in New York for many years and has now moved back to Moscow. This can't be the man who *committed* the murders, he'd be far too old. So our thinking is that he took the contracts and passed them on to a much younger man.'

The priest nodded. 'I understand. But you also think the older man's an ex-KGB officer, or you wouldn't be here.'

'We can get closer than that,' I said. 'Volodya also told me he was a KGB man who defected in the last days of the Soviet Union. Afraid, according to Volodya, of reprisals from the families or friends of his victims.'

'Victims?' Father Nicolai said. He was thinking, head down, fingers smoothing the huge cross round his neck. 'This sounds more specific.'

I glanced at Dronsky. We were both trying to follow Nicolai's train of thought.

'If these are Volodya's words I'd make a guess that this man worked either in a KGB basement, an interrogator, a *boxer* they called themselves, or that he was a camp guard. Probably quite senior. In other words someone whose victims would know him by name. Would be able to identify him for a reprisal attack.'

'We have something else,' Dronsky said. 'A list of the connections of a man who almost certainly took out a contract on his lover, an actress here in Moscow. There are nearly fifty names on the list. One of them *could* be our man. Could be.'

The priest took Balkhin's list, studied it carefully, then began walking back and forth, stopping to open a wooden draw here, another there.

'So . . . is he traceable?' I said. 'Or are we going to have to narrow it down further?'

The priest crossed over to one of the banks of filing cabinets. 'I suppose at some point we'll get all this onto disc. For the moment though, you can come here and actually handle the files, see the original photographs.'

He slid out several wooden drawers, selecting files until he had three stacks on top of the cabinets in front of him.

Dronsky and I looked on. For myself I'd never seen a KGB personal file. Even in themselves they looked sinister. A thick grey board cover edged with red and a window on which the subject's name, rank and number was written.

Bringing the three stacks of files to the table where we were sitting he gave one to Dronsky, one to me and kept one to read for himself.

'There are roughly three dozen men,' he said, 'out of a hundred or more who might fit your basic facts. Some appear on your list from Balkhin. They all defected in 1980–90. They were what we call American defectors, men who presented themselves via an American intelligence officer, rather than say British or French or West German. If we divide the work we can get through a dozen files each without too much difficulty. That should cover the most likely cases.'

I looked down at the top file on my stack: Alexander Kochevnikov, Colonel. No: 6347127.

It was, I suppose, a not unusual case. A man of 52 in 1987, he had been an officer in Soviet interior towns most of his life. He had served in Gorky, in Smolensk, Tomsk, Rostov. And then suddenly in the 1980s he had been posted for security duties, spying on his friends in the Stasi in East Germany. What he'd seen there, the mild affluence, the widespread ownership of a cheap motor car, but perhaps most of all a nightly diet of West German television, had its effect. His children were by now in their twenties. His wife was back in Moscow. With his East German girlfriend and a bagful of middle-range Stasi/KGB documents, he had organised a visit to West Berlin and surrendered to the first American officer in uniform he had encountered.

There were a dozen reports, as his senior officer tried to account for what had happened, pathetic attempts of some low-ranking KGB general to save his own backside. Then there were clippings from the American print media, *Newsweek* and *Time Magazine*, the *New York Times*, the *Philadelphia Inquirer* and a dozen smaller newspapers which added the declassified American side of the story. And finally a report from a Soviet agent in Washington named Notre Dame which described his debriefing.

Kochevnikov had been debriefed at Langley and resettled, finally, in Seattle on a small pension. His new CIA name, supplied by Notre Dame, was Henry Krakov and a long fictional background was appended.

I could *feel* he was not our man. He was a minor administrator with no violence in his background. He defected under pressure from his girlfriend in East Germany. I studied his picture, looked into his dull grey eyes and just could not see this man as the spider at the centre of a web of assassination of seven women.

I looked up at Dronsky who was just closing a file.

His almost imperceptible shake of the head showed the same result, perhaps even indicated he was thinking along the same line as myself. Did we make a mistake asking an unworldly priest to help us trace a man like this?

I read through three more grey, red-bordered files. All three fitted a few of our outlines – lived in New York, returned to Moscow – but none had anything other than a run-of-the-mill KGB background in administration, mostly at the Lubyanka headquarters in Moscow or as junior officers at the Washington Embassy, although one of them appeared on Balkhin's list as a friend of the old goat.

My mind wandered as I opened the next file. Olchenko, Boris Ivanovich. I looked at it for a moment and stood up, the chair legs scraping the stone floor. I had to call Alex before she left for JFK. I told Dronsky and Nicolai I would be back in a moment or two and went out into the courtyard under the looming scarlet church. Listening to the phone ringing, I imagined Observatory Point and tennis courts and the sheer glitz of the party that first night I was there.

Five thousand miles away, Alex picked up. 'How's Russia looking?' she asked when I said her name.

'About the same – chaotic, dangerous, interesting . . .' I looked up at the blood-red church. '. . . colourful. But I'm not in Moscow at the moment.'

'You haven't forgotten I was coming tomorrow?' she said. There was a real anxiety in her voice.

'Of course I haven't,' I said, then realised that the anxiety was really about the operation scheduled for the day after her arrival. 'Listen Alex, I've been checking up on the Nevetsky Clinic. I met Nevetsky himself.'

'And did you approve?'

'Definitely. He's brimming with confidence. I think it's looking good.'

She was silent.

'Are you OK?'

'Can't wait.' She paused. 'I mean that,' she said. 'However scared I am. And I'm scared.'

'I can imagine.'

'Tell me about the notary.'

This was the part I wasn't looking forward to. I told her first about my visit with Dronsky to the waste ground her grandfather was supposed to own. 'Whatever was the real source of the money, Alex, it wasn't a straight value-for-money sale of that property.'

She mused on that for a while. 'We'll have to talk more when I get to Moscow, Constantin,' she said. 'What about the funeral arrangements?'

I described Katerina's final wish that she should be buried at Sin City. I was preparing to launch myself into the difficult task of telling Alex what Sin City was, when she cut me off.

'I know, Constantin,' she said.

'You know about Sin City? You know what it is?'

'Yes,' she said flatly. 'A vast whorehouse.'

'She told you.'

'Katerina had secrets from me but that wasn't one. She never tried to conceal her time in Sin City when she was young. She wasn't ashamed of what she did then. They were hard times for her. I think she was just proud to have survived them.'

I made arrangements to meet her at Sheremetevo Airport the next day. Olga and Stack would be with her, of course. What Ben Rushton and the rest of the funeral party were planning to do I had no idea at this moment.

'Listen, Alex, I have to go back.'

'Back where?'

'To the monastery,' I said. 'I'm taking instruction from a priest.'

'And growing a long black beard?'

She was laughing. I loved it.

Then the smile went out of her voice. 'You'll be there tomorrow, Constantin.'

'I'll be there,' I said.

41

I returned to the archive room and silently took my place.

'Nothing too promising so far, Chief,' Dronsky said. 'My list is all basically administrative or border guards.'

I got back to work.

It wasn't material you could read and dismiss from your mind. It lodged here. It evoked old stories, old ghosts. I read of men and women who had worked in enterprises, made friends, and denounced them for trifling indiscretions. The trial details and sentence were always appended: in Stalinist times ferocious labour-camp punishments for a joke about the Party or for being a distant relative of a suspected 'traitor'. Between the mid-Fifties and mid-Eighties you could see things becoming marginally easier. But the labour camps still thrived and the psychiatric hospital was developed as the prison camp of the Soviet future.

We worked long hours. When the light began to fade Father Nicolai renewed the vodka bottle. Dronsky sat back in his chair, stretching, yawning.

I accepted a small thumb of Nicolai's vodka and was about to tackle the last of the files before me when something stopped me. A sense of something left undone. I looked round at the piles on the long table. I shouldn't say this, definitely shouldn't say this to Dronsky, but some premonition, *post*monition perhaps in this case, was telling me I had brushed aside some thought, some idea that might be helpful.

I struggled back through the last two hours. Struggled through almost a century of the slime we Russians had made and lived in, like pigs in a sty. Olchenko! I had it. Boris Olchenko. The file I had been about to read before I went out into the courtyard to call Alex. I never finished reading it.

Disappointed, expecting a more significant epiphany, I got up and searched for the first pile of documents I had examined. Taking the Olchenko, Boris Ivanovich, file, I carried it to where I was sitting. But as I dropped it in place and small spurts of dust emerged from between its yellowing leaves, I began to feel a curious sense of excitement. All right, brothers, I know you'll find it hard to believe. But before I read that file, before I flicked open the grey, crumbling cardboard with the faded red border, I knew Boris Olchenko was my man.

I turned to the inner title page: Olchenko, Boris Ivanovich. (1929– ?) Entered service: 1947. Rank at time of disappearance: Captain. Date of disappearance: December 4 1983.

Born 1929. A gulf yawned within me. I had not noticed the date of birth. The chances were that he was long dead.

But the premonition was still strongly with me. I pulled the file back to me and began to read.

Boris Olchenko was born and grew up in a village outside Kharkov. The year of Olchenko's birth was the opening year of Stalin's merciless attack upon the peasantry. Land collectivisation brought starvation to untold millions, especially in the Ukraine, as activist youth groups rooted out peasant sacks of grain and turned families off the land and sent the adults to camps, the children to harsh orphanages.

I had to sit back and breathe in hard. Memories of stories told me of those days opened free passage to the phantoms of my imagination.

I was half aware that Dronsky and his brother were looking at me. 'A possibility,' I said as coolly as I could, and continued reading.

First posting: Sergeant. Special Anti-Guerrilla Unit in Ukraine. This was Russia's secret war. The war which the Soviet Union fought against the Ukrainian Nationalist Forces between 1944 and 1952 and which Stalin succeeded in keeping from the Soviet people and his supporters in the press and universities and coffee bars of the comfortable West. Even to this day few Westerners, I've noticed, know of the hundreds of thousands killed in battle or executed in the village main streets of the Ukraine.

Executed. So Olchenko's next role in the NKVD/KGB was a natural step. After suitable training, he became a travelling executioner. There were firing squads and there were hanging parties. My hand began to shake as I turned the pages. He became a specialist in the hanging of Ukrainians, men and women captured in the forests as they fought against the Soviet State. He was awarded First Grade Status.

A Specialist First Grade in hanging.

There were several faded photographs from the time. Olchenko as a sharp, ferret-faced young man, quick, intelligent you would say. Medium height perhaps. Light sandy hair curling from the side of a jaunty uniform forage cap. Wearing breeches and jackboots and, recognisable even in monochrome, the dark blue tunic of the NKVD soldier. Olchenko and others receiving instruction in the cutting and erection of a birch gibbet, two ten-foot 'A' frames with the hanging bar between. Other photographs showed snow deep on the birch trees, the hangman in his prime, pictures of Ukrainian Nationalists, mostly women, hanging from gibbets erected in farm or forest or the middle of burning town squares.

I turn the page. Olchenko alone now, older than the earlier pictures, in summer woodland, jacket discarded, shirtsleeves rolled up. Satisfaction shows in his hands-on-hip stance as he surveys his work. I recoil from the six dogs hanging there. But, most of all, I recoil from the sight of a small boy in the corner of the picture, laughing and pointing up to the improvised gibbet.

I am deeply moved. Small boys can be infinitely cruel and touchingly kind. They have both characteristics, or perhaps capabilities, in uncritical quantities. I can't erase the memory of my own son lost to me about the same age, six or seven. I look again at the haunting photograph. In my ears I hear the gibbet squeak, the boy's cry of excitement . . . but the voice, straining with pleasure, is my son's voice . . .

Nicolai and Dronsky are looking at me as I raise my head. They know I have something. For a moment I can't speak. I nod. Then when I've brought myself under control, I tell them. 'I've got him,' I say. 'Olchenko, Boris. Travelling hangman for the Soviet anti-guerrilla forces in the Ukraine.'

I turn the file and push it across the table. While they read, I get up and walk over to the arched window. I can see the church from here, glowing red in the weak autumn sunlight. In the United States students, young people like Rosalie from Ellis Island or professionals like Polly are gearing up for the most important election on earth. Millions of dollars' worth of commercials will be running on TV; a third of every page of newsprint will be devoted to the candidates; millions of phones will be ringing in millions of offices; posters chuntering off the presses; mountains of hamburgers and rivers of Diet Cokes consumed while polls are polled, guestimates are made, confidence rides high or hopes are dashed.

And I stand here, in a silent archival monastery, six hundred years old, and watch the sun set on the grotesquely beautiful church of Dimitry of the Blood. And try to push from my mind the image of Olchenko standing, in shirtsleeves and breeches, hands on hips, surveying the hanging by the neck of six swollen-tongued dogs. A demonstration of the hangman's art to his small son.

42

To my surprise the monastery owned a state-of-the-art photocopying machine. When we left Dronsky's brother to drive back into Moscow I carried to the car a thick wad of papers on Boris Olchenko's career.

Father Nicolai shook hands with me, and embraced Dronsky. He stood for a moment looking towards the distant shapes of Moscow's skyline, dark against smoky yellow clouds. 'Snow soon,' he said.

There seemed to be something infinitely sad about him. He stood for a moment with his arm round Dronsky's shoulder, as if reluctant to let him go. 'If there's anything else I can do . . .' he said to me.

'Nothing right now,' I said.

He was clearly disappointed. 'I like to see this archive used. Especially the section we were working on.'

'Foreign historians must come here?'

'They do. But Russians are perhaps too shamed. I think we are a people at odds with our past. If Russia is ever to emerge from the nightmare of its history, then Russians need to know what happened.'

'Do you think they care, the majority of our people?' I asked him.

I was willing him to say yes. But he pulled on his beard, shaking his head. 'No . . .' he said despairingly. 'And things can never get better until they do.' He thought for a moment. 'We're exiles, all of us. Exiles in our own land. Exile has played such a part in Russian life. Exile to Siberia, to the West. Compulsory exile, or voluntary defection. All Russians are exiles in some sense. Desperate to leave, desperate to stay. Exiles,' he repeated. 'All of us.'

Dronsky had a music station on the radio as we drove back to the city. Russian new country music – town boys reinventing folk songs which were tedious enough to begin with. Dull, almost unbelievably repetitive stuff, it always surprised me that he got anything from it.

'I don't understand where you're going, Chief,' he said, eyebrows furrowing. 'You believe Olchenko's our man?'

'The man who took the contracts, yes. He had the connections in New York and Moscow. Requests filtered through his criminal network.'

'And the killer?'

'I'm not sure yet,' I said. 'I think we have to know more about Olchenko's contacts in New York.' I reached in his top pocket and took a cigarette. He handed me his lighter and I lit it. I was feeling a building sense of triumph. We didn't know *who* had commissioned Katerina's death. We didn't yet know *why* for sure. But I felt certain these things would become clear as we unravelled Boris Olchenko's life. Again I looked down at the photocopied documents bound between card covers with rough string. When Dronsky went home I'd spread them out on the desk at Station 13. I'd open a clear bottle – and I'd find the answer.

The balalaika was close to driving me mad. 'Ilya,' I said with excessive politeness. 'Would you mind . . .'

He reached forward, cigarette dangling from his lips, and flipped stations. It was the evening news. An item on the war in Chechnya, the Fourth Chechnyan War, had just finished with another claim of a spectacular advance against the guerrilla army. And then a bombshell.

'From the United States,' the announcer said, 'news that could alter the course of next month's election for the presidency. Today a young chambermaid at the San Francisco Mallet Croxton Hotel claims on a leading talk show that last month she witnessed the presidential candidate for the American Unity Party, Ben Rushton, perform a sexual act with an unknown woman. The witness dates this act at barely a week before Rushton's wife was found murdered. Rushton, who will shortly be on his way to Moscow for the funeral of his Russian wife, has so far made no comment.'

A Russian commentator in San Francisco took up the story. 'San Francisco is no stranger to Russians and since the 1990s it has had a growing legal immigrant population. I'm standing on Russian Hill which goes back even further. When American Unity Party candidate Ben Rushton came to the city, his advisers undoubtedly had in mind the large number of Russian voters that a man with a Russian wife might be able to influence. While he was here he spoke twice to enthusiastic Russian audiences in Russian. But if the young chambermaid Elvira Santos is telling the truth, Mr Rushton's interest in San Francisco was not confined to politics . . .'

I could almost hear him licking his lips as he continued.

'Miss Santos's claim is that she was on duty at the exclusive Mallet Croxton Hotel when Rushton's party, which had reserved the whole sixteenth floor, arrived in San Francisco. About ten-thirty she had been going off duty when she paused, as she often did apparently, at one of the staff restroom windows to look out over the Golden Gate Bridge, on a misty night one of the great sights of this whole coast. Whether you consider she was rewarded by one of the Pacific coast's great sights depends on your view of life and current politics.'

I could hear his smirk. He summed up. 'Beyond the allegation that there was a sexual act in progress, and that presidential candidate Rushton was the male participant, we have no further details. But *what the chambermaid saw* may very well alter the whole outcome of the American election, due to take place in ten days from now.'

*   *   *

We stopped at the end of Dronsky's street in Fili. I declined his invitation to dinner and took the car on to Station 13 in Red Presnya. It was only when walking across the parking lot, the thick bundle of Olchenko files under my arm, that I realised how badly shaken I was by the news item from San Francisco. Sitting next to Dronsky, smoking his acrid pre-rolled cigarettes, the American presidential election seemed almost immeasurably distant. But alone, pausing on the uneven steps of the station, the full force of Elvira Santos's accusation came home to me. Sarah Rushton's name would emerge within hours. However *positively*, as Polly would say, the American electorate had reacted to Katerina's murder, it would not accept Ben Rushton's innocence in the murder of the niece he was sleeping with. He would become guilty, almost by osmosis. And with days only before the next and final Bernheimer, the Russian announcer was right when he gloatingly suggested what the chambermaid saw was going to lose Ben Rushton the American presidency.

I got into my office, or rather Dronsky's office, and locked the documents in the safe. The duty sergeant, who remembered me from when it really was my office, brought in a half-litre and a plate of lamb-filled pelmeni dumplings and sour cream. I fought off V. I. Lenin who considered all food introduced into Dronsky's office belonged first to him, then the mice he was too lazy to catch. When I had got him backed up against the rear wall, at a safe distance from the pelmeni, I started work.

My first call was to Hanratty. I'd got to him by a process of elimination. I didn't want to speak to anyone at Observatory Point, especially Alex, until I had some idea of how the news from the Mallet Croxton Hotel in San Francisco was being received.

Hanratty picked up after two or three rings. 'Vadim,' he said. 'Good to hear from you, Chief. Don't tell, you called to say how sorry you were to miss my retirement party last night. It was a blast. Nuclear. Listen, I'm now a free man.

I've been looking at the travel brochures. Russia's not so far away, uh?'

'Congratulations on the pension,' I said.

'But that's not why you called.'

'No.'

'OK. Your boss is in deepest shit. You heard?'

'I heard. I just wanted to get some bystander's take on how it's all going down there.'

'Bad, Chief. Bad for Rushton, two ways. First, the matrons of America are outraged that he was screwing someone else just days before his wife is garrotted. And when they find out it was his niece . . . The niece who has just been murdered . . . oh boy! Listen, I'm no political expert but as a voter I'd say your man's chances of election are out there in Long Island Sound, sinking for the third and last time.'

'It's the chambermaid's word against Rushton's.'

'She has *video*, Chief. The edited shocking and disgusting act will soon be available to all upright Americans who can't tear their eyes away. Elvira the chambermaid is what the newshounds are calling her. Actually, she's the senior floor manager at the hotel. Slim but busty, pretty with a sexy glint in her eyes. Great TV material.'

'So how could she *see* into one of the suites, for Christ's sake?'

'Architect's miscalculation is what the San Francisco mayor's office is hinting. The staff restroom window on all floors was extended three inches last summer to comply with a city ordinance. This gave more ventilation but also better views. Press up against the wall and you angle straight into the bedspace of the major suite on each floor, apparently.'

'So Elvira knew what she was doing?'

'Enough to take her camera. She's been fired from the hotel – but I don't suppose she's that worried.'

I popped a couple of pelmeni and cut the glutinous taste with the sharp sting of a good mouthful of vodka.

'What the hell you eating there?' Hanratty said.

'Dumplings,' I said. 'You mentioned *two* strikes against Ben Rushton.'

'OK. The first is political. Obvious. He's out on that one alone. But last night, my retirement night, the State Police lieutenant . . .'

'Miriam Cohen?'

'She'd had a few. Quite a few. She began whispering in my ear.'

'Whispers about the investigation? I can't imagine Miriam Cohen . . .'

'Didn't I mention we were in bed? Pillow talk, as I live and breathe.'

'Tell me. Just the public interest part,' I added, just in case.

'She says DeLane was never totally satisfied by Rushton's account. First he changed story. Second the fact that someone had gone over Katerina's music lodge, looking for what nobody knows. Third of course he's balling his niece.'

'No,' I said. 'Too much of a risk for him to put the finger on her too. Immediately after his wife's death.'

'You're assuming he's working alone, Chief. Let's say him and Yado are in this. Or him and Maddox. Maybe the second conspirator starts to panic and jumps the gun.'

I grunted uncertainly. I didn't like this speculation. I wanted to get back to my files. 'So, according to the amorous Miriam, what's DeLane's next move?'

'Her point was, up till now, DeLane couldn't get ballsy with a presidential candidate. So it became an investigation where the natural suspect is off limits. But now along comes the svelte and lovely Miss Elvira Santos. And the great American public will be ready to go along with any investigative steps against Rushton that DeLane orders.'

'Miriam Cohen whispered all that in your ear?'

'She also pinched my ass. Your man's finished, Chief. He'll be lucky he doesn't find himself on Murder One.'

I put down the phone and was already lifting the glass to my lips.

I called Observatory Point to talk to Alexandra and the phone was picked up right away. The call-screening system was at last in operation. It took me five full minutes to establish my identity with the woman Secret Service operator. When I was cleared I asked to be put through to Alexandra.

'Ms Alexandra won't be back here this evening,' the voice said. 'I understand her plans are to go straight on to the airport from the wedding reception.'

'Wedding reception? What wedding? Whose? Her wedding?' Even I caught the alarm in my voice.

'You didn't know? Mr and Mrs Stack were married this morning in Greenwich,' the voice said smugly.

'Olga,' I said. 'Olga married Stack?'

'First thing this morning. Quietly, given the circumstances.'

'Thank you . . .' I said. 'Thank you.'

Strange, the feelings that grip you when you're presented with a shock, surprise rather, like that. For a moment there I really did think Alexandra had been married, although who to, I suppose I had no time to guess. I replaced the phone and drank a thumb of vodka to my new brother-in-law, then went over to the safe and pulled out Boris Olchenko's life history.

43

A scrap of paper, part of a journal, or letter from Olchenko to someone equally enthusiastic about his work, described a mass hanging at Magadan in 1953. Twenty-nine women were to be hanged for staging a protest against habitual rape by the work-guards. Olchenko described, for his correspondent, the problems peculiar to the task. *Hanging a woman is more demanding than a simple male execution. Never forget these are public hangings conducted before the whole camp prison population, paraded for the occasion. Camp officers, even if personally convinced of the guilt of the condemned woman, will be on the lookout for anything disturbing in the conduct of the hanging. Vomiting should be achieved in her cell so that the condemned woman has an empty stomach when she is led out onto the camp square. Her hands must be tied and her skirt secured with a cord. She may well need to be gagged beneath the black hood.*

Having pointed to the difficulties when women prisoners are involved, it is worth adding that there is a certain satisfaction to be gained in surmounting them.

I saw Olchenko's face then, almost like a trick of the camera, fading in through the yellow page, a face sharp, eager, as he scribbled by lamplight his inadvertent confession ... *A certain satisfaction to be gained when women are involved* ... Reaching for the bottle I poured the last of my vodka. Who could he possibly have been writing to? Who, I wondered, was to be accorded this sinister confession of pleasure in his work?

Olchenko went on to cover the technical details of

acquiring timber for building the gibbets, the delicate question of the order of precedence – old before young? Ringleaders first, or last? And, the most troublesome detail to any public hangman, the sub-zero temperatures, the maintenance of the ropes in suitable condition. Of course, in all these matters Olchenko was experienced, as a travelling hangman one of the most experienced executioners of the Gulag administration. *My system*, he wrote to his correspondent, *is to take two kilos of lard, zhir, and carefully grease the brittle, frozen noose. I then place it, or them if it's a multiple hanging, under special guard overnight, in a hut with a stove which will bring the temperature to ten degrees above zero. Throughout the night before the hanging, which usually takes place at dawn, I allow the ropes to 'cook' gently in the zhir. This way, they become smooth and supple, unlikely to break under the strain, even in the most severe temperature. This is a system I have invented myself and you should know I have already received praise for it from a number of our most senior camp commandants. Finally you should know that it's my practice, once the condemned is cut down, to touch the eyes with a dab of wax or candle grease. I understand this was common in English hanging prisons in the past. I carry a stick of red sealing wax with me whenever possible. My conclusion is that the sealed eyes are a matter of both practicality and decorum. Inspecting officers do not appreciate staring into the dead eyes of hanged women.*

After this section in his file came the account of the day he gave himself up to the Americans, a section supplied and forwarded to Moscow from Washington by the Soviet agent Notre Dame. A note by a Soviet Military Intelligence, GRU colonel whose smudged name I couldn't read, told the reader: 'We were indebted to our agent, Notre Dame, (Captain Carla Love of US Military Intelligence) for the following. By chance she had flown into Berlin with a US team from Washington during the week of Olchenko's defection and was thus able to supply debriefing notes.'

I sipped vodka, wondering who this woman, Notre Dame, Carla Love, had been, young enthusiast or middle-aged believer, unable to let go of a dying faith? But I could find nothing more in the file on her.

During the debriefing Olchenko was perfectly candid:

Officer B: How many hangings did you carry out?

Olchenko: Without reference to my notes I can't say accurately.

Officer B: I make it eleven hundred hangings.

Olchenko: That could be the correct number.

Officer C: Of these how many were women?

Olchenko: Probably no more than ten per cent.

The man had hanged a hundred women. I got up and made myself some coffee, first pushing V. I. Lenin along the shelf where he lay with one of his front legs hanging down, between me and the Nescafé. He gave a faint hiss of disdain and settled down again further along the shelf. I looked at the clock over the cracked glass door. One-thirty a.m. Time to sleep for a couple of hours before I went to the airport to meet Alex. I was heavy-eyed with lack of sleep. Perhaps I had been wrong when I assured Dronsky that the Olchenko files contained more answers for us.

I made the coffee and sat back at the desk. V. I. Lenin opened his eyes no more than slits to convey his contempt at my time-wasting, and went back to sleep himself.

There were twenty or thirty pages of question and answer in the preliminary debriefing in Berlin. Mostly technical questions about the material Olchenko had brought with him, and the men who had been his superiors and subordinates in KGB, Minsk. Then a dozen or so questions about his family. My eyes flicked to the end.

Officer B: What was your relationship with your wife?

Olchenko: I put her out. Sent her away. *(Pause)* Beatings did nothing for her. She was a slut. Known in the neighbourhood. She consorted with other men in my absence.

Officer B: What happened to her?

Olchenko: I believe she was last heard of in a soldiers' brothel somewhere. They gave soldiers' whores three years.

Officer B: And then what?

Olchenko: Disease.

Officer B: Among the documents you brought with you was a journal, detailed, addressed to an intimate . . .'

Olchenko: Correct.

Officer B: In it you describe, in detail, methods, even the pleasure you derived from your . . . profession. Particularly, on the days you were required to hang women prisoners.

Olchenko: I have pointed out it was a more demanding task.

Officer C: So who was the journal intended for? It dates from the 1950s, it's obvious you put a lot of effort into it.

Olchenko: Correct.

Officer C: So who was it for? Who was it intended for?

Olchenko: For my son, of course. For the son, Vikenty, I hoped one day to have.

I have found the killer. Beyond the fact that he was once, long ago, called Vikenty, or was once intended to be called Vikenty, I know nothing about him. But I have found the murderer of Katerina and Sarah, and the dupe, Luke Bassenger. I pick up the photograph of the dogs hanging and the little boy laughing, pointing. I can almost hear his piping voice.

I get up from my desk. Only movement can control the agitation I feel. Many men, I suppose, might write to the son they sometime hope to father. But what sort of man writes, to the son he dreams of having, detailed notes on how best to hang a woman?

I sit in the half-darkness of my old office and call DeLane. I have no idea what time it is where DeLane is at this moment but he answers his cellphone almost immediately. I give him the Olchenko name. With an effort I tell him about the boy Vikenty, and I can hear DeLane taking a deep, deep breath.

'So Volodya came through before his heart attack,' he says, satisfaction pouring through cyberspace.

'*I* came through,' I remind him. 'Both with Volodya and here in Moscow.'

'Credit,' he says, 'where credit's due.'

'So now what about you, DeLane? Now we have the original Russian name of the defector, how quickly can you get me the name your intelligence people resettled him under? His name and his son.'

'You sure it's the boy?'

'Certain.'

'OK, I'll go to work on it.'

'DeLane,' I say. 'Don't just go to work on it. Spend every single waking second on it.'

I cut him off and stare into the deep shadows climbing the walls. The green lamp casts a warm glow onto the scratched desk. V. I. Lenin's eyes gleam a smoky yellow as he lies, a dark shape, on the shelf opposite. I cross my arms and lower my head. I have a few hours before I am to drive out to the airport to meet Alex. But I'm too restless, brothers, too disturbed by what I have read in those KGB papers, about the corruption of a seven-year-old boy.

44

Then more thoughts strike me. Motive, I start worrying about in the middle of the night, and it becomes very clear to me there can only be one motive now for the two murders, Katerina and Sarah. It's to protect Ben Rushton, of course. But ... who is it who's prepared to pay the cash price of two murders to protect Rushton? Lots of people, Katerina once said. And Sarah herself agreed. But plain, ordinary common sense must make anyone start with Rushton himself.

And now this woman at the San Francisco hotel, Elvira Santos, has come forward with her film. Is *she* safe? Going public with video of Sarah and Rushton in bed together is like inviting the hangman into your loft. Yet Elvira Santos can't know that. I feel sick in my stomach. Will DeLane tell her? I try to call him but this time there's no immediate pickup. I'm invited to leave a message and I leave enough to get him to take some steps to protect Elvira Santos. I hope.

My mind's racing. My stomach's heaving. I'm not the man to be at the centre of a murder investigation. I'm not like Dronsky, imperturbable. At this moment I'm not sure I'm even breathing regularly and my tinnitus is like a peal of handbells in a great empty cathedral.

I look across at the shelf where V. I. Lenin is lying. He has lifted his head as if following my thoughts. He gets up onto his two front legs, sitting high like an Egyptian cat-god. He hikes his shoulders in a way that cats have. Sometimes it seems to mean: worrying will get you nowhere. This time it is different. I sense that about it. What V. I. Lenin is saying is – it's possible.

'Possible,' I say to myself, 'that Ben Rushton himself is the instigator, the man who has taken out the contracts. He has most to lose.'

Then I realise that I'm talking to a cat. To V. I. Lenin, for God's sake. To a cat who wouldn't be among my favourite hundred cats even if I were an irredeemable felidophile. Which I'm not.

Vodka cures. In Dronsky's desk I find several two-hundred-and-fifty-gram bottles of fifty per cent spirit. Guaranteed seven years old. I open a quarter-litre and tip the bottle. My tongue, roof of my mouth, insides of my cheeks, all sting and burn. I swallow one gulp that nearly chokes me. I count ten and take another. The pain is exquisite. But I'm back on track. Perhaps vodka kills more than it cures. But tonight it has restored something in me.

Not my faith in Ben Rushton. He is not the man I once believed in. But that doesn't make him a killer.

I improve. Two years ago I would have jumped him with the certainty that he arranged the killing of his wife. Now I'm only nursing suspicions. But they're suspicions that won't go away.

I drive out to the airport in the pre-dawn. I drive slowly, partly because I have time and need to think. Partly to take in the people camped on either side of the highway. Foreign medical teams were rumoured to be setting up for TB vaccination in the morning. But Dronsky had told me that most of these teams were not German or French or Italian as they claimed, but Russian *racketiry* employing smart young girls with a few words of a foreign language to charge fifty dollars for a quick injection of water. Clean water if you're lucky.

Smoke from the roadside campfires drifts across the road from the airport. Inside the building glittering boutiques are open even in the middle of the night. I check the arrivals board. The flight's on time. Landing in five minutes. Lights flash to announce a plane has just landed from Berlin, one from Rome, and a third from Washington – so Alex and party from New York will have to wait until Customs clear the other arrivals. I buy myself coffee and a croissant 'shipped in from Paris an hour ago'. Inside the Tsar Ivan Café the atmosphere's warm and opulent and comfortable. Outside the building, the poor wretches are singing Russian folk songs round their campfires.

I'm sitting there watching a stream of German and Italian businessmen come through. And then a trickle of Americans, obviously from the Washington flight, when my eye is caught by a group of similarly dressed big men, black overcoats and black fur hats. They have stopped in a half-circle just before they emerge into the foyer. I'm curious, then see a short stocky man in dark green overcoat adjusting his fur hat in a mirror held by one of the encircling group – Jack Yado.

And behind him, to my surprise, Clinton Maddox is walking with Hanratty ambling by his side. Hanratty in parka and with cigarette in the corner of his mouth, staring aggressively at the Russian signs.

I get up and cross to the arrivals area. Yado and his team have disappeared into the elevator which will take them to the hospitality rooms above. Maddox and Hanratty are left to shuffle forward behind a hundred or so other passengers.

I wave to Hanratty. He sees me and edges over, Maddox behind him.

'What's going on?'

'Hi Chief. This is my new boss.'

'I asked Hanratty to join my team,' Maddox says irritably. 'Obviously as a Unity Party man I have no official entitlement to protection.' He gestures towards the Secret Service agents disappearing into the elevator with Yado. 'In the circumstances, I feel the need to provide my own.'

'After what happened to Sarah Rushton,' Hanratty says, his voice heavy with solicitude, 'Mr Maddox was impressed by the need for an experienced personal protection officer.' He turns away from Maddox and rolls his eyes at me. 'Mr Maddox invited me to fly down with him to Washington and take this trip with him.' He flicks his cigarette end into a sand bowl. 'An offer I was honoured to accept.'

Over Hanratty's shoulder I see a group from the New York flight being escorted to the VIP elevator – Alex, Olga and Stack and Polly. Maddox is fuming at what he feels is a notable slight to him. 'Polly,' he says. 'How the hell does she rate the treatment?'

A Secret Service man stops me as I move towards Alex. There's no doubt about their efficiency but their manner can be a little brusque and overdramatic for my taste. I recognise him from Observatory Point. He recognises me. He swings me firmly by the arm until I'm facing him.

'We've reserved two floors of the Royal American Hotel. You know it?'

'I know it.'

'Good. These are the travelling arrangements, Vadim,' he says. 'You have a vehicle?'

'I have.'

'You take Alexandra Rushton and Polly Mason. We have an American limo for Mr Yado. Mr and Mrs Stack will ride in the escort car bringing up the rear.'

'What about Maddox and Hanratty?'

Maddox has overheard. 'You have to understand we're part of Mr Yado's party,' he says. 'We're booked at the same hotel.'

The Secret Service man looks at him a moment. 'OK, sir. We'll take you in the escort car. Mr Hanratty can go with you, Vadim.'

'Hold it,' I say. 'I can't take three people and their luggage. I have a Renault Economy, not a Rolls-Royce.'

'OK,' he nods crisply. 'The limo can handle the extra

luggage. Just so that you know. We're regarding this whole movement – of all or any of the principals – as fraught.'

'Fraught.'

He gives me his crisp, Secret Service nod. At that point, neither of us knows how right he may be.

In the small Economy we're cramped. Alex sits next to me, one suitcase on her knee. The others have already been transferred to the limousine. Hanratty and Polly are in the back, Hanratty at least enjoying the enforced proximity.

It's the first chance I've had to talk to Hanratty without Maddox there. 'Good to see you here,' I tell him.

'I retired, Chief,' he says. 'And like I say, the next day Maddox calls. Come over, he says, I got a proposition for you. So it's personal bodyguard, the guy's nervous as hell. Are you ready to leave for Russia, he asks. I say what's to stop me now? And before I know it I'm flying Learjet down to Washington – and on here.' He peers out at the campfires by the roadside. 'Looking around me, I'm not sure it's the best move I've made in my life.'

Polly is not speaking but in the rear-view mirror I can see she's moved by the plight of the people that line the road. 'Maybe for the first time,' she says, 'politics mean more to me than percentages.' After that she keeps quiet.

I turn to Alex. Obviously she can't see much, can't see the shivering people gathered round the fires, just perhaps pinpoints of light at ground level.

'People, Alex,' I say. 'People waiting, hoping for a vaccination they think they can trust for their children.'

She knows what I mean. Tears well in her eyes. We bounce over potholes, deep scars in the asphalt that could wrench the steering from your hands.

'I've hardly been back in Russia for an hour and I'm beginning to feel the desperation,' she says.

She asks me if there's still much damage from the recent Civil War and I tell her it depends which area of Moscow you're in. The northern suburbs and Red Presnya suffered the worst of the shelling when the Nationalists besieged the city. The rubble's been cleared from the streets now but in some areas virtually no rebuilding has been done. Most of central Moscow, I tell her, looks like a vast rubble heap criss-crossed by glittering streets of cafés, jewellers, fashion houses and auto showrooms. Unreal city.

We ride on in silence for five minutes, even longer. She looks straight ahead, perhaps wondering, as I found myself thinking in New York, whether she could ever again live in this strange land. It's now what? Nearly twenty years since she's been here. Her blinding was a millennium present.

We have crossed the railway at the side of the Belorussian Station and have turned left into the streets beyond Tverskaya which I calculate will bring us down on the Garden Ring just above the Royal American Hotel. Each time I turn I check in the rear-view mirror to see that the limousine is with us. But the driver, a young Uzbek, keeps tucked just behind us, thirty or forty metres back, the Secret Service car behind that.

Away from the airport the drive is quieter. I ask Hanratty: 'The threatening call to Alex, did you find out how anybody managed to get through to her?'

'There's only one way it could have happened, Chief,' he says. 'We have to face it. It was an in-house call.'

'Someone in Observatory Point?' I am aghast, in the pristine meaning of the word. Struck with terror. The man, the Russian-speaker, who had threatened her on the phone was *inside* the house. No hoaxer. No sadistic joker. No joker at all.

'I've had no time to tell you,' Alex says. 'There was another call before I left for the airport. Just moments before I left.'

'In Russian again?'

'Yes. Not fluent but good enough.'

'He said the same things?'

'He said he was only thinking of me. Of my welfare. He said that if I went through with the operation I would follow my mother to the scaffold.'

For a moment I am speechless. The man who killed Katerina was in the house. Announcing that his next victim was Alex.

We have just turned a corner and are running past a small park. I glance in the mirror, waiting for the other car to make the turn. My attention is caught momentarily by the leafless trees of the park, black skeletons against the city lights. Then suddenly the trees, the railings, a phone kiosk, are all lit up by a bright yellow light. Followed a fraction of a second later by the dull thud of an explosion that opens into a lion's roar.

And round the corner behind us the limousine buckets on two wheels, flame pouring from the back. As it crashes into the iron railings of the park a figure, perhaps two, are thrown from it. It's difficult to be sure in the balloon of black-edged flame. Then, as the Secret Service car brakes towards it, it explodes again, a harsher sharper crack. Alex, I realise, is screaming at me.

I brake and swing the car round. 'The limousine's crashed,' I tell her. 'It's on fire. The escort car's crashed too – but everybody's out, I think.'

I make a half-circle in the wide, empty street and drive towards the burning wreck.

Alex is calm suddenly. 'I can see the flames,' she says. 'What about Olga and Stack, are they out?' She has forgotten Yado in the limousine. She leans forward towards the windscreen as we pull close, staring without speaking.

I stop the car about fifty metres from the burning wreck. To Alex I throw one of those superfluous pieces of advice like stay in the car or keep your head down. I am running now across the road at a diagonal towards the burning limousine. I am coming at it side on. The tyres have caught, two bright rings of flame. I see the outline of the driver. He is burning, his head and shoulders bright as the tyres. In the back is thick darkness and, from a broken window, pluming black smoke.

I change direction and run round to the other side. I stop as the heat scours my face. I run forward ineffectually, two, three, four steps, aware even now that I am making a gesture in case anybody is watching. Smoke catches the back of my throat, sharp as acid. Is it burning flesh I'm smelling?

I crouch in fear. There is someone on the ground just paces in front of me. He is writhing in agony with smoke rising from his back, from his hair. I hesitate in terror. It's too late, he'll be dead in seconds.

Then *act*, something says. Certainly not courage. But equally not the mindlessness of the automaton-hero. I pull the front of my jacket across my face and run forward. One, two steps, then stop in disbelief at the tangible wall of heat. I am about to turn when the blackened figure moves again. I throw myself forward, grip a wrist and turn my face from the heat. Hanratty comes hurtling through the curling smoke and flame. He takes the other wrist. Like hunters hauling a carcass, we run, dragging someone across the road.

The heat hits me. I can barely breathe. I look back and see the burning pitch on the road surface is spreading towards us more quickly than we can drag the man free. I am nearly on my knees. Hanratty pushes me aside, towards the cooler air, and bends to take the man round the chest. With his heels trailing, his clothes smoking, Jack Yado is pulled to safety.

Alex and Polly are in front of me. Polly has taken off her coat and throws it at me. Away from the heat, I can breathe again. I wrap the coat round Yado.

Hanratty has gone back into the smoke. Secret Service

men from the following car are shouting but I miss the meaning of words. Olga, thrown from the escort car, is lying in the gutter. Stack is beside her. He looks up and shakes his head at me but I can see Olga is moving, struggling to move.

Somewhere in my pocket I have a phone. I can't think of Moscow's emergency number so I call Dronsky. Quickly I tell him what has happened and listen to his calm voice. Then I close the line and look down at Yado. Polly and Alex, using God knows what sight and instinct, have made him as comfortable as possible. Alex is kneeling, holding his head, talking softly to him. Polly is kneeling beside her. He's breathing and miraculously his face, at least, has not been badly burned. But he is bleeding from the nose or ears. His Secret Service escort, I know, is still in the blazing car. Alex must know this too because she asks nothing about him or the driver as I kneel beside Yado praying for an ambulance to arrive.

But it's Dronsky who arrives first. Ambulances will be there in minutes, he tells us. And while he's speaking there's a klaxon somewhere behind us and blue lights flashing. Dronsky takes charge of everything. He starts to give directions to the paramedics. Yado is taken in one ambulance. Olga is carried to another, and I see Hanratty, limping, being helped by Polly towards it. I walk Alex back to our car.

'Olga . . .' she begins. Then tries again. 'Olga . . .'

'She'll pull through.' I parade the cliché, but she's too upset to notice. 'Stack's with her. She'll be on her way to the hospital in minutes.'

'What happened?' she asks. 'Did the limousine driver lose control as he took the corner?'

'I didn't see,' I tell her. 'Something like that. It must have been.' I try to sound as if I mean it.

'And Olga's car crashed into the back of the limousine? Is that right?'

'We'll know when the police have been,' I say. 'They'll check tyre marks, take measurements.'

'But there was an explosion. I heard that clearly.'

I'm trying to hurry her away. If it was a bomb, there was a target. Maybe Yado. Maybe Alex.

She drops her head forward as she walks. 'Let's pray Olga will come through.' I sense she means *pray*, not like I pray which is really just wishing with fervour, usually for something that will directly benefit me. She means pray – and I suddenly realise that Alex believes in God.

We get into the car and sit there smoking, windows open, I, at least, watching the fire consume the limousine and the two human beings inside it. Yado has been lifted and placed in the ambulance, Olga in a second ambulance. When the fire engine arrives, firefighters tackle the flames with foam and cool the road surface with hose water.

As the smoke begins to clear I see two squad cars are on the scene. Dronsky is talking to a militia sergeant from the leading car, giving him some details which the militiaman writes down in his notebook. After a few minutes he takes one last look at the hissing, sodden wreck and walks over to us, bending at the passenger window to acknowledge Alex, then signals that he wants to talk to me. I get out of the car and we walk together a few yards to the street corner.

'What happened, Chief?' is his first question.

I shake my head, then push the words out of my parched throat. 'It was already burning as it came round the corner, burning from the first explosion.'

'There were two explosions?'

'One just before they turned the corner. Then a second, a more powerful, sharper sound as the car cracked and disintegrated.'

'OK,' he says slowly. 'What are you going to do?'

'About Alexandra? Take her to the hotel.'

'She'll need time to get over this, won't she? A few days at least. There'll be no operation until then.'

I go back to the car and get in behind the wheel.

'Wait,' Alex says, 'where are we going?'

'To the Royal American. I'll take a room next to yours.'

She shakes her head. 'No,' she says, firmly. 'I want to go to the Nevetsky Clinic.' She pauses. 'Now more than ever. You must understand that, Constantin.'

Yes, I think I do. She wants to take part. In whatever's going to happen in the next days or weeks, she wants to take part as fully and with the least physical impediment as possible. Yes, I think I understand that.

We go to a twenty-four-hour café and drink cups of coffee and talk about Olga. I've called the nearest hospital twice but they can't locate her. Alex makes no attempt to ask me any more about what happened, how it happened, was it an accident? She has an extraordinary capacity to contain her curiosity, to listen and think before she speaks.

She asks me about Olga and I tell her the truth. That she was thrown clear of the crash. That she was alive, moving when Stack was bending over her. That there's every chance that she's received very little in the way of injuries.

She relaxes. She begins to tell me stories about Olga that reveal a whole different aspect of my sister which I completely missed. I only saw, from the much younger brother's point of view, what I took to be the domineering, jackbooted manner. Alex saw something that I hardly caught more than a flash of on Long Island, her real affections, the struggle she had to show them. She must, Alex says, have had a hard life.

I tell Alex about her, as a teenager, permanently assigned by my mother to stand in line at the butcher's or grocery store. My mother had a powerful, a selective streak of sadism. My father, and Olga, suffered more than I did. Once, I remember, in a trivial family argument, she sneeringly hinted that Olga, fat and not beautiful as she herself had been, was a foundling, was not her child. I was seven years old at the time and Olga a young adult, but I remember the crushing effect it had on her.

Alex is dabbing tears from her cheeks but she wants me to go on. She wants to know more about the life Olga never talked about. I tell her about Olga not long before she left for the US, a snow-sweeper on the streets of Murmansk, or working the docks, chipping ice from the steel hawsers of the fishing fleet. Yes, I say, to Alex, Olga had a hard life. A very Russian life.

And then I think of Alex's own Russian life and swallow my coffee, quickly, choking a little on it to help me get control of the emotions welling up in my throat, too.

45

Half an hour later, we crossed the courtyard of the Nevetsky Clinic. I guided Alex towards the concrete stairway then up to the double, ochre-painted doors at the top. 'The building's a Seventies or Eighties clinic for the *nomenklatura* of the day,' I told her as I rang the bell. 'Decorated hideously in reddish paint. Inside it's clean, efficient, comfortable enough. Maybe not quite like the American hospitals you're used to . . .'

She put her hand on my arm. 'Listen,' she said. 'I know what you're doing, Constantin. And thanks, but it isn't necessary. I've met Dr Nevetsky. I know he's the best chance I've got.' She smiled. 'Whatever his hospital looks like, I shall only see on the way out.'

'You win,' I said.

We were taken through registration by a young man in a pale blue short-sleeve medical shirt and led up to the first floor where Alex was assigned to a room. Room 12 was large, clinical, dominated by fittings for medical equipment and a high white bed. Three bad cracks ran down the wall and a fresh coat of white paint would have helped. But Alex was right, of course. She could only possibly see any of this on her way out.

'Dr Petrov will examine you first, Madame,' the male nurse said with tsarist courtesy. 'Dr Petrov is a generalist. His examination is to confirm that you are fit for tomorrow's operation.'

I turned to Alex. 'You'll make sure you tell him.'

'The explosion? I don't see it's relevant.'

'If you don't . . .'

'You will.' She nodded. 'OK, I'll tell him. But it won't make any difference.'

I waited outside while Petrov carried out his examination. As he left he stopped in the corridor beside me, young, plump with metal-rimmed glasses.

'She's OK for tomorrow?' I asked.

'She's a fit young woman. She tells me she plays tennis.' He shook his head. 'Remarkable.'

'But she also told you what happened on the way here.'

'She told me. I just called Dr Nevetsky. He wants to speak to you.' He gestured. 'Floor above.'

'He's here already?'

'Yes. Something must be troubling him.' He left me staring out at the smudge of dawn fire in the eastern sky. There was a greyness in the air which you couldn't yet call light, but dawn was not far off. I turned and climbed the stairs.

I found Nevetsky in his office. Two dark green shaded reading lamps threw spools of light round the desk, leaving deep shadowed areas between. He was standing beside a fireless fireplace, his head and shoulders in shadow. 'Come,' he said. He moved forward into the light and I was struck by his furrowed cheeks and the pinkness around his eyes. My glance slipped to the glass of vodka on the mantleshelf. He pointed to a tray on the desk with a bottle and glasses. 'Help yourself,' he said. 'Don't look shocked. I've a clear day. No operations.'

'Dr Petrov said you wanted to see me.'

He nodded, then turned his back to me and leaned both forearms on the high mantleshelf. His head dropped forward onto his clenched fists. 'Constantin,' he said, speaking to the wall a few centimetres from his nose. 'You said I could call you that?'

I didn't like the atmosphere in the room. The atmosphere he was creating. I felt the total difference from when I was last here. The belief in himself, the belief in the success of the operation that he had conveyed, had seeped away. He was, I think, about to tell me something about Alex's operation. Something bad.

I moved impatiently. 'You've got something to tell me. Go ahead.'

'You're right.' He took his glass and straightened up, turning towards me. 'You haven't poured yourself one,' he said, suddenly active, fussing towards the vodka tray on the desk. 'After what happened on the way here . . .' He stopped. 'Or I can get you coffee sent up?'

First light outside was pale against the windowpanes.

'In a moment,' I said. 'First tell me what you have to say.'

His small ruse to delay the moment had to be abandoned. 'Yes. It's only fair.'

I waited.

'I think it would be unwise to go ahead with the operation,' he said deliberately. 'That's to say,' he added, 'I think Alexandra will decide not to go ahead when given the full facts.'

My stomach churned. Disappointment surged through me. In a fraction of a second I saw four, five snapshots of Alexandra receiving the news, from the first stunning shock to her expression as she absorbed, with that terrifying dignity she could muster, yet another of life's devastating blows.

I looked at Nevetsky. He was watching me silently, with unfeigned sympathy. He came forward and poured a heavy thumb of vodka. Silently he handed me the glass.

'The full facts . . .' I took a good tip and swallowed hard. Then another to help me pick up the thread. 'The full facts, you said. What are the full facts, Doctor?'

'There are complicated considerations,' he said carefully, eyeing me from under his brows.

'Are you talking about the accident? Or new medical data?'

'No . . . yes, in a sense.' He looked at me, hopelessly flustered.

I wasn't going to take this. 'Had you already decided not to operate? Even before you heard what happened on the way here?'

He sat down, heavily, at his desk. His eyeglass clinked gently on the top button of his waistcoat. 'My assessment of the medical risk was too . . . optimistic.'

I stood staring down at him. I knew he was an unusual, even a strange man. I also knew he was lying. And I thought I knew, without being absolutely sure, that he wanted me to *know* he was lying. I pulled up a chair and sat, opposite him, at the desk, leaning forward towards him. 'You've just discovered, or become aware of additional risks?'

'Let's say the eye is at the same time both a simple and a delicate organ, Constantin . . .'

'You saw her in New York a month ago,' I said harshly. 'You received the full reports and conclusions of her American ophthalmologists at the same time. You made your decision – it was positive. You built up a mass of hope, as you would have in any blind person. She travels all the way to Moscow. And now you tell me you've changed your mind. *When* did you change your mind, Doctor? *What* changed your mind?'

He poured himself vodka, a small thumb this time, restrained. 'It's a question of medical facts . . .'

I pushed my face closer. 'New medical facts? How could there have been? You haven't seen her since New York.'

'No new medical facts. You're right, how could there have been?' He sipped his drink, winced at the burn on his tongue and looked straight at me across the desk. 'I'm asking you to suggest to Alexandra that she should not go ahead with the operation. Will you do that?'

'On what you've told me so far – no.'

'I'm telling you, Constantin, *I* can't go ahead.'

'But you won't tell me why. You're asking me to go down and shatter every hope she has of recovering some of her sight. What the hell's happened? Has someone been to see you?'

I threw it at him. I knew there was someone in America who wanted to prevent the operation. But I had no reason to believe there was someone in Moscow who equally wanted that. I think I said it more as a measure of my frustration, more perhaps to force him into saying *something*.

He was standing now, we both were, on different sides of the desk. 'Accept what I've said for God's sake,' he said in a low, controlled voice.

I could see he was trapped in a cat's cradle. Of his making, of someone else's – I couldn't guess. 'No,' I said. 'I won't accept it. Tell me what's happened.'

This man was brave. His dark eyes held mine. 'Two men were here less than an hour ago. They gave . . .' he smiled wanly, 'what are, in Moscow, impeccable references. One of the city's biggest criminal names. One of the men who came here even carried a photograph of himself, with his arm draped round his master.'

I didn't ask who this was. I knew there was no chance of him telling me. And no chance, under any circumstances, of discovering who had hired him to send his thugs. Instead I asked him, 'What did the emissaries ask you to do?'

'They had a range of demands,' he said coolly. 'The first, the preferred option was that I should let her die under the anaesthetic.'

I was rigid with shock. 'Christ on the Cross,' I said. 'They wanted her *dead*?'

His face was taut, white. 'I explained that medically it was certain that I would be discovered to have done it deliberately. Not true of course, but it was enough for them to step down to their next most favoured demand.'

'That was?'

He lifted his eyebrows. 'To make sure that the operation was unsuccessful. Even to destroy what little sight she has.'

I was cold. My hands, my cheeks.

'Drink,' he said.

I shook my head.

'Is this a woman you love?' he asked.

I thought about that. 'Yes . . .' I said. 'I think I do.'

'What will you tell her?'

'That depends on you.'

He walked back towards the fireplace. Stood with his back to it. 'The plan was for Alex to leave for Murmansk for her mother's funeral as soon as she had recovered here?'

'That was the plan.'

'I will propose to you an alternative. Unrelated to these events, I was in process of moving my practice to Paris. You'll be surprised to learn that a surgeon can travel light. All the necessary equipment will be found in a good modern hospital anywhere in the world. It just means moving forward my plans to leave Moscow.'

'You want to do the operation in Paris?'

'No. Alex is going to Murmansk for her mother's funeral. By good fortune there is one of Russia's best equipped hospitals there. The Lermontov Infirmary.'

'My wife was once a surgeon there,' I said with effort.

'Your wife? The way you speak . . .'

I nodded. 'Yes, she's dead. Three years ago.'

His hand went to his forehead. 'Vadim . . . of course. Dr Natalya Vadim. I once met her when I was operating at the Lermontov. She . . .'

'Was murdered,' I said.

He stood for a moment without speaking. 'Tell Alex that certain instruments have not arrived on time,' he said smoothly. 'And after the operation can we agree that whatever the real result you will announce a failure, if anything a reduction in sight.'

'Of course.'

'It'll give me time to leave for Paris,' he said. 'Something I should have done years ago. But I was reluctant. Reluctant to leave Russia.'

'I know that reluctance,' I said.

He nodded purposefully. 'So . . . There'll be a delay obviously. But a day at most. I'll operate at the Lermontov day after tomorrow, at noon.'

I went down to room 12. A militia sergeant stood guard on the door. Dronsky was with him. 'I've just been talking to Alexandra Ivanova,' he said. He tapped his notebook. 'I've got the basic facts.' He stood, running his hand back and forth across his brush-cut. 'Your sister . . .' he began.

I waited.

'She'll be all right. She's at the Veterans Hospital. Her husband is with her.'

'And Yado?'

'Mr Yado's critically ill.'

'You mean he won't recover?'

'God knows, Chief.'

From a shelf behind him Dronsky produced a small strong black coffee. He nodded towards Alexandra's door. 'I'll wait for you here.' He gave a muted smile. 'She's a lovely girl. She's got courage, uh?'

I drank the coffee in one mouthful and went in. Alexandra was watching, or listening to, TV. She sat barefoot, wearing a short white robe. Somehow, by instinct, she was aware of my glance towards her brown legs. 'The hospital robe's a little short, perhaps,' she said, standing.

'Or the legs a little long.'

She gave me a brief smile. I could see how much the night's events had drained her. 'What did Dr Nevetsky have to say?' she asked, switching off the television.

I hesitated only a moment. Then explained, I hope as

smoothly as Nevetsky had to me, that instruments had not arrived. That he had agreed to operate in Murmansk.

'That's extraordinary,' she said. 'Extraordinary.'

'Not for him,' I said. 'He operates in hospitals all over the world. By chance he knows the Lermontov in Murmansk particularly well.'

She shook her head, still baffled. 'Very well then . . . Very well. And when will this be?'

'The day after tomorrow,' I said. 'You'll be scheduled for midday. Russian doctors call it the lucky hour.'

46

I left Dronsky and drove to the Veterans Hospital near the Belorussian Station. It's known as a hospital for veterans, but in fact it's a private clinic for the Moscow wealthy.

It was still not six in the morning but it took me almost an hour to push my way through the reporters and to establish my identity as Olga's brother. Even so I was given a tough-looking male nurse to escort me up to her floor.

Olga occupied a room with Stack at her bedside. I didn't stay long. She was greatly distressed that Alexandra was going on ahead of her to Murmansk. But she insisted she would obtain her discharge at the earliest possible moment. Her back had suffered some strain, one hip was bruised. 'Here . . .' She pulled down the sheet. I averted my eyes . . . She would survive, that much was more than evident. I left Stack, infinitely attentive as ever, and went down the corridor to see Hanratty.

'Goddam knee,' he said from his bed. 'They're checking it out, but God only knows when I'll be able to get back up. How's Yado?'

'I only have press reports. He's in a bad way.'

'American politicians live for ever.'

'Kennedy didn't.'

'Sure.' He was quiet for a moment. 'In the chaos,' he said, 'I didn't see Maddox. Did he come through OK?'

'He's fine. The Secret Service have got him sealed up in the Royal American. He's their responsibility now. Anything I can get you?'

'Listen, can you smuggle me in some Scotch? And a pack of cigarettes? Could you do that for me, Chief?'

'No problem here. Just ring the bell. This is Russian five-star luxury. And Ben Rushton's campaign chest will be picking up the bills.'

He grinned. 'I like it. So tonight I'll order a rib-eye and trimmings.'

I turned to go. 'Someday I'll tell Yado what you did,' I said.

'Forget it. By that time I'll be back in Florida.'

When I returned to my old office in Station 13, V. I. Lenin glanced up in something Dronsky would call sympathy and raised his paw in salute.

I grimaced at him but it made no difference. Infinitely devious, was he trying to persuade me that his show of sympathy was genuine? I didn't believe it. V. I. Lenin and I were old combatants. Live and let live was the closest we had ever got to an understanding.

It had been as hard a night as any I'd had for some while. There's a point in exhaustion where you can lean back against the door jamb and close the eyes and the next thing you know you're awakened with a jerk as the knees give way. Somebody told me once that horses have the advantage that they can lock their knees.

What about cats? I wondered. But then why would cats need to lock their legs? They spend half their life sleeping anyway. Or in the backyard yowling for sex like a demented rock star. Not a bad life. I raised a hand to V. I. Lenin. He gave me a derisive yawn.

Outside in the big hall I could hear the detective room filling up with people and banter. A moment or two later Dronsky came in with two cups of coffee. 'Did you get any sleep?' he asked.

'Sated,' I said. And yawned as I reached for the coffee.

It was a dark grey, overcast morning as we pulled into the Militia Explosives Centre on the Arkangelskoye Road. Beyond the heavily guarded parking lot a long flat-roofed dark green clapboard building looked more flimsy than its present use suggested. Lieutenant Kotsev of the Militia Engineers was expecting us.

A young man with a closely shaved blond head, freckled face and a shy smile, Kotsev, I saw, wore the ribbon of the Russian Eagle above the flash of his bomb-disposal unit. It was a prized combination, awarded to anybody who had defused a terrorist bomb in a public place.

Kotsev led us into his office, a large timber-floored room with maps of Moscow and engineers' diagrams of the sewer system, water and electricity systems and the subway, covering the walls. He offered us coffee and busied himself drawing up two comfortable chairs.

'First Captain Dronsky and former Captain Vadim,' he said, 'I am assuming that your time is short so I will go straight to the matter before us.'

'So, what do you make of it?' Dronsky said.

'When a vehicle explodes there's always a possibility the driver is using one of the additives he can buy under the counter to boost his mileage. Most of them pose a significant risk of a gasoline explosion. But that usually results in a fire in the motor.'

Agreeable as the young lieutenant was, I didn't want a lecture. 'This was an American Embassy limousine.'

'A Russian driver,' he said. 'Uzbek.'

'But in any case you think this was a bomb?'

'There's no doubt about it.'

'Your preliminary conclusions then,' Dronsky said.

'Preliminary conclusions. First that the key to what happened during the night is the detonator. Fragments of it have been recovered, some of them hurled clear by the explosion but still exhibiting the giveaway traces of packing grease on the mechanism.'

'Packing grease,' I said. 'What's the significance of that?'

'We can't yet identify the explosive charge, but the detonator is commonly available on the world's arms markets. It's a last-century vintage, but usually reliable, British pencil detonator. Very simple. You set the time you want on the cap of the pencil and push the point into the explosive. Inside the pencil an inner sleeve is depressed by the controlled pressure of compressed air. When two chemicals come into contact at the set time, up to twenty-four hours, the detonator explodes. Usually very accurate, very reliable.'

'But not this time?' Dronsky asked, looking up from the cigarette he was rolling.

'No. Probably because the detonator had not been stripped down properly and re-oiled for use.'

'So the action of the time setter was slowed.'

'Yes. Each minute on the setter cap could take any amount of time as the compressed air inside tries to push against the congealed grease. This is when an unexploded device with this type of detonator becomes particularly dangerous. It could explode the following day, or next week. Or it *could* explode in your face if you try to dismantle it, even moving the detonator a centimetre or two.'

'So what happened here?' I said. 'The original time setting got stuck. And . . . ?'

'As the luggage was thrown about being unloaded from the aircraft or loaded into the limousine at Sheremetevo, the detonator got separated from the explosive. Ten, twenty centimetres would be enough.'

'And in the normal movement of the limousine, the grease lost its battle to hold the pressure of the compressed air?'

'Correct.' The lieutenant straightened in his chair. 'The detonator fires, too far from the explosive to detonate it, but it does ignite the gasoline tank in the limo. That was explosion one, muffled . . . Isn't that how you described it to Captain Dronsky?'

'Yes. The second explosion was much sharper. A powerful crack.'

'This is what I believe happened then. The second explosion was the gasoline fire igniting the explosive. It requires intense heat to do that. Of course.'

'But none of this tackles the most important question,' I said. 'The question why. Is this an attempt on Yado's life?'

Lieutenant Kotsev was shaking his head vigorously. 'Please come over here.'

We crossed to the far side of the room. On a grey plastic-topped table were a dozen burnt and twisted objects.

Kotsev took a pointer. 'This is part of a suitcase,' he said. 'Strong. Good quality. Note the difference between the burns on the inside and out. On the outside the flame effect is evenly distributed. That's the gasoline explosion. Inside you have sharp scarring burns characteristic of a powerful explosive.'

'So one of the unloaders at Sheremetevo airport slipped the device into the suitcase.'

Kotsev pursed his lips.

'No?'

The young lieutenant shook his head and used his pointer to tap the table beside a piece of blackened metal. 'The detonator cap. Still showing the time it was set by whoever did this. When the device was planted, the case was still in America.'

'Wouldn't American Airport Security have detected the explosive, Chief?' Dronsky said.

'Not if the Secret Service escorted the luggage through.'

'The detonator tells the story,' Kotsev said. 'There is no doubt that the device was set before the luggage left America.'

I stepped back from the table. There were too many consequences of that fact for me to work on for the moment.

'More than that,' Lieutenant Kotsev was saying, 'I think the target of the bomb was the owner of the case.' Again he used his pointer. A small metal plate riveted on the side of the suitcase read: ALEXANDRA RUSHTON.

Lieutenant Kotsev looked efficient, earnest and was, from the evidence of his Russian Eagle, undoubtedly brave. But did he know what he was talking about? The time setting, he told us before we left, was for an explosion in thirty minutes. If he was right, the packing grease had so clogged the detonator that it took some twelve hours, including loading and unloading on a transatlantic flight, to function.

All this, he assured us, was very possible. But how did the device get into the suitcase? And where exactly? Here, Kotsev could be of no help. The only real answer was at Observatory Point itself before Alex packed – or in a brief absence during packing. So . . . someone who had not taken the flight, Alison Bryson or Rushton himself. Or one of the security team from the FBI? Or an even wider band – Polly's team of youngsters wandering 'in error' into the wrong part of the house. Possible. Although they would have had to get into Alex's bedroom or sitting room unseen by Olga or Stack. I thought about that. Not at all impossible when I considered it. Security once inside the house was not tight. So assuming we were also talking about the man who made the phone call, we were looking for an adequate Russian speaker with access to the house – and reasonable freedom once inside.

I put these points to Dronsky. 'You have to face the facts, Chief, that the hand of the clock points to Rushton again.'

I shook my head. 'He's not going to target Alex for all the votes in New York. He's the man who rushes back every possible morning to play tennis with her.'

'Then there's only one answer.' We were walking from the green clapboard building and out across the parking lot. 'Breakfast,' he said, as we reached his car.

'Breakfast!' I thought of Dronsky's love of fishburgers. I shook my head queasily.

'You need something in your stomach, Chief. There's a place I saw down the road . . .'

I stopped him. I'd seen it too. A fishburger bar. 'Dronsky,' I said. 'Find me somewhere we can get a good coffee vodka for breakfast and I'll join you with pleasure.'

47

I slept on the cot for a few hours and drove to the Nevetsky Clinic at dusk. The radio carried a long stream of news bulletins about the bomb attack on the US vice-presidential candidate. The flickering neon news ribbon, stretched on steel braces across the Garden Ring Road, read: *Attempted assassination in Moscow of US candidate vice-president Yado: Channel Pravda – 9 o'clock news.* At the Chekov crossing a competing channel was giving less away. Old habits die hard. Their ribbon read: *Top American seriously injured in Moscow. The best footage on Moskva 20–20.*

At the clinic I parked and walked back to the main gates. Through the old railings I could see a man in the courtyard pacing about in the chill wind and drawing on a cigarette. I crossed towards him and stopped before the modern concrete steps. The lights showed the pink walls bright red. 'What are you doing here?' I said to Dronsky.

'Just getting away from the kids' bath-time,' he said.

'You can't get enough of bath-time, for God's sake. You're a besotted father, Dronsky.'

He grinned sheepishly.

'What's the latest on Yado? The news strips have him at death's door.'

'I called the Veterans Hospital half an hour ago,' he said. 'He's stable but he's not going to be flying to Murmansk. Your sister's OK. She's being discharged later this evening. The duty doctor told me the building was surrounded by TV trucks hired by Americans and Europeans. He was furious that a team of US burns specialists is on its way for Yado. He insisted Veterans has the most experienced burns unit in Russia. The Americans don't trust us – that's the truth, he said.'

'The truth is nobody does.' I looked up to the light from Alexandra's room.

'She's all packed, ready to go,' he said. 'It's touching, Chief. She's like an eager child waiting to go on her first vacation.'

'She isn't a child,' I said, more sharply than I'd intended.

He looked at me. 'No, sorry, Chief. You're right.' He gave me one of his appraising looks from under his heavy eyebrows. 'She certainly isn't a child.'

'What's she doing now?'

'Watching television,' he said. 'Or maybe just listening to it. Anyway, she's got the Moscow News on. It's full of Rushton's visit to Russia for the funeral. Full of the bomb, full of detail on her operation which they report is happening here, tomorrow. It's a family newscast.'

'Did you talk to her?' I asked him.

'About who could have planted the bomb in her suitcase? She says your sister and Stack were the only ones in the room.' He paused and shrugged.

I was let into the clinic and up to the first floor. A uniformed second-shift replacement for the sergeant Dronsky had put on the door sat reading a football magazine with a sub-machine on his knees beneath it.

I went into the room and stood, leaning back against the door jamb. The television was on. She was in the armchair, sleeping lightly. Her single surviving case was packed. I took it out of the room and down the corridor to the washroom. Resting it on the table I opened it up. I didn't really expect anything resembling a pencil bomb but I moved clothes aside with care and, I suddenly realised, a slightly trembling hand. The clothes, I saw, were all new. Up-to-the-minute designer labels. Bought by Alexandra for the new Alex who expected to step out of this clinic.

Closing the case I took it back to Room 12. As I put it down she opened her eyes.

'There's a flight at nine o'clock,' I said. 'Arrive Murmansk just before midnight.'

'OK.' She stood up. 'I'm ready.'

I thought of Nevetsky's question: is this the woman you love? The consequences were beyond my power of perception of the future. I watched her move about the room, bending, straightening, smiling (vaguely) in my direction. And Nevetsky's question churned within me.

The old house on which the present concrete block was built had had, like many old Moscow houses, brick wine and food cellars underneath. These had been excavated by Nevetsky as an exit from the clinic unknown to the press. With Dronsky's sergeant carrying Alex's case we were led through the narrow passages by Dr Nevetsky. His plan would be to sleep overnight at the clinic and make a brief announcement to the waiting press in the morning, talking about his hopes for the operation and leaving the reporters to assume it was taking place, as planned, here in Moscow. He would then use the same tunnels, drive to the airport and fly to Murmansk.

Emerging into a narrow lane somewhere behind the clinic we saw the unmarked police car Dronsky had arranged parked alone in deep shadow. There was no sign of the press as we drove towards the airport.

'You must explain to me, Constantin, what you are seeing. This is the last time, I promise you.'

The plane banked across low hills. In the moonlight, they were grey with snow, ridged like a frowning bald head.

'Murmansk was founded by the last tsar, Nicholas, as an all-year-round port,' I told her. 'It might have one of the worst climates in the world but it's touched, no more than licked really, by the tongue-tip of the Gulf Stream.

It's what makes it an ice-free port, although step back a mile or two and every lake and river on either side of the Kola estuary is frozen solid.'

'But what are you seeing?' she said. 'I felt the plane bank. We must be lining up on the city.'

'These are just hills, low hills, covered with thin snow. The wind doesn't allow for deep settling. And what? There's the remains of several nickel-processing plants. All closed down now. And the outline of a gold-mining camp at a place called Pork where the slave workers lived who mined the ore. Now we're coming across the Gulf of Kola. There's mist, there's always mist,' I said. 'Rises from the sea which is much warmer than the air around.'

'Mist . . .' she urged me. 'And what can you see through the mist?'

'It's quite a light mist tonight. So I can see the lights in Murmansk's centre. It's a square we call the Five Points. And I can see the tower of the Regional Government Building and the lights of the Lermontov Infirmary. I can even see its floodlit façade.' I could hear my tone of voice change. 'And Sin City, five or six miles upriver. Bright lights of a dozen colours sparkling through the mist. By God, I can almost smell the barbecued reindeer steaks.'

She touched my arm and I turned up my palm to hold her hand. 'OK,' she smiled.

I held her hand tighter. She thought I was offering reassurance, but the truth is I needed to take it from *her*.

This was my city. My birthplace. An ugly, icy, cement-block sprawl with a bitter climate and, in the long winter, week after sunless week of Arctic darkness. But it was the place my life had been lived. The place my son, lost to me, blown away by the winds of war, had been born and spent the six years of his life when I knew him. And the place my second wife, Natalya, the woman I always think of simply as my wife, had died.

The truth was I was afraid to bring Alexandra here. I was afraid that I should always see her with Natalya standing behind her. In ways that hurt, I recognised their essential similarities. They were both strong women. Both capable of a commitment to a future that I had not yet learned to face, and perhaps never would. There were superficial similarities too. They were tall, blonde Russian women . . . the one a lawyer, the other a doctor.

I stopped myself thinking just there. Natalya would never be forgotten and I would never want to forget. But what I feared was that their very similarities would merge them into one – seamlessly fusing them together into a third woman, threatening my past with Natalya and my present with Alexandra.

'I talked to Dronsky quite a lot in Moscow,' she said.

'Quite a lot?'

'He likes to talk about you. About meeting you.' She paused a moment. 'He talked a lot about Natalya.'

Could she always tell what I was thinking?

'He told me the memory of her could never stand between you and another woman.'

'He said that? Dronsky said that?'

'He said that she would have hated that to happen. Is that true?'

I leaned over and kissed her temple. 'I hadn't thought about it until you asked,' I said. 'But – of course it's true.'

48

The most attractive way to enter Murmansk is along the river road into the centre of the city, but the difference from any other route is marginal. Granted, you miss the port itself and the listing cargo ship, the *Lenin*, crammed full of nuclear junk, too frightening for anybody to clear. But you still see the empty tower blocks and their tier after tier of shattered windows. Even the very poor have abandoned these habitations. Some chronic alcoholics live there among the rats and roaming packs of stray dogs. For the rest, the people have gone. South to St Petersburg or Archangel. Some even to Moscow. Once a city of half a million, Murmansk now barely counts itself a hundred thousand. This is a measure of our despair.

Nobody denies Roy Rolkin has done much for Murmansk in the three years he's been governor, the elected dictator of the Kola region and the city at its centre. But he can do nothing to bring people back to the harsh winters, the brutal monotony of the buildings, and the permanent pollution haze we call Anastasia which hangs like a brown-cloaked witch twenty kilometres to the south, ready to engulf the city.

The Lermontov Infirmary is a bright, stucco-faced haven in the middle of all this cement. As a building it is all Murmansk has of grace; as a hospital it has a deserved reputation in European Russia. Its floodlit façade, pierced by long, eighteenth-century windows, shines pale blue under heavy white eighteenth-century dog-toothing, a building in the style of one of the great palaces of St Petersburg. It is of course named after Mikhail Lermontov, the writer whose bronze statue dominates the cobbled forecourt. The inscription at the base of the statue is the ambiguous title of his great novel: *A Hero of our Time*. Only with difficulty had I persuaded Roy not to erect a statue of himself next to the writer.

I had not been to the Lermontov for three years. It carried heavy memories of the time my wife, Natalya, had worked here – but I still enjoyed that up-all-night feel that airports and hospitals and TV news stations have. In the main hall the receptionist greeted me like an old friend. People who had worked with Natalya stopped and talked. Alex stood next to the marble statue of Roy, which, having failed to find a place for it outside, he had insisted on being erected in the lobby. Fortunately, on this occasion at least, she would not be able to read the shameless inscription, composed by Roy himself: *Roy Andreivich Rolkin, Governor of Kola and Mayor of Murmansk. Without his comforting presence this would be a lonelier planet.*

From reception we were taken to the Department of Ophthalmology where Nevetsky's assistant, the dour young Dr Petrov, received Alex and began to put her through her second series of tests in two days.

As Petrov wrapped the blood-pressure band around her arm, Alex pressed him for details about the length of time she would have to remain bandaged after the operation.

'I know from other operations that Dr Nevetsky has performed that, when the bandages are removed, you will in all probability see less well than you do at the moment. The brain needs time to adjust to the new messages it will be receiving and learn to interpret them.'

I left them as the tests began. Outside a short stocky man, with eyes that seemed in dire need of surgery, was standing in the corridor. Murmansk's head of plain clothes police, Captain Pinsk, was an old friend, a man who had worked for me in the past. I had arranged with him to have a permanent guard on Alex's door. In Russia, these informal arrangements are not at all unusual.

'I've assigned ten men,' he said, his eyes rolling uncontrollably. 'They'll take positions in the corridors and outside in the courtyard under her windows. Watches will change every eight hours. She'll be all right, Chief.'

It was almost two o'clock in the morning when I stood with Alex in her room. 'Don't come back tomorrow until the operation's done,' she said.

'You'd prefer that?'

'I want to fix some things, things that are important to me, in my memory. One of them . . .' she smiled, 'is this very hazy view I have of your face.'

'Keep it that way.'

'I'm serious, Constantin.'

'Why would you want to fix a hazy image in your memory? You'll have a better view tomorrow. Or the day after.'

'In case I don't,' she said flatly.

Waking up to the alarm in my own flat, in my own bed next morning, I felt I could sleep for the rest of the day. But I stumbled up and, American habits dying hard, I flipped on the TV while I prepared my face for the world to see. With a mug of coffee before me, I called Dronsky in Moscow. He liked to wind me up by telling me how much V. I. Lenin was missing me. He claimed the cat had been mooning about in a desultory fashion ever since I left. Not even consolable with a fishburger.

We talked about arrangements for the funeral and both crossed our fingers for Alexandra's operation – but I felt strangely confident about it. Confident about Nevetsky.

Dronsky left me with one curious titbit of information. A journalist he knew pretty well from a Moscow radio station had been in touch. The journalist said there was some sort of rumour going round about this San Francisco hotel woman, Elvira Santos. Basically the story was that Rushton was refusing even to mention it in his answers.

The suggestion was negotiations were in progress at this very moment.

'You mean he's buying her off?'

'That was the suggestion.'

'But Rushton would have to pay a fortune. This is not a DNA-smeared dress. This is film. The American TV companies would pay untold millions for it. And if this were going on, his financial man, Clint Maddox, would be back in the States, negotiating with her lawyers. But he's in Moscow. Getting ready to leave for Murmansk.'

'Maybe they're offering her the iron fist in the velvet glove.'

'You mean a big cash payment but also a big reminder of what happened to Katerina and Sarah, gift-wrapped along with it?'

'Who knows, Chief? Certainly not me. Just forget about it. V. I. Lenin sends his best. He means it. He's a very sincere cat.'

What bothered me was whether *Dronsky* meant it. Sometimes I think he does.

I put down the phone and thought about what Dronsky's journalist had said. I could believe Rushton trying to buy back the videotape from Miss Santos. Any politician would. But if there really *was* an iron fist in the velvet glove, the same iron fist that had been used against Katerina and Sarah, it placed Rushton behind it all.

I felt sick at the thought. Most of all, I felt out of my depth. I had spoken to Ben Rushton a few dozen times. I had seen him under stress and strain. I just couldn't believe that the man who had invented that crazy tennis for Alexandra was capable of organising the killing of his wife and mistress – and maybe most of all the attempt on Alexandra herself.

Somehow, what happened to Elvira Santos, whether she went ahead and sold her multimillion-dollar piece of videotape for public showing, or whether she simply and quietly withdrew the accusations – and her tape –

must give me a strong pointer to what was happening. And Clint Maddox, the easy-voiced Southerner, would be the key. He was a hundred per cent loyal to Rushton, everything down to body language confirmed that. If there was to be any negotiation, iron fist or velvet glove, or *both*, I thought Maddox would handle it. But not from Moscow. If I suddenly heard he was flying back, I thought I would know what for.

I knew I couldn't make arrangements for a big funeral like Katerina's without Roy. Roy knew it too. And beamed as I arrived in the governor's private quarters, a huge penthouse apartment above City Tower. A few quick minutes were spent on Yado's condition but it was clear that Roy was already moving on, ready to exploit the presence of Ben Rushton in Murmansk to the full.

Within five minutes of my arrival, Roy had turned his attention to the things that, for him, counted.

As he laid out his ideas for the funeral, my sense of alarm increased. At four kilometres from the airport the hearse carrying Katerina's body would be met by a battalion-strong guard of honour. To the clash of well-timed cymbals the troops would solemnly goose-step into Murmansk, past City Hall where Roy (and Rushton and Alexandra of course) would take the salute as the flags dipped for a distinguished daughter of the Kola region and the city. The whole team, plus reserves, of Murmansk Dynamo would be lined up in blue club strip with a special fleece in club colours. Notables (if he could find any) and honoured guests (like me) would be in a special stand just behind the team. Most of his planning assistants, he said, thought it was great.

I told him I knew who his planning assistants were. Girls who'd have to think it was great. Otherwise they wouldn't get to share his bed this month – which meant an immediate redundancy and loss of job.

He asked me what I thought. I told him he'd lose all

respect from Rushton if he enacted this self-serving farce. Play it down, a slow drive through the city. The City Hall flying a single Stars and Stripes at half-mast. Roy, in the governor's limousine – the smaller black one, not the white monster he favoured – bringing up the rear.

'Bringing up the rear. Fuck your mother I'm paying for all this. I don't bring up the rear.' He walked back and forth in the long room overlooking the port. There were a few fishing boats unloading down there on the quays but very little else now. Nickel had been overmined in the last century and Murmansk tourism had acquired its own particularly unsavoury connotations.

'In a funeral, the rear's the only place,' I said.

He was thinking hard.

'OK,' Roy said, pouring us both vodka and strolling the length of the room to put my glass on the low table in front of me. 'The funeral's fine. I've no problems with that. "Presidential candidate's wife buried in Murmansk – Regional Governor speaks movingly of a Child of the North." Great – couldn't be better. But this Sin City burial – can't you *do* something about it, for Christ's sake?'

'What can I do?'

'You saw her lawyers. You have the testament. Just leave the last couple of lines out. We'll bury her up on Martyrs' Hill if you like. Big porphyry sarcophagus. I'll pay.'

'It's the city's money.'

He grinned. 'But I control it.'

'Roy, Katerina Rushton wanted her burial in Sin City to underline her origins. I don't know why – some sort of revenge on Rushton perhaps. But it's a dying wish. It has to be respected.'

'Respected – you say she was a crazy woman and a lifelong whore. What is there to respect?'

I finished my drink and stood up. 'Yes, she was crazy in some ways. But I liked her, Roy. So what she was a hooker? She looked after her daughter through it all. She deserves to have her last wish honoured.' I shrugged. 'In any case, it's too late. Too many people already know about it.'

Leaving Roy, I picked up my car from the City Hall car park and drove down to the Lermontov. We were still only at the beginning of winter, and far off the beginning of the long Arctic night, but the light was already quite different from Moscow and New York. This grey light from a weak low sun, wreathed in mists, was neither day nor night, but it required all street lamps to be on and shops in the city centre brightly illuminated. The rest of the city, the grey concrete areas, lay half-lit and resentful in a ring round the glittering centre. It was Roy's belief that as long as the main shop and bar and café-club streets were lit, and Murmansk Dynamo stadium lights burned brightly on Wednesday and Saturday game nights, the voters would vote his way. Perhaps he was right.

At the Lermontov, I didn't go into Alex's room, but stood watching her for a moment through the round glass port set in the door. She seemed full of confidence, sitting up in bed wearing what looked like heavy orange swimming goggles. Petrov and Nevetsky stood in the far corner of the large, high-ceilinged room discussing a long printout Petrov was holding.

When Nevetsky left the room I followed him down the corridor. 'She's been meticulously prepared,' he said. 'We can do nothing now – except get on with the operation.'

I followed his flat tones. He was a man, I guessed, uncomfortable with my gratitude for what he was doing, for the personal risks he was taking. 'I'd like to thank you,' I said.

He brushed the idea aside.

'However it turns out,' I added.

He looked up at the corridor clock. 'I must get myself

scrubbed up,' he said, lifting his hands in parody of a medical soap opera.

Then his eyes met mine and he was crossing the fingers on both hands.

I stood in the waiting room at the end of the operating-theatre corridor. I had just seen Alex wheeled by, an inert white form on a white trolley, a white scarf tied around her forehead, serene but for the brutal reminder of the orange goggles she wore. A game show was playing on TV behind me. There were three or four people in the room whom I'd hardly registered. An old woman, a pensioner I'd guess by her clothes, offered me bread and sausage. 'She'll come through it,' she said. 'We Russians do. Look at the last century. The rivers ran with blood – and yet Russia survived. We have faith in ourselves. That's what brings us through. Blind faith.'

I patted her shoulder and declined her bread and sausage. I had had enough of blind faith. I leaned against the door jamb and my thoughts moved back automatically to Observatory Point. Of course I knew that that world, too, was an illusion. Most Americans didn't live that way. But they still didn't live as we did, with TB epidemics that we were perfectly capable of defeating if the gangs had not been fighting for the vaccines; with inequalities as gross as they had ever been under tsar or Soviet; with brutal camp punishments for minor offences when our rulers were stealing billions of roubles from the state coffers.

And then, as I thought about Ben Rushton and whether a Rushton presidency could possibly mark a new beginning for Russia, his name was spoken on the TV set behind me. I turned. A newsflash had interrupted the game show. I saw Rushton and Alison Bryson escorted by six or seven identically dressed Secret Service men. Cameras were flashing, microphones, shaggy as bears' paws, were being thrust towards him. A Russian voice identified JFK airport where Mr Rushton was just leaving for his wife's funeral when he had been given the news.

What news? At a table set up against a glass wall Rushton stopped and the others fell back. A girl came quickly forward and attached a microphone to his jacket. As he spoke his words were translated into Russian by the reporter: 'I can only regret that my wife, Katerina, is not beside me now, to hear this extraordinary news. It doesn't mean we've won – but I've no doubt it means we *will* win on Thursday.'

Across the screen a red strip giving the latest, and last Bernheimer poll result of this election: Governor Colson, Republican – 38%. Ben F. Rushton, American Unity Party – 38%. Senator Henry Bass, Democrat – 24%.

Rushton was still speaking. 'As you all know, tragedy has haunted this campaign. The FBI and other law enforcement authorities are investigating both the death of my wife and niece and the circumstances of the explosion in Moscow where vice-presidential candidate Jack Yado was severely injured. Latest news there is that he is in a grave but stable condition at Moscow's Veterans Hospital where he is being attended by American doctors. A decision on his ability to continue to serve as vice-presidential candidate will be made by him in the next days. I will of course be seeing him in Moscow on my way to my wife's funeral in Murmansk.' He paused. 'And a final word to you, the American people.' He looked directly at camera. 'For your vote of confidence I thank you – for your boundless sympathy at this time, no words can express my gratitude.'

A journalist yelled, 'One question Mr Rushton. Ms Elvira Santos in San Francisco claims to have in her possession videotape of you and an unnamed woman . . .'

Rushton turned to him, stony-faced. 'I've heard claims. I have one comment, sir. It is not possible . . . I repeat, not possible for Ms Santos to possess the videotape I have seen described in the press. There'll be no further comment on the matter.'

Voices brayed in protest.

'Miss Santos has not identified the woman . . . Will you, sir?'

'Do you accept that Ms Santos might have videoed you in that room? Do you accept it was physically possible . . . ?'

Rushton calmly collected his papers. No further word about Elvira Santos in San Francisco and her snatched videotape. He lifted a hand in salute and stepped away from the table.

Supremely confident.

I saw Nevetsky only briefly after the operation. He was dressed in a heavy topcoat and fur hat, waiting outside the theatre for his bag to be taken out to his taxi. I went forward and shook his hand. 'Everything went as planned?'

'Yes.' His mouth was tight with tension.

I had seen surgeons like that after a difficult operation. 'You'll go to Paris?' I said.

He shrugged. He knew he must have, to some extent, the life in front of him of a man on the run. On the run from the *possibility* of revenge by the people he had refused to bow down to. He wasn't shrugging because of that. He was shrugging away the answer to my question: Where are you going now? From now on he wouldn't be handing out answers to all and sundry.

An hour later I was standing at the door of the waiting room as she was wheeled out. Her face was bloodless, a heavy bandage across her eyes. Petrov, still in green, his mask hanging, was at my side. 'There is no reason to believe it was not perfectly successful,' he said in his deep, unemotional voice. 'Dr Nevetsky has left me full instructions. She is to sleep undisturbed . . . undisturbed . . . until the morning.' Then suddenly he allowed himself a smile. It was slight, but coming from Petrov instantly and tremendously infectious. Within a second we were grinning like fools at each other. 'It was brilliant. I don't understand the process, not at all. But one day I'll have Nevetsky's courage – and perform it myself.'

'When will we know?' I asked him. 'How long?'

'Sometime after the bandages come off tomorrow. Healing is not an exact science. Now let's find ourselves a thumb of pepper vodka.'

49

Throughout the night, I stayed in Alex's room. Her head was locked in a white leather clamp and her hands loosely tied down. But her legs thrashed under the agitation of disturbing dreams. Time and again she formed Olga's name. I quickly understood that, for Alex, Olga was more her mother than Katerina had been in the last fifteen years. Once or twice she asked for me.

Just after eight in the morning she had awakened enough for me to moisten her lips with water and to tell her the operation had gone absolutely according to plan. She smiled wryly, caught in the leather head-clamp. 'But according to plan doesn't mean guaranteed success. You must remember that, Constantin,' a touch of Russian conversational didactic entering her tone as if I, rather than she, was the overanxious patient.

We were still waiting for Petrov's arrival when I was called out into the corridor. A message had just arrived for me from the US consulate at the port. The consul, Margaret Burns, would like to see me right away. Mr DeLane had called her with some information.

We have a full-scale consul in Murmansk and, if the truth were known, a revolving team of American environmental and nuclear specialists. Everyone knows, ourselves included, of the threateningly decrepit condition of the old Soviet northern fleet. Radiation levels are given with the weather report on the morning *Polar News*. It's one of those post-Cold War deadly stand-offs. The Americans are too eager to clean up the mess – the Russians are too sensitive to let them do it. Meantime the US maintains a formidable presence in Murmansk. Principally in the person of the plumply overweight Ms Margaret Burns, *Mrs* Margaret Burns as she insists, the woman I'd met in St Petersburg when I first collected my US visa. When I arrived at the new consulate overlooking the port she recognised me immediately and greeted me in a friendly way but I could see the concern in her features.

'A message from DeLane?' I said. 'I thought he was on his way here with the Rushton party.'

'He is. They'll be arriving in Murmansk tonight. But this can't wait.' She indicated I should help myself to coffee and I got up and poured some for both of us.

'DeLane's message is to be passed direct. From me to you. Unwritten. Unofficial.'

I handed her coffee, a gesture of acceptance of her terms.

'As I understand it, Constantin, you're interested in a 1980s Soviet defector named Olchenko – and his son.'

'I'm interested in knowing the identity he was assigned when he arrived with his small son in the United States.'

Mrs Burns nodded slowly. 'And the case involves an American woman who was jailed for twenty years for spying against the US. An intelligence officer.'

'From KGB records,' I said, 'I know her name is Carla Love, a receiving officer for American Military Intelligence, handling East-block defectors before the Berlin Wall came down. She passed back to the Soviet Union vital details, like relocation addresses in the US. Most vitally of all, newly assigned names. Her activities allowed the KGB to trace and assassinate at least a half-dozen of the key defectors of the period.'

'But the man you're interested in, Olchenko, was not a key figure?'

'No. The KGB, I guess, would have left him alone. But I need the name he was assigned in the United States. Olchenko's dead now. But I'm convinced the hitman can be traced through Olchenko. I believe our killer is

Olchenko's son.' My mouth was dry. On the edge of discovery it always was. 'Mrs Burns,' I said, 'what did DeLane get on Olchenko?'

'First thing,' she said, 'was Olchenko's death certificate. He was buried in Moscow four months ago. Death by natural causes. Influenza/pneumonia. He was a very old man.'

'But his *name*.' I felt the savage excitement of the hunter surge through me. 'The name they gave him when he defected. The name he lived under all those years in America, protected by the FBI? The name they gave Olchenko and his son.'

'I'm sorry, Constantin. DeLane doesn't have it.'

'Doesn't have it?'

'He asked me to make it clear that nobody on his level, even if he knew it, could give you that name. It would need to go to the top of the tree at CIA, FBI, Justice, and maybe others. And they'd fight about it for a year. This is before it went to court.'

Hope flowed from me, like energy. I was lost in this world of dealing and counter-dealing. I had never understood the complex rules. I didn't now.

We stood next to each other by the big window overlooking the port. The mist rose from the grey morning water, the snowfields rolled greyly away towards the Finnish border. I knew it stank of fish out there, but inside here there was a faintly perfumed warmth. The coffee was excellent, the carpets thick. In the old days, defectors chose the West for less. Was that what I was? At heart, some sort of defector? Not for perfumed air and thick carpets, but for the freedom to make a life without the arrogant and often incompetent certainties of living in Russia?

'So,' I said. 'Did you just call me out of the Lermontov to pass the good news that DeLane could do nothing to help?' I was tired. My good nature was slipping.

'No,' she said. 'I have a message. It's this. DeLane asked me to tell you that this woman, Carla Love, who assigned

Olchenko his American name, left America when she was released from prison. She came to Russia with her lover, a woman, now dead.'

'She lives in Russia?'

'She's hidden herself away in a tiny village. No transport, no phone. And now, no lover.'

'This village – where is it?'

'Takarsk – just outside Archangel. Just over an hour's flight from here. New York to Buffalo. There and back in the same day, Mr DeLane made a special point of mentioning.'

Archangel is an hour and forty minutes from Murmansk. In summer. In winter the prop jet Tupolev fusses about the apron until the control tower declares an ice-free run. Then the twenty-eight seater gathers speed down the runway, jerks alarmingly into the air and battles through the heavy brown cloud that sits like the rim of an unwashed teacup around Murmansk Airport.

Murmansk to Archangel is a flight of about five hundred kilometres, or in miles just over three hundred. Straining, rattling, spitting ice from the wings we flew south and east, across the Kola Peninsula, crossing the frozen White Sea. We landed at Archangel Airport in mid-afternoon and climbed down the aluminium accommodation ladder into a wind as chilling as anything I had felt further north. Thin snow flurries skittered across the concrete apron in front of us. Heads down, bundled against the wind and grimacing at the stench of kerosene in our nostrils, we struggled into the cement-block reception hall. Before the Civil War Archangel had boasted a modern airport. Prolonged shelling from one side or another left it a statuesque ruin on the far side of the runway system.

Takarsk was a village of twenty or so painted wooden houses on the steep bank of a frozen river. As I drove

435

down to it in my hired 4×4 Kamka I could see great patches, ten or fifteen metres across, of coloured snow. Bright green and blues and yellows ran down the curving river bank like greasepaint on a clown's face. What stained the snow I had no idea.

It wasn't difficult to find the house occupied by Carla Love. An old woman, bundled in a coat made of reversed rabbit furs, pointed to the end house, a small green and yellow two-storey building with a red banistered balcony running along the upper floor.

The door was opened by a woman in her late sixties. I could see immediately that she was not a woman from a small village in the Archangel *oblast*. She had something about her, something totally elusive but immediately perceptible as Western. I wondered if it was a lack of fear when a stranger knocks on your door.

'I'm Chief Inspector Constantin Vadim,' I said, resurrecting my old rank. 'I'm looking for Carla Love.'

She pursed her lips. She didn't hear English at her door every day.

'I take it you're Carla Love.'

She nodded briefly and stepped back, pulling wider the door.

'Come in quickly,' she said. 'It's too cold out there to talk to you on the doorstep.'

She led me into a small room with a good-sized iron stove. The wooden walls were warmly hung with a sort of cord matting, highly coloured. I fingered it. 'It's local, is it?'

'And very effective. You were no doubt wondering what the great splotches of colour were on the river bank. It's where the locals dye the matting. It's the village's only industry.'

Did she have a faint vodka lisp? The lip muscles get affected. The mouth slackens before the brain.

'Take your coat off, Inspector,' she said. 'I have a feeling you'll be here some time.'

I watched her as I handed her my coat. Her clothes were worn but well kept. American clothes, I'd guess. She had grey hair that was neatly brushed and her lips carried the faint blush of lipstick. But her expression conveyed neither friendliness nor hostility. It was the dull-eyed expression of a woman who had spent a long time in jail.

'You want to talk to me about the past, no doubt,' she said, pouring tea and gesturing me to a seat at the deal table.

I looked around the room with its two kerosene lamps shafting light across the sisal wall hangings. It was little more than a peasant hut in a bitterly cold corner of Russia. Not at all the sort of comfort she'd been used to as a US citizen. Not even, in all probability, the conditions she'd enjoyed in her American penitentiary. 'Why did you come to Russia?' I asked. 'You're not Russian. The Cold War's all over now. Why not stay in the US?'

'There were personal reasons . . . but that's not the whole story.' She stood with her hand on the samovar, looking down at me. 'I'd given my life to the Soviet Union,' she said. Her face twisted. 'I'd never been to Russia, of course. Throughout my time in prison, I promised myself I'd come the moment I was free. It was no longer a Socialist land . . . But there would still be, I was sure, signs all over of the great social experiment that had taken place here.'

'There *are* signs all over,' I said. 'Socialism has left its imprint. *Si monumentum requiris, circumspice.*'

'What?'

'The Englishman Sir Christopher Wren's epitaph. But he was one of the world's great architects. Not a blundering murderer like Stalin or Brezhnev. I can understand why you came. But not why you're staying.'

'You're one of those, are you,' she said, 'who'd leave Russia to waste away?' She sat down at the table and pushed a glass of tea towards me.

I looked at her. 'I'm not sure. It's not that easy a

decision,' I said. I felt, for some reason, bitter towards this woman who had grown up in a cocoon of glib decisions.

But she surprised me. 'No,' she said. 'I can imagine, for a Russian today, it's not easy to decide to stay.'

'But you, an American. You've chosen to stay here. You haven't told me why.'

She took some cigarettes from a drawer and lit one. 'My father was a college professor. At Harvard. My mother taught school. Comfortably-off Americans with a house in Cambridge, Mass. Brattle Street. A cool, leafy yard in summer; a warm clapboard house in winter.' She smiled. 'Not unlike this – hung with carpets, except they were valuable Persians. School for the little girl at Peabody, on Linnean Street, with the other professors' kids. Civilised coffee and dinner parties. Charitable contributions and good causes discussed. Except – my parents were members of the American Communist Party. On the secret list of course. In those days they were called sleepers.'

'When did you find out?'

'While I was still skateboarding down Linnean Street I think. It was like I always knew, although that couldn't have been the case. Anyway, very young I knew there was an exciting secret. My dad could be called on at any time. Of course he wasn't. He was one of a few thousand who got their kicks from standing way back from the edge. He taught English at Harvard. The secrets he was prising out of *The Tempest* were of no interest to the Soviet Union. What we didn't know was that long-termism was the name of the spymaster's game. They weren't interested in my poor old woolly-headed dad. Or my mother. They had their sights on twelve-year-old little me.'

'When did you know that?'

'Can't remember. It was all too smooth and flattering. Somebody would come to the house. A woman, usually. An American woman. And I'd be taken out and talked to and shown awful, shocking things in South Boston. And

438

there *were* some, of course. Poor people living rough, you know. By the time I was eighteen, I had a social conscience the size of a basketball. I was desperate to protest, march, demonstrate – but that wasn't allowed. On the outside I was a calm, neatly dressed college student. Inside, every political hormone was jumping like I was on yoppo.'

'You applied for intelligence work?'

She shook her head. 'After my Master's at Columbia, in 1978, someone approached me. I suppose Moscow had somehow arranged this. I never discovered. Two years later I was a very junior officer in the United States Intelligence services. Someone sitting at a desk in Moscow must have felt very pleased with himself.'

I asked if I could take one of her cigarettes. She pushed them over and gave me a light. Then she got up, took two small glasses and a green decanter and poured a clear vodka that smelled of fish. Tasted of fish.

She nodded as she watched me grimace. 'There's a certain amount of fishbone added during fermentation of the vegetable matter,' she said. 'It's a delicacy.'

'I'll spread the word.' I finished my glass and she poured me another.

'What is it you want to know?' she said abruptly. 'I don't suppose you'll tell me why.'

'Back in the 1980s, you were a reception officer – first in Berlin. Then in charge of a number of debriefing centres and safe houses for defectors in Paterson, New Jersey.'

'You're well informed.'

'These old espionage documents are being traded back and forth these days. You received a Russian defector in December 1983. A man named Olchenko.'

'What did he bring with him? I remember them, if I remember them at all, by what information they brought.'

'Nothing much I'd guess.'

She sighed. 'It's nearly forty years ago. Seventy shadows passed before me in that time. Oh, one or two big names. But mostly rubbish. Nothing to offer.' She paused, glass to her lips, then swallowed. 'Olchenko ... no. I don't remember Olchenko. What did you want to know?'

'You gave them all, after the debriefing, names and Social Security numbers.'

'And designated areas to live in.'

'I want Olchenko's resettlement name.'

She poured more fish-smelling vodka. 'Tomorrow,' she said, 'if I had a phone, I could probably get it. I have a friend,' she added in explanation.

I took out my cellphone and put it on the table. 'You have a contact you can call? Do it now.'

'Tomorrow morning is the soonest I can get him at his office. His wife wouldn't appreciate a call from me this late. I'd get nothing – and only alienate him.'

I had no choice but to wait until the bureaucrats of the new Lubyanka opened their doors at 9 a.m. tomorrow morning.

Desperate for company, she asked me to stay for supper. I suppose, in one sense, I *did* feel sorry for her. She had been manipulated by those nice, caring New England parents who had indulged their fantasies about the Soviet Union in comfort and safety. And meantime they had conditioned their daughter to be an acolyte, ready when called upon, of the florid god Brezhnev.

There are a hundred forms of child abuse. Against her parents, Carla Love never really stood a chance.

From a booth in Archangel Airport I phoned the Lermontov and got a benignly non-committal report on Alexandra. I asked them to pass on a message that I'd called as soon as she woke up, and turned to the problem of sleeping what remained of the night in the long cement-block hut that passed as a departure lounge at Archangel International Airport. A big TV set was permanently on at either end of the hut. Three glowing pot-bellied stoves heated the long room, each surrounded by a low iron railing. Ten or fifteen men sat around each railing, their chairs tipped back, feet on the guard rail. Some dozed. Some tipped vodka and chewed a hamburger. There were few women except for a pair of very young girls who wandered from one group of men to another promising the use of a heated van in the parking lot. From time to time a man would heavily lift his boots off the rail, hitch his trousers and follow one of the girls outside. I was reminded of trade at the Pirate.

The departures board stood propped on the counter, a tall blackboard which was brought up to date with a damp cloth and chalk. The women behind the food bar, frying hamburgers and pouring tea and vodka, received telephone messages every so often and wrote up the new flight information. The flight to Moscow was delayed for lack of fuel. The St Petersburg plane had a technical fault . . . Ice on the wings and runway, it was announced, would hold up our Murmansk-bound Tupolev until early tomorrow morning. If this was even close to accurate I still had a reasonable chance of getting back for Katerina's funeral.

I stood in line for the phone again. The nearest TV showed pictures of a long convoy of horse-drawn sleighs. A children's burial. Fifty boys and girls from an Archangel orphanage, dead from tuberculosis, their bodies wrapped in cloth. The grave a huge pit. For the camera there was some effort not to tip them in too roughly. But a mass grave is a mass grave.

I came to the head of the line and called the Lermontov again. The duty sister said Alexandra had been up but of course was still wearing bandages. At the moment she was being examined, but all the signs were good. With that I had to be content.

The young whores had gone home. The single bar-girl slept behind her counter in a canvas-backed chair. Men rose to throw logs in the stoves or stamped around to wake themselves before checking for a change on the noticeboard. Archangel is a couple of hundred kilometres below the Arctic Circle and a strong grey light appears with the late dawn. At nine o'clock I called Carla but her friend, she told me, was away from his Lubyanka office for the morning. She would call again at midday.

Looking like a pack of shaggy wolves, my fellow passengers and I stumbled out across the apron to board our Tupolev at just before eleven o'clock. Belted into the freezing aircraft, every one of us pulled out the hip flask of dubious vodka we had bought at the departure-lounge bar. I sniffed mine and was dismayed to discover it didn't even smell of fish.

Sitting in the Tupolev on the runway while they chipped the last of the ice from the wings, I had plenty of time to think about Olchenko and the name he had been assigned by the Langley resettlement authorities in their New Jersey safe house. Carla Love had outlined the process followed for all defectors of minor importance. News of a defector would bring a debriefing team scurrying over from the US to their point of entry in the West, usually Berlin. Within twenty-four hours the subject would be transferred by a special CIA flight to Trenton, New Jersey and be established in a Paterson safe house where an in-depth team would meet him. Carla Love's speciality lay in the last stage of reception – the Defector Protection Program not dissimilar to the FBI's Witness Protection Program.

Her responsibility was to bed down the defector safely in American life, organise language-laboratory sessions in English, assign a name and background, a driving licence and Social Security presence and to choose an area in which the defector would be required to live under the watchful eyes of the Agency. It was a felony for any member of an agency to disclose details of a defection and an identity could only be revealed by order of a judge. Civil liberties groups would automatically oppose any such order. I began to see the extent of DeLane's problem in obtaining Olchenko's American identity. But *I* had a connection beyond the arm of the US government. In Carla Love, I had another source.

50

Landing in Murmansk was coming back home. I savoured the familiarity of the airport, even nodded to the big, proud bronze of Regional Governor Roy Rolkin. 'This would be a lonelier planet without you.' A smaller version, with a similar inscription, now stood in the foyer of any number of Regional or City buildings. Collecting my car I took the river road, driving along the Kola–Pechanga Highway for a few kilometres until the city lights and buildings fell away behind me. The sky light was dark grey up here so that the mist, which in winter rose permanently from the river, looked pale against the snowfields behind it.

This is a season when the bleak landscape makes the mind desperate for colour. The priests were not wrong with their decorated churches and swinging lamps. Desperate for it up here in Murmansk, people seize on the colour and lights the Ice Fair has to offer.

As I breasted the low hill I could see Sin City stretched across the frozen lake before me. Early in the long winter season it has a more orderly appearance, at least at a distance. The grid system on which the militia and the fire department insist is still just apparent. Soon wooden additions will be built, narrow lanes will be blocked, or forced out of shape, a café or a whorehouse will collapse or burn down – and the whole highly coloured mass of false casino-Kremlins and brothel-churches, a Potemkin village on ice, will lose any shape or coherence it has and visitors will again see it as the ramshackle fun palace, the rambling, dangerous, exciting casino-brothel they have named Sin City.

A hole had been opened in the ice, perhaps five metres long by two metres wide. Weighted lengths of deep red cloth had been hung over the sides of it, blackening as the freezing water lapped at it. Banks of candles stood on gold benches brought from the surrounding whorehouses. Red flares sputtered and smoked from stakes driven into the ice.

It was clear the Sin City militia had lost control. TV vans ringed the burial site. Presenters did their to-camera pieces in a dozen languages. Reporters pressed as close to the centre of the event as they could while photographers held cameras above their heads and strobes flashed out across the surrounding hills.

Among the packed crowds I recognised a hundred faces, denizens and concessionaries of Sin City, crammed shoulder to shoulder with the visitors, their breath visible as a cloud magically disappearing above their heads. From a half-dozen different directions, bands, kettledrums and fifes vaguely concerted their music. Business was not ignored. Girls, naked under thick furs, plucked men from the crowd. Hawkers sold vodka by the paper cupful and hot reindeer sausage from trolleys and braziers.

Up on the hill road above the lake I could see a convoy of headlights approaching at a funereal pace. The militia units now began to force open a path from the edge of the lake to the burial site in the middle. My old friend Captain Pinsk marched an arrowhead of militiamen into the crowd. Forcing people back, they held the two sides twenty metres apart by lines of men armed with short truncheons which they used to poke and slap at the crowds trying to surge forward. What was planned and what was chance no-one could say. But as the hearse led the way onto the ice a burst of flares on the hillside caused a drift of red mist across the lake. The muffled drums played. Old women chanted. Potent incense floated invisibly in the freezing air.

The hearse was followed by Roy Rolkin's limousine. I caught a glimpse of Ben Rushton and Alex in the back. In the front, window wound down, Roy, against my advice, sat in the passenger seat wearing a black overcoat, a cravat at his neck and holding a black top hat to his chest, for all the world like a funeral director. In the back seat I could see Alex sitting upright, a black sable hat low on her brow, her face in shadow. Behind the limousine were other cars. I saw Olga in the back of one and a glimpse of Stack beside her.

Behind the convoy a foot procession formed. As they passed where I stood I saw acrobats and tumblers careering across the ice, a group of twenty or thirty whores in their working dress as SS officers or cloaked dominatrices, croupiers with their money slides, like pool sticks held across their chests in the port arms position, majorettes throwing and catching black-edged imperial Russian flags, babushkas and small children, a whole section of the people who worked and lived in Sin City and who saw, in this funeral, one of their number coming home.

Alex was wearing wraparound dark glasses as she got out of the limousine next to Rushton. Tears were streaming down her cheeks. Rushton, in black coat and black silk scarf, looked stunned at the spectacle around him. A ring of lights glared down on them.

Secret Service men struggled as reporters tried to get close to the funeral party. I saw Olga knock a photojournalist to the ground and caught a glimpse of his camera skidding towards the hole in the ice. Then Olga was at Alex's elbow, murmuring into her ear. Rushton moved forward, locked in a phalanx of Secret Service men. I saw Polly and Alison Bryson, distinguished in black, and DeLane somewhere in there in the middle.

For the television cameras it was an unrepeatable gift. The leading presidential candidate – better in some ways than the president himself – was standing on the edge of a carpeted ice hole in the midst of a huge and garish brothel fair surrounded by real and false priests, real nuns for all I knew, mixed with similarly dressed girls from the Virtual Convent behind the Kremlin Casino.

And yet the whole hotchpotch ceremony was strangely moving. The open steel coffin was brought forward and set on a low trestle. Rushton, his arm round Alex, stepped forward and first she, then he, bent and kissed Katerina's forehead for the last time. Sombre drums and a single flute played as the coffin was sealed and the bearers lifted it on straps to hold it for a long moment suspended over the ice hole.

In the bitter cold, a woman, dressed in the habit of a nun but one of the girls, I'd guess, from the garish convent-brothel behind us, sang in an ethereally clear voice the Farewell to the Dead.

What could have degenerated into farce became high ceremony as Rushton whispered to Alex and she slowly raised her black-gloved hand, the signal to lower the coffin into the depths of the lake.

'Pure Hollywood, fuck your mother,' Roy said, suddenly next to me. 'I'm entertaining the candidate-president of the United States at City Hall at seven this evening. You're invited.'

He placed his silk hat on his head and moved forward. Even members of the US Secret Service stepped aside to give him access to the graveside.

51

At Sin City the funeral is over. It is no longer an open grave. A thin sheet of ice ripples and bends with the mysterious movement of the depths below. A Sin City carpenter has built a huge Orthodox cross and he and friends are lashing it to a frame so that it will be locked into the ice by tomorrow morning. The cross is painted gold. The name Katerina is in red. As are the dates, 1965–2020. When the ice melts it will sink with the rest of the flotsam of Sin City.

The TV vans are pulling away. Some reporters are picking up background stories from the girls who are mostly going back to their workstations. The main party has already left for City Hall. Before I follow I must change my clothes and make another call to Carla Love.

I walk with an old fortune-teller I have known for some years. She dresses as seers, psychics and fortune-tellers should, in down-at-heel boots and a yellow and green polyester silk dress under a moth-eaten fur. I have sworn to myself I will never consult such a one again. It's too Russian a thing to do. And I may well be on the road to becoming an American.

'You're well, I hope, Captain,' she says.

'Your cards have obviously not told you I have resigned,' I say. A friendly jibe.

'Oh yes,' she says confidently, but I know her to be a fluent liar. Then she does say something that shocks me. 'A beautiful woman, the sightless one.'

And suddenly I'm desperate to ask her if she'll remain sightless. If the operation has been a success.

The old lady knows it. She's cleverer than I. She smiles,

the rubbery lips drawn in and pressed together, unimpeded by teeth. She is looking up where fireworks of all colours chase each other round in circles across the sky. 'There,' she pointed and sang in a cracking voice: '*In Russia's land we find our way through circles of deceit / The smiling mask cannot conceal your neighbour's cloven feet.*'

Suddenly, I see it's a bitter smile. She is shaking her head. I don't understand her but I'm desperately afraid for Alex.

Firecrackers are going off all around us. The drums and fifes are sounding. The whores singing. For a moment my head spins. Then I fight back to sanity. The old woman can know nothing. She has a sharp eye and probably saw me watching Alex at the graveside. Beyond that it's guesswork and the desire to entrap me again as a customer.

I give her a few roubles to buy hash. She takes it with one hand and unfurls the other, dirty lined palm upwards, an invitation to consult the cards in her tent.

I tremble on the edge. But one thought saves. I could never, *never*, tell Alex that I have consulted a fortune-teller.

Driving back to the city, the image that stays with me is of Alex standing by the graveside as the coffin is lowered. Very tall, very upright. Sable fur hat and fur-trimmed long, plain black coat. Apart from the dark glasses, you might have put her in a film of *Eugene Onegin* or *Anna Karenina*.

I've forgotten the old lady's bitter smile. My thoughts are concentrated on the image of Alex by her mother's grave. Is it possible she was *standing* with more confidence? As if she already knew that Nevetsky's operation has succeeded? But she couldn't possibly have known that yet. All the same there was something different. Something that showed on her face too, in the angle of her head, the set of her lips.

In my apartment I take a shower, put on a suit and tie and take my reserve cellphone. For the third time I ring Carla and this time she is not engaged. I had begun to suspect that she had been playing me along, using the phone to call all her old pals in the US. But now she answers.

'Carla, it's me, Constantin. Have you had any luck?'

There's a pause while, I suspect, she throws down a quick vodka. 'I got through to my friend, yes. He's left his wife for a masseuse.'

'Did he have access to the files?'

'After a lot of grumbling, yes. He's the sort of man who likes to remind you how big a favour he's doing you . . .'

'Carla . . .'

'Ah. You're anxious to know the name we resettled him under. Much good will it do you. I remember him now, Olchenko. Pale-faced, shocked by what he'd done, defecting. He brought nothing worth talking about. Low-level tittle-tattle from various KGB headquarters around the country. He was an executioner . . .'

'I know. A hangman.'

'A travelling hangman. Revelled in the job. A pervert, of course. You'd have to be. But this one really got his time out of hanging women. He told me he'd hanged over eighty altogether. Mostly in Siberia. Kolyma.'

'You resettled him.'

'Them. He brought his son with him.'

'I know.'

'Six or seven years old at the time. Nice little lad. When they were cleared at the New Jersey safe house they were sent out West.'

Having a child as I have had causes blocks in the thought processes. In a sense you're in denial all the time. Little boys can't grow up to be evil men.

And I suddenly realised who the son was, who the son must be. Reddish hair like his father but grey now. The only one who was around throughout. The only one who might have gained access to Observatory Point as Alex was packing to leave for Moscow. I felt it as a powerful intuition.

'You want the resettlement name,' Carla was saying.

'I want his name,' I repeated dully. 'Give it to me.'

'Back then, I had a colleague, Colm O'Leary. At just that time he was suffering neighbours from hell. It amused Colm to name Olchenko after them.'

'Stack,' I said.

'No,' she paused. 'For a Russian you couldn't get more Irish – Hanratty.'

Hanratty!

52

City Hall is Murmansk's only new building. It rises fourteen floors, clad in marble, from the centre of the city. Glittering with lights, it contemptuously faces the dark twentieth-century workers' tower blocks long abandoned on the low hills beyond the new city limits.

I pulled my Toyota to a stop at the chain-link gate to the parking lot and signed myself in, waited for confirmation from inside and drove into a space indicated by the sergeant of the guard. I could see that everybody else was already here. Murmansk's limousines were lined up, the drivers drinking tea in the reception hut on the far side of the lot.

I turned off the radio and sat for a moment in the car. I was thinking about Hanratty, trying to unwrap the rough-affable New York cop, the no-nonsense salt-of-the-earth figure who had plodded through to uneventful retirement. The real Hanratty, of course, wasn't like that at all. To begin with he almost certainly spoke Russian. Perhaps even close to the fluency of a native. And he had been scarred, not as he jovially claimed by his mother's Irish cooking, but by his Russian father's obscene obsession with the hangman's trade.

On the spur of the moment I took my cellphone and dialled his number. It rang, four or five times and somebody pressed the button.

'Hanratty,' I said.

'The same. That's you, Chief, uh?'

'The same.' I took a deep breath. 'How are you doing?'

'Good. Fuck it, I say good but my knee's killing me.'

'What's that noise in the background?'

'A Russian beauty in a white uniform is adjusting my traction.'

'How long will you be there?'

'Torn ligaments take time they tell me. But thanks to Yado being here, too, I'm getting the best of treatment.'

'You're still in the Veterans Hospital?'

'Where else?'

'Missed all the fun, uh?'

He picked up something. 'Fun? Mrs Rushton's funeral?'

'Bad choice of phrase. But it was really something.' I couldn't let it go. I needed to tell him something. 'She maybe died hard, at the hands of a cowardly fucking lunatic, but she would have appreciated the send-off.'

'I'm sure. Listen, Chief. I can't stop to chinwag as my old mother used to say. They're serving dinner. Tonight we got pelmeni. And lemon vodka on the rocks. Gotta build up my strength.'

'Do that,' I said. 'Take care.'

'Call again, Chief. Any time.'

I closed down. Opened up and called Dronsky. In a few sentences I filled him in.

'I'll take a squad down right away,' Dronsky said. 'At least he can't get far with that knee. I'll make out the charge on the road.' He hesitated. 'Just as long as he really was still at the Veterans when you called him.'

In Roy's penthouse apartment, which occupied the whole of the fourteenth floor of City Hall, the main room held close to two hundred guests. I took champagne and minute smoked-sturgeon rolls and entered the fray. Most of the men were in extravagantly cut dinner jackets, some white with black silk-stripe trousers, some French grey. Ben Rushton was in the middle of a group of men and elegantly dressed young wives. He wore a dark business suit and vest of the same material and managed to look more appropriately dressed than any of Roy's political colleagues. Alison and Polly were in the same group, Polly looking surprisingly at home in a long copper dress with split skirt and high heels.

I took a route across the room that hugged the wall round to the big windows which overlooked the city. Alex was talking to Roy in one of the alcoves. She was wearing big round dark glasses but no bandages underneath. For the second time in a couple of hours, I was stopped dead by her. It was as if she had cast off an earlier, younger Alexandra. Talking to Roy, one hand holding a glass of champagne, the other stretching a long palely tan arm to rest casually on the inevitable head-and-shoulders bronze of him that looked out over the city towards the Gulf, she presented a picture of extraordinary self-possession. I stopped watching her stroking Roy's bronze skull for a few moments before walking towards them.

Roy turned, as suave as he gets. 'I was telling Alexandra that Murmansk is on the brink of revolution,' he said. 'A revolution which will restore the city to its former wealth and population. But this beautiful woman only wishes to talk about phrenology.'

'Phrenology?' I looked towards Alex.

'A study of personality via prominences in the skull.'

She ran her hand over the brow of the bronze beside her. 'Is this, would you say, Governor Rolkin, a passable likeness?'

'You must call me Roy. Governor is way too formal. A good likeness? Well, let's see. We should be asking Costya that. He's known me since we strutted together in the Young Communist Pioneers. The Brezhnev youth of the day. Well, Costya, does it do me justice?'

'What could?' I said.

'No sour remarks, Costya. A likeness?'

Alex was smiling.

'Not bad,' I conceded irritably.

'I must leave you,' Roy said. 'New arrivals.' He leaned

towards Alex. 'If you find him morose these next few days, he's worrying about the way he let down the team.'

'The team?'

'Murmansk Dynamo. I sent Costya to New York to buy us a star player . . .' His eyes tightened. There was remembered hostility there. 'And he failed me miserably. This week we lost our last chance of promotion.'

It struck me forcibly: this was the first time since I was a child that a Dynamo match had passed without me knowing the score.

When he had gone I watched as she trailed her hand thoughtfully off the bust. 'In a way,' she said, 'I can see why he's your best friend.'

I flinched at that. 'He's somebody I've known longer than anybody else alive, except Olga, of course. But I have very uncertain feelings about him.'

'I can understand that, too,' she said.

We stood together for a moment. I could have told her about Hanratty right then. But even the thought of him brought a sensation of slime in the throat, a sensation I didn't want associated with her.

'What are you thinking?' She put a hand on my arm.

'That you looked magnificent at the funeral,' I said.

She smiled. 'The only way I have to imagine what I look like is to go back gently twenty years and remember what Katerina, my mother, looked like. I'd be pleased to look like that.'

'In your new clothes, I think you probably do.'

'I brought them from America,' she said. 'My new appearance was to match my new sight.'

'*Will* match your new sight,' I said firmly.

She put her arm through mine as I manoeuvred her through the knots of people in the huge room. 'You haven't asked me, so I imagine you know,' she said. 'There's no sign of improvement yet.'

'The last thing Nevetsky said to me was that it could be

days after the bandages are off before you became aware of any change.'

We stopped at the buffet table and I handed her another glass of champagne.

'Is it important to you that my sight improves, Constantin?'

'Important? Of course it is.'

'I mean,' she said. 'For instance, if you were falling in love with me, would you, you know, back off if Nevetsky's operation had not succeeded?'

'What a crazy question!'

'I don't think so.'

'Then put it this way,' I said. 'If you were falling in love with me . . .'

'Which I concede is much more likely,' she said.

'. . . would you back off if the operation hadn't been quite the success you hoped?'

'What a crazy question,' she said, lifting her champagne glass to me.

The strange spell this woman bound me with had taken my mind off DeLane. Now I saw his tall, stooping figure moving through the crowd towards me. She had to know now. I held up my hand to DeLane as he came slowly forward. 'I have something to tell you, Alex. I went to Archangel yesterday.'

'Olga told me. Why?'

'To see Olchenko's American resettlement officer.'

Alex lifted her head as DeLane joined us. 'That's Mr DeLane, isn't it?' She faced him. 'I didn't know you had come for the funeral.'

'Only just made it.' DeLane shook hands with her and turned to me. 'Did you see her? Did you see Carla Love?'

'She lives alone in a village outside Archangel. She's on a pitiful pension from Moscow.'

'I should feel sorry,' DeLane said. 'Could she tell you anything?'

'She told me she resettled Olchenko and his little boy in 1983. Olchenko was given language-laboratory teaching in English and taught a trade. Another trade, that is. American plumbing, I think she said.'

'And the resettlement name? Let's hope to God they didn't go for Smith or Jones.'

I put my hand round Alex's waist. 'Carla's colleague thought it was some sort of Irish joke. They registered Olchenko and his son as Brian and John Hanratty.'

'Jesus Christ . . .' DeLane said quietly. 'Hanratty.'

I looked at Alex. Her face had changed again, hardened in a way I'd seen before, hardened and taken on an expression of utter determination.

'Hanratty,' she said. 'He hanged my mother, then came to the house to invite me to beer and pizza in the Broken Bottle.'

She frightened me.

'I'll get onto my own people at the Veterans Hospital,' DeLane said.

'It's been taken care of. The local police will be there by now.'

'OK,' DeLane hesitated. 'Perhaps I slipped up here.'

'I don't see how.'

'I ran a check on every local cop on the investigation. It's Bureau practice.'

'And . . . ?'

'Hanratty came through as just what he claimed to be. A twenty-year, clean-record, small-time cop. Only thing I didn't pick up was that he applied for his Greenwich posting just a couple of months before Mrs Rushton was found dead. He made careful preparations.'

'The serving-cop cover worked for him. I think a check would show he was on furlough when the British judge was murdered. All the rest were a night's work away from New York City. Except the two Moscow killings, of course.'

Dark-eyed, DeLane nodded gloomily. 'I was warned

by Abby Cunningham that anything to do with you wouldn't be that straightforward, Vadim. But it's appreciated. OK?'

'OK. But call the Veterans,' I said. 'I want to be sure he's safely tucked away.'

Alex, her head bent, was talking to Olga. I joined them. 'The doctor said she should rest as much as possible,' Olga said. 'I'm taking her back to the Lermontov.' She turned and Stack was at her elbow.

Alex lifted her hand. 'A few minutes longer,' she said. 'There's something I still have to do.'

None of us asked what.

I felt a strong compulsion to say something to Alexandra. I wasn't sure what it was. I knew the tone but not the content. I leaned forward and kissed her on the lips. 'What we were talking about. It wouldn't make any difference at all. You know that,' is what I said.

I hadn't spoken to Ben Rushton since Observatory Point and my stomach churned with doubt as I saw him crossing the room towards me. In the same room the idea that he had paid for his wife's assassination, for his niece's assassination, seemed so totally crazy. I now knew Hanratty to be the killer, but I had to keep reminding myself that someone had pressed the button. And too many things for comfort pointed towards Rushton.

As he walked across the room, I remembered my test. I looked round quickly for the tall figure of Clint Maddox.

Nowhere. I realised I hadn't seen him at the funeral.

Rushton was a few steps away. At a few yards, or camera-ready, he still looked great. But I was struck by how worn he looked really close up. 'A presidential campaign, Vadim, is the equivalent of fifteen rounds with a good heavyweight once a day,' he said.

'Only three more days,' I said. 'And from what the polls say, you're going to make it.'

He grimaced. 'Maybe.' Putting his arm round my

shoulder and steering me away from the two Secret Service men who stood in close attendance, he looked out over the city towards the sentinel tower blocks. 'DeLane just told me about Hanratty,' he whispered. 'I was shattered. I always imagined the man who killed Katerina to be some anonymous ruffian.'

'I don't think it works that way, Mr Rushton.'

'No.' He took his arms from my shoulder. 'But somehow it doesn't seem possible that he could be such an unremarkable American cop – and do what he's done.'

I was thinking about our camp guards and Lubyanka officers, the banality of evil, it's been called. But I said nothing.

'I feel bad,' he said, 'because I suggested Clint Maddox should take him onto the staff.'

'I didn't know that.' My ears pricked. 'Where is Maddox?' I said. 'I don't see him here tonight.'

'No, he won't be. He's filling in for Jack Yado as campaign manager. He's already on his way back to the States.' He paused, took a glass of champagne from a waiter and walked towards the window. 'I don't mind telling you, I'm swimming, Vadim. Drowning a little even, in all these happenings.'

I couldn't hold back any longer. Didn't see why I should. 'Let me ask you,' I said. 'Has Clint Maddox gone back to settle with the hotel supervisor, Elvira Santos?'

'Clint's gone back to take charge of the campaign.'

'And the Santos video of you and Sarah?'

There was a long pause. 'That's already settled,' he said very slowly. 'I've no apologies to make to you, Vadim.'

'Of course not. Cash?' And when he frowned, 'Will she settle for cash?'

'Cash?'

'Of course. An admirer willing to put up a very considerable amount. At this stage of a campaign, they tend to come over thick and fast to the man they see as the likely winner.' He turned and looked over the room, dismissing me.

I followed his glance towards Roy. 'Has our regional governor hit on you yet?'

'Hit on me?' He looked back at me as if surprised I was still there.

'You know he's looking for a key place attached to the new administration. *Your* new administration.'

Rushton frowned. A neutral frown. It didn't say I *know*. It didn't say I *don't know*.

'As an associate. He thinks he's just the man for your new Aid Supremo.'

'And by your tone, you don't.'

'No I don't.'

'Yet he's a friend. A very close friend, I hear.'

'A friend? I don't know. Like a brother, almost. When you've known someone this long you don't get to choose whether they're a friend. This close, it means something different.'

'But you don't think he should have the Aid job.'

'I'm absolutely certain,' I said.

I watched him move forward towards Alex, his Secret Service men in a loose circle. Polly had come up to my shoulder. 'He's a good man, Costya. Don't lose track of that.'

'You think I am?'

'On the edge.'

'Is he strong enough to fight off people like Roy Rolkin?'

She thought for a moment. 'I hope. I really hope.'

At the entrance to the apartment Ben Rushton had just said goodnight to Alex. Polly had come forward and hugged her and dropped back discreetly among the guests standing around the door. In turn, Roy extended his hand. 'I'm so sorry it was this unhappy occasion that brought you to Murmansk,' he said grandly.

The very first shiver of cold passed down my back as I saw that Alex had not extended her hand. Instead she stood there, taller than Roy, neither moving towards him nor stepping back. Olga, I noticed, looked at her, puzzled.

'Your mother . . .' Roy seemed to gather himself up with a deep breath. 'Mrs Rushton must have been a very extraordinary woman.'

Again there was no answer, no movement even, in Alex's face.

Roy applied his political voice. 'To have grown up here, in the very worst of times, to have known the Ice Fair in its earliest days and still to have risen from that to become the wife of a man who, I think we all believe, will be the American president-elect in three days' time . . . your mother must indeed have been a very extraordinary woman.'

There was an intimidating silence.

'You would know, of course,' Alex said low, level and hostile.

Roy's face froze.

I saw the interpreter's lips moving at Rushton's ear.

'I would know . . . ?' Roy's voice trailed like flattening smoke.

'As her pimp in Budapest I can believe you found her extraordinary. Extraordinarily profitable.'

'I think you're mistaken,' Roy said, just keeping the snarl clear of his tone.

'No,' she said. Utterly sure of herself. 'You were her pimp.'

His eyes, strange eyes, seemed to slant even more. They were fixed on her as he forced a smile. Then, with a slight shrug, he turned to those on his right with the same *what is going on here?* smile.

'You collected her for work each night,' Alex said coolly.

'I don't know what you're saying,' Roy was losing

461

ground now, waving his hands, appealing to the people around him. He turned to me. 'Costya, for Christ's sake. What *is* she saying?'

'You came to brief her on her client for the night,' Alex said. 'I have no difficulty recognising you. I could see then, remember.'

I couldn't immediately work out the significance of what was being said. Alex was saying she recognised Roy from the time she and Katerina spent in Budapest. She was saying that Roy, as a young man, had been her mother's pimp. So he would have known her, maybe even kept in touch with her. And somehow Alex, now blind, had recognised him.

Was all this possible? I remembered Roy had spent time in Budapest, once as a very young man, later in self-imposed exile. And whether, or how, Alex could have recognised him . . . God knows.

I couldn't work out where that took us, but I knew by Roy's face that it changed everything if he really had known Katerina all along.

I stepped forward and grabbed his arm. 'Is it true, Roy? Is it true what Alex is saying?'

'Of course it's not true, fuck your mother,' he muttered under his breath.

But she stood there, her face white with anger. 'He knew her all that time ago. And that makes all this a masquerade. Before my mother died she told me she was being threatened by someone she knew many years ago. Someone who stood to gain a huge fortune if Ben won the presidency.'

Roy stiffened. The room was completely silent. Everybody in the huge apartment was now staring at him. 'A blind girl,' he said contemptuously. 'Conjuring faces from twenty years ago. She's accusing me on the basis of God knows what – my voice? What else is there?'

He dragged his arm away from me and turned to Alex. 'You're mistaken. I never knew your mother. I never moved in *her* circles. Believe me – you're very badly mistaken, Alexandra Ivanova.'

Then he turned and walked away from her, between the guests falling back before him, and banged through the double doors into his study.

53

We were in the lift going down, Alex, Olga, Stack and myself. I didn't want to believe what she'd said about Roy – it had too many sinister consequences. More than that I couldn't believe that she could recognise his voice, or whatever else it was, after twenty years. I thought back – would I remember uncles and aunts long dead, remember them by their voices? No . . . there was only one sure sense. Sight alone would identify them.

'You think I'm wrong, Constantin,' Alex said, in a low voice.

'Right or wrong,' I said, 'he'll never forgive you.'

'I'm right, Constantin,' she said firmly. 'Why all this pretence that he never knew Katerina? Work that out and you'll know I'm right.'

'If you're right, it's obvious enough. He didn't want to be put on the spot. Didn't welcome being called a pimp by Katerina's daughter.'

Olga and Stack kept quiet, exchanging unhappy glances.

'There's more to it than that, much more,' she said, again her voice low, as if she were only now working out the full implications of what she had said up there in Roy's apartment.

The lift doors slid open and we stepped into the hall.

'You were eight years old when you last saw him. *Twenty years ago*. You can't remember a voice over twenty years.'

'It wasn't the voice,' she said angrily. She stepped forward. I reached out to pull her off course as she nearly walked into the bust of Roy standing in the middle of the lobby. We stopped in a cluster around the smiling, confident face of Roy on his plinth.

'If it wasn't his voice . . .' I said. I let the words trail away.

'If it wasn't the voice,' she said. 'What was it? Is that what you're asking me? You've heard of Braille?'

'Of course I've heard of Braille.'

She reached up to the bust, ran her fingers across Roy's face. 'They're good likenesses, you say, these busts of your friend all over the city.'

Her fingers were moving over the surfaces of Roy's face, down the shape of his nose, tracing the lips, exploring the cheeks and ears . . . 'I can read them, Constantin. As surely as I can read Braille. I can read the shape of this man's face. And it's the same. The same face I saw when I was a child in Budapest. Can't you understand that?'

'You can say this is a man you last met twenty years ago? I can't believe it.'

She gripped my arm. 'For Christ's sake, you can say that. You can say you recognise a man. Why not me? You've got to work out what it means. I never knew his real name when we were in Hungary. Katerina called him Stevan. But I remember him from those days in Budapest. Katerina was in her mid-thirties. He, of course, was young, very young. An adventurer. In his early twenties. And he was free with the chocolate, liked to tell silly jokes. He was good to Katerina too. Not the sort of pimp who beats his girls up. As long as they were performing well for him, they got good treatment.'

When I put her into the car I was still uncertain. She sat with Olga in the back. Stack driving, a pistol on the passenger seat beside him.

'I must go back upstairs. Take Alex back to the Lermontov,' I said to Stack. 'I'll be an hour at the most. I must speak to Roy.'

'Speak to him,' Alex said, holding open the car door. 'But will you take his word – or mine?'

'I don't know,' I said. 'I'm sorry, Alex, just now I really don't know.'

'You're dazzled by him, aren't you? The way Katerina was. He's a villain who can do no wrong.'

'For Christ's sake,' I said. 'I know he can do wrong.'

'Then believe what I say.'

'I have to talk to him, Alex.'

'All right,' she said. 'Talk to him. And let him run circles of deceit round you as he has since you were children.'

Russian circles of deceit. The old woman. The fortune-teller's lines: *In Russia's land we find our way through circles of deceit* . . . I leaned forward to say something more to Alex, perhaps to ask her if she knew the folksong, but she slammed closed the door. Her head was turned away from me as the car pulled out of its place in the lot.

I stood there for a moment in a temperature twenty, even more, below zero. It was all beginning to come home to me. If Alexandra was right, Roy's involvement with Katerina could be much more than that of a youthful pimp.

Flurries of snow skittered in circles across the parking lot. A man was crossing the asphalt towards me, tall, slightly stooping. It was DeLane.

'Oh my God. What a climate!' he said.

I opened the passenger door of my car and he climbed in. I walked round and got in beside him. 'Did you contact the Veterans Hospital?'

'I spoke to your friend Dronsky.' His big, dark eyes widened. 'By the time he arrived, Hanratty had discharged himself. Even when you called his cellphone I doubt he was still in the hospital.'

'Christ on the Cross,' I said. 'No trace of him?'

DeLane nodded. 'Dronsky's good. He had all the

cab services from the Vets Hospital checked out. They identified Hanratty by a slight limp. He took a cab to Sheremetevo Airport. Booked a flight to Murmansk. He's on his way here. Maybe even here already.'

DeLane was arranging cover at the airport. I was doing over eighty kilometres down the Pushkin Boulevard, weaving between cars, jumping at least three set of lights before I saw the pale blue stucco façade of the Lermontov in front of me. Taking a gap in the traffic, I gunned the car straight across the round-point and into the cobbled courtyard of the hospital. I didn't need to recognise the car Stack had been driving. It stood between a hospital Kamka and a laundry truck, all its doors wide open, like a new model at a motor exhibition. I was out of my car, slithering across the iced cobbles. I saw Stack's hand, palm up, under the driver's door. Blood was running, coursing down the wrist. Olga was sitting in the corner of the back seat, her face shocked-white. A huge and spreading bruise across the left cheek and temple.

She was moving her mouth. 'Hanratty,' she said. 'Hanratty.'

'What sort of car?' I said.

She shook her head. 'He'd never been to Murmansk . . .'

She was rambling. I struggled to understand the non sequitur. 'He said he'd never been here?'

'But his father had.' She vomited gently down the front of her coat, effortlessly, like a baby. 'He said his father had worked here once.'

I pulled myself out of the car and hit the emergency siren on the hospital Kamka next to me. When two orderlies came running from the main doors of the Lermontov, I looked once quickly at Stack. He was lying on his back across the front seats, his arms trailing. His chest was a mass of blood and torn clothing. Olga was unconscious.

It seemed to me I might have time to make one single guess about where he had taken Alex.

One only. 'His father had,' Olga had said. Olchenko the hangman had visited Murmansk. Where?

54

I talk as I drive. Talk into the empty car, the curtain of white beyond the windscreen. It takes my mind off what Alex is going through. It's a bad night tonight with a Meteo that forecasts heavy snow and blizzard winds. It's a bad night tonight because if I'm wrong here, Alex, I know, is dead.

I'm heading out towards an area roughly between the city and the Finnish border. It was a forbidden area in the past. In Soviet days the gold mines out here were notorious. The ones I described to Alex from the air. Each one had its own labour camp attached to it, all subordinates of the main mine and prisoners' camp at Pork. Prisoners – zeks they called themselves – men and women, were forced to work eighteen hours a day in dangerous, ill-maintained mine shafts. Most Soviet camp systems had little difficulty in controlling their zeks. They were too isolated to make escape a possibility. But in the Pork complex security was a serious problem. The presence of Western borders only a hundred kilometres or so away acted on the zeks' imagination like marsh lights flickering their seductive invitation.

In the whole of the Soviet gulag, the rate of attempted escape was highest at Pork. Most were recaptured. It was why Pork received regular visits from the travelling hangman.

But the mines lost their importance as the price of gold declined in the last years of the Soviets and the city of Murmansk closed them down one by one as Brezhnev's rule came to an end. Pork itself was the last to go. I'd heard that the last guard detachment had set it on fire before they left, in some pointless attempt at eradication of all the pain and misery the zeks had undergone here – or perhaps in simple fury at their *own* wasted lives.

I switch off my lights as I pass over the last hill. The camp is not difficult to see. The moon is full and dramatic, shining off banks of snow clouds building just out over the sea – but also silhouetting the big iron-mine derricks which surround whatever's left of the camp at Pork.

Here on the main road there's still the faint tyre marks of two or three cars that have passed in the last few hours. Mostly they're obliterated. What I'm looking for, straining my eyes to see now, is a turn-off with a single vehicle's recent tracks. The sign that my guess was the right one, that Hanratty has passed this way.

And as I drive, forcing my eyes to focus on the white slopes of the roadside and dragging myself back from the mesmeric effects of the shifting white planes of the endless snowfields beyond, I see something, marks where a vehicle has turned off between two split marker stones. This was once the road to Pork. A road taken by a car in the last half-hour, a car that can only be Hanratty's.

So this is not going to be a simple rescue, brothers, I know that. Fairy tales are not called fairy tales for nothing. I know this man has a lead of half an hour. Time to prepare. Time even to have achieved his object.

I give the car some throttle and it slides and slips on the downward slope. At the bottom of the shallow valley there is a cement bridge over a frozen stream. The real pine forests of northern Russia end hundreds of kilometres to the south of us here so the hills around me are bare, white humps. Except for the steel derricks and the cluster of long huts made shapeless by their roof-loads of snow.

I stop the car. I take Stack's gun and the heavy flashlight everybody keeps in the car in the Arctic north. I open the door. The wind chill slashes at my face. It has started snowing. Not a heavy, comforting fall but thin icy points that tear at the face. The cloud has reached in from the coast and the moon seems to race across the sky, finding gaps here and there to spill light down onto the bald hills.

The wind is kicking up snow in agitated flurries all across the hillside. I've been out in weather like this a hundred times. I know it. The blizzard is waiting, crouched, to come roaring in from the sea.

The stories were wrong about the camp at Pork. I can see that not much more than a very small section of it was burnt down. I am standing now between two lines of huts. I see some parts that were damaged by fire, a jumble of blackened beams iced with snow, the tar-paper roof having burnt away. But most of the prisoner huts are intact. To me they look as if they might be occupied, even now, by silent, frightened zeks.

I follow the tracks of Hanratty's car. The wind, rising in short, increasingly ferocious bursts, tugs at me, like a supplicant in a doorway. A broken shutter on a distant window begins to slam and bang with every gust. A wolf howls somewhere on the low hill behind the camp. Along the alley, between the huts, I walk into the blasts of thickening snow, fearful for Alexandra, frightened for myself.

At the far edge of this hut, I stop. The appel square, central feature of all camps, everywhere, stretches across to the administration buildings. Snow covers the broad rectangle; and the double channels cut by a vehicle's tyres bisect it in a straight line to where a single dark car stands.

I move quickly round the edge of the square, as quick as I can go through the thick layer of snow there. The moon peeks or sometimes stares. If Hanratty is standing at a window, up in the two-storey administrative block, he's seen me. And I'm dead.

For a moment I press myself against the rough wood-work of the entrance to the block. Green-painted. Faded stencilled words in red. I can hear the howls, the out-of-time ululations of wolves on the hills around the camp. I shiver pitiably. If there were someone to pity me. I count to three.

There's nothing natural about risking your life, brothers. But I know it's fatal to push open a door cautiously, to peer round staircases or creep forward step by step. Instead, I hurl myself in through the open doorway. I'm shouting, screaming even, for Hanratty, for Alex. I'm more frightened than I've ever been but I keep the loaded pistol, eight rounds jammed into the handgrip, I keep the pistol held in front of me.

Hanratty fires first. A huge thudding explosion that seems to shake the whole structure, bringing down snow like plaster dust. I know he's on the open staircase or the landing of the floor above me but I'm not sure where. I fire wildly in that direction – then think of where Alex might be. But this is not a time for thinking.

I throw myself forward, climbing stairs two at a time. Accurate pistol shooting is for the range, steady, two-handed stuff . . . In the street, the house, the back alley, most shots miss. I blast two shots into the darkness above me and receive a thunderous reply that tears a big splinter of banister from under my hand. I fire again – is that three or four? Then two bullets from the landing, one that splits a board-wide hole in the plank wall, a second that cracks above my head. I spin round with shock and see it has hit Hanratty's car outside and torn a fistful of rubber from a deflating rear tyre.

I reach the top of the stairs and fire again. And this time I hear a yelp from Hanratty. Only a yelp. But sharp, like a dog.

On the landing I see a door swing open. There's moonlight in the other room and snow falling through a hole in the roof. I point and fire. I miss, of course, but the wild ricochet bounces round the room. The splintering woodwork and the shattered window has him crouched, looking in all directions. And I am in there with him – delivering a kick that cracks his head and sends him sprawling. For a moment I watch him. He is unmoving.

I raise the pistol to kill him. To put a bullet in the back of his head. Then I see a coil of thin rope draped over a broken chair. I take it and bend over the slumped body. I twist his arms behind him and start binding his wrists together. I know I'm wasting time. Alexandra could be hanging in the room next door. I'm wasting time but I don't have the courage to shoot him in the back of the head.

Alex lies on the floor, coat off, freezing in her thin black evening dress. Her hands are tied behind her back. There's a loop of the thin cord round her skirt just above the knees. An old cloth has been pushed into her mouth. But she kicks and struggles. Even more when I call to her.

I am bending down next to her in seconds, pulling the cloth from her mouth, untying her wrists.

It's only now that I see the boards prised loose in the middle of the room to make a drop-hole. Only now that I see the thick hemp noose dangling from a crossbeam above my head. It's only now that real anger, of a sort I've seldom known, boils in me. My hand buzzes and tingles for the gun. I could, I think, quite easily put that bullet in him now.

But I untie the cord around her knees and draw her to her feet. Her coat is on the bare boards next to her, part-way slipped into the hole created by the missing boards. I lift it out, tearing it on a nail and think what that hooked sharpness might do, tearing at the flesh of a falling body.

'He said you would never guess,' Alexandra is saying. 'He said you'd never guess where he was taking me.'

I want to ask if she can see. If her sight's improved. It is now thirty-six hours since the operation. Nevetsky had said there could be slight but definite indications before forty-eight hours. Instead I tell her exactly where the missing boards are – and, reluctantly, about the rope hanging from the beam above us. 'We have to get to my car,' I tell her. 'Hanratty's car's done for. Mine's only three or four minutes away.'

'Is he dead?' she asks me. 'Did you shoot him?'

I tell her Hanratty is in the next room unconscious, bound at the wrists. He can stay there. We'll send a militia unit back.

I see something different in her stance. A refusal. 'I'm not leaving him to escape. Give me your gun,' she says. 'Drag him in here and put him in that corner. I can cover him from here.'

Beautiful faces can relay a determination beyond others. Beyond that was the almost insurmountable problem of helping her through the blizzard. I feel weakness in my legs, fear of the struggle with the wind and the icy snow. I capitulate. 'You've used a gun before?'

'I can see movement,' she says. 'I can *hear*.'

The thunder of the wind on the plank walls causes a flicker of doubt, but no more than that. I hand her the gun, watch her thumb checking the safety catch and feel satisfied she'd at least handled one before.

In the other room Hanratty is struggling and grunting. Blood from his nose and torn cheekbone is smeared across the floor. I tie his ankles with the last of the cord and turn him over onto his back. To my surprise he has an easy, laconic grin on his face. 'Underrated you, Chief,' he says.

I take his coat collar and drag him through the door, along the landing and into the room where Alex is standing. 'Never underrated her,' he says.

The wind drops for a few seconds. Both of us turn our heads at the howling outside. There's a lot of Hanratty's blood smeared about. Wolves pick up a blood-scent quickly. Russian peasants believe they're all witches. Those sly, flinching eyes are the giveaway. I go to the window and knock a pane of glass out with my elbow. When I shine the torch into the darkness, the beam picks up the yellow eyes of one, two, three animals, wolves prowling back and forth making twisting figure eights in the snow. I turn back into the room.

'OK,' I say. 'I'm putting him in the corner.' I haul Hanratty into place. 'Sit up,' I say and hear my voice as a frozen croak. 'Only move if you're planning suicide.'

I give Alex the flashlight to keep trained on him, then fill Hanratty's heavy Czech gun with a full magazine from the loose rounds in his pocket and place it on the floor beside her. 'I'll be five minutes,' I say. 'Ten at the most.'

I run down the stairs and stop halfway. A wolf stands in the hall. They're afraid too, I remember being told. I shout. Once only. It turns, a serpentine movement that takes it only as far as the doorway. I shout again and it hesitates, then slinks away into the snow-streaked darkness. But I can see its moon-shadow, waiting.

I run between the huts, the wind so strong on my back that twice it brings me down, once onto my knees, once rolling me over until I thud against the wooden step at an entrance to a hut doorway.

Clearing the huts I am out in the open, flayed by a crosswind now as I fight my way towards the car. An Arctic wind can move the snowscape like sand dunes in the desert. I kneel, shielding my eyes from the slash of ice. My car is nowhere where I left it, or thought I'd left it. New drifts have formed. As I try to plunge through to where I think the perimeter road must be, old barbed wire tears at my legs. I should not have left Alex there, some litany plays in my head. I should not have left both guns in the same room. Wire claws me as I thrash about among its invisible coils. If Hanratty can free just one hand . . . I feel sick and frightened by my own foolishness.

I can't force myself forward. Coil after coil of wire rises from the drift of snow. I trample one way, then another. I kick and scream at the serpent coils to fall back, to stay back. And then, in this freezing hell of hidden steel barbs and shifting snow shapes, I hear a shot fired.

I stand stock still. The pistol shot comes from across the appel square. From the headquarter block. From where I have left a sightless woman to guard a fiend.

I can see my blood on the snow as I wrench my torn legs free of the wire, but cold anaesthetises pain. Turning into the full face of the wind I begin to stumble back, fighting my way through the blasts that come roaring between the huts, forcing my way out onto the open appel square.

I take no precautions against being seen now. Each pace kicks up a cloud of snow which freezes on the chest and shoulders of my coat. Every ten paces I tear the breastplate of frozen snow from me. When I reach the headquarter building I fall to my knees in the entrance, head hanging for a few seconds, the perfect target, before pushing myself to my feet and beginning to climb the stairs.

Once clear of that wind, energy comes back to me. Don't ask what I'm thinking as I run across the landing and burst into the room. The truth of course is that I'm not thinking. I'm no longer thinking. I'm incapable of thinking.

The flashlight is rolling slowly back and forth as the building shakes under the buffeting of the wind. Alexandra is sitting in a corner, her legs tucked in beside her, one gun on her lap, the other where I have placed it on the floor.

Hanratty is, it seems at first, standing in the middle of the room. I catch his teeth gleam as the torch rolls closer to him. Catch the reflection of light across his eyes and the blood dripping from his face. He seems suddenly small, eight or ten inches shorter than me. I remember a moment's puzzlement at this. We are of much the same height, but his head is positioned so much lower than it should be. Then the torch rolls again, like some fairground wheel of fortune. By its light I can see that

Hanratty's feet are through the wide hole in the floor. In the room below the wolves, who have mounted some empty packing cases, are leaping and snapping at his legs. I snatch up the flashlight and point. He is perhaps *just* still alive. His face is horribly swollen. His lips drawn back in a pointless last gasp for breath. The rope from the beam above supports him around his broken neck.

55

The drive back from Pork through the eye of the blizzard had taken over three hours. Three of the worst hours of my life. Hours of a woman sobbing where she lay on the back seat of the car, hours in which the woman I had been on the edge of loving became a stranger. Perhaps showed herself to have been a stranger all along.

The car skidded and bumped as we crawled back onto the main Murmansk highway.

'I shot him,' Alex's voice, thick and unrecognisable from behind me. 'That was the shot you heard. I don't even know for sure if I hit him. But I think I hit him in the hand. I forced him to his feet. To stand on the edge of the hole. I was forcing him to stand below the noose. I think he'd lost a lot of blood,' she went on. 'He began to ramble about pleasure. He said he subscribed to the pleasure-pain principle. Pleasure could only be derived from the pain of others. The greater the pain . . . you know . . . He said that killing was the only thing that had ever given him pleasure in life. He would, he said, be eternally grateful to his father.'

'Did you ask him who . . .' I hesitated, scared of the answer I would get. Only in that moment did I realise how much I had been shielding myself from discovering it was Rushton. 'Did you ask him who had taken out the contracts?'

'I asked him if it were Ben.'

'And . . .'

'He laughed. With a rope round his neck, he laughed. He saw my pain. He thanked me for the last scrap of pleasure I had been able to give him. Then he stepped into the hole in the floor.'

'Tell me,' I said. 'Don't take it alone.'

'I could hear him thrashing about. Jerking like a puppet. A good hanging is supposed to break the neck of the victim, Hanratty told me that. This one was different. He stayed alive, all that interminable time you were out looking for the car, Hanratty stayed alive. Fighting with the noose. And the wolves were getting bolder. I could hear them in the house below . . . tearing at his legs.'

The heater in the old Toyota barely worked. My teeth were chattering with shock and cold.

'I tell you, Constantin, I needed this purging. I needed to kill him.'

'For your mother?' I said, an incorrigible desire to impose some pattern on what she'd done. 'You made him hang himself, for Katerina?'

'For *me*,' she almost screamed the words. 'I made him hang himself for *me*.'

I drove on through the rolling waves of snow at eight kilometres an hour, listening to her wild, breathless sobbing, her fists battering the seat beside her in the back of the car.

'He told me,' she said, minutes later. 'He told me I'd never see again.'

'He didn't know about the operation,' I said.

But he did, of course.

'He knew,' she said tonelessly. 'He knew more about the operation than I did. An operation as false as any Potemkin village. Nevetsky did what he was told. Nevetsky did the operation as Hanratty ordered.'

'I don't believe it. What difference did it make to Hanratty whether you would see or not?'

'You know why, Constantin. You know why . . .' Her voice had dropped to a whisper. 'The question isn't what difference it would make to Hanratty whether I saw again or not. It's what difference it would make to *Roy Rolkin.*'

They were the last words before she lapsed into an impenetrable private grief. She stayed at the Lermontov that night, awaiting Olga's arrival from the morgue where Stack's body had been placed. When Alex saw her she clung to her like a wounded animal, shoulders moving in an almost silent sobbing which slowed in pace for four or five minutes at a time, then picked up again as if she were suffering direct waves of physical pain.

Ben Rushton came to the Lermontov at about three o'clock in the morning. But she refused to see him and he turned, shocked, and came out into the corridor where I was waiting.

'What is it?' he said. 'What have I done?'

I didn't answer.

He glanced towards his Secret Service people and gestured to them to drop back to the end of the corridor. He kept his voice low. 'She doesn't think that I arranged all this? That I paid for it?'

I didn't answer. I wanted a thumb of vodka. And then another. And a cigarette.

'She can't think that,' he said.

I put my hand up to stop him. 'She doesn't.' I was through counselling presidential candidates. 'At this moment,' I said, 'she just doesn't know.'

Did he look relieved? God knows. He simply nodded that he understood and we faced each other in silence.

I'd never seen a man so pumped out by events. He stood resting his back against the wall, his eyes closed. 'Did she really hang him?' he said.

'She forced him to hang himself,' I said. 'Forced him at gunpoint.'

He expelled breath and straightened up from the wall. 'Could you *imagine* it from Alexandra?' he said. 'Did you ever see a quieter, more gentle girl?' He looked at me suspiciously. 'Did she really . . . did she really do that?'

I felt she deserved some defence. And more than that, if he *had* put out the contract, I felt he should be left with no protection from the sordidness of the details. 'When I got back to the hut,' I said. 'When I found him hanging, I cut him down. Not as easy as Western movies would have you think. All sliding arms, his great swollen head cracking against mine. His legs torn to shin bones by the wolves.'

'For God's sake,' he said, grimacing. 'Did you leave him there?'

'A team will go out when the blizzard drops. There won't be much to find. We left the rest of him to the wolves.'

I glanced at his face and saw how pale it had become. How the pouches under the eyes had become more prominent.

'On the way up to the camp,' I said, 'Hanratty had forced her to listen to his life story. How they'd first come to the States and lived in a cabin in the woods. And his father had taught him to trap animals in humane traps, then practise with them to teach him the hanging trade. They'd walk miles, Hanratty told her, to snare their neighbours' dogs. And they'd take them back, a long string of eight or nine of them. Then calculate the weights and drops – and hold a hanging party.'

'How old was the boy?' Rushton said. 'How old was Hanratty?'

'By then seven maybe. Nine or ten before Intelligence allowed them to move on to New York. After that it goes dark until Hanratty was nineteen. That's when he made his first application to NYPD. It's when he hanged his first woman.'

'Who was she?'

'He was still practising. A young runaway he picked up in Grand Central Station. Then an old bag lady. But this wasn't what his father had taught him the trade for. This was still practice. When he was in his mid-twenties, an NYPD badge holder, he took his leave in London. He hanged a woman there, his first on contract. A British judge.'

We were walking through the corridor towards the entrance. There were perhaps four or five Secret Service people around us, easily recognisable by their pressed suits, the women in skirts and pumps. Russian women wore trousers in a Murmansk winter.

'Did you get the news?' Rushton said. 'The other news?"

'No.'

'Yado,' he said. 'He died in intensive care late this afternoon. My campaign's in a thousand pieces, Vadim. The last polls all over the country were putting me ten clear points ahead of Governor Colson. Senator Bass nowhere. Now I'm a candidate without a running mate . . .'

I think I asked automatically, not because it was what was first on my mind. 'And what now, when all this breaks loose?' I wasn't pressing him for any sort of answer.

'Alex acted in self-defence.'

'She didn't hang him in self-defence.'

He looked at me. 'I'm sure you agree the story could be legitimately rewritten there. For Alex's sake.'

'For Alex's sake?' I laughed.

He looked at me. He knew much had changed between us, but not quite how much. 'Electorally,' he said, 'what happened up at that camp at Pork is no difficulty. What I need now is to announce a running mate. Maddox maybe . . .'

I turned away.

'What is it, Vadim?' he said. 'You've got something on your mind – say it.'

'I have Roy Rolkin on my mind. I want to know what

it means if Roy Rolkin really did know Katerina years ago. Are you telling me you've given no thought to that in the last six hours?'

His face tightened. 'I don't know . . .' he said slowly.

'You really don't know? He sent his people to buy off Elvira Santos for you, didn't he? Cash down and some appropriate threats. I know how Roy works. You know that. He wants that Aid Supremo job. You know that, too. And you're going to give it to him. You don't have a choice.'

'I need to think,' he said.

He stopped in the lobby and held out his hand. There were many people watching us. He smiled, warm, but muted as bystanders must see the occasion demanded. He was a politician. He saw the importance of knowing when to stop talking and start shaking hands.

I couldn't let him go like this. I called to him and he turned – and half a dozen Secret Service people turned with him.

I went forward. 'We haven't finished,' I said.

He frowned.

'How about in here?' I opened a door, any door. It led into a cramped office off the lobby. A desk, shelves of blank hospital files piled high. No window.

'What is this, Vadim?' His body movement signified protest, but he gestured to his minders to stay where they were and followed me in. 'What the hell is it?'

'Unfinished business,' I said.

He stood against the packs of blank medical reports, pale-faced and angry. But his eyes never went to the door as I kicked it closed. He had been expecting this or something very like it.

His head suddenly jerked forward. 'Before you say a *word*,' he said. 'Before you blunder into something you don't understand and start throwing accusations about . . . I never knew it was Hanratty. I have no idea who was paying him.'

'But you know Katerina's money never came from her father.'

He didn't answer but one minute blink of his eyes admitted it.

'When Katerina found out herself, she asked you to give up the money. It's what she meant on that recording when she asked you to give up politics. *Be a man*, she said. She meant regain your independence from your paymasters.'

'Unknown paymasters.'

'Maybe.'

'For Christ's sake, I have Russia more at heart than either of my opponents, doesn't that count for anything with you?'

My problem was that, in this, I believed him.

His eyes narrowed. He put it into words for me. 'What you have to face, Vadim,' he said, 'is that without the tainted Ben Rushton in the White House, there will be no Russian Aid Program. The epidemic will march on unchecked. In the villages, the bodies of children will continue to be tipped into mass graves.'

It was as if he had grasped me by the throat. I pressed my back against the wall.

'Listen, Vadim, the tragedy is that I never believed these threats against Katerina – not for a moment. In this room I'll admit I was taking money from the only source I could find who'd take a risk on me as candidate. The Russians themselves. Of course I was naïve. Of course, I didn't know who I was mixing with. But I didn't collude in the murder of my wife and niece. Those murders were ordered and paid for by people over here, Russians, protecting their invest-ment.'

He stuck out one long arm to brace himself against the wall in the narrow room. The white cuff was inches from my left ear. 'One crime, Vadim . . . I'm guilty of one crime only: an infringement of the campaign-funding rules. And every American political figure has been guilty of it at some time. You're not going to block my way to the presidency for that?'

He was far too clever to offer money – or even a lucrative post. But he was expecting to get away scot-free. I thought of Katerina, of Sarah – and most of all of Alex – and her lost opportunity to see again. At the very least he'd risked them for his own ambition. He wasn't going to get away with all that.

He thought I was hesitating. 'You've got to put all this behind you, Vadim,' he urged me gently. 'It's the only way to get what you want – and what Russia needs. And, dammit, it's the right way.'

I came very close to hitting my first presidential candidate. Instead, I made him a proposition.

It was one of those if you don't – I will propositions. He didn't like it at all.

'It's impossible, Vadim. We're at the end of a long, long campaign. Do you expect anybody is going to agree?'

'You are,' I said.

Then I went out into the lobby of the Lermontov and called Roy.

I crossed first to a night bar on the other side of the square from the Lermontov and ordered a quarter-litre and a pack of cigarettes.

I sat on the high bar stool in the half-darkness and listened to Frank Sinatra and watched the silk-clad girls dance slowly with their customers beneath the revolving globe of mirror glass above their heads.

Before I finished my vodka one of the girls came over and asked me to dance. We moved round the floor clutched tightly together, pressing loins, our thoughts light years apart. She offered her name as Zoya and I told her mine was Vladimir. At the end she asked for champagne and suggested a curtained booth and instead

I gave her a handful of dollars from my pocket and went back to my vodka.

It was an hour before I finished the quarter-litre.

Then I took a cab down to the Dynamo Stadium where Roy was waiting.

56

From where we stood at the top of the stand, I could see that the blizzard had passed over to the other side of the Gulf of Kola and was sweeping away like cavalry across the bare hills. Slowly, we began to walk down between the banks of blue bucket seats. 'So let's have it out in the open, bratkin. You believe the blind girl was right,' Roy said. 'You believe I knew Katerina before?'

'You tell me,' I said. My voice echoed in the empty stadium.

He shoved his gloved hands into the pockets of his topcoat. We weren't looking at each other. We were looking down to where the moon served as a single floodlight on the pitch.

'OK. I knew her, just as Alexandra says. Katerina worked for me when I first went to Budapest. Sad thing was she thought she could do better for herself in Moscow. Wasn't there a month before she got herself involved in a piece of gang warfare, Alexandra standing beside her on the steps of a church.'

'You heard about it at the time?'

'Fuck your mother, what do you take me for? Katerina had worked for me – but we were friends. I flew back to Moscow as soon as I heard about the girl's injuries. I put up the money for her to go for surgery in Paris. Before that she couldn't see a thing.'

'You put up the money for Alexandra to go to Paris?'

'What did you think happened? You thought the Moscow *racketiry* had a whip-round for the surgeons?'

He never made it easy, Roy. 'So you kept in touch with Katerina over the years?' I said.

'She was too old to do business by then of course, but we met for a drink together whenever I was in Moscow. Then suddenly she's getting married. Some vek in the World Bank she'd been giving Russian lessons to. Mr Respectability Rushton. Could the world be a funnier place, bratkin?'

'But it wasn't the last you saw of her.'

He took his hands from his pockets and batted them together. 'Why are you asking?' We sat on the end of a line of blue plastic seats and he pulled a quarter-litre from his pocket and stuck his feet up on the seats in front. 'Why are you asking when you already know? I saw an opportunity. An opportunity for us all, fuck your mother. Not just for me. For the whole collapsing country. For four, maybe even eight years, we might exert a controlling leverage upon the American presidency. First we pay the president's way to power. Then we tell him our price.'

'*Your* price.'

'OK, it was my idea. My money.'

'Rushton didn't know you had arranged for Katerina's fake legacy? He didn't know where his wife's money was coming from? He entered the election thinking the seed money was put down by a legacy from Katerina's father. Is that how it was?'

I knew it wasn't.

'That's the way he wanted it played.' Roy laughed. 'So when I called Observatory Point for the introduction to Yado I knew you'd never give me, I was laying down smoke. Establishing my first contact with candidate Rushton after the kosher *American* money had started flowing into his campaign. That way we all looked squeaky clean.'

Roy unscrewed the cap of the vodka and passed it to me. 'When Alexandra blurted at my apartment, Rushton followed me into my study. He demanded an explanation.' Roy chuckled. 'The bare-arsed cheek. *Demanded* an explanation. So at first I played along. I told him that his twenty-million-dollar campaign fund came from the city entertainment tax on the whores and gamblers of Sin City.' Roy laughed.

'How did he take that?'

'Very well. Suitable anger. Outrage.'

'You mean he already knew?'

'He knew. Katerina had told him. One night soaked in vodka and self-pity.'

'And Rushton, what did he do?'

'He told her to keep it quiet,' Roy said slowly. 'I don't deny it must have been a nasty shock to him. He told her that the very first Bernheimer poll of the election was about to place him in the presidential race. So anything about the inheritance should remain between Katerina and him. When she told me that I knew I had him in my hand.'

I drank a mouthful, held it in my cheeks and swallowed. The new AstroTurf pitch, permanently heated, misted green before my eyes.

Roy took the bottle back. 'She was unhappy about it. Strange woman. Husband with a good chance of becoming president and she goes screaming off the rails. Begs him to get out of politics.'

'She told you?'

'Open about it.'

'What did you say?'

His eyes narrowed. 'I told her to be very, very careful. I'd put in too much to lose now.'

'And the Aid Supremo was to be your prize,' I said. 'Infinite dollar funds to divert your way.'

'The big prize . . . yes.'

'And the vaccination programme?'

Roy shrugged. 'Depends how much money there was left over. I was planning to do what I could.' He clapped his gloved hands. 'Dog Death – we could do without it, uh?'

'If it didn't cost too much.'

'Russians have always fed off Russians, Costya. There's nothing new in that. Be reasonable, fuck your mother.'

'And Olchenko . . .' I said.

'Crazy, like his son. An old man when I first met him, barely still alive. But reliable, everybody told me. I was worried about Katerina from the beginning. But I thought it through. I put a holding contract out as soon as Katerina began to go off the rails. Cost me, of course. But Olchenko's boy was put in place. Standing by. I hoped to God it wouldn't be necessary. Christ on the Cross, don't blame me. I warned her enough times.'

'And why did she go off the rails?'

'Guilt, Costya. When she saw all those poor devils dying a dog's death. More good and harm is done in this world by guilt than any other human motive. Guilt is the cornerstone of reality.'

This didn't sound like Roy. I'd heard him maudlin in his cups, aggressive, exuberantly cheerful. But never philosophical before. Did *he* have a gun in his pocket?

'When Alex's last big American operation failed, Katerina broke down. Guilt eating at her. She began to blame the way she'd spent her life for Alexandra's blindness. I had her babbling drunk to me on the phone every other night. She was always on the edge of crazy.'

'So she had to go. And Sarah . . .'

'She had too much to hold over Rushton. And clever, too. Safer to put Olchenko's boy onto her.'

We sat on looking silently out across the pitch.

'Ah,' he said. 'I meant to tell you. I bought the goalkeeper you saw in New York. Paxton, is that how you say it? Five million dollars, sight unseen.'

I nodded. 'A good buy.'

'In the end,' he said, 'decisions have to be made.' He stood up and began walking down the steep steps towards the pitch. 'You've learnt that,' he said over his shoulder. 'You've made your decision.'

'How do you know it isn't a decision to kill you?' I shouted down to him.

He turned and opened his arms. 'Could a Russian kill a friend? The old proverb, remember. Russian friendship binds deeper than vice.'

I started down the steps and stopped just above him. 'Pushkin's Eugene Onegin killed his best friend in a duel,' I said.

Roy grimaced. 'Onegin maybe. But that was fiction. Real life was different. It was Pushkin who was shot. By his worst enemy.'

'Friend . . . enemy . . . it's not always easy to tell.'

He shrugged. 'Give up these dreams of conscience, Costya. This is the life you live. A Russian life. It's never been any different. Never will be. We're none of us angels. You've killed in your time, we both know that.'

'But I didn't put a contract out on Alex.'

'Nor I. I could have, but I liked the girl. Always had since she was this high. So I got Nevetsky to do an unsuccessful operation. That way, she wouldn't recognise me until Rushton was safely in the Oval office.' He laughed. 'Lot of good that did me. Braille! Who would have thought it?' He paused, his slant eyes on me. 'But I never put a contract out on her. That was pure Hanratty. His work excited him. He developed a dangerous taste for it. And I thought he was the ultimate professional! Stay away from people who mix business and pleasure, bratkin. They're dangerous, fuck your mother.'

I didn't know if I believed him that he hadn't put Hanratty onto Alex. Never did know if I believed Roy. But he had loosed a lunatic on Katerina and Sarah. He had delayed, and probably prevented for ever, Alexandra's recovery of her sight.

I looked down at Roy standing next to the bronze figure of himself looking out over the pitch. The plaque carried the same preposterous dedication as all the other plaques on all the other bronzes of Roy placed about the city. Yet strangely, the words mean something. They hold some sort of twisted truth. For me at least, this planet would be a lonelier place without him.

All the same, I called his name – and when he turned, slowly, puckish eyebrows raised, I shot him.

Twice in the chest.

57

Ben Rushton returned to America in an incomparable blaze of media attention. Four news helicopters with searchlights were permanently in the air above Observatory Point. Secret Service helicopters were called in to buzz clear the skies for the presidential candidate of the American Unity Party to fly in to land on his own lawn.

As his helicopter landed a bank of lights glared from a low hill just past the main gate where the TV vans and newsprint reporters from all over the world had been corralled. Secret Service men spilled out of the helicopter to take up positions around the machine. A few minutes later, Rushton appeared in the doorway and walked, ducking automatically to a point beyond the slow circling rotors.

In Murmansk I watched the scenes on TV. The sense of anticipation was visible on the face of every news presenter. They stood, most of them young women, doing their pieces to camera with the lights of Observatory Point in the background. Their faces were rapt, aflame with involvement in the rumours that were sweeping across America. I was watching Jan Petersen reporting live. Known for her impeccable studio presentations, she was nevertheless out tonight in the freezing fog coming off Long Island Sound, a woollen scarf wrapped round her head, a thick pea-jacket collar turned up. '*No-one – but no-one, knows the score at this moment,*' she was saying. '*No-one, that is, outside the library room in Observatory Point where I have often had the pleasure of talking to Ben Rushton. I think we can be sure, from the lights we can see over there in the house, that deliberations are taking place.*

Our information is that there will be an announcement from the Point later this evening. Meanwhile the wildest rumours are flying through the international press corps. One, I have to describe it as a persistent rumour, is that Ben Rushton, shattered by the events of the last week, the loss of his wife, his niece and his running mate, Jack Yado, has decided to withdraw completely from the presidential race. Yes – to withdraw in the hour before victory.'

I switched channels. BBC International were treating it more cautiously. A man with thinning hair, wearing a fawn topcoat, was saying: *'None of these resignation rumours has any basis that we, or anybody else, can trace. But five hours is a long time in international rumour-mongering and there's still no sign that the story of an impending resignation is to be officially denied.'*

I switched channels until I reached Polar One. Murmansk Dynamo were playing with black sashes across their chests for the mysterious death of their proprietor, His Honour the Governor of Kola Province, Roy Andreivich Rolkin. He was, of course, known to have had enemies.

Undeterred by the black sash, Dynamo were doing well. In a friendly against Racing Club de Paris the score was 1–1 at half-time. It should have been 10–1 to the French but Paxton had swooped and dived and used his prodigious armspan and anticipation to muffle every shot the French team had mustered. Looking at it another way the true score was Racing Club de Paris 1, Paxton 10.

I switched back to Connecticut. Something was happening. TV vans and reporters had been allowed through the gate and were clustered in a semicircle on the drive around the front door. Ben Rushton was coming out. He wore jeans, a denim shirt and a blue cardigan. Clint Maddox, Alison Bryson and six or seven Secret Service men were in the background. There was no sign of Alexandra.

The mist rolled across Rushton's face and he shivered visibly in the first November chill as he read from a prepared statement. 'Today, two days before America casts its vote, circumstances are such that I have been forced to consider my position as a presidential candidate. The most obvious elements I have been presented with are, of course, the deaths of my wife and niece. And the loss in Moscow of my running mate, Jack Yado. Other considerations will emerge in the next several weeks, after my lawyers have conferred with the Justice Department.' Was he talking about Roy? About the phoney inheritance fixed for Katerina? Not quite. 'I have to accept that even on the basis of present knowledge acquired only yesterday, about the origin of some of our Unity Party funds, I would wish to stand down from any opportunity I might have of becoming president of the United States.

'In the last hours, members of the Unity Party and in particular our chairman Clint Maddox have therefore discussed this matter with senior Republicans and Democrats. I myself have talked to both Republican and Democratic candidates in this election. There has been, as you can imagine, an amount of good old-fashioned horse-trading in order to retain the paramount element of my Russian Aid Program. This, I am satisfied I've been able to do – and I now wish to announce that I have accepted the offer of the Republican candidate, Governor Colson of California, to become his new running mate, on the free and willing withdrawal of his vice-presidential partner, Congresswoman Irene Cameron.'

His hands, holding the notes, were shaking. Nothing to do with the November chill. 'I am therefore speaking to you tonight as your candidate for the vice-presidency of the United States in the Republican interest.'

58

I had decided to let Alex call me. That last night in the camp at Pork had been so traumatic and the discovery that Nevetsky had *deliberately* failed the operation so devastating, that I couldn't blame her for not wanting to see Russia – or me – again.

The election was without surprise. There was of course a great deal of discussion about the legality of a vice-presidential switch at that stage of the campaign – but the deal went ahead. On the night, Governor Colson won in one state after another. His strong chin and alert eyes seemed to fill every screen. There were a few nodding references to the votes Rushton had brought in, but a new king was about to be acclaimed. Nobody had time to think of the man who handed him the crown.

Time went by quickly. November passed and December. I watched the January inauguration of President Colson and saw Vice-President Rushton there in the background of the ceremonies. Colson had already rewritten his Russian policies to include a Health Aid initiative. Rushton had offered full co-operation during the special prosecutor's investigation into the origin of his deceased wife's inheritance and her funding of the American Unity Party. The only interest in Rushton now was in the investigation.

Late in January the phone rang. It was Alex. 'I have to speak to you,' she said, without preamble. 'I have something to say.'

Her voice was formal. Maybe even a little severe. Like someone about to discuss money matters. An awkward loan outstanding.

'OK,' I said cautiously.

'I've spoken to Dr Nevetsky. He called me from Mexico. He didn't apologise. He simply said *his* life and *my* sight had both been at risk. He considers he took the best possible decision.'

'He must have said more.'

'He said that he deliberately operated on me at the limits of technology. In effect, he did half an operation. In two or three years' time, when the technology catches up, he would be honoured to complete the work with every hope of a very significant success.'

'Jesus.'

'So I have a date three years from now.'

I could hardly speak. 'That is . . . marvellous.'

'OK,' she said crisply. 'That's item one.'

'There's an item two?'

'Yes.'

I caught the hesitation. 'Go on.'

'There's a state of affairs I want to resolve, Constantin. I need your co-operation.'

'What state of affairs?'

'I'm sure you know I've never been with a man.'

'That's the state of affairs you want to resolve?' I could hear my voice trail away.

'I've sent a plane ticket,' she said. 'I thought Venice would be a good place.'

I only hesitated a fraction of a second. 'It would.'

It was.

Perhaps for the first half-hour in the hotel room above the narrow Canale Moise, Henry Miller looked down over her shoulder. But he was soon forgotten. I had imagined I would be somehow tutoring her in her deflowering and perhaps in the first few awkward moments as we undressed each other, that had been so. But it was something soon and easily abandoned in the body warmth of the quilted bed. Not surprisingly, she made love quite differently from any woman I'd ever met. Most obviously, she used her hands and her mouth for eyes, so that she never seemed to surrender wholly to her *own* pleasure, never seemed, even in the most ecstatic moments of the night, to be somewhere distant from me. From the first kiss, the first fondling to penetration, from penetration to detumescence, it was an act performed together.

Sometime during that first night as we lay in bed and the lights from the canal boats slowly arched across the cracked and ornate plaster ceiling of our hotel room, we decided we would stay together.

'Where we live,' she insisted, rolling nakedly towards me, her breasts brushing my chest, 'Russia or the United States, will be your call.'

It hurts more than I can easily say, but I called the West. I can't deny that I saw Alexandra more as a Westerner than Russian. In the end, I tell people, that was the deciding factor.

But it wasn't, of course. For myself, I never realised how much Roy Rolkin, or the idea of Roy, tied me to Russia. From childhood he had been there, part of my life even when we were apart, showing every Russian face – kind and cruel, generous and grasping. The decision about where to live was already taken when Alexandra called me from the United States. It was taken in Murmansk Stadium, when I pressed the trigger twice and heard his shriek. Of pain or shock, I'll never know.

I'll miss Dronsky. I'll miss the knowing looks of V. I. Lenin, and the casually raised paw. But I think I belong somewhere else. If I'm ever to start again, I belong with a Russian-American woman, not necessarily in New York or London or Paris. Perhaps even somewhere I haven't alighted on yet. Like Argentina or Australia. I appealed to Alexandra to narrow it down.

I had made the major decision. I had called the West.

I left it to her to call where in the West.

She told me she had already chosen.

Established like a medieval university in the old buildings beside the canals, with faculties housed in palazzos and wine warehouses and grain stores, the new Venetian School of International Politics has preserved Venice without reconstructing it. Teachers are drawn from all over the world. They include formal scholars like Alexandra, the newly appointed professor of Politics and the Rule of Law: and less formal journeyman scholars like myself, appointed to a minor readership in Russian Twentieth-Century Archive.

Our household, of course, includes Olga. Since Olga and I have begun to speak to each other in English I notice a slow sea change taking place in our relations. The truth is we have effaced our common past. Since we have learnt to see each other as human beings, we get on remarkably well. It has left me wondering, as I walk the canal paths of the city, whether it's not language rather than manners that maketh man. Whether it's not the raw unrestrained exuberance of the Russian language that's at the root of our troubles. But then, I suppose, the sheer unrestrained exuberance of Russians is at the root of the Russian language.

Just occasionally I miss the *impossibility* of my country. I am surrounded by polite Americans, Englishmen, Swedes, Germans, Italians . . . But the parties where we get wildly drunk and dance and shout from the windows of our huge apartment over the Canale Grande, these are parties attended by at least a critical mass of Russians.

I'm surprised and delighted to watch Alexandra slowly changing, relaxing all those high tensions she has lived with so long. Olga whispers to me that she gets more Russian every day. Perhaps, she says, it is in anticipation of motherhood next year. Despite my surprised expression, Olga insists this is to be. She attends a psychic fortune-teller in the Via Moise every Friday night in the hope of making some other-worldly contact with Stack. Sadly so far without luck, but she's come back with some interesting titbits all the same. One of them is the idea of Alexandra's impending pregnancy.

Of course I don't believe a word of what the old psychic says. I threw away fortune-telling and that whole dark but magical side of life long ago – but what's the harm, I say, in sharing a thumb of vodka and a glass of tea with Olga when she gets back on Fridays? As long as Alexandra doesn't know what we talk about.

Summer evenings here have a magic of their own. After supper Alexandra and I walk down to the Piazza San Marco and sit at a café. Drinking coffee I describe to her the fading light on the old buildings, the Venetian world as it goes by. From time to time, one of her students stops to say hello. Every young male in the university seems to be hopelessly smitten by her.

We grow closer by the week, as she learns more of me, and I of her. Here in Venice, on neutral ground, I find myself watching for signs that she is becoming more and more American in her ways, in her brisk manner, her sense of humour. Or more and more Russian.

I know why I watch her like this. Somewhere in me there is still an ache for whatever it is makes up the core of Russian life. It's not commendable. It's something to do with the ever-present fight for life in Russia. The combat. The exciting uncertainty. The sheer unreality. Is it that that keeps us on edge?

If that's what I'm missing, do I communicate it to her?

A strange moment happened between us yesterday evening as we sat at the Café Folciano. I felt it as some additional mysterious transfer of warmth. Nothing much set it off. We had been talking about the modest successes of President Colson's Russian Health Aid Program. Signs, thank God, that the disease was slowly receding in the big cities, that the vaccinations and treatments they call DOTS were getting through. While she talked, Alexandra had been thumbing through the London *Times Higher Education Supplement*. Articles on academic pay mixed with ads for scholarly posts all over the world.

She could not, of course, read. But she was counting the pages. When she reached page six she folded the paper in two, folded it again and placed it in her lap.

'I have a question for you, Constantin,' she said.

I knew her face so well. I knew this was serious. 'A question. OK . . .'

'*If* we were to have a child,' she said, 'where would you want that child to be born?'

Moving my head forward, I could see that the folded paper in her lap showed one advertisement that occupied most of a half-page. It was an English journal, so . . . 'There would be worse places than London,' I said. 'Or New York, if that's what you wanted?'

For a moment she was silent. Then she placed the folded journal, and its big advertisement *in Russian*, in front of me. A professorship in the new study of the Rule of Law. Would there ever be circumstances, she wondered, in which I would consider living in Novgorod?

Will she lose all this . . . this knowingness, this sixth sense, when she goes to her rendezvous with Professor Nevetsky in Mexico next year? God knows. But then there are many things I'll never know, I realise that.

One thing I believe I know is that we both feel a need to be part of what is happening to Russia. To be part of the remaking of the motherland. We won't, of course, be rebuilding, because, unlike Americans after their Revolution, we have only rubble behind us. Yet we are a deeply conservative people. We *want* to salvage something of our past. That's the heart of the problem that Ben Rushton, flawed in almost every way though he is, clearly understood and put into his programme.

Today's Russia won't change by revolution or a sudden,

jolting, uprooting reform. There is a Russian journey, as there has been a journey for other nations, and successful journeys are slow and steady and as uneventful as possible. I say some of this to her.

That's it. My two copecks in the hat. My answer. I take her by the hand and we leave the café.

'If there's been one real flicker of the Rule of Law in the whole of Russian history,' Alexandra says, 'it was in Novgorod before Ivan the Terrible crushed the city and imposed Moscow upon it. Did you know that?'

'I think I'd heard,' I tell her. I am thinking back to Dronsky's brother in the monastery archive. Our slow steps ring down the arcades of the Piazza San Marco. I've loved this place, but I think I've always known it was a stopover. One day we would have to decide to go east or west. And tonight we have.

And so the world turns, brothers. The world turns.

MONSTRUM

Donald James

'Brilliant . . . on this performance, Donald James deserves to be on the very first rank of bestselling authors'
Jack Higgins, *Express*

Russia in the early years of the coming century, at the end of a savage civil war. Newly arrived in Moscow, Inspector Constantin Vadim is assigned to investigate a series of horrifying murders by an elusive killer that people call the Monstrum.

But Constantin is neither professionally nor personally the ideal man for the task. He is a provincial policeman who has never investigated a homicide – and a fatal attraction to strong women threatens chaos in his personal life.

Yet he does not lack a certain kind of courage. Against all odds, he pursues his investigation as it carries him through Moscow's kaleidoscopic world of privilege and poverty, sex cults and sinister politics to a place where the evils of Russia's past and present meet.

'A first division horror thriller to keep you awake in the early hours' *Mail on Sunday*

'The thriller of the year, *Monstrum* combines the best of *Fatherland* and *Gorky Park* with a dash of *The Silence of the Lambs*' *The Times*